BOND
AND
SONG

BOND
AND
SONG

Mera Akiana

Published by Vale of Gold

Author Contact:
https://meraakiana.com
books@meraakiana.com

Cover Design: johnny_an
Author Photo Copyright: Emma-Jane Photography
Author Photo Headdress: Samantha Walden Tiaras

ISBN: 979-8-9885142-0-6 (hardcover)
ISBN: 979-8-9885142-1-3 (paperback)
ISBN: 979-8-9885142-2-0 (ebook)

Library of Congress Control Number: 2023910938

First Edition – Third Printing

Written in British English
Printed in the United States of America

A percentage of all profits generated through the sale of this book is donated to philanthropic for-purpose (nonprofit) ocean and nature conservation organisations.

Thank you for doing good with your reading!

To the authors in whose stories I found solace, shelter, and my sanity:

Thank you for singing my soul home.

To the reader:

May the stories that sing to your soul find you.

PROLOGUE

THE LOUD

IS THERE ANY SANITY IN offering myself up to save a world I've lived apart from for most of my life? Alas, sanity has been slippery ground under my feet for a while, setting me careening and grappling for purchase. Sanity has left me without a solution.

This final fall into madness is a choice.

I wrap my arms around myself and follow the path of the blood spiralling down my thigh as I'm buffeted in the blow ravaging the bluff. Earth's laboured lament, livid as the night. The ferocious elemental embrace returns my thoughts to the cave below, to the sin I'm leaving behind.

Submerged in sorrow, my heart shudders against the suffocation. I've made my choice, yes, yet letting go of love is harder. I know—more viscerally than most would be privileged to—that our love is a web spun through space and time. But will I remember it, when no reason remains and I don't even remember myself?

In the end, it is sense that has always known, not sanity. My senses that are sound, that sing a song my mind can't follow. The whole world is inside me. All of life, and all of that love that is *everything*. It was there in my senses before reason ever fathomed it.

My eyes snag on iridescent wings, arresting me in awed stillness. *Sister?* I track her tumbling through the darkness. Each beat of her wings pulses hope into my heart—life—life—and then...

Illumination like sunbeams penetrating the deep below the waves.

The fragile butterfly dances in the gale because she doesn't try to stand against it. She remembers she *is* the Wicked Wild and becomes it.

The secret to the power of the witch is that the fire she burns with is not that of her pyre.

And her spells are woven in the fabric of life.

So this last leap off the cliff isn't just a surrendering. The Dark leap is a fall into glorying grace.

It's a homecoming.

1

THE LOUD

3 years & 7 months ago, evening of April 30

FRAGMENTS, ALWAYS FRAGMENTS, SNEAKING UP on me unawares, yet elusive like the deer in the woods of the estate back home are supposed to be.

My eyes flash up to the grand floor-to-ceiling glass panes on the far side of the room, answered a split second later by the brilliant glory of fire poured from the sky, a bolt of wild freedom and burning power. My muscles clench in a minuscule lurch towards the world behind the glass before contracting further to keep my behind on the plush cushion of my chair. The vestiges of my breath shudder out of me with a quiet whimper.

For a moment, bronze-framed smaragdine eyes brimming with feeling stare back at me. The velvet melody of a husky murmur wraps around me.

Fragments.

Memory or imagination? Dream or vision?

Real or conjured, I'll take being lost in the...windows...to the unfortunate reality of the banquet going on around me. I have a whole kaleidoscope of those pieces. *My mosaic of madness.*

Grimacing, I force my eyes back down to the stiff table cloth. It calls to mind bleached bone. Focus on lifting the fork. The unmistakable aromas of sage and laurel filling my nose don't match the caramelised carrot on the tines. My hand stills.

Ephemera, wisps of something, a vexing sense of almost knowing and almost remembering.

Like fragile beams of a far lighthouse peeking through thick billows of fog when you're bitter cold and near-drowned, reduced to a puppet fighting against the strings that none too gently make it dance. You know you won't reach safe harbour. But for a moment, the light made you feel less alone.

The scents flip over to browned sweetness and my arm resumes its motion. I finish chewing and swallowing and manage another four bites. My masochistic musings tumble on, my mind trapezing along the well-worn loops of my confusion, before I allow myself to stop wondering for a minute and just...

Experience the storm. *Better.* Its wild and unleashed company raging outside feels more friend to me than the multitude of controlled people milling about in here, with their multitude of pushy and pressing agendas.

At least the food is delicious. Another three bites.

"Where did your thoughts go there, Miss Zatinsa?" The slick fifties-something seated on my right grazes my hand. I hadn't cared enough to memorise in what capacity he is here or who he is representing.

The sensation of a thousand slimy hooks needling my limb spreads from the point where his fingers make contact. It isn't intense enough to hurt, but it feels awful all the same. It also ruins the delightful swirling unfolding across my sternum from the spices in the dish.

I glare at the man, and crystal coldness edges out the slime as he registers my expression. Really, why is he surprised that a teenage girl does not appreciate this particular flavour of his... attention? His anger comes next, and I flinch with the scalding now radiating through me from that featherlight touch of his fingers.

"Far away," I reply, and yank my hand from his. There, Mother, I didn't sabotage your oh-so-important relationships by —gasp—ignoring someone.

Dignitaries and politicians and heads of state. I'm sure they aren't all bad people, know, in fact, that there are those who have sacrificed much with the honest intention of help and service. But they're still...people. I don't do well with people. This crowd? Skewed towards too much manipulative intent born from ambition turned greed, or competition turned arrogance.

Which is woeful for the world. And hell for me.

I attack the broccoli artfully crowning the roots on my plate with more vigour than necessary. I have had about as much battering as I can take from the sly prodding and requests laced in avarice exchanged all night up and down the table, over glasses of champagne and across piles of potatoes. They have been ricocheting around the room as energetic bullets that no-one but me has been bothered by.

Next course.

The storm, at least, tearing through me where I primly sit as I do my best to go through the motions of dinner, brings with it spaciousness and power and life. It itches at me, calling me to join it and give myself up to it. Dark expanses are yawning open inside me from its lashing winds. But it gives me room to breathe.

My pleasant seat neighbour swats at a bee that found herself lured from who knows where to his unfinished dessert. She's as lost and in the wrong place as I am. The impact sets her floundering, and my stomach reels as if in free fall. When she finds her wings, I link my thumbs and spread my hands in my own imitation of wings, hovering just above the edge of the table. Unerringly, she flies home to safety, and I clap my hands around her in a protective bubble.

The hours drag on, intangible constraints holding me captive. So does the dinner, despite dessert being done. The mingling phase of the evening preceded the sit-down phase. It seems this phase is endless.

My body is aching most everywhere, my muscles are rigid from hours of defensive tension. Only the pure, sweet aliveness of the gentle buzz in the dome of my hands brings me comfort. Much more of this and I'll dissolve into one of my *episodes*, and wouldn't Mother just love that?

My lips hitch when my eyes fall, and fasten, on the grandfather clock with its swinging pendulum. It's the most endearing thing in this stately room. It becomes my favourite thing when—at last—it strikes midnight. The deep and melodious sound of it rolls through me like lush waves of silk, from my hips up to my head.

Briefly, I feel myself relax, and I catch the curious gaze of the statesman opposite me. He's Greek, and his sea blue eyes are kind as he notices the first sign of contentment I must have shown all evening. I allow him a small smile, and feel a slight ray of warmth from him in response, joining the silken waves.

May 1. *Happy birthday to me.*

I shoot up and flee the room, rescuing myself and the bee.

3 years & 7 months ago, evening of April 30, Sacred Song

Sin nearly ran from the revelry.

"Brother—" His best friend broke off. What was there that Fern could say?

It's Sacred Song?

Yes, Sin was vividly aware. The Sung's highest celebration of the year, the one filled with ritual that every Sung boy spends his whole youth dreaming of fully participating in. His instincts should drive him right into the depth of it.

And they did—a magnetic force coaxing him to get lost in the gyrating bodies generating as much heat as the spiced fires burning in great chalices throughout the Court while the festivities were getting into their swing. And yet, defying the tugging in his loins, his feet carried him from his people and the seductive thrums of strings and drums, out into the quiet night pulsing with humid warmth.

The fragrance of sage and laurel in the air was lost on him. Nausea was clogging his throat.

There are many Queens who'd accept your Bond with delight?

He couldn't escape that knowledge with the hope he read in the looks of many Queens at whatever Court he went to. His own innate need to Bond had been growing uncomfortably insistent. But he didn't want any Queen. He wanted a Queen he couldn't have. A Queen he knew existed, but of whom he had no idea who or where she was.

And here was yet another Sacred Song, and still he hadn't found her.

Sin braced himself against a tree, his toes cramping around small rocks and digging into the ground as the urge to retch passed over him.

Just celebrate with us and forget everything for a night?

He could never forget. Wouldn't ever let himself forget. Didn't want to forget. He had let her slip through his fingers, had let her go once. Had let her be lost in the Loud, and she was paying the price daily. So was he.

The music was fading behind him. Sin fell into a sprint, finding a modicum of an outlet for his frustration in the punishing pace. He ran and stewed in his thoughts.

He should've found a way to hold on to her that day. With all he'd seen in her eyes, with what she'd said, the way she'd acted, he should've done something to bring her in, to take her back to Court. He should have been her shield and prevented the years of her extensive palette of pain. Or the worst, that tearing sadness he had felt from her since, somehow echoing through to him through this bond that wasn't a Bond.

Like now. Sin stumbled, caught himself, and gritted his teeth against the sudden sensation of being riddled by bullet holes. It came and went. Nothing more than an echo.

For him. For her...

Sin's fraught anguish fuelled him through the close to three hours his feet clipped to his destination. He'd taken to travelling from Circle to Circle, sometimes even the Loud, looking for her, clinging to the hope that she may have been Sung in, that he might finally find her again.

Find her, know her, be with her, shield her. *Love her.*

He'd only just returned from Ember Court eleven days ago. His mother had been euphoric to have him home, had greeted him so warmly. Sin bounced back to Storm Court more than any other place, and she always received him with an outpouring of affection. But she knew as well as he did that he wouldn't stay long before moving on.

So where next, she sighed yesterday.

Maybe visit with Mrak and Jave at Crystal Court?

Night was deep around him, but Sin's body knew this route by heart. Light or dark, he could jump each brook and leap each rock without one wrong tread. He'd carved out his own peculiar path of a half-life among the Sung, yet he kept feeling the need to return to this beach. As if she might suddenly pop back up by the water's edge.

The only place he'd ever truly met her.

There. Sin slowed when he could make out the scraggly old tree, stopped when he reached its low branch. It touched the sand in places, knobbly elbows leaning on the ground for support. To make his torture exquisite, Sin settled back into the same spot in the tree as he had then.

The worn memory played out in front of his eyes as if he was living it, as if he'd reverted to being that overconfident stripling, his mother's gentle scolding ringing in his ears. Exploring where he wasn't supposed to, far beyond the Court, he'd discovered the girl. His Queen.

Even all these years later, Sin was spellbound by the phantom of her that his memory conjured, time stilling around him—and he still shuddered from the moment the spell broke.

When she had taken all the life with her.

He collapsed back onto the thick branch, uncaring about the bruises the poky bits earned him. No, there was only one Queen he would ever offer his Bond to. Ever wanted to celebrate Sacred Song with. And that had nothing to do with his oceans of guilt and regret, but everything to do with her.

He'd felt it with a brilliant irrefutable certainty that had made him want to howl to the heavens, whilst the hum of the Dark Song had sung all around him. Miracle upon miracle. He'd sat next to her and decided he would work harder than all the other males to become a male strong and worthy enough of a Queen like her. He would learn all he could about every facet of the Court Dance, and he would court her until she accepted his Bond, and he would offer his life in devotion to her Dance.

She was his Queen, the only one there'd ever be for him. Overconfident, young, and foolish or not, it was a knowing that didn't care about age.

It had been true.

So he *had* worked harder. Had tirelessly prepared for her. He'd been her sin that day, she'd said. When she spoke those words, he'd known that much more than just being her sin... He had become *her Sin.*

His vision of her gracefully loping away from him with that feather in her hair morphed, showed her grown into the female she would be today. When he ached and craved to be her every sin. Every delicious, wicked, and glorious one that took her straight to paradise.

Sin groaned and slung his arm over his face. *Not helping.*

He twitched up. The vision faded. He opened his eyes—and ground his jaw when he saw only the desolate beach. Bereft of her now as he was then. Not even an eagle circling above, who might share in his misery. Understand his loss.

Sin clenched a tight fist around the polished moonstone hidden deep in his pocket.

Kicked at a rock.

Loosed a roar, and heard it break into a half-sob, as if punched in the gut by the vacant space and folded over the emptiness.

Those few precious minutes with her on this beach... They had been the best day of his life, and the start of his nightmare.

2

11 months ago

I STRETCH UP TOWARDS AWARENESS with the dream clinging to me like tree sap, forming threads between me and what feels like a whole life I've just visited. Or lived. Sometimes I wake up feeling more exhausted than I'd been when I went to sleep.

As a child I was convinced it was all real, everything I saw and...felt...while I slept. I'd delight in recalling every detail of it that I could upon waking, revelling in the sense of hope it gave me.

I've learned better since then.

Nothing good ever came from brooding, Zaja.

With a small huff, I sit up in bed and scowl at my stiff muscles. I stupidly look into thin air for a bit, bracing myself. There's not much to see anyway. My room is as devoid of things or knickknacks as it is overfilled with sensations.

Another day filled with nothing and far too much.

The blanket is bunched up next to my body—like usual, I wrestled it off me during the night. The softness of it under my fingers where my hand has come to rest on it shivers through me like skittish wraiths chasing across a fairy lake. Chill and fresh early morning January air wafts in through the open window, washing over me like dew settling deep in my cells, while Cat butts up against my bare thigh. Her purring is full of love and sends golden warm waves pulsing through me, overriding the dew chill. Around my feet Dog is curled, his tail rhythmically clopping on my shin. While Cat's love is more languid, his has an edge of expectation and excitement to it, making it fizzy as it bubbles up through me from my leg. The creaking of the barren tree branches outside reverberates through my joints as one of the squirrels leaps onto my window sill. Over and under all of it lies that constant pressure, rubbing over me like a heavy coat.

It's one of my more peaceful moments.

Up you get.

A flash of green eyes flickers across my vision—again—as I stumble to my ensuite bathroom. I shove it aside, along with that crushing sense that something is escaping me—that there must be *more*, somehow—that tends to accompany me throughout my otherwise solitary days.

I turn on the tap and hear a roaring of water out of proportion to the stream hitting the sink.

Waterfall, I think.

* * *

Leaving my room, my eyes snag on the little metal rectangle next to the door jamb. Who has name plaques next to rooms in their own family home? I suppose this one was installed before my parents realised how much rather they'd undo me if they could.

I wander through the spotless halls of the estate. It takes a full three minutes to get to the library. Some *Daina Fund* passed down through the generations paid for it all. Cat and Dog saunter beside me. Who knows if my parents are home—it won't make a difference to how much I'll see of them either way. Not running into anyone else, I may as well have been the only person here. *The ghost in the castle.*

I smile at Cat and Dog as we walk the polished wood floors. "Best friends," I whisper. Dog's wet nose nuzzles my wrist. Cat does a smooth twining loop around and between my legs that doesn't cause either of us to miss a step. "Yep, the best." Along with the horses, the birds, the squirrels, the deer living in the woods. In summer I spend more time living and sleeping in the grounds than I do in the house.

Animals always have pure intentions and emotions. There is nothing smudged there, nothing blurred or twisted or tainted. Joy is joy, fear is fear, aggression is aggression. They are upfront and honest about what is going on for them, and act accordingly.

Animals are safe.

People? Not so much.

When I was five, my parents had a visitor, one of their rolodex of important business partners, and I dissolved into tears of pain and rage after he'd felt the need to grip me by the chin to impart some self-righteous life lesson. My mother threw up her hands at my unreasonable behaviour. I stormed out into the grounds and returned with Cat on my heels a few hours later. She hasn't stopped following me around the house and grounds since. Dog arrived briefly after. Not that my parents were particularly pleased with the idea of shedding, furry animals running wild in their pristine estate, but they've bowed to it.

Schooling had become home-schooling had become self-study by the time I was eight. Minimalise triggers, reduce the potential for *episodes*. Eventually it was easier for my parents to just...treat me the same way they regard the one piece of art in the estate I happen to love—useless, best packaged away in bubble wrap, and left forgotten in a room with a closed door and catching dust. They remember me occasionally, but mostly I'm relegated to something to be dealt with only when it pops up on the calendar, like a routine health checkup or the trimming of the hedge. Every now and again guilt hits them, and they insist I'm there at one of their events. We all suffer through it and are sufficiently reminded why it isn't a good idea.

It hasn't happened for a while now.

I don't like people, people don't like me, animals flock to me. It's been established I'm incapable of functioning normally and being part of society. Let the isolation and half wild existence continue.

But for how long?

I shake my head like a bird shaking off water as I step over the threshold to the library and inhale deeply. Books. My other best friends. Internet first though today. I head to my favourite—the only—stuffed chair, ready to park myself behind my laptop screen. My butt hits the generously upholstered seat a wink before the vision takes over.

Velvet dark suffused with rainbow colour.

A circle of women.

Beyond, on the outside, men positioned in a looser circle.

I taste celebration, reverence.

Intimate connection.

Power flowing in currents, being woven and building.

The pressure I always feel has eased up, and instead there's a resonant hum.

It's over as suddenly as it started, leaving me blinking with the sweet shock of colour and sensation that is igniting instead of suffocating.

Then the pain slices its hooks into me.

Most of my pain—a companion I'm intimately acquainted with—goes outside in. This one is just...in. Deep within. My chest caves and my breath becomes choppy as I ache. My torso makes little circles, one half of the infinity sign spinning around and around with the loss of the other. It felt like a memory.

"Absurd," I mutter.

It wasn't a memory. So there's nothing tangible there for me to cling to, nothing to mourn and grieve in remembrance. Doesn't change that it hurts worse than the burning in my veins when hate gets pinged between people. Breathing through my nose, I try to accept that my life is one of being stranded on a raft of vague emptiness and cryptic flashes in a sea of nothing and sensory overload. I don't feel particularly successful.

Hey, at least you tried, Zaja.

When my crumpled chest smoothes out a bit, I finally boot up the laptop. My latest addiction are travel docs, vlogs, you name it. Anything that allows me to see the peaceful and perfect places that exist out there somewhere.

I've made good use in the past ten years of all the time my sparkling social calendar affords me. Master's in biology and anthropology, finessed with hours of research in all corners of the internet. It still hasn't illuminated how I can be socially functional, fit in, and have a life. I may have an abundance of visions—but I lack a vision for my future, coming up blank whichever way I turn it.

"Not good with dying the resident ghost of the Zatinsa estate, Cat." Which is pretty much option one.

Cat yawns.

"Why, thank you for that vote of confidence on my liveliness." But she's right, it's my current modus operandi. As good as dead. And equally exciting.

"So what about exploring paradise, hm? The heaven that is Earth?" What about those green eyes? What about...love?

Voila, option two: Get out there. Experience what the world has to offer. And very possibly be crippled by all the scents, sounds, sights, sensations, emotions, intentions, and energies ripping through me in the attempt. Which again results in— blank.

Dog growls from where he's kindly warming my feet, and I'm tempted to growl back. Not at him. Simply at...life.

The floor tilts a little. I grip the armrest. I feel myself slipping, flipping back and forth between lives like pages in a book. It's been like that the past few months. The flashes near constant now, one after the other, minute after minute, demanding my attention like they had when I was younger.

Maybe it'll help me fill in what I'm missing in this picture, I'd thought at first. What if the only way to *remember* me is to lose hold of myself in the same breath, I think now. *What if the price is my sanity?*

Because my haywire senses are packing up my mind and taking it along on a road trip into the nether lands crammed with an excess of sights.

And we've reached the next stop.

* * *

My mind is generously dumped back to the present.

Thick silence. Library.

Sharp to blurry to sharp, my eyes regain their focus.

Which is latched onto said favourite artwork of mine: An onyx statue webbed with gold veins. A woman, with majestic self-possession and power that remind me of Nike of Samothrace. She is suspended in stillness whilst amidst throes of feverish dance. The sweeping folds of her gown that caress and just barely conceal her curves appear almost translucent, similar to the effect Strazza achieved when he Veiled the Virgin in marble, and there is grace even in her burning fire.

So much life in that frozen form. I can't help but be awed by it whenever I look at her.

I don't know where she came from. I simply found her one day, lovelessly discarded in one of the endless undisturbed rooms of the house. Mesmerised, I brought her here and installed her in pride of place, where the sun adds to her glow.

Still too shook up by my latest sojourn in who-knows-where and the subsequent dark misery of my mind to concentrate on my intended internet surfing, I slam the laptop lid closed again. I'll come back later to plan my fabulous, spectacular, imaginary trip. A journey to witness the wonders of the world. Never mind I've done enough mental journeying to last a lifetime.

My leg twitches, and I get up just as the first few rays of sunlight fall through the large windows, caressing my dancer. Sometimes I like to play a game with myself. I wander along the shelves of the library, letting my fingers trail the spines, pull out a random one, and open it to a random page.

I look to see what my finger has landed on this time—the library is big enough that even after my lifetime thus far spent in here, I've yet to land on the same tidbit twice.

In yourself find the vale of gold.

I snap the book shut and thrust it back into its place on the shelf.

Right.

Hastily, I stride three shelves over to pick up another tome— one that I've been working my way through these last few days. Mythology and anthropology fascinate me. Patriarchy wasn't always a thing. Women, and the moon, the dark and the mysterious, they were all worshipped and revered once. Recognised as powerful. Nature was respected. There were incredibly advanced societies where power was balanced and neither man nor woman was oppressed. And surprise, everyone flourished.

I wonder how much of this stuff they keep in their own library my parents have actually read? Sitting in positions of power and change-making as they do? Because I may not much be part of the world out there, but I've sure spent a lot of time looking out on it, and I know something's askew there.

Pacing in a slow circle, the polished wood cold under my bare feet, I page through the volume to where I left off yesterday: Moera. The triple goddess, older than time, who holds the destiny of men in her hands. She is many in one, she is refracted into three, spinning and weaving fates. For some reason, the idea comforts me. I imagine myself one of the three sisters, who are one and the same, yet as three less alone, who weave the threads of existence, and thus from nothing create something.

Then I tremble from the thought of holding that much power in my hands. That much responsibility.

"What do you think, Cat? Fatalism. Yay or nay?"

When I'm full up on mythology for the day and can't stand anymore of my own babbling, I return the tome to its home and head outside to the grounds. The biting winter wind rushing up my nose wraps around my brain and helps me to stop thinking. I throw a stick for Dog. Then I pick up my own to swing around and pretend I'm a Samurai.

Capable. Noble. Graceful.

Loved.

I don't know if Moera decides my fate or I do. But I can always try.

I puff out hot breath and watch it contort itself into shifting nebulous forms.

January. *This year something will change.*

3

OLD COURT

11 months ago

SIN RELISHED IN THE CLANG of stick against stick.

With his mind narrowed in on the vibration travelling up through his arms, the swift and sure dance of his feet on the sandy ground, and the sweat slicking his body as the sun beat down on them, he could almost ignore the constant worry that ate through him like acid. He twisted and pivoted, then swept his arms in a move meant to gain him the upper hand over both his opponents—if he hadn't faltered because he was distracted.

That can't happen, he berated himself.

Quaden and Jalen exchanged a glance he could read only too easily before Jalen started talking. "You've never considered Bonding?"

Oh, he had. Considered it everyday.

"No." He whipped down his staff so sharply it sang.

Parried. Feinted. Attacked.

Quaden and Jalen had company in not knowing what to make of him. Sin knew that he'd become a bit of a name among the Sung years ago. Accepted to Heart younger than any other Sung. Vagabonding about since, like a youngster circling the Courts to find where he fit, despite having grown beyond that age. Offering the polite and expected contributions without fully committing or integrating himself anywhere. The puzzle pieces didn't fit together anymore.

For a while Sin might have questioned which way that pendulum swung. By now he was sure it had landed on infamy.

"Songs." Quaden grunted. "You must be chafing."

Sin met his blow. *You have no idea.*

The stark need to Bond natural to a Sung male with the makings of being Heart was forceful enough to slowly rob him of his sanity. Because he *had* chosen his Queen, *had* considered who he wanted to offer his Bond to, *was* ready to offer it.

The problem was his Queen was missing, wasn't among the Sung.

He had no way of finding her.

Could only wait until the Song sang her in.

Lunge. Strike. Victory. The satisfaction didn't even penetrate his skin.

"Brothers." With a nod, Sin excused himself to go clean up.

"Bond and Song," they chorused after him.

If only.

While the water sluiced down his body, Sin's thoughts yet again returned to her. His ephemeral Queen. How was she doing? He wasn't feeling anything from her right now, so that was a good sign.

He also hated it. Anytime he didn't feel her, he wondered if he ever would again. If he'd lost her for good. If something had happened to her. If the Loud had eaten her up.

Selfish. Sin rubbed down his body with a little more roughness than necessary. How rarely were the sensations echoing through to him from her pleasant ones? He should be glad for any minute there was silence and emptiness. Any peace she might have. Songs knew she had precious little of that, and it was his fault. He wouldn't be surprised, wouldn't hold it against her, if she never accepted him.

If he'd ever get the chance to face her and find out.

* * *

With jerky movements, Sin threw on loose pants and went to find Vala. She was about to start her work for the evening, and he hurried through the sprawling maze of Old Court so he wouldn't be late. He hated leaving any Queen waiting. He'd already been too late once. He swore he never would be again.

"Lady Vala." She was a young unbonded Queen, a strong one, and whenever he was staying at Old, he conspired with her when she Danced. Sin greeted her with a warm smile even as his hand and head flowed in the customary spiralling gesture of respect.

Vala preferred entering the Dance out in unbounded nature to using one of the courtyards, so he positioned himself to her left and they started walking. The tinkling of the wind chimes gave way to the chirping of dusk.

"I had a dream about being Bonded last night."

Sin liked Vala. She was gentle and soft-spoken, with eyes that looked deep and saw much. It was an honour to contribute to her, and they worked well together. He knew there were those in Old's Heart who were waiting for him to present her with a moonstone and offer his Bond. He also knew that she wasn't among them. It was because of that that he replied easily. "Oh yeah?"

"Mh-hmm." Her vibrant eyes were teetering between cheeky amusement and sorrowful longing.

Well, he knew that feeling. Sin hoped she would be forming her Constellation soon. Vala was a wonderful Queen and deserved to have a formidable Bond. As it was, conspiring with her allowed him to feel useful and needed, and he was grateful she trusted him with the task so frequently. Was he worthy of it? Another question altogether. He had the strength and skill, sure. But...

The tips of his ears grew hot. Recently, he had taken up the habit of mentally replaying his days at night, imagining it was *her* instead of Vala that he had contributed to, had shielded. Had offered himself and his strength to in whatever way he could. Sin cleared his throat with the thought of how much further he spun the extent of his devotion in his fantasies compared to what filled his days in reality, when he imagined it was *his* Queen he was offering his life to, not any Queen.

He cleared his throat again. "Do you think you might like to join another Coven?"

As far as Sin was aware, it didn't look like there were any young males at Old Court who were likely to join Heart anytime soon, and none of the current ones belonged in her Constellation. There might be a Heart male available who suited her and matched her strength in another Court. It was more common for males to travel between Circles, but there was a fair amount of movement between the Covens, too. They were all connected in sisterhood in the Dark Song, so in a sense, all the Hearts housed the Queens of one large Coven, anyway.

"I'll listen to what the Song tells me."

Sin grunted. Yes, she would. She was a Queen, after all.

Hopefully she wouldn't have to wait for her Bond much longer. Being a Queen, it wasn't likely. And even if it did take a while, she was sure not to get as lost in the meantime as he had. She was female.

"Here." Vala halted. She looked up at him. "Here is good."

Sin scanned the area once more, then he nodded. There was soft grass under their feet, rock protecting them on one side, and space to move. It should be safe, and she should be able to complete her Weaving undisturbed. "Go ahead."

His mind focused, his senses extended, as he calmed and controlled his energy. He took a defensive stance close enough to reach her, and far enough to allow her room. His breathing slowed, then matched, joined, twined with Vala's. When a Queen Danced, she unveiled her soul. It was a Sung male's honour, one of the ways of their devotion, to breathe with her and become the guardian of her soul for that time. This was what it meant to conspire.

Vala's eyes closed as she began. In the slackening and flushing of her features, Sin read the exact moment when she entered Dark Song. Its caress whispered over him, raising the hair on his skin. Songs, how his body railed at him with the need to Bond, to connect with the very essence of the female in that deep and intimate way. To experience the gift of the Bonded Dance, where devotion redounded to fulfilment untold.

Wicked Wild. Sin gritted his teeth. This wasn't a Bonded Dance. There would be no touch, and the caress was as much as he would experience of the Song.

Keeping his knees bent and loose, Sin watched Vala as she began to move. Her Dance was big, untamed, and vibrant today. Her colourful skirts flared as her body twisted and beads of sweat began to form on the exposed skin of her upper body. Sin had to circle and step with her as she whirled, his attention split between her and their surroundings.

His toes left the ground. Before they met the soft blades again, a crippling loneliness crushed his chest, wholly wrenching his focus away. His world narrowed to nothing but the feelings and sensations he received from *her*.

He'd been wrong before. He'd give up ever feeling her again if it meant she wouldn't feel *this*. How could she be this ravaged with loss—and survive it?

Sin's muscles clenched with useless power, his jaws gnashing, adrenaline cursing through him with the urge to protect but nowhere to go. A wild animal lived under the skin of every Heart male, a creature that lived to love and seduce, and to roar and defend. It lived barely concealed, oh so close to the surface, its primal sensuality always oozing from their pores, its snarling rage the slightest hint of provocation away. Being unable to do anything for the Queen of his devotion—it was as deftly stealing Sin's reason as the pain he felt from her. A long growl rumbled through his chest, going to war against the intangible.

Desperately, Sin tried to push something back through to her. Comfort. Reassurance. *Being there.*

"Sin?"

Anything beautiful he saw around him, or good he'd felt. Anything that might delight her. He fumbled with it, didn't know how to grasp on to the diaphanous, tenuous connection between them.

"Sin."

He didn't know if anything ever made it through to her. Still, he always tried. It was all he could do.

"Sin, take a breath."

Take a breath... The voice filtered through his hazy mind as the serrated edges of her mellowed.

Take a breath...

Vala. She had been Dancing. He had dedicated himself to conspiring with her. Sin reoriented to the ground under his feet, the low sun in the sky, the warm and humid air.

Vala was looking up at him, her eyes wide and concerned.

Her Dance finished.

Songs! How long had she been finished? "Are you alright?" He hadn't kept her safe while she Danced, hadn't been there for her when she returned from the Dark Song, to anchor her or help her adjust. Sin gripped her shoulders as if he could squeeze a response out of her.

"Are you?" Vala replied softly.

"Lady, forgive me." His voice was choked. "Vala, truly, I'm sorry."

They'd been lucky, but he didn't want to imagine what might have happened. He'd left her wide open and betrayed her trust. A Sung female Dancing in the Song was a wonder. A miracle and mystery of feminine strength. It also made a female deeply vulnerable. She *always* deserved fully focused protection.

This... How could he go on like this? Contribute to any Queen? He was a Heart male, one of the strongest and most capable the Sung had known, and he was flailing. No good to the Queens who were here—nor to the one who wasn't.

He'd been distracted for years, yes. Never had he lost hold of himself so completely.

Vala placed a hand on his chest, and it occurred to him that she might have witnessed and felt a great deal of what he'd experienced. She had been in the Song... Reading the currents of life itself as they flowed in and around them. How much had she put together? Her hand was warm with gentle power. "Strong heart and Song's caress." Her eyes were serious, yet free of accusation or reproach. "She will come, Sin."

He'd always yearned for his Queen. It came with being born a Sung male of Heart temperament. But by now he'd been alive longer waiting, for *her*, specifically, than not. The one time he met her was more than half his lifetime ago. So...

Will she?

STORM COURT

12 years & 4 months ago

"Sinu, don't you dare!"

Too late. His mother's voice was swept away on his tailwind as he raced from the Court with a shout of glee.

He may be a boy, but he was ready to grow up and become a respected Heart male. He'd be the best and strongest there ever was, and he'd be Bonded to the best Queen, and he'd offer his devotion and help her Dance in the Song with all of his power and skill.

Sinu ran and ran, whooping and jumping, his feet flying as far and fast as his mind. Today, he'd run farther than his fear. Today, he'd run faster than the wind. Today, he'd bravely explore the unknown.

And then he'd go home and tell his mother about it!

Sinu relished the power in his muscles. His heart was pumping. He flew through sun and shade, across rock and dirt and grass and sand. He scooped water from a brook he leapt across, stripped a few berries off a bush he passed, picked up a stick and practised his warrior moves.

Maybe this was far enough and he should turn back? No. He was fearless and strong. He'd keep going.

Eventually, the sun had slid across the sky by about four handswidths. He must have run around half the island by now! He'd definitely never been to this beach before. There was a lone scraggly tree with a low branch dipping over the sand, perfect for lounging on. That's what he'd do.

The rough bark was warm under his thighs as he found a good spot. He'd sit and rest for a minute, and then—

Who is that?

He wasn't alone. Down there, by the water's edge...was a girl. Sinu stilled. Had she noticed him arrive? He didn't think so. He drew in a big breath, and held it, and stayed very still in his spot on the low branch.

When it ran out, he did it twice more.

And again.

And she still hadn't moved one bit, in all that time! At all! Was she alive? Real? She looked real. And alive. Even if she was frozen.

Sinu studied her. Her knees were drawn up, her hands placed flat on the sand beside her. She was slight. Probably a few years younger than him. She reminded him of a perching bird. What was she doing? And why had he spent the same amount of time sitting in absolute stillness, watching her, as she'd been sitting there?

Of course, she was a girl, and he was a boy, so she could hear the Song, and he could not, so there was that. Maybe she was listening. But every girl among the Sung could hear the Song. They were probably listening all the time. And he'd never done this before with any of them!

Oh! What if she wasn't Sung? *What if she is—from the Loud?* Sinu's heart sank like the stones he'd tossed into the water some way back.

Argh! He wished she would just move!

As if he'd willed her to, the girl unfurled and flowed to her feet. She began to sway, and flutter her hands on the breeze, and then she was dancing. Sinu had never seen anything like it among all the Sung. Her body bent in rhythm with the waves rolling to the shore, and he could have sworn the birds above him sang for her—their song rising with a quickening of her steps, and falling as she slowed. Her hair flew around her.

Now she looked free as nature herself.

Most strangely of all, with each of her twists and turns, she was somehow freeing something deep inside him. And the more she danced—or Danced?—the stronger the caress of the Dark Song ghosting over him became, making the hair stand up on his arms and tingle on his scalp. Sinu found he had raised a hand to his chest. It was as if a warm glow wanted to burst him at the seams! He couldn't decide whether he wanted to run across the beach for joy, or freeze for fear of being discovered intruding on her dance.

She must be from a different Court, he decided. No one in Storm Court dances like this. Not even the Queens in the Heart when they were lost to the Weaving Dance!

Watching her, he felt himself like a bow being pulled.

Until the girl tensed and came to a jarring stop. She turned and looked directly at where he was sitting in the low tree. At him? All the life that had been coursing through her rolled up and in, back towards her, and shutters and curtains closed and dropped all over her.

No! I'm sorry.

The glow in Sinu's chest disappeared. Like sitting in one of the hot springs and have it suddenly vanish around you, leaving you cold and miserable and confused. The power of the Dark Song ebbed away from him.

Everything felt all wrong.

Sinu wanted to make it right. No, he needed to make it right. He propelled himself off the branch and hurtled towards her. Then his brain caught up. *Don't spook her, Sinu!* He needed to slow down. If he startled her she'd fly away.

Only she'd become stock-still again, completely frozen, just glaring him down as he got closer. He stopped a few paces from her. She definitely seemed a little younger than him, but it sort of didn't matter. There in her wide eyes...whole worlds and lifetimes. *Wicked Wild!*

Sinu furrowed his brow as he stared at her and contemplated what he saw. Wariness. A flash of anger. And a sadness that wrapped her like cobwebs. He felt an odd crack in his heart. He wanted to hug her and not let go until she felt peace.

Then he realised what this meant. Cold fingers traced down his spine. Sung males took care of their females. He was learning how to do that every day. It was important—the most important. No girl he'd ever met in a Court had a look like that in her eyes.

So she couldn't be from another Court. Any Court.

But then Sinu noticed the deep reverberating hum that had blended with the familiar caress, travelling through his bones and filling his soul with sound. He was hearing a glimpse of Song. Through her.

She was giving him access.

Without touching him.

She was a Queen. *A Queen!*

A crazy powerful one, apparently, if she could do this! The world got a little wobbly.

And he was still staring at her without saying anything! But there wasn't silence. It was filled with the hum of Song—so what was she hearing? *She must be hearing symphonies, the full Dark Song, if she's that powerful!*

Sinu noticed a gleam had entered that stark expression in her eyes. Like she was curious about something. Her shoulders relaxed. She seemed to breathe a bit more deeply. Like she was drawn in water colour now instead of pencil. Like all her lines softened.

A lot.

It made him feel like he'd conquered the world.

Sinu grinned at her and sank down onto the sand. She hesitated a moment longer, but then she followed and sat down, too. She didn't face him, rather looking out at the ocean as she hugged her knees, perching again—but she hadn't flown away. She had sat down with him. She was still here with him. Sinu's feet jiggled about a bit until he managed to get them under control.

The girl—Queen—may have been looking out, but Sinu looked right at her. She was fascinating. Emotions he didn't even know seemed to roll through her eyes from moment to moment. Like mirroring pools reflecting a whole world around her that only she knew.

He watched every slight rising in her chest from her breath. It was the only thing about her moving, since she was completely still again otherwise, and silent—totally opposite to the vibrant stirring of life she was causing all around her. She didn't even seem to realise.

The Dark Song's caress was far more than skin deep with her around. It slid through Sinu's bones. Songs, he was able to hear its hum! He'd only once before heard it, a few months ago, when he'd gotten to hold the newest baby in the Court, who had been really happy, and because she was a Queen, and still a baby, she'd automatically given access in that moment, so he'd been lucky...

And now he could hear it again, because of this girl next to him. Even the waves seemed to draw closer up the beach to her, reaching out like tongues wanting to lick her. How would she taste if he tried licking her? He'd never wondered that about a girl. His brain was hazy and crystal clear all at once. In a fuzzy sort of way, more in the animal part of him than his mind, he was aware of a golden eagle lazily circling above. As if he, too, had been drawn close by the girl.

What should Sinu say? Do? He wanted to connect with her. *But how?* She didn't seem local. He wouldn't get far with his native language. But anyone spoke at least some English, right?

"...beautiful." *What? No!* Well, yes, but—he'd meant—

Songs, why was this so hard? Why was his heart pumping again like it had done from all of that running earlier? Why was he so hot all of a sudden? What happened to his tongue? Sinu choked against the tight croak in his throat.

He was strong and courageous, training to be the best Bonded for the best Queen!

He tried again. "I'm Sinu." But this attempt came out weird, too. Wonky. The whole second half swallowed up when his voice broke halfway through his name.

"Sin," the girl echoed. Her voice was lovely, like the gentle murmuring lullaby of the waves. It made his ears feel tingly. Every part of him felt alive and like it was straining to listen to her. "My parents don't like for me to talk with people." She wrinkled her nose a bit. Chewed her lip. The corner tilted up.

Finally, she looked at him. Her eyes were lit up and laughing. Not outright, more like a secret she was hiding—but he could see it. And they were asking a question as well, that he prayed he knew the answer to. "So I guess you're my sin today. Thank you."

All the breath whooshed out of him. She was... Magnificent. He'd heard the adults in the Court use the word. Now he knew what it meant.

A laugh bubbled up and out of Sinu, and he sketched a bow. "My pleasure and privilege." He'd often heard the Heart males say that, too.

She blinked at him.

He grinned again and opened his mouth to say more, but the eagle swooped down in a graceful loop and landed on her small shoulder. Sinu rocked back. His Queen didn't even startle—as if she'd expected the majestic bird, been aware of his movements this whole time. She reached up a hand to stroke his wing as she continued to watch Sinu.

Like she was searching his face for something. Was she finding it?

The eagle nuzzled his head against her cheek. Then she dropped her hand, the eagle took off, and she looked after him with a smile on her face. For a second she looked completely serene.

Sinu smiled. A light golden feather had settled on her hair—it must have come loose as the bird nuzzled her. He reached up to fish it free and give to her. Not that she acted as if this had been any memorable sort of occasion worth keeping a feather to remember it by, but he certainly thought it was. He thought this moment was as special as she was. And he wanted to be able to offer her something.

Only, when he went to pluck the feather out, she flinched away from him. Like it was instinct.

And then she cocked her head, her eyes went distant, focused on something behind him, and all the relaxation slipped right out of her. She glanced at him with fear in those wide eyes—and then she bolted.

Sinu scrambled around. *What in the Songs just happened?*

That golden feather teetered in her hair as she was darting away. He felt like he was that feather on top of a cliff's edge. Breath filled his lungs to call after her, before she was totally gone, to ask her what was wrong and to wait and—

She'd disappeared. He hadn't even learned her name. There was nothing to hold onto but his memory of her.

What was he going to do now?

34

4

7 months ago, evening of April 30

"I TRUST YOU'RE NOT PLANNING to go on like this, Zajasang."

I suppress a shudder while I watch my father chew his steak. If there is one reliable thing in my life, it's this dinner with my parents. Once a year it will happen. Some years, defining it as *with* my parents may be a bit generous, since all it means is that we breathe the same air inside a reception room filled with other people. Tonight it truly is just us, in the dining room of the estate.

With sleek and modern lines, the room could have just as easily been a conference room as a family dining room, and there is a good chance the only people to have set foot in the place over the last year were the cleaning staff. The one lone thing I like about it is the view of the grounds. Most of the estate's rooms facing this direction have floor to ceiling windows, and it's their best feature.

Maybe another child would have had a life of warmth in this cold place. I have dinner once a year the night before my birthday.

My father's brows are raised as he shakes his head. "Near feral and refusing to participate in society."

What a pandora's box of a statement. I narrow my eyes. "I have master's in biology and anthropology." He does remember that, doesn't he?

"We have given you your freedom, dear," Mother joins the fray. "We feel it may be time for you to pull yourself together."

And there it is. My parents haven't *seen* me when they look at me since they saw a child throwing an overwhelmed tantrum.

I stare at them as I continue eating. The taste of the beetroot bounding through me is almost enough to distract me from my focused glare. No meat on my plate. One of the many ways my parents and I don't match up.

My stoic silence doesn't ruffle them. Irony of ironies, they probably approve of it. My parents live by dear Ben Franklin's words about decorum that never snoozes and composure that can never be convinced into a jig as if they get up in the morning to breathe them, settle down at dinner to eat them, and hold onto as a mask that might deliver oxygen any moment in between.

"You ought to go abroad and gain some experience that will set your path for your future."

I allow myself a quiet sigh. My parents aren't bad people. They do care—somewhat—and mean well. They just don't know what to do with me.

We continue eating in silence.

"You don't sing, dear, do you?"

I snort. Where did that come from? I do sing—just not in a way anyone would enjoy. Well, the animals don't mind it. But in the sense that she means...

I drift off into the swaying of the trees and the flight of the birds, the clatter of our silverware fading into dim awareness. Realities flip, forests and dinners replacing each other. Slides swapped out on a projector. If they could appreciate how much fight I was putting into maintaining composure and proceeding with a dignified dinner my parents would be jubilating.

The plates are being cleared when my mother murmurs into her napkin. "Follow the Song. Follow the Song, wasn't it?"

I'm spooled in like an elastic snapping back. She gives herself a little shake, folds the napkin, and drops cloth and thought with equal dismissiveness.

"What—what did you just say?"

"Oh." Her embarrassment and annoyance buzz around her as she rises. Were she a horse, she'd be swishing them with her tail like pesky flies. A sliver of discomfort slithers towards me from Father as well. "I'd forgotten about it. A great-grandaunt of yours left some cryptic instructions that were passed down through the family, for the girl born on May 1. She was the one that named you, actually."

That is...not what I was expecting. "And?"

"And I just remembered that the other part of the message was that 'she must be told to follow the Song.'"

My mother waves her hand through the air, gesturing for my father to follow, and she hurries from the room. Her mind has passed on to other things, her energy smoothed over.

The dinner is done, I'm forgotten.

And she just gave me the most meaningful thing I've ever been given by her for a birthday.

For weeks now, I've been slipping between vision and reality like walking on a frozen lake. And with every slip, I've been hearing song.

Melodies overlapping and tangling together into harmonies. Song like bright sunshine and aegean blue tempest waves. Song like Franklin's mournful armonica and Water's ocean harp, like ancient whales and crystal bells, song like the handpan and the gong pulling it from another dimension, song like a million voices weaving together. Song like a deep hum quavering through my bones.

Song that accompanied me in the dreams of my childhood, and that I pushed down and away into a locked and shrouded room of my soul.

Song that has been demanding to be heard, and that no one else ever has.

Song that I've never told anyone about.

I get up and stand with my fingertips pressed against the window glass. The reflection of my wide eyes floats among the stars.

Someone knew about me. Someone knew about the song.

There might be someone out amongst those stars to look back at me and see me. If I ever want to find them...

I'll have to leave the estate.

* * *

I spend the rest of the night wandering the grounds, chasing a grasp on the implications of this revelation. Failing as it keeps evading me. Some great-grandaunt foresaw my birth and left instructions. That somehow were passed down and honoured. *It makes no sense whatsoever.*

And it's the first shred of hope I have to cling onto in—well, ever. It's a smidgen of possibility that there is something more to my madness. I'm hesitant to pile my hopes onto an ancestor who sounds like she was just as lost as me, but maybe, if she was lost in the same way...

Before I finish the thought, I'm ripped into a whirlwind of grief and pain rasping through me like sandpaper, physically whipping me about. I have just enough sense of self left to wonder how I'll come out of this not bleeding.

Shrapnel shatters my collarbone. My stomach convulses from aching emptiness. A knife opening my throat. On and on it goes, and with each new sensation comes a new image, a new knowing of a whole world, a whole life.

It is a body larger and stockier than mine that gets torn apart by the shrapnel, in a world of grimy smoke and fire and sliding mud under my feet, yet I feel it as if that foreign body were my own.

It is a body younger and smaller than mine that is crippled by hunger, with shackles around my ankles and the wooden slats swaying beneath me, yet I feel it as if that was mine, too.

I see the world in different colours and from the wrong angle when the massive blade slides across my throat, and yet the anxiety pounding through that different body...

Vision after vision give way to swirling darkness, and the pain flows from everywhere and swallows me whole, and I don't know how there'll ever be any relief or I'll ever make it through.

Then I'm spit back out into the here and now with soft grass and mulch under my feet, and I'll never know. I hope.

My body—I pat it down to reassure myself of its dimensions—still shakes. Through my trembling I try to thread my thoughts. Maybe, if she existed, this great-grandaunt, I don't have to be alone in my madness. Maybe there are others alive now, others like her. *Like me.*

Follow the song.

There was song in that kaleidoscope of chaos. Keening, aching song.

Oh no. No no no. I don't think I'll ever want to follow it. Not if it leads into a prism of pain.

With a sense of frantic back-paddling and the taste of copper in my mouth, I tumble against a tree to catch my breath, the rough bark digging into my skin. Calm steadiness invades, a quiet river. A squirrel clambers down onto my shoulder and wraps its fluffy tail around my throat like a warm necklace. My swimming head rocks back and I lift my gaze to the stars.

Breathe, Zaja.

Breathe.

My vision blurs, and another starry sky overlays mine, this one so filled with shining lights it fills me with awe. A magical carpet of galaxies and suns and more stars than we have numbers to count. It's like seeing the universe itself.

Instead of cold tree bark I feel a warm, hard chest at my back, lifting and falling in slow rhythm, and the brush of lips on the column of my neck.

It feels so good that tears prick my eyes.

It feels so much like the embrace I have desperately needed for years that a sob rises in my throat.

A soft and gentle hum shivers through me like a caress.

Follow the song.

How?

Maybe this is worth braving the world for. Maybe this is worth leaving the safe sanctuary of this passionless estate behind. It has confined me as much as it has kept me from being ripped apart out in the world. Alas, the walls aren't holding the world back anymore. Sensations battle me down anyway. So where do I go?

This last vision, the one that came with the familiar and steadying scent that makes the coil in my chest unfurl, fades away. I sway after it, from my hair to my toes.

Of course. *A moment ago I didn't want a vision, now I do. Fabulous.*

Needing to expel the jittery energy of my mind I push myself off and resume my roaming. The estate spans acres of forest. I won't meet anyone else out here who walks on two legs. At the stream I scoop a few mouthfuls of chill water, then I march on. I kicked my shoes off a long way back. Dog will have returned them to the house for me by morning.

I don't want to stop, don't want to face the literal music.

So I walk.

When the night turns darkest in the early morning hours and one of the deer nuzzles me between my breasts, soft pink velour sweeping through me... I admit to myself that I may actually need to take my parents' advice.

Go abroad.

Just not the way they imagine.

I kiss my friend on her forehead. "If I'm going to go mad, then I'll go on my own terms, right?"

And maybe I'll find someone. Something. A way to turn it off. To fix me. *Anything.*

Or maybe the onslaught will give me the final boot out of my mind within a day of leaving the front gates. Frankly, it seems more likely.

I hate how much I yearn for a world that terrifies me. And I hate the terror more. Frozen fear threads through my veins and thaws with the heat of my anger in a tedious, torturous cycle. Because I know that if the onslaught of sensations and emotions and energy won't kick me over the cliff, then the visions will.

And it won't matter if I'm out there or in here.

Gah!

I keep walking.

My feet turn numb from cold while still alive from the currents of energy flowing in the earth beneath.

I keep walking.

My legs grow tired and my eyes feel strained.

I keep walking, as I see not two feet in front of me and far too much.

Only when dawn tiptoes across the sky do I curl up and sink into another life. Only when I can't stay awake any longer do I embrace the song I know will inevitably greet me...yet I have no idea how to follow.

Or if I dare to.

* * *

Water clings to my skin as I step out of the shower. *Another day.*

I cocoon myself in a thin linen towel snugged around my shoulders. *Second will follow upon second.*

My hands clutch the edges in front of my heart. *Eventually, it will end.*

I stand there.

I don't move or think. One thoughtless, eternal, perfect moment of fragile peace.

Shallow and empty.

False.

When the day ends, night will come.

Snap out of it.

I take a deep breath, getting ready to make myself get on with things, when I pitch into swirling colours shot through with black swaths. This body is similar to my own, swaying with large sweeping movements. Like the conductor of a symphonic orchestra, I'm moving and directing the eddies of energy. It's taxing. There is an underlying sense of sorrow.

There is also song.

A sense of completion follows. Satisfaction. I become aware of the tickle of sand under my feet as my vision clears to lush green surrounding me. A pair of arms snags me around the waist. Just as contentment begins to flow through me in great soothing waves—

I'm back on the mat in front of my shower. Gritting my teeth, I growl. *Seriously?* It's been twenty-four days since *the dinner*. It's been double that of days and nights filled with visions that alternately taunt me and torture me.

Getting dressed is an unbalanced dance of hopping and slinging my clothes around. Cat and Dog are wisely giving me room. I'm a boiling kettle about to spill over.

I want to go.

I can't go.

I can't stay.

I'll break out there.

I'll break in here.

I want to go.

I want to go.

I storm out into the grounds with my head haphazard in the flowing armhole of the loose dress that barely made it onto my body, stomping farther and farther from the house. When my feet have eaten enough earth that I feel a teeny bit less suffocated and my own boiling whistle is shrilling alarmingly in my ears, I scream. It's a good, loud scream that startles all the animals.

That's the only effect it has.

Besides the tears it seems to have summoned. What self-respectable thunder comes without rain, right?

Green eyes. Beautiful, tender green eyes. I want to find those green eyes.

I have to go out there.

I can't. Those few trips my parents dragged me on I scarcely endured, and they were all private planes and minimal human interaction and...years ago. Before everything became this strong and wild in the way I feel it. Before the constant visions heaped on top of the sensory overwhelm.

My shoulders crumple. *Another day it is.*

I trudge towards the library. Realising that my outburst is over, the animals cautiously approach again and accompany me up to the house. Cat and Dog step inside with me, weaving between my legs and rubbing against me. In colours and tastes and temperatures, I sense their upset and desire to comfort. We make our way through the halls like a whisper of wind, and the thought of my books and research brings a modicum of soothing. I have a sense of control in the library, of ownership over my life.

Then I cross the threshold.

Everything appears untouched. Old-fashioned globe sitting on its angled axis on a round side-table to the left. Seven books out by the chair ahead to the right. Endless shelves and vast windows. My domain and safe haven just as I left it.

Apart from the black shards scattered across the floor.

Apart from the glinting slivers of gold.

And the empty spot where the dancing woman lived, who was so alive in her frozen state. Who glowed in her darkness. Who had been solace and promise to me.

Now she is shattered on the ground, broken in an unperturbed world.

Something fissures inside of me. My resistance capitulates, tumbling down in an icefall of corroded pieces and glacial clarity.

My decision is finally made.

A flash of verdant green.

A teasing, comforting scent.

A snatch of a deep velvet voice.

Song, colours, darkness, connection, belonging, sand, green, water, touch, laughter.

Follow the song.

Yearning is its own kind of song.

I spin the globe.

5

Vigil Court

6 months ago

My body is juddering, I can smell my own sweat, and my mouth feels powdery, as if I've pulverised the crowns of my teeth from grinding them incessantly.

But the grin splitting my face is wide enough to border on unhinged. *I survived the last few days.* My legs may be quaking and threatening to fold, but I'm standing. Multiple thousands of miles from where I started. Hundreds upon hundreds of miles from any continental land mass.

I need a safe place to play dead pronto.

"Thank you," I say to the boy who ferried me to my destination. He can't be more than fifteen years old. My voice is so soft and rasping I'm not sure he even hears it.

"My pleasure, Lady!" He looks like I've put a whole tray of fresh warm cookies in his arms. I'm not sure what to make of that, or of the *Lady*, for that matter. I decide that maybe I don't mind it. It was said in earnest...reverence?

My breath isn't too far off a death rattle. With effort, I draw the lush air into my lungs as deep as it'll go. Mhmm. Flowers, soil, ocean. Most importantly: Clean. Pure. It gives me hope that I may not keel off that cliff quite yet. The air settles through my system like a soothing mandala, a few bursts of life here, sheltering softness there. Colourful birds, some lizards and cats come to investigate me. A monkey swings itself onto my head and joy cascades down my centre.

Definitely grinning.

The boy has been hanging back, watching me. Almost like he was available should I need his further assistance, since he already took on the job of impromptu ferrier—but he wasn't going to force it onto me. I can tell he's gearing up to say something now. To spare us both the embarrassment of my social ineptitude, I propel my legs into motion. Picking the most obvious, busiest path between bamboo and wood structures decorated in flowers and shells, I'm headed into the heart of all that bustles here. My eyes widen and ears sharpen and tongue tastes. Every sense straining to take it all in and experience it to the fullest. The baffling irony doesn't escape me.

The local people are beautiful. Soaked full of the life around them, and radiating with it. They are also a mind-boggling hodgepodge, based on what their features reveal about their origins, and yet it's clear they all belong. This is their home.

A home that overflows with contentment.

Two girls amble past me with arms linked at the elbows, immersed in their avid chatter. One of the two is lithe, the other a little plumper. Both of their lines are soft with peace and self assuredness. I catch snatches of their words amidst lots of giggling.

"...any Queen who wouldn't accept his Bond?"

"The Song knows I would!"

I suck some air through my teeth. *Good. That's good, right?*

Like a fish surrendering to a strong current, I let myself be pulled along, head on a swivel, gaze sweeping across the many women of all ages going about their business. I envy the majestic poise and confident grace with which they hold themselves in their airy and flowing gowns of gossamer, revealing enough I'm astonished to see them outside a red carpet.

Sweat trickles down my spine. I fiddle with the fabric of my cotton top sticking to me. I think I might like one of those gowns for myself. Though looking at the men here... My cheeks heat with blood.

Where the women rest in open strength, the men are arrows sharpened with purpose. Their cut may be varied...but the energy aligning them to their target is cohesive. I watch a few of the men manipulate wood in a working courtyard of sorts. Loose linen covers some of their chests, others are bare to the sun, their smooth muscles rippling with each movement. Easy bantering accompanies their focused and skilled artistry. There is a shared lilt to their voices—everyone's voices in this place— like birds that have picked up the tune of the leaves and wind and waves, and it coloured their song.

Suddenly and in synchrony, the men halt their well-oiled flow and look up at me, expressions of surprise clear on their faces. I duck my head and hurry on, casting about for somewhere else to anchor my attention. *I don't see you, you don't see me.* It works for children.

"Lady." The stocky middle-aged man my flitting gaze latched onto exudes an intense, unmissable sensuality that kisses my skin. To my amazement, it's neither uncomfortable nor creepy. It's rich, yet void of conscious intention. Part of his natural essence. It feels more wild animal than human.

Huh.

I spin in a slow circle as I totter on, my jaw growing slacker as I go. Now that I've noticed it, am actively seeking for it—I can't feel anything pushing at anyone. Everyone's energy is regulated and held in check, not nudging at anyone else, not leaking or oozing or pressing. Simply flowing in the way of life. Children barrel past me, half-naked and squealing. They're a speeding train of exhilaration whistling past—but yep, even they know how to keep their energy contained around them. I think back to the boy who ferried me. I was in complete peace next to him, despite the close quarters of his small boat.

My feet stutter. I haven't had any visions overcome me for the past several hours, either. The closer I've gotten to this place. After months of constant slipping...silence.

Serene, steady, safe, singing silence. *Miracle upon miracle.*

I reach the perimeter of a large circular area where the bustle is most concentrated. Throngs of people are winding their way through more or less permanent open-air stalls. Instinctive caution honed over years of self-preservation at last arrests me. And yet, despite the teeming mass... No one is bumping into or crowding anyone in an unwelcome way. They all move as if they are aware of one another, as if they are performers of one grand dance, and respect is their maestro. Everything here, all sounds, all scents, all *people*—it all blends in with nature. There are no obtrusive, jagged edges.

It's an observation so intriguing it lures me out amongst the offerings of ripe fruit and vibrant vegetables, nuts and grains, swaths of linen or gossamer, plants and seeds and herbs, gemstones and jewellery, tools, wood ware, woven baskets, books, an eclectic assortment of all sorts of things—but no fish or meat, I note. I ramble through it all, the buffet of sensations wearing my battered body down no matter how pure.

A handsome young man close to me in age inclines his head in my direction with a warm smile on his lips while we pass each other. He shares in that charismatic sensuality the stocky man carried. Several of the men here seem to carry. "Lady."

It must be a local custom. He is the seventh to have done it.

He comes to an abrupt stop, almost doing a double take, appearing nearly as puzzled as I feel. He isn't the first one to have done that, either.

The young man's wide eyes are fastened on me. Tendrils of his boyish excitement unfurl and tickle in my chest.

Odd.

A finger nail tickles behind my ear.

Oh! I finally remember the small monkey still riding along on my head, and the assorted flock trailing me. *So that's it.* Of course. This must appear unusual to—well. Anyone. I do my best to return at least a shy imitation of a smile. Maybe I should ask him about finding a place to sleep? Though the absolute fascination has doggedly kept me going, I might collapse any moment now.

Solitude. Rest. Sleep. Ask this friendly young man for help to find those.

It's a good plan. A plan I'm fully on board with. Only something beyond fascination or reason or will takes over the minute I make the decision. It keeps making me put one foot in front of the other until I stand on a pristine beach. Out on the ocean, where the sky kisses the waves, rise the contours of another island.

And I know that *that* is where I'm going, like it or not.

I let my small backpack drop to the sand at the foot of a palm tree, pull my shirt over my head and shuck off my shorts. *Uh oh.* I'm definitely just being pulled along now. Not that my opinion on the matter seems to make a difference at this point... but I'm strangely fine with it. Who has the energy for sanity anyway?

Besides, I'm comfortable in the ocean. One of the times my parents dragged me along on a trip, I swam to the Mokes and back; a distance most people prefer to kayak. Turtles accompanied me the whole way.

I'm supposed to follow the song, aren't I? Well, I sure am following something now.

Three steps to the waterline.

Should I be concerned that my legs and arms have been trembling for a good hour?

Two.

At least I made it to here. May the rest be up to Moera.

One.

The waves whisper and murmur a song of sirens with seaweed for hair as they sweep over my feet, and I sink in.

* * *

I wade out of the water that is molten gold lapping through me. Step for step, the sand under the soles of my feet transitions from wet to warm and dry.

A moment of absolute stillness and silence. Just me, and the ever-present pressure, heavy like compressed millennia. The anvil upon which I've been crushed in torment as far back as I remember.

Now it cracks.

It crunches and shifts, and a storm of transcendent sparkling colour swirls through me as my ears, no, my whole being, fills with harmony layered upon harmony, song that I hear as much as I feel it, song that feels like all of life.

It flows through my veins with gentle loving trembling touch, it rushes over my bones with wild harshness, it rises and falls and sparkles and dances. It sounds rich and full and magnificent, more complex and beautiful than any symphony

I've ever heard, as if there were whole worlds to be discovered within it, lives hidden in its echoes.

Now this...this is song.

All of it I take in within a split second, in the void between one heartbeat and the next. And that next one singes with electricity.

Because some part of me recognises this. It's so very, very familiar. Through the heights and depths of the song one rich and vibrant harmony stands out, wrapping itself around my spine like gilded tendrils of endless darkness. It is a deep hum and a full melody, it is powerful and centred, sovereign of itself, demanding and gentle, full-bodied and full of mystery. It rolls through the land out into the sea, through the air and the water, through every plant and flower and slant of sunshine. It fits into my soul like a missing piece, it says *welcome*, it calls to me and I find that a part of me calls right back to it.

Recognises it as itself.

Has long since answered it.

Rolls out of me in a mighty wave to complete it, my body blissfully bowing with it.

Another second has passed.

The harmonies that weave over and under one another lift in unison and rise to a crescendo. My own arms lift with a lightness I've never known, as if buoyed up by the air itself. I have just enough time to marvel at my arms like I've never seen them before—*is it really gone?*—before swarms of birds burst out of the foliage and arrow right for me, followed by flying foxes, and monkeys, and frogs, beetles, geckos, snakes, even cats and wolves and seals—they all emerge from the jungle, the trees, the rocks, from caves and coves and crevices—and I am the centre of their vortex.

I sink to my knees just as they all arrive, and there is nothing but feathers and furs and pads and scales and noses and claws running over me, nudging my neck, scenting my wrists, lifting my hair; nothing but exuberant joy and love and welcome exploding through me in sensation and colour and that wild, glorying song. I sense lithe and massive bodies tunnelling through the waves behind me, only to break the surface in jubilation and hang suspended in the glinting fire of the sun for a moment of magic.

The air, the energy, my every cell is saturated with the hum and roaring song of teeming, reckless, unbridled life. Amongst all the sensation, the wonderful, pain-free, overwhelming sensation, only one conscious thought is left to reverberate through me.

Home.

I want to know this place. I want to discover the scent of every flower, trace every cleft in every rock, I want to dive off every cliff and curl up in every cove, I want to fly across every beach and rest against every tree. So I rise to my feet—have aeons passed? Was it a blink in time?—and head inland. The animals keep step with me, with twitching ears and swinging tails and cocking heads and watching eyes and lots of chatter, and a brief laugh sneaks out of me.

Just like Cat and Dog back...not home. A weird sensation sits in my chest. But the smile remains on my face.

For hours I wander the island, never alone, that song always rolling through me. It's comforting, reassuring. As I go, I drink from a stream and munch on berries growing everywhere in abundance. My most astonishing find is a vast...palace, of sorts, hidden in the depths of the island; its treasured, protected heart. When I first discover it—and it takes my eyes a good minute to even realise it's there—I just stand and gawk. Gawk at what I can glimpse of it, at least. It's a building, a human-made structure; yes. But it might as well have been grown by nature herself. Imposing night dark rock flows seamlessly into graceful woven bamboo. There are more swirling and round lines than straight ones and right angles. The whole thing says 'majestic' more effortlessly than any toiled for palace I know of. And it beckons with more magic than a Disney castle.

When I'm about to pass through the first elfin gate that reveals itself to me, my posse that accompanied me since the beach remains behind, stopping a few paces from the gate.

"What, no good?" I turn around and ask them.

A myriad of creatures look back at me. Not a single motion or fidget. But not a single ruffled feather or hair of bristled fur, either. No metallic tang. No heat or cold rippling through me.

Alright, then. Off into the unknown I go.

I enter a tunnel of rock, the darkness around me becoming more complete with each step. It's only from admiring the gate before that I can fathom the improbable heights of the ceiling. Any outside noise or echo soon is swallowed up. Pressure builds around me. But, ah, does it feel glorious! So different to that rasping pressure that has long accompanied me; this one tastes of midnight and freedom as I trail my hands along the stone. A sleeping dragon with the power to wake, rage, and roar. A cocooning weight that is shelter and relief. And, oh, how the hum sings here!

When my brain determines I must be walking into the heart of the mountain, I emerge into wide open courtyards instead, complete with cloisters and trees stretching to the heavens above. I climb spiralling stairs that appear to float on air, and find myself on terraces and balconies and whole courtyards in their own right, levels dappled with sunshine, where a scented breeze snakes around me. The concept of walls as foundational to building seems to have been skipped over. It would make a western architect's head spin.

I absolutely love it.

The palace sprawls and sprawls. It feels alive, in ever-moving flow between emotions. The pulse under my feet guides me like Ariadne's red thread while the hours tick past and dusk descends. Everything is deserted, undisturbed, and in perfect upkeep.

Who created this place? *Who belongs here?*

At last I follow a dead-end corridor to its final, well-protected round door on the left, a piece of massive ebony wood carved with breathtaking artistry and finesse. It swings open silently on a central swivel. The rooms behind it—is rooms a good name for them?—hide one more archway. Beyond it is an inner courtyard with no other access point. Night-blooming flowers, lushly dark and heavy, mingle along the black rock walls.

In this courtyard, a tree grows, her bark deep ash and onyx, near as ancient as the island itself, growing tall as if reaching beyond the sky into the heavens and the eternal darkness even beyond that. Twilight filters through the branches above, and I spy the full moon rising in the sky. Power, vast power, flows through the tree's trunk. Where her mighty roots delve into the earth, they form arches. Arms opened in an endless embrace, ready to wrap around a back and shelter.

I sink into them, drop down through the earth into sleep. Deep, blessed sleep.

Until some time in the night I come to. The flowers are iridescent around me, limned in the white-gold of the moonlight. The song flows through me still; tinkling melodies and deep hums and loving caresses.

And the song carries a name, dropped into my soul like it's always been there, sent by the island like a long-lost friend saying hello. Welcome back. Welcome home.

Amea.

I know without knowing how that it means *mine.*

I belong here.

56

6

EMBER COURT

6 months ago

SIN CAREENED INTO WAKEFULNESS. THE moon hung in the sky above him, a silent symbol of hope to keep him going. No matter how often she disappeared into darkness, she always returned into full brilliance. Indeed, she would reach her apex as Bright Moon the next night.

After ascertaining he wasn't needed in Heart, Sin wove his way through the dark to find some distance and solitude. He had become well-acquainted with the depth of night that preceded dawn, so restless had he grown these last few weeks. When had he last slept through the night?

Sin groaned. He could do with dawn arriving in his life, not just his days.

When he reached and climbed a large rock formation out in the land and settled in, the horizon was beginning to tint shades of blue and violet. His ears picked up the clashing and rasping of the ribbed horns of two topis meeting. Sin could make out their silhouettes as they pranced and charged, and he had half a mind to join in their fight. Maybe it would rid him of some of this pent-up energy...that was dangerously turning into uncontrolled rage.

He hated having to admit that to himself. Not even the caress of the Dark Song, that, as a male, he knew he was blessed to feel as viscerally as he did, offered the comfort it usually held. Sin clenched and unclenched his hands as he waited for the sky to turn orange. Each day burst into existence in a fiery spectacle here, and left the same way, too. As if each day was full of pride, and not a single one wanted to be wasted.

Every one of his was wasted until he could spend them by her side.

For weeks now she had been getting more and more distressed. The last couple days had been a continuous stomach ache. Helpless fury had built up inside him to the point that Elu had taken him aside and told him in no unclear terms that if he didn't get himself under control, the males of Heart were asking him to leave. Sin understood—Elu was shielding Adara and the other Queens. He would do the same for his Queen.

If only she were here and his to shield.

As it was, he had become so unfocused that he was useless to the Court that was graciously hosting him as a guest—again—while being equally useless to his Queen who was out there somewhere. By all appearances on her own and in pain. And still out of his reach.

Sin pummelled the dusky ochre rock next to him. A splinter flew lose and the skin of his knuckles broke open. The redness of his raw flesh seemed to bleed into one with the vermilion sky that signalled the sun was moments from making her grand entrance. He drew back for a second punch, then froze a hair away from making impact.

For one never-ending heartbeat, all he felt and knew was *her*.

His whole being became so attuned with her, Sin felt like they were merged into one. He felt her more clearly than he had ever before, as if previously cobwebs had clouded his sight and silt had clogged his senses.

Sin collapsed onto his elbows as his whole being staggered, uncaring of the sharp sting of his bone meeting rock. All he felt, as the sun rose over the horizon with the glory of a Queen ascending her throne, was the impossible intensity of life rushing like whitewaters, of her joy set free, of love taking flight, of fierce rightness and serene goodness. He even heard a snatch of *melody.*

Dawn had come. His dawn.

Only one heartbeat had passed.

With the next, a ripple rolled through the energy and hummed through the Earth that he knew had been felt by every Sung in every Court. And while that first heartbeat belonged to no-one but him, with this second he was no longer the only one privy to what was happening.

With the third, he realised what it all meant.

The first—his Queen had been Sung in.

The second—the Dark Queen had come.

The third—

My Queen is Dark Queen.

* * *

For one further suspended fraction of eternity, Sin sat unmoving, the newborn sun as blinding as the knowledge settling into his heart.

This is glorious.

This is terrible.

He scrambled up and sprinted hard back to Court. He needed confirmation. Immediately.

Short hours before, Sin had left a mostly slumbering Circle. When he skidded to a halt on hot dust as he reached its borders now, it was awake and aflutter, filled with chatter and smiles and glowing gazes. The Dark Song's caress slipped up his arms and slid down his spine. He grasped the first girl he saw by the shoulder. "Has Vigil Court—?" But he knew there had been no confirmation before he received a reply from the girl looking up at him with shining eyes. He read excitement and expectancy in his people, tasted anticipation rife in the air, but there was no celebration.

Yet.

So Sin strode through the mingling females and males, the younglings darting about, until he reached Heart. An unbonded youth who had just recently joined Heart was brimming over with his hands shaking, and spilled as soon as he spotted him. "Did you feel it? We all felt it. The Queens started Dancing right away. They were frantic, Sin, and the males—!"

Yes, as frantic as he felt, no doubt. He was already past the youth, on until he came upon the grassy plain where the Queens had assembled, their Bonded in tow to assist. They were entering into Dark Song, as he knew Queens all over the world in all the Courts would be, so they could meet their Sisters in the beyond-space of the Weave and pass along information amongst one another.

Pass along the news of a new Dark Queen.

Sin fastened his eyes on Adara and Elu as he waited. Thank the Sacred Song and Wicked Wild he had trained to be a Heart male for as long as he had, conspiring with Queens from a younger age than any other male among the Sung; otherwise it would have been impossible, with the chaos roaring inside him, to regulate his breathing and check his energy.

But it was necessary. Queens were vulnerable when lost to the Dance, and Heart males accordingly volatile when they conspired with them; dedicated both to protecting the female and to preventing any disturbance of her Dance. A Bonded's temper especially rested on a knife's edge when his Queen Danced, whether he conspired with her as anchor in a Bonded Dance or as guard only in a Weaving Dance.

The Queens of Ember had arranged themselves in a circle, facing one another. They were an average-sized Coven of sixteen. A Bonded or Heart male stood with each, and more were gathered around them. The males present would have pounced on Sin had he barrelled in flailing about—which is why it had been smart of the youth to stay back. Wouldn't have been easy, but was the right thing to do.

Elu stood behind Adara with his arm wrapped around her waist and a hand on her thigh. The other Bonded anchored their Queens similarly, some holding their hips or rib cage. Adara's movements were gentle, a subtle waving of her body. She wasn't doing any work in the Song, she was there to meet with her Sisters. An expression of intent euphoria formed on Elu's face, his strong body rocking with slight tremors every now and again, his hands on her steady thanks to the potency of his concentration.

It was its own kind of torture to watch them.

Unbearably long minutes later, Sin felt Adara's focus returning. She turned and tucked herself into Elu's chest as she adjusted, and Elu closed his arms around her and scented her temple. Sin envied him for being able to be for his Queen whatever she needed. To be strength in devotion to a female was a male's privilege and source of true bliss. Reverence that redounded was the Sung males' way of life and contentment.

Maybe now, finally, Sin would have that privilege, too. He bit down on the torrent of impatience that wriggled through him. Songs, he needed her to say what he already knew—

"The Dark Queen has come." Adara's voice was melodic and filled with happiness as she took on the role of spokesperson. "The Vigil Sisters confirmed that a Queen just passed through their Court and swam out to Amea. She's not from Vigil and the Sisters confirmed that no Queen has travelled from any other Court, though that was more of a formality—Vigil shared it was quite obvious she had only just been Sung in." A pause. "We have a Dark Queen from the Loud."

Sin distantly registered an unbonded male peeling off to spread the message through the Court while the significance of that last statement sunk in for the males around him. Sin's brain was hung up on the fact that for the first time, *he knew where she was*, where he'd have to go to get to her. He itched to run and go this instant.

"Vigil is of course giving her due space," Adara continued, "and, for now, will wait for her return from Amea to greet her. So we expect to learn more within a few days, and to find out who she is."

The words were ice water sluicing over his skin, freezing Sin to the spot. He, sole among all the Sung, already knew who she was. He'd met her, shared some time with her, shared years with her in his heart.

But, *due space*.

He'd known she was his Queen. He'd known she was an exceptionally strong Queen. What he hadn't counted on, hadn't acknowledged as a possibility when suspicions arose in his mind, because he knew *she was from the Loud*, was that she was also Dark Queen.

Which meant she needed time, time for the Dark Song to ravish her.

Which meant he had to wait to be Sung in to Amea before he could go to her.

Which meant troves of males might vie for her.

Which meant—

"Elu." His voice came out strangled. Apparently the panic in his expression where there should have been only elation was enough for his friend to grab hold of him and step away from the group.

"Brother?"

"She's my Queen."

A single raised eyebrow. "How—"

"I met her when we were kids."

Two brows. "So you—"

"Yes, that's why. Elu, I've felt her ever since, and I could never find her, and I felt her earlier, and... *She's mine.*" Sin surprised himself with the bite in that last statement. It went beyond the desire to Bond.

Clearly, Elu had noticed that, too. "Alright," he said slowly. "So you'll offer her both a Dedication...and, in time, a Devotion."

"What if she doesn't accept me? She's Dark Queen!" Sin's hand cramped around the stone he hid in it. "What if another —"

"Sin, brother," Elu interrupted him. "Her accepting you has nothing to do with her being Dark Queen. And getting close enough to court her—"

"Her whole life she's been lost in the Loud. Think about what that means, Elu, for a Dark Queen." Sin could see him grasping the implications as his expression darkened, and still Sin was certain what Elu imagined didn't come close to what he'd felt from her, over and over. His fist met his own stomach as if it held a knife, and it did nothing to quell his nausea. "What if she doesn't even Sing me in? She may not forgive me.

Once she realises, once she understands…" And he might need to wait months to find out. After all these years, wait months to even be able to fight for her. Wicked Wild, this truly was terrible. He'd have to sit on his haunches and learn about her from other people. How could he still *not even know her name?* Sin groaned.

Elu clapped him on the shoulder with a shake of his head. "Strong heart and Song's caress, brother." What else could he say?

Even if she Sung him in. Even if she accepted him. Even if this connection between them meant he would become her Bonded. Even if it meant he was worthy of becoming…her Dark Destined. Sin's whole body locked up. His heart thundered and his lungs gasped for breath that wouldn't come. Even if he'd finally have the privilege of being with her, having her—there was a much greater problem than all of those.

What if I lose her to the Dark Song?

Because that was a far too real possibility.

7

Amea

6 months ago

Feeling languid and enveloped in gooey warmth, my muscles for once so very relaxed, I wake up to something soft and wet nudging my cheek. There's bark at my back and a heavy, toasty mass of strength and life wrapped around me from the front.

"Love you too, Dog," I mumble in my daze. I've woken up like this many times out in the grounds of the estate during summer months. My hands and face buried in soft fur, I hum at him and try to sink back into sleep.

A lengthy, rumbling purr answers me.

Decidedly *not* canine.

I flutter my eyes open and stare into large, beautiful, luminous pools of aquamarine surrounded by fur of snow and ash, a handsbreadth away. Blinking once. Staring back at me.

There's tree in my back and a tiger in my front.

As if bored with my lacking reaction already, he opens his jaws in an impressive, lazy yawn, and then has the audacity to—*I swear this tiger is grinning at me.*

Roguishly.

In self-satisfaction.

I burst out laughing, and my stomach muscles hurt from having forgotten how to laugh like this. I snort and bellow and hiccup, and I think I might have drooled a little, too.

At some point amidst my hilarity I've rolled onto my back, and the tiger is now my mirror: On his back, head lolling to the side. He's massive, all brawn and power. He looks nothing but adorable.

When I've calmed down enough that my breathing evens out a bit, I'm entranced by his eyes again. I let myself be lost in those crystal depths, and as if rising up from the bottom of those pools, a sense of remembrance settles into me. Flashes of dreams from long ago, long forgotten childhood memories of the future, slices of lives lived in other times.

"Zurea," I whisper.

And get rewarded with a big swipe of wet tongue across my face.

Which sets me off laughing again.

* * *

Zurea pads along on my left, tall enough to reach up to my waist, often rubbing against my thigh, scenting my wrist, and altogether never leaving my side. There is so much more exploring to do...especially if this is meant to be my new home. *Could it really?*

The jungle is wild and untamed, and I relish in the spongy soil rich with power radiating into my feet, the juicy leaves sliding against my skin cool as silk, the vibrant, sometimes spicy scent of the flowers that bloom in unapologetic abandon. The air is rife with the chatter of toucans, macaws, hornbills, geckos, monkeys. The teeming life overflowing all around me is woven through with overlapping melodies that seem to emanate from between the folds of the world itself. I've never felt so much sensation at once in a way that's left me so…giddy.

Drawn in by the sound of thundering water, we step through a tangle of vines. Rainbows dance in the spray, billowing like sprites above the clear water of the pool forming at the foot of the waterfall. My fingers tap at the hollow of my throat as I stare up at it in wonder. *It's magnificent.*

I'm still enchanted by the sparkling diamonds of the water refracting the light, the mist settling on me like a protective layer, when two heavy weights fall against my upper back and the world spins. "Zu–," I squeal, before I meet with the surface and go under. Trying not to swallow water in what I can't decide is outrage or mirth, I pop up and try again, "Zu–!" This time I'm cut off by the large splash of white tiger landing almost on top of me. "Rascal!" Gaiety wins out. I swat at him. "Impolite, sneaky, too large for your own good, ras–!" The rest of my tirade is lost when two legs pounce on me and dunk me. Coming up for air, I'm blubbering with laughter. "Wait, wait!" I suck in oxygen. "You know you're stuck with 'Zuzu' now?"

My gleeful cackle bounces off the rock face, and *Zuzu* huffs.

We are doing an odd water dance, one front leg wrapped over my shoulder, one around my ribs, and Zuzu's head snuggled next to mine. I wrap my arms around his back, returning the embrace, and we spin in a lazy circle while my breath regulates.

We splash about some more, until I decide tiger-induced break time is over. After clambering out of the pool side by side, Zuzu shakes himself off. Right next to me. Leaving me just as doused as I had been a second earlier–when I'd still been *in* the water. Zuzu grins at me. It's warm enough that half the wet has evaporated by the time I've pushed my hair out of my face. "Hah!" I crow in triumph, and grin back.

We find our way up a cliff that juts over the edge of the island, majestic and formidable, a steady incline narrowing to a blunted point. It beckons me to run, run past the drop, run and keep running into the beyond. My hand in a tight grip in the fur of Zuzu's neck, we walk along until we reach the edge.

There is nothing but glittering ocean and blue sky before us. Space, so much space, and endless room to breathe. An eagle circles high above and dolphins are playing far below, with us suspended in between. Sitting beside me, Zuzu opens his jaws into a deafening roar. So I open my mouth into a roar of my own.

Until we become one, roaring out into the world, until our roar becomes one with the roar of the wind.

I feel myself dissolve and become nothing and everything, loosing substance and folding into the fabric of life.

Finally.

I'm halfway gone when Zuzu rubs his head against my belly. Warm ripples of gold, limitless lakes of midnight, fierce shards of burning ice spread through me from his touch. Love. Devotion. Protection.

They tug me back, reel me in to the disturbing feeling of my cells fitting into each other again like puzzle pieces aligning. *Whoa. What was that?*

Those pieces...they're wobbly. Very wobbly.

I take a deep breath and look down. Can Zuzu feel everything inside of me trembling? Undecided on whether to wiggle closer together or further apart?

Aquamarine eyes are looking back, bold and relentless. Demanding.

"Alright." I whisper and trace my fingers between Zuzu's bright eyes. "I'll stay."

On the island—Amea.

In...myself.

At least I'll try. At least for a little while. And see what I might find.

* * *

Uh oh. I pause my swimming a little ways from the shore. It looks like I have a committee waiting for me. Do I really *need* supplies? I suppose interacting with people was to be expected on a supply run... But being intercepted by them right on the beach?

One of the turtles swimming with me bumps me in my behind. *Yeah, yeah. They were very nice yesterday.* I get swimming again, much slower than before, despite my turtle friend's energetic assistance. Instead of mostly diving, as I tend to prefer, my head stays firmly overwater. The better to see them, and all that.

Maybe the island is supposed to be off limits? Oh goodness. As deserted as I found it, it's obvious someone's taking good care of it. It may be a sacred place of the local people. I switch to treading water once more, and am rewarded with another bump—accompanied by a nip. *Yes, just give me a minute!* What if I crossed boundaries I shouldn't have? I should have considered this yesterday before barrelling right in.

Well, that would have required my limbs to be under my control...

I scrutinise the people on the beach. Three women—one girl, a young woman my age, and one gracefully carrying the signs of being an elder. All wrapped in gauzy gowns. A few steps behind them, two men—one tall, maybe a touch older than me, the other virile and a match to the oldest of the women. They stand a good distance from where my backpack and clothes still sit under the palm tree, but there's no question they're here for me. No anger though that I feel…or hear in the melodies of the song.

It'll be fine.

Almost to the shore now.

When I emerge from the waves and stride for my discarded shirt, the men politely turn to give me some privacy. It hangs close to mid-thigh on me after pulling it on, and I decide I'm covered enough.

This is it. Moment of truth. *Deep breath.*

As I pad over to the women, that breath fills with tart juicy apple and popping fireworks. It's the middle one, the one my age, who looks like she's accomplished a herculean feat in holding herself back until now. "Welcome home, Sister!" she bursts out. She sweeps across the remaining distance between us like unstoppable gale winds, her left hand on her heart, and places her right hand on my chest before I can protest.

Sandstorms of rainbow colours, more of the apple, rushing tingles. Below it all the calm of a lake. And a jubilating melody all her own.

"Tama!" That's the eldest one chiding. Tama drops her hand and steps back.

Following her movements, my eyes catch on the moonstones both her and the elder wear on delicate, braided golden chains, just long enough so the stones come to rest above their hearts. They are beautiful. Luminous. Like their wearers.

The youngest smiles at me with her head half-ducked. "May we meet in the Dark Song, Sister."

I have no idea what that means. But *song* sounds promising that I may be on the right track? And it doesn't look like I'm in trouble. I give her a small smile back.

The men choose that moment to step up, saving me from having to figure out the right thing to do or say. Their sensuality laps over me, and the force of their focused attention on me is...intense. Just like yesterday, in the marketplace. Yes, that's where I've seen the younger one before! He's looking at me with even more awe now than he was then.

There is no monkey on my head this time.

This is all so weird.

The sentiment makes me want to laugh. Who knew my life could get any weirder than it already was?

The older one lifts his left hand to his chest like Tama did. I tense, anticipating that he'll approach me, too. Instead he sweeps his right in a spiral shape from his crown to his heart, with a respectful dip of his head, and extends it towards me with his palm facing the sky. There's grace and beauty in the gesture. I certainly prefer it to him trying to shake my hand. Or jutting his hand to my chest like Tama did.

"I am Baro Ranita-Chosen Anthea-Bound."

Wow. That's a mouthful. And I have no idea what any of *that* meant, either. For a minute I just stare back at him. Two gold bands sit on his finger. One is plain, the one above it is inlet with a small round smoky quartz of deep chocolate brown. Unfortunately, he's still looking at me expectantly, so I give him my own best version of a long and strange name. "Zajasang Maaya Zatinsa."

A smile breaks out on all of their faces, and the melodies lift off into angelic carolling.

"Queen Zajasang," the marketplace guy says, as he repeats the same gesture the older man made. "We are the Sung."

Queen Zajasang. *Queen?* "Zaja is fine," I tell them.

"We are Queens, Witches, Sisters, Goddesses... All the same thing, isn't it?" Tama winks at me. Her grin is nearly as wide as mine had been when I stepped off that last boat the day before.

I swallow. This has all been jolly, but... maybe none of this is real? Maybe I'm still in bed back at the estate and this is just another one of my really lengthy, really lifelike dreams. That's more likely, right? Than a singing island and Queens and slumbering with a tiger. Not great signs of intact sanity, are they? Nothing's felt like a slip or a vision since yesterday, but—

I don't know. *I don't know!*

My breath is coming faster, and my eyes start to flit around, trying to hang onto something that will tell me this is real.

Please let it be real.

"This is confusing for you." Marketplace guy's baritone voice cuts through my rising panic. His energy expands around him a little, calm and steady, while he takes a careful step closer. It actually makes my system settle a little in response. "We didn't mean to overwhelm you. We are glad you've come. Do you want help taking your things to Amea?"

Amea. He knows the name of the island. Is this good or bad? Does that make it more or less likely this is... What even is reality?

When I don't say anything, he continues, "I'm Tavo." His build is strong, an unyielding rock towering over me. But his energy is all puppy friendliness, and his eyes are warm.

I like you, Tavo. And how often has that happened? "I...was hoping to take some supplies back with me." Enough of my wits about me to seize the chance to correct a possible earlier mistake, I hurry to tack on, "If it's alright for me to go back?"

This seems to equally please and baffle them. Tavo nods. I read only openness from him. Alright.

We set off in the direction of the market, a gecko scuttling along with us. They give me space to breathe, and no one tries to touch me again, but a bubble of steady calm still hangs around Tavo. I find myself falling in with him, keeping a step away. He shifts to walk on my left, then matches his pace to mine.

When we pass any of the local people, their smiles are radiant, and they repeat that greeting-bowing-spiralling gesture in my direction, whether they are men or women. At the stalls, Tavo insists I keep my money. "No money among the Sung. Whatever you need is provided, freely given. All give and all receive."

I hum. It sounds beautiful, if a bit fantastical.

Tama trails along with us. Some of the women call her Sister, and some of the male vendors address her as Queen Tama, or Lady.

"You called yourselves the...Sung?"

"Yes, the Dark Song Sang us in. Well, for some of us, it Sang our ancestors in. I was born into the Circle. Here at Vigil Court, actually. My parents were born into Circle, too, though my mum is from Ember." She still hasn't drawn a breath. "I can't imagine what it's been like for you living out in the Loud. I've only been twice, and I wasn't a fan. Did you like it?"

I glance at Tavo, who looks faintly amused, then back at her. There were a lot of...words...in what she said. But did I like where I've been living? "No."

Tama nods vigorously, her curls bouncing. I get the impression that it'd be a marvel to see her in stillness. "I don't know if there's ever been a Dark Queen who grew up in the Loud! We're so excited you've come. I bet you all the other Courts haven't stopped celebrating since yesterday!"

"Let's get her back to Amea, Tama," Tavo says.

Yes. Amea. Zuzu. My shoulders relax.

Tavo sails me over on a type of sailing canoe. He handles the ropes and tiller with suave expertise, never coming closer to me than the distance I set when we walked. The ten minute ride is exhilarating. I love the feeling of gliding over the waves, the wind teasing my hair, shooting soft needles into my scalp with each gentle tug, the sun warming my skin and filling me with gold dust, the wonderful scent of the ocean enveloping me. The song that never ceases mirrors my experience, flying with me as I fly over the sea. A pair of humpbacks breaches in exuberant greeting. I turn my head to smile broadly at Tavo, and find his eyes already on me. His smile just as broad as mine.

Maybe I've just made my first ever human friend.

He lets me hop off in the shallow water by the same beach I landed at yesterday and hands me my few things. He doesn't get off the boat, doesn't suggest to take the supplies anywhere, doesn't ask to join me on the island. I breathe a quiet grateful sigh.

"Welcome home, Queen Zaja."

Then he leaves me to be on my own.

* * *

My body curves backwards, my head tilted up in blissful trust, my heart wide open and reaching to the heavens above. A braided cord of golden energy connects my chest and the infinite beyond, feeding into the eternal spiral that governs and rules all life. The flow gives and receives, comes and goes.

A strong, warm hand is spread high between my shoulder blades, supporting my weight without hindering the energetic charge emanating from my back. Almost like...wings. Unfurling.

My long hair is playing in the breeze, teasing the backs of my thighs. Another hand, also on bare skin, steady in my lower back, now hotly sliding down and outwards, over my soft curving flesh, coming to rest low on my side with the thumb just grazing my hipbone. My breath is deep, running through me, coursing along with the pleasant shivering tingle. Skin on skin, my front is pressed into another, wrapping around me and sheltering me, taking on the weight of my body leaning into....*him*. He grounds me, anchors me in presence, in this body, in this life.

His hair tickles the underside of my chin as his worshipping lips trail down my arched throat, then linger in an endless, burning kiss on my sternum. I am the waxing crescent moon, shining brighter and brighter in the face of his fire.

The glowing, glossy lava of his reverence mingles with the tendrils curling from the golden braid, and I become nothing but a flow of brilliant energy, carrying in it the dust of plains untouched for millennia, the impenetrable darkness where space is folded and the deep ocean becomes the same place as the vastness between stars, carrying in it the first beat of an unborn heart, and the fragrance of a lily. I become no thing and every thing, and am anchored only by the taste of his devotion, of that sweetly dark blaze.

Until I'm me again, reclined on a thick tree branch jutting out over the ambling water below. Blinking rapidly, then twice, slowly.

So much for my plan of indulging in some calm, uneventful resting. My blood feels hot, my body so alive it's an excruciating kind of ecstasy. My gaze darts between the foliage and sky above me as I try to reorient myself, as I wait for my body to calm down, as I listen to the gently melodious song humming around me—even as the wildly moving, epic symphony of a moment before still echoes through me.

Lolling on his tummy on another branch a few feet away, Zuzu is studying me.

Great. A *tiger just watched me—watched me what?*

Tavo dropped me off a few days ago. Visions are once more my constant companion. But they feel different now. They don't come with a side of pain. They all take place here, on the island. They come with a sense of knowing and understanding. They feel like *remembering*—sometimes forwards in time. I huff. That should be unsettling, right? It feels familiar though, from the dreams of my childhood.

I drum the heels of my hands on my temples. My head is stuffy with questions and my body overly sensitive—even more so than usual. A different kind of sensitive. "I need to cool off, Zuzu."

I roll sideways and splash into the water below. Submersed in the fresh current gliding through my veins like soothing gel, the glint of a stone that's been polished smooth hits my eyes. It sparks a memory, and I swim in thoughts of one of yesterday's visions as I float.

People—Sung—were greeting me with that same spiralling gesture Baro had made. I witnessed some other women being acknowledged the same way. *The Coven,* that sense of knowing whispered. Those called *Queens.* One of these women sashayed up to me. She could have been Tama's grandmother, a young vibrant sort of grandmother, and shared her exuberant energy as well as looks. "Sister," she said, and placed her hands the way Tama had done, one over her heart, the other over mine. This time, in the vision, I replied in kind and completed the circuit by placing my hands in the same way, slipping one hand under hers, the other over. I noticed the moonstones—there was one hanging around her neck, and four rested on my chest.

Rising to the water's surface and turning over, I let the stream carry me on my back. Those moonstones I saw in that vision yesterday—I've seen them before. On the other island. Vigil Court, Tama called it. I'd seen some women there wearing them on fine gold necklaces, hanging over their hearts. Some wore one, others two that had been cleverly set together.

It meant they were Queens, I realise.

Bonded, Amea whispers, the knowledge dropping in like a stone into the river.

Bonded Queens.

Like a puzzle coming together, the Sung are beginning to make sense to me, their dynamics revealing themselves with each vision. Which I'm less perturbed by now. For the first time, it feels like my life might fit. Like I might come to be someone to these people, similar to the women whose eyes I've been seeing through since arriving here. Someone who belongs.

I clamber out of the water in search of some fruit, my hand buried in Zuzu's fur as we walk. Bonded. *So what does that mean?*

The world tilts and fractures. I feel the Bond between me and the man who is acting as my anchor, feel the strength he freely offers for me to draw on as I weave and braid strands of energy with movements resembling a dance. I feel how he becomes my touchstone the deeper into the energies I go, feel how he becomes a shield and sanctuary to allow me a moment of rest, when the intensity of the storm of emotion and sensation that rages in the depths becomes taxing.

I also sense the pleasure that awaits me in that storm, sense the bliss of dancing in that much life, sense how the melodies are living harmonies here, how the song I not just hear but also feel is *Song,* how it is the totality and essence of all those wild energies of life.

I sense how I can let the experience of Song flow through the Bond, and share it with the man. My Bonded.

Then I snap back to the feeling of Zuzu's fur between my fingers, hardly missing a step. "Bonded Queens," I grin at him. "I guess I have an idea now."

And so many new questions.

8

AMEA

5 months & 2 weeks ago

"WE COME BEARING FRUIT, WISDOM, and all the answers you seek!"

Tama's curls are vibrating with the force of her enthusiasm as she's standing on the beach, her arms full and a stupendous grin on her face. I feel my own lips quirk in response, but I keep a few feet back, with Zuzu standing tall and stable by my side. My eyes slide over to the young woman standing next to her, also loaded with goodies.

"Sister," she says, her voice a clear, arctic stream, melodic in its crystal tones. Her eyes are filled with as much spunk as Tama's. The two of them next to one another make me think of an Italian harlequin—one all creamy brown gleaming beauty, the other opalescent grace, and together more mischief between them than could possibly be healthy.

Both of them notice Zuzu now, and their eyes grow huge as they look back at me. For some reason, that causes a full smile to rise to my lips. I give them a shrug. "Sisters," I respond, and delight enters their eyes.

We remain looking at each other another moment, and I taste the roiling chaos of their tart and sweet excitement, warmth, and curiosity. There's juiciness from Tama again, like when I first met her two weeks ago, and the slight saltiness of frozen snow from her companion.

Zuzu gives a huff. I watch as the new girl's brow raises increment by increment. When it can't go any higher, she tells him sagely with a dignified nod, "Strong heart and Song's caress." And Zuzu begins his rumbling purr.

Well, then. "Whyever say no to wisdom?"

And that's all the encouragement they need. Tama starts bustling toward me, and I begin leading the way to the Palace. Mrak, I learn, is also a Queen—I thought so from the moonstone hanging around her neck—and just arrived from Crystal Court, far up in the north. I wonder how many there are?

"So why did you come here?" And please don't ask me the same thing.

"You Sung me in." She says this the way one might state the air is hot and humid.

"I...did?"

"Mhhmm." She grins at me. "Marvellous, too." She does a little hop-skip.

Marvellous. Is that all the wisdom she's going to impart?

* * *

"Queen Zaja," Tavo says, his smile brimming with happiness, as he performs that sweeping, spiralling, bowing gesture I've come to grow familiar with from the visions. It's only ever offered to Queens. "A pleasure to see you again."

He forms one end of a loose crescent formation of five men who just landed on the beach. The full moon hangs bright and low above them. Tama and Mrak have been with me two weeks, and for the most part I'm still waiting for that wisdom they promised.

None of the men move a muscle after that, and they hang back much closer to the waterline than the girls had. Probably because of Zuzu's snarling.

Looking into Tavo's kind eyes, I realise I'm happy to have him here. Rather than feeling the need to preserve my solitude —as much as there is of that with the two firecrackers around—I like the thought of him joining us. He brings steady calm with him. "Welcome, Tavo."

Zuzu's snarling stops. I don't think I imagine the slight relaxing of shoulders all along the crescent. The side of my mouth twitches.

Next to Tavo is a young man who can only be Mrak's twin. A gold band glints on his finger. "Queen Zajasang," he says. "Jave Mrak-Bound." The unmovable glacier to Mrak's darting icy stream.

Also from Crystal Court is Dashuri, regal and reserved like Jave. Then I meet Sehe Tama-Bound, who wears a gold band, and finally my eyes come to rest on a tall and lithe man with skin the colour of rich soil. Reverence rolls through the lilt in his deep voice as he performs the greeting. Instead of feeling embarrassed, I find myself at ease in the power of his sombre gaze. "Anda from Ember Court," he finishes their introductions.

With all of them through, I let my gaze roll back along their crescent. None of them seem more than a few years older than me, and as varied as they all appear, they share two things in common. There's a gravity to their energy, that steadiness of their focused attentiveness that promises rest and reassurance.

Then there's the sensuality that pours off them and warms my skin. As the focal point of their half circle, I'm inclined to fan myself.

I meet each of their eyes, taking my time as I taste their energy. They remain silent, respectful, willing to give me however much time I need—even with Zuzu still baring his teeth at them occasionally. "Welcome to Dark Court," I finally say.

For that's what Tama and Mrak deigned to explain to me is happening here: Supposedly, as Dark Queen, I'm establishing the Court on Amea, and Sung in those men like I did them. Never mind that apart from Tavo I've never met a single one of them. But I called them, and it's up to me to grant a formal invitation to stay. There are more complex dynamics to the whole thing that make my head spin, about Heart males—the ones with that overflowing sensuality—and the Coven and Bonded.

Bottom line: I'm the Queen they've all been waiting for. They all act awfully convinced of this being so, and cement it further in stone with every person who arrives.

I wonder if they've gotten me confused with someone, and just how long it'll be before they boot me off the island. I've been shut away in the estate my whole life. How am I supposed to be anyone's Queen? And why?

* * *

Ignorant of my doubts, a Circle bustles into life around me. There's the Circle at large, the lifeblood of the Court, and there's the Heart—the Coven and Heart males. When I observed to Tama that many of the men and women and children arriving to establish this Circle seemed to be from Vigil Court, content to hop their lives one island over, she looked at me like that ought to have been obvious. "We *are* called Vigil Court, Zaja." Yes. Well.

Every time I go wandering, I discover something new. Hammocks hung. Hundreds of small prisms that glitter in the sun, refracting the light and throwing rainbow patches on waxy green leaves, smooth tree bark, on the skin of passing Sung. Every change respectfully blends in with nature, never taking action to remove it, only to emphasise its beauty. Rather than feeling overrun, Amea feels adorned. Surveying it all, I overheard Mrak whisper to herself, uncharacteristically serious and reverent, "And so the Dark Court has returned to Amea."

I try not to think too much and go along with it.

A few weeks in, I find I wake up in the mornings with a light smile playing on my face. "I think I'm almost looking forward to what the day might bring," I tell Zuzu with dramatic wonder. "What world is this?"

He dignifies this with a sluggish sweep of his tongue. Along my face.

Yeah.

"Anyway," I clear my throat, "I'd say it's time for—"

I stutter into stillness at the feeling of phantom hands on my waist, accompanied by a husky velvet chuckle. That deliriously good, masculine scent floods through me. Even my bones seem to soften. The sensation of him is so visceral, I turn to check he isn't truly behind me. Then it's gone, and only a gentle burning fire in my chest remains.

"Time for dunking my head in cold water," I mutter.

Those flashes have become persistent. Well, they've been persistent for a good long while. But now they're so very vivid, nothing like the fleeting impressions they used to be. Not as easy to write off as imagination. Which, granted, could be really bad news. When madness starts flirting back... Only, I don't feel like they are bad news.

It's not dread they trickle down my spine, but anticipation.

I throw open the heavy ebony door to my rooms on its perfectly smooth swivel. Sitting high on the island, the destination of Dark Palace's most protected hallway, they're the jewel only reached after traversing the rest of the Court. One with the onyx cliff, my bedroom yawns open to nothing but stars nearly close enough to touch and ocean calling up from far below. It has two exits—one tucked away, leading to the hidden courtyard and majestic tree that embraced me through my first night on Amea. The other, more obvious one, is its connection to my sitting room, a few steps below and slightly set back. This one is also open to nature, albeit on the opposite side to my bedroom's view over infinity. Archways supported by smooth columns, vines and flowers wrapped around some, lead out to a lush private courtyard, rich with jungle. On its opposite side the layout of my quarters is mirrored, minus the infinity view and hidden courtyard access. Those rooms are currently unoccupied, but have their own door out to the hallway. Theirs is the second-to-last door before my final one—the one I've just flung open.

To find myself nose to nose with a stranger.

"Who are you?" The surprise in my tone is mirrored on the admittedly lovely face opposite me, and for once, I don't believe the credit goes to Zuzu by my side.

"Oh," she says, nothing else forthcoming.

A moonstone rests on her chest, and there's a male a step behind her with an equally stunned expression on his face. The flavour of both of them is earthy, sun-dried, twined with the harsh metallic tang of their awe dipped in disbelief. All of it backed by a lot of power, the Queen's Song strong and demanding notice. Her feel reminds me of Mrak, though her colouring is Mrak's polar opposite.

Thankfully, Dashuri chooses this moment to make his presence known, his head of white blond messy curls popping around the solid wood of the swivelled door. "Pardon us, Queen Zaja, we—"

The amazonian beauty cuts him off. "Want to make yourself useful, Sister?"

Dashuri closes his eyes with a heavy exhale out his nose, his fingers coming to pinch the bridge of it.

I find myself chortling. "Lead the way."

Satisfaction sparkles in the deep brown eyes studying me. A touch of approval, too, I think, which is confirmed when she shoots her hand to my chest with a quick, "May we meet in the Dark Song—" an incline of her head, "I'm Adara."

Friendship, and a recognition of kinship, spread through me from her touch. I've been around long enough to know to complete the circle between us with my own hands, though it still freaks me out a tad each time one of the Sisters does it.

"Queen Zajasang," the male says as he sweeps his hand from his brow to his heart in that graceful spiral and extends it out to me, "Elu Adara-Bound from Ember Court."

I thought so.

My curiosity is piqued by the mix of exasperation and heat in Dashuri's eyes as he regards Adara. I get where he's coming from—she exudes strength and sensuality in equal, large, measure. I wonder what Elu has to say about it?

I'm reminded of other present mysteries to intrigue me when this flaming meteor of a Queen turns on her heel and strides down the hall, not bothering to check whether any of us follow. We stop soon after in one of Dark Palace's many courtyards, this one with cloisters on all sides. Adara rounds on me. "You've learned how to Weave?"

"Mh-hmm." Still figuring it out somewhat, but between the visions, Mrak and Tama's instruction, and following instinct since arriving on Amea, I guess I'm getting the hang of it.

When I landed on that beach, the explosive awakening to the Song blasting through me was like a shroud being ripped away. From there, it's a little like taking a turn in your brain you never have before, a pivot and dip between the folds, and this whole new path opens up before you. In this case, that is the pivot into the Song, where life essence is tangible to be woven at will.

"We discovered an oil spill on our journey." Adara's expression is grim.

So is mine. Oil spills in the oceans are devastating in their destruction. "We better fix it." I hope we can.

She gives me a determined nod. "Let's Dance in the Dark."

The more immediate plane of the Song, that one dip away from regular reality, is a world of marbled vibrant watercolour, with bursts and streaks, melody and flavours of emotion. But the more of that power unique to Queens that you have, the deeper into the spiral you can go, and the rainbow turns to velvet black and sighing gold, to harmonies and storms, to maelstroms of energy and emotion. To everything and nothing. That is where the Song becomes Dark Song. It's the difference between dipping a toe, or jumping whole into the river and diving the depths of its currents.

I watch as Elu moves to stand behind Adara, an arm slung about her waist.

"May I, Lady?"

"Thank you, Dashuri." He steps behind me and falls into the attentive guarding stance—a good two feet away. Only Bonded share touch with a Queen when she Dances. The support a Heart male can offer without touch is less, but touch during a Dance is too intimate a thing to share randomly. To say this will be taxing is putting it mildly, I expect.

My gaze connects with Adara's. I take a deep breath. "Welcome to Dark Court. May we meet in the Dark Song."

And so we do.

9

4 months ago

I WHIP AROUND A CORNER, fly down the hall, whip around another, and duck through an archway. My heart is drumming wildly and the blood is hot in my cheeks. Maybe I'll just hide for a minute?

"She's magnificent, isn't she?" Ah—not alone.

I cringe, then realise it's Vala. My hiding plan may not be foiled yet. I blow out the breath I was holding. A gentle Queen who has fast become a good friend, Vala arrived not long after Adara; Jalen her escort, though not her Bonded. Both of them from Old Court.

I focus on her question and make myself properly take in my surroundings. My heart abruptly slows. *Yes, yes she really is.* Sitting proud like a Queen on her throne, she is all graceful curves and seductive beauty and delicate mystery, singing softly as the wind grazes over her. "What is she?" I ask Vala.

Dark Palace is as nested as the petals of a rose. There are courtyards on ground level, flying balconies large enough to be courtyards in their own right on higher levels, little alcoves everywhere. Moving through the palace is a constant flow from light to dark, from open to protected, from shadow to sun. We've come out to one of the flying levels I'm sure you can only find if you know to look for it.

Or are fleeing mindlessly from a male like a startled cat.

"A Witch Harp." Quiet joy shines in Vala's large eyes. "The Coven plays her together, or a Queen might play her as she Dances."

Witch Harp. Following the undulating waves of her overall arched frame with my gaze, her gleaming deep blues like underwater crystal or frozen ocean, her black strings like spider steel, her gold snakes and winged dragons slithering along her harmonic curve and soundbox, twining around her columns and fiercely roaring at her crowns... I decide the name fits.

"Will you teach me?"

Vala's smile is radiant. "Oh, we'll have so much fun by the time Sacred Song rolls around again!"

It's breathtaking how beautiful Vala is, when you look close enough to notice. And yet there's something slightly jagged in her that I recognise. Another conversation, for another time.

"And that is...?"

"The Sung's highest celebration. It just passed a few months ago. It's marvellous!" She bounces on her toes. "Fire and dance and music and—" Her grin turns a tad sheepish. "It's a celebration of you, really..." At my raised brow, she flutters her hand in the air. "You'll see. Or we'll explain when the time comes. Or you'll know. Or your Bonded will show—whichever. Whatever. You'll see."

"Vala," I chuckle. "Are you flustered?"

"No!"

I'm laughing now. "You sound like there's something scandalous you can't spit out."

"No!" Her cheeks are flushing. "No, truly. It's beautiful. We're the Sung. I just...feel a little behind, sometimes. And I don't have a Bonded, yet..."

And the dull hollow hiding behind her eyes is back. Maybe this is the time for that conversation, after all.

"That's unusual?"

"A little." Vala strums her fingers along the Witch Harp in a slow glissando and sighs. "Queens enter into Bonds earlier than males, generally, to receive the support for their Weaving. The males tend to be a few years older before they offer a Bond to a Queen, so they're confident enough in their training, and can be sure of their decision, their desire to Bond with a particular Queen."

"Because a Bond is lifelong."

"Well, if a male ever asks to be released from his Bond, that request is honoured. Or the Queen can choose to undo the Bond. But either is extremely rare."

I hum. "So it's a big decision for a male to offer a Bond. Because it means service." My voice pitches a little too high on that word.

"No..." Vala shakes her head. "I mean, yes, with a Bond a male offers his life to you in service to your Dance—that's what the words of the Bond Song are all about." She glances at me to check I'm following, and finds I'm not. "The ritual during which a Queen accepts an offered Bond and creates the energy weave between the two of them," she clarifies. "It's always done on a Bright Moon. You'll experience one soon enough."

"Ah." I nod for her to continue. "Service?"

"Right. For a Sung male, to offer his strength in contribution to his Queen, to be able to offer her his protection, his power, his dedication and devotion—his power *is* in his devotion—it's the highest honour and fulfilment. Well, next to marriage," another glance and aside for my benefit, "and that ritual is the Wedding Song."

This may be the most in terms of straight up explanations that I've gotten out of any of them yet. Some of it I've gleaned from the visions and the knowledge Amea seems to drop into me, but I greatly appreciate the clarifications.

"Do the men really feel that way? I mean, can we be sure this is not just patriarchy reversed, but with the same flaws?"

Vala doesn't swat my question away. Her head sways while she searches for the best way to explain. "Not everyone is born into Circle. People, males, are Sung in—they knew the way of the Loud before—and they can choose to leave again. They don't." Her foot taps slowly, as if each tap helps her order her thoughts. Helps her find the words to describe what to her is natural and self-evident, is a life-long lived experience. "Among the Sung, we accept that we are all different. Some of us have soft strength, others dark, others hard, all kinds of different strengths. Our sovereignty as females comes not from our position in our society or our relationship with the males—it comes from our connection to ourselves and to the Song. To life."

She plucks a few more strings, incredibly harmonious for all that they are played haphazardly. "Every Sung, whether Coven or Bonded or Circle, does what they are uniquely able to do in order to contribute to the great web of us all. To the Song. And we cherish each other for who we are. We meet each other in reverence no matter who we are, as we meet the world around us. Reverence redounds. We know this to be true strength, and true happiness."

Vala cheekily raises her shoulder. "Don't the Sung males seem rather satisfied to you? Don't they ever put you in mind of a preening chimp, or a prancing stallion? Proudly peacocking for all to admire?" She's giggling now. "A dancing bird-of-paradise?"

Oh, that comparison is brilliant. Their dances are *quite* fabulous. All that puffing and masterful sidestepping and slinky bobbing and rhythmic head-waggling. I burst out laughing. "And indeed, admiration they receive."

My tense back relaxes. Vala's right. Sung males aren't shy about showing off their majestic masculinity, and Sung females aren't short on offering appreciation. It's a joyful, light-hearted reciprocity. The primal wildness of these men isn't just allowed, it's celebrated. As is the women's. And each enjoys the other's, knowing there is nothing to fear from it, and so much to receive.

Vala confirms the thread my thoughts have followed. "There is great pleasure in the way we dance with each other, each leading or surrendering in different circumstances, and in the way we dance with the Song through one another. And for Heart..." She purses her lips. "Same as a Queen, the stronger a Heart male is, the more he needs the Bond. They yearn for it. It's a," her hands flutter emphatically, "natural urge. It allows him to be intimately connected to her."

"Because the Bond is sexual?" I squeak. My blood is hot thinking of the three moonstones resting by the side of my bed at this very moment...the three Bonds offered to me in short order by Tavo, Anda, and Yako over the last couple of days. The same Yako I ran from with the grace of a panicked hen to land me here with the Witch Harp and Vala. He arrived the same day as her, yet where she is all gentle goodness, Yako is fierce demanding power. He's from Crystal, same as the twins and Dashuri, but he doesn't have any of the reticence of the other two Crystal males. I snort inwardly. No, Yako is all impatient fire, much more like Mrak than like Jave or Dashuri. And he's not been shy in seeking time and closeness with me. Not sexually. Always respectfully. But the sincerity and intensity of his and Tavo and Anda's intention... knowing they are waiting for me to... it freaked me out.

So I ran. Avoid the scary thing. I'm good at that.

Vala observes me with obvious amusement. "Mm-hmm." Her shrug is the most nonchalant I've ever seen.

My eyes grow as big as that of the dragons gracing the Witch Harp, which plinks in indignation as my knees fold and I sink against it.

Vala cracks up laughing. "Oh, you should see your face right now!"

I glare at her. "So it's not?"

"It can be. It doesn't have to be."

"Meaning?" I swear, a wicked imp hides underneath that gentle exterior. I pluck a few strings with my nail.

"Meaning it's your choice." Suddenly Vala sobers, her whole expression turning serious for a moment. "Remember that, Zaja. It's always your choice. Everything. Your choice will always be honoured here."

I hold her somber gaze and nod. This is important to her.

She watches me for a moment longer, then, apparently satisfied, continues her explanations. "You know Mrak is Bonded to her brother. You'll be relieved to know, their Bond is not sexual." I stick my tongue out at her. "Mrak may meet another male who belongs in her Constellation, and be sexual with him. Both her Bonds would have equal value and strength, the one with her brother and the one with the other male, but one would be sexual and the other not." I nod to show she hasn't lost me yet. "A Queen could also be Bonded to two males and be sexual with both of them, if all of them are happy with that, or all her Bonds could be platonic and she is sexual with another female, if that is her preference."

"But sexual or not, the Bond is always intimate," I repeat her earlier statement.

"Yes." A slight pause. "Besides the practical functions, the shared experience of Song through the Bond... There's a kind of deep comfort and connection it brings. A truly supreme celebration of life. Or so I'm told."

I regard her in silence. She comes to sit next to me, and we look out over the lush jungle and ocean beyond. With Vala, silence is always peaceful, never strained. Two butterflies ride in the breeze before alighting on our knees. Vala is so still I wonder if she's holding her breath.

"You long for it?" I ask.

"Yes." Simple truth, and so much feeling in that one word.

One of the butterflies dances up to the tip of her nose. Lazily, he beats his wings. A true butterfly kiss. I pluck another string with the pad of my pinkie.

"I know," I say to Vala, and we share a gentle smile.

When the butterflies take off, twirling around one another, she twitches her shoulders and clears her throat. "Where it gets tricky is that if a Heart male falls in love with a Queen, he'll want to be Bonded to her, too. Could you imagine not sharing that special intimacy when you're in love and you could?" Vala shakes her head, her brow wrinkled in a frown. "The drive to Bond with a particular Queen might be strong enough to override that risk of falling in love with another Queen," a pointed look in my direction, "but as I said...tricky." She sighs.

"Oh, the perils of Queendom!" I joke. But I can see how the interplay of love and Bonds can get complicated. My head hurts trying to keep it all straight. My heart hurts knowing Vala is waiting for a Bond that hasn't found her yet. "How do they know? The males. That a Queen is the right one for them to Bond to? Other than the falling in love stuff."

Vala shrugs. "I don't know, it's a sense. The animal inside them will know. They'll start trying to scent her wrists, neck, and temple a lot."

Right, putting that aside to think about later. "How does she know whether to accept?"

Another shrug, and wry grin. "I don't know, it's a—"

"Sense?"

"Yeah. A feeling in their energy, their Song. It'll call to you or it won't."

I wrinkle my nose. Call away then... I'm listening. And could really do with a hint.

Vala looks at me, then she bumps her shoulder against mine. "You may also just want to think about whether you want to have that kind of close connection with the male in question. Simple as that. It's not all deep mystery and sacred magic." Pause. "Sister."

We crack up laughing. My head rocks back—and I see Yako standing in the archway, grinning down at me like the cat that got the cream.

10

3 months ago

ADARA IS GUFFAWING. THAT'S THE only word for it. It's bellowing enough to have startled the lovebird snoozing on my shoulder into anxiously hopping side to side. We *were* enjoying a quiet moment in one of Dark Palace's many courtyards. I had just been contemplating how we were two peas in a pod, both so far outside of our natural habitat and comfort zone our world was unrecognisable.

Apparently, my pokerface isn't as beautifully blank and neutral as I thought it was. I suppose it's the heat in my cheeks that gave me away, or the slight involuntary widening of my eyes. Gave my innocence away. Because as much as I think it's wonderful—well, to have Adara right in front of me with the hands of two men all over her is...making my blood flow.

Hadn't I just been thinking about lovebirds?

"Will you do it, Queen Zaja?" Dashuri asks with quiet intensity that is soft pressure snaking along my bones. My eyes dance over to Elu's. His gaze is open and calm. Peace and contentment radiate from him, soft dew and sunny rays. Nothing hidden.

They all want this. They want Dashuri to join Adara's Constellation—in itself nothing hugely extraordinary, though it is evidence of the depth of Adara's strength to have the capacity for two Bonds. What does make this fascinating, at least to me, having grown up sheltered and out in the regular world as I have, is that they're making it abundantly clear that they intend for both of her Bonds to be the sensual kind. And what makes it nerve-wracking is that they are asking *me* to Honour their Bond Song.

I swallow through air that sits in my throat with the thickness of an elephant's hide. Or is it a serpent squeezing? I have no idea how to do this, what it involves, what is expected of me. It's obvious it means a lot to them that I be the one to preside over the ritual—*Honour* it. Well, I don't think it has so much to do with me personally as who I am to them. "Yeah, I'll do it." My mouth seems to have amassed a desert. The words feel sandy on my tongue.

Dashuri's shoulders drop, his biceps loosening where they're wrapped around his Lady. Elu smiles a quiet smile. Adara has calmed down but is still wearing a shit-eating grin.

"Of course you will, Sister." She winks at me. Then she takes my hand, squishes it, and says, "Thank you, Queen Zaja." Honest joy shines in her eyes and floods through me from her grip in place of circulation.

"You're welcome, Queen Adara." Somehow, the whole thing suddenly is terribly moving, and my voice croaks just the slightest bit.

They saunter off, ostensibly to leave me to my snoozing, and I watch their playful pecks and teasing smacks. "Look at that, lovebird." It's been all of a month since Adara and Elu arrived and met Dashuri. And yet, none of them shows the smallest niggle of doubt. "When you know you know, I suppose." It must be nice.

Thus, a few days later, the moon is plump and bright above us, the soil rich and dark below. My feet are bare. I love the gown I'm wearing: Light and flowing as always, it rises high on my chest, while in the back one single twisted column runs along my spine, leaving the rest of my skin to be kissed by moonlight. Low on my back, fabric takes up again and flows out behind me. Little interconnected chains of gold adorned with pearls and gems web around my arms, head, and hair.

The whole Circle—still growing in numbers daily—has gathered around in a natural clearing deep in the jungle, turned out in beautiful garments and celebratory spirits. The Heart forms the immediate circle, the Court at large right behind. There is Mrak, beaming, her moonstone proudly worn on her chest, holding hands with Jave, her Bonded twin. There is Tama, also wearing her moonstone, bouncing on her feet, with her Bonded Sehe standing close to her behind her left shoulder. There is Vala, nodding at me in encouragement, and Jalen, who travelled with her from Old Court, standing on her left. Directly opposite me stands Elu, tall and proud, his Dedication—the gold ring signifying his Bond—gleaming on his finger. Before all of us, in the very centre of it all, Adara and Dashuri are facing each other.

I'm too nervous about the role I'm meant to fulfil to get too worked up about being stuck in the middle of a crowd. Besides, Zuzu stands two steps back to my left, Yako beside him, while Tavo, my gentle giant, is to my right, and Anda beside him. Between those four, I'm practically cocooned in a sphere of calm.

Time to be a Queen, Zaja.

With a resolute nod to myself, I begin, welcoming us all to this festive occasion. My voice is steady enough, but too constricted to build up much volume. The Sung save me by nixing even the quietest murmur amongst themselves. The jungle stills and listens, too. I get out my words without too much stumbling. Then all that remains for me to accomplish is to witness Adara and Dashuri as they do their part.

The ritual is brief, a few words only, but when I sense the ripple in the Song when their Bond is formed, when I hear the beauty of the new harmony that forms between their Songs, I realise it is utterly beautiful and pure. Witnessing that connection being spun between the two, not because it was forced or pre-ordained, not because it magically snapped into place, but because they want it and chose it and created it, my mind is suddenly made up about those three moonstones waiting next to my bed.

On the next Bright Moon, I will return to stand in her mystical light, and it will be my Bond Song. I will accept and have three Bonded. Tavo, my first friend. Anda, my sombre strength. Yako, my fierce fire. The decision feels easy, graceful.

What rocks through my system like a cold gale is the familiarity of the feeling of the Bond spun before me.

Because it already hums from my heart to another.

7 weeks ago

"You'll like this." Tavo gently elbows me, a cheery smile on his face.

"Ooooh, yes, you'll love it!" Yako says.

"It's pretty special," Tavo adds.

"Like you," Yako echoes.

With a playful half-roll of my eyes I look at Anda. Is he about to join in with his part in this little Bonded choir? One of his brows lifts almost imperceptibly in his otherwise composed, impassive face. I press my lips together, a laugh trembling behind them, and turn back to the two jabbering males with puppy energy flanking me.

The whole of Heart Court is trekking across the island together. It's one big, happy group trip, complete with chatter and laughter and friendly teasing. Wherever it is we're headed, which everyone's taken great pains to conceal from me, I see idyllic picnicking and squealing splashing in our future, based on the swirls and eddies of energy currying me.

"Do you miss your home Courts?" There must have been other people they used to do these sorts of thing with, before they up and left for Amea. Because I arrived. My chest tightens a little.

"I'd like to show you Ember one day," Anda surprises me by speaking first. "I think you'd adore it there. But I wouldn't want to go back without you."

My features screw up in a frown. "Why not? Anda, I don't want—"

"You're home now." He says this in a way that somehow conveys he means it in every sense: That I've come home, and I've become home.

"Anda—"

"Trust in me, Zaja."

I clack my teeth, trying to process this. My fretful silence only lasts a few steps, before Anda offers his arm to help me clamber over a mossy fallen tree that nearly reaches my hips. This—his touch—I find easier to accept than his words. *Life truly has changed.*

"For a Bonded, a Queen is his home," Yako says, the fire in his eyes blazing. "It's...it's even in our most basic greeting."

Bond and Song. The Song is sacred to the Sung...as is the Bond.

"Zaja, for a Heart male, it's all we long for while growing up," Tavo says. "Impatiently. We don't even expect to stay in the Court we grew up in, since it's so possible for our Queen to be in another Circle."

"They're all...they're all Sung. So we feel home and connected in all of them."

My shoulders are still tense. I strip a leaf of a fern and chew on it–better than continuing to mistreat the inside of my lip. And besides, it's tasty.

Anda reaches out to tug me to a stop. "You didn't steal us, Zaja. You gave us the greatest gift of our lives."

The other two nod emphatically.

"Being called in by the Dark Queen? Getting to see the mythical Amea?" Yako winks at me, though I can tell he's dead serious beneath the joking demeanour. "Every male in Crystal was green with envy and wanted to be me."

"Not the Bonded ones," I retort.

"Ah, I think even them." It's such an unlikely comment to come from Anda that it wrenches a short laugh from me, which peters into a few reluctant giggles. Anda smoothes a peck to my brow while Yako and Tavo chuckle, and we set off again.

"What–what about you?" Tavo asks. "Do you miss...where you grew up?"

The last bit of mirth dies in my throat. Memories of the estate fill me, of the...loneliness. The fear. "No," I croak. "I don't miss it."

Picking up my hand to swipe his thumb over my wrist and briefly bring it up to his nose before letting me go again, he says, "We want you to be happy, Zaja."

I give him a soft smile. "Right now... I really am."

And in this moment, it's the truth.

"So is he, I think." Yako waggles his eyebrows while jutting his chin at Jalen. Walking some paces ahead of us next to Jave, his eyes are fastened to Mrak ahead of them, who's telling a story to Vala with helicoptering arms aiding her narrative. Unaware that all of our attention is now on her, she throws her head back in laughter, completely entertained by her own story. A burst of delight and a flame of desire emanate from Jalen.

"He is," I smile, then crinkle my brow a little as I worry about Jave.

His connection with Mrak is profound—as Bonded, and as twins. If Jalen is hoping to join Mrak's Constellation and be her lover... I focus on Jave, whose gaze is flitting back and forth between his sister and Jalen's rapt attention. And pick up... The gentled rose of affection. Affection, friendship, and contentment.

"So is Jave," I breathe with a relieved sigh. The guys grin at each other over my head, then turn radiant smiles on me. Interesting. I wonder if I might have a chance for some girl-to-girl interrogation of Mrak once we reach...wherever it is we're going?

It's fascinating to observe relationship dynamics among the Sung, to watch who is drawn together as Bonded, and what shape the Bond takes, and how it all interplays with matters of the heart, and of desire. It seems there are no rules, so much more open acceptance than in the world I grew up in, and simultaneously, all the rules—the carefully respected guiding threads of the Court Dance which keep the complex web from crashing in on itself. Adara is living her life by her design, and obviously very pleased with that life. Tama has Sehe, her Bonded, and he is her best friend—no more, no less. Who will she love? My eyes snag on Vala just as she smiles back at me over her shoulder, full of loyalty and goodness. A kind, strong Queen. Where is her Bonded? *When* will she love?

Sacred Song... Sing in the right one for Vala. I send the call out into the Song, wide and deep, set it shimmering along the strands of energy that wrap the globe. Her Sung is out there, has to be.

The thought echoes in my mind. He is out there...

Suddenly I think of a different him. I see green eyes looking at me, hear a snatch of a darkly velvet voice. *Sing him in, too,* I whisper into the spiral. Even if my voice may be wobbly and my belly may tremble... I want to know him. *I'm ready, now.*

With my eyes unfocused I listen to the low hum singing back while I take the last two steps to crest the ridge we've been climbing. We've reached a sort of natural balcony, and right in front of us... My jaw falls in awe.

It's like a vein of passionate love come alive.

"Firefall," Anda murmurs.

"Firefall." The name fits perfectly. Illuminated by the sun just so, the waterfall looks like it's pouring molten fire, and the Song hums.

6 weeks ago

"Mrak, a storm is coming." Much wetter than the refreshing ocean moisture coating our skin as we lay sprawled on hot stone by the shore.

She clucks her tongue. "I'm already here, girl."

Adara chuckles from where she's lounging in the sun a few rocks over.

I suppose Mrak isn't wrong. "Another one, then. The drenching flashing kind."

Now Adara pipes up. "Oh, I'm sure she drenches alright, Sister."

"Songs," I mutter, but my lips are twitching. "I expect you'll tell me now that you flash, too?" I regret it before it fully leaves my mouth.

Both of them are chortling.

"Oh, yes, often. So easy to do as well in these gloriously gauzy gossamer things," Mrak says while fingering her gown and swishing it around in the air in demonstration. I raise a hand to cover my face. She continues, "I tell you, it took a little more committed effort in Crystal."

Adara is wiping tears.

Fine. I give in to the hilarity fizzing through my blood from where Mrak's arm touches mine as we lay beside one another. Once I start they're off again, too, and it takes us a minute to stop bouncing the giggle back and forth and finally calm down.

"Seriously, a non-Mrak storm."

"And?"

"And... The storms keep *tugging* at me." It's more than feeling them coming by the increasing force with which the water is slapping against the rock below us more and more loudly, or the way the wind is singing more urgently, or the air is tasting brinier. It starts long before any of those things become noticeable.

A soft smile plays around her lips. "They're calling you to the Queen's Dance, Sister."

"It's a time I should Dance?" I prop myself on an elbow.

Months ago, I experienced my first. Six weeks ago, I Honoured my first Bond Song. Two weeks ago, I accepted Bonds of my own. Altogether, I've grown familiar with the Dance since coming here. I thought.

Through the Weaving Dance, we balance and heal. We weave the energy strands, flow the energy where it's needed. It's like...gardening. Like honouring the Song by anchoring into the grid that spans the globe and doing what we need to based on what we see and feel.

When the Weaving we need to do is more intense and we go into the deeper levels of the Song, deep into the spiral, where the rainbow colours give way to onyx and gold, where the Song has teeth, we rely on the assistance of a Bonded. With the Bonded Dance, we can heal, we can hold another through their pain, we can soothe, we see visions of what can be, and hold and weave and seed them to create them. The Bonded hold the frame, so we can hold the vision. With the Bonded Dance the Sisters also meet with one another in that whirling wild beyond time and space, to connect, to glory in it, to pass along information, to Weave together.

All one Dance, and those—Weaving, Bonded—its different rhythms. *Queen's Dance?*

"No, this is different." Mrak looks at Adara. "We only know this from what's passed down through the Sung, of course, from the times there were Dark Queens in the past..."

"It's not to Weave," Adara says. "Not directly."

"The Queen's Dance is for you," Mrak says. Then her grin turns arch. "And for everyone around." Her grin really turns impish now. "You're sort of taking your breaks off. So we can all become drenched and flashing storms."

And Adara is snorting again.

Great. I'm glad they're so amused. With a huff, I plop back down. "That cleared it right up for me, Mrak. Thanks."

"How about following the tug, Zaja?" Adara says. "What's the worst that can happen?"

Oh, I don't know, anything? Every day here is a trip through the wardrobe or down the rabbit hole for me. I've gone from ghost of the castle to heart of a Court—a whole system of Courts. I have Bonded and a Coven and my work is dancing and weaving the invisible. I sleep cuddled up with a tiger—

granted, that's not utterly out of left-field given my history. Letting that one slide. Just like with this whole Queen business I'm still sliding between living in this world and the space between worlds…

"Yeah, what's the worst?" I mumble. I sit up and sling my arms around my knees, staring out at the water.

Mrak and Adara clamber down to the sand. "May we meet in the Dark Song, Sister."

It's a softly tossed farewell, and I return it by rote, my mind churning like the whitecaps. The visions don't worry me as much anymore. They're alive, but I feel less out of control. I can…flip back to the right page. But what I experience in the Song—in the Dark Song, when I venture that deep—that scares me. It would be far too easy to lose myself there. I bang my head on my knees. *I've only just begun to find myself.*

Find myself. The thought echoes around my mind with each bang of my head. As if driving it in, like a nail into a wall, might make it hold. Find myself. When I emerge from my mental carpentry, the girls are gone—even Anda and Jave, who had lingered at the edge of the trees, giving us space yet close enough to keep us in their sight, have gone.

It's just me.

And the pull of the storm.

It's here now, gaining power with each second, becoming feverish, and each howl of the wind and fat drop of rain pulls at me to…to…to *join* it. To dance with it. Slowly, I climb off the rock. Slowly, I wander to the centre of the beach. Slowly, I close my eyes and stop thinking.

Slowly, I allow myself to feel.

Everything.

And then I begin to move.

All around me the island is soaked as the elements whip themselves into a wild primal dance, and I revel in it. My bare feet skip and stomp on the soggy sand, my hair plasters to my cheeks and down my back, swinging like wild snarled rope spitting droplets as I twirl. The thunder claps the bass to my dance, and there is nothing but the glory of the power that is all around me...that is me. I feel each drop as it crashes on a leaf, each molecule as it hums with electrical charge.

I open myself up to all of it and become it. It is instinct, now, ancient female instinct, to enter the storm rather than shy away from its mad intensity, to know that its power is my power. To become it and throw off the shackles and limits of this painfully beautiful life. To be reborn to it as the night itself and all the stars. It's like laying down the armour, ceasing the constant struggle to hold myself together, and simply surrender to shattering—only to discover that come apart I am everything.

I am the darkness and the bolt of lightning that cleaves it.

So I lose myself to the Dance, wild and free and wicked, my senses stretched out far beyond the boundaries of the island. I feel the sun-heated scales of the lizard as she lavishes on the desert rock. I am the golden eagle as he soars on the icy mountain wind. I feel the life humming in the rich earth of the mossy, fog-clad forest. I am the palm bending on the other side of this island, and the stars colliding in the far reaches of space. I feel the cool caress of the rain on my skin in the same moment that I feel the fire embrace the log in the hearth in the Dark Palace.

My feet pound on the sand and my hair arcs as I become nothing and everything and life itself. I am in the breath and heartbeat of every being in the Dark Court, on Amea, feeling their lust, their hunger, tasting their desires, their dreams, soothing their fears in my velvet arms of darkness, and revelling in their joy.

I've never felt more present in my own tingling awakened flesh.

I've never been less of myself.

And as wolves everywhere take up their moon song to say *We are here. We recognise you. We honour your Dance*, I am among them just as much as I am dancing on the sodden beach, and I am free. I am the unbearable, exquisite ecstasy of life embraced. That, I discover, is the true power of the Dark Queen's Dance.

At last the storm ceases, and I fall to the ground in a trembling, sobbing heap, my limbs limp and spasming, my tongue tasting snot and sand.

I cry with the awe for this feeling of unfathomable freedom I just grasped. With the bone deep grief over my years of frozen death.

Over the understanding that I can become the sensations rather than be assaulted by them—that because of being me, I can be free of being me. I hiccup and sob and shake.

There was a razor edge just one breath away. An edge of stepping beyond the point of no return, of losing myself in the Wicked Wild. Wholly. Completely.

One breath away from ending up shattered like the onyx dancer at the estate.

I'm crying hardest because of how glorious it felt, and how tempted I was.

11

Present day

Wicked Wild, how in all the Songs was this happening right now?

The Queen Dances.

Throughout the throng of Sung Sin was torturously trapped in the middle of, like a wildfire trying to outdo the storm raging over the island, the hushed whisper was passed from rosed cheeks to gleaming eyes to fluttering hands, was passed in knowing gazes, muscles clenching and unclenching, bodies tightening with the sensation of wires come live. All Court activity ground to a halt and suspended, the Sung had come out and congregated in the Dark Palace to share in this experience, like they might assemble on another night in festive spirits to witness a comet passing. Sin's own breath was coming faster, his skin responding to each touch of fabric and movement in the air.

"Bond and Song, brother."

He didn't register who it was that clapped him on the shoulder, so fiercely was he concentrating on clinging to control. Even now he felt the echo of her ecstasy, and everything in him demanded to go find her, Bond to her, claim his position in her Court and life—and to witness her Dance so he may taste the Dark Song.

Get it together, Sin! Who did he think he was? He hadn't even met her yet—had scarcely arrived on Amea. None of that seemed to matter to his body. All that wild creature inside him cared about was that the Dark Queen was Dancing the Queen's Dance. His Queen. *You have no claim on her*, he growled to himself.

Songs, he needed—he needed to—he needed to wait. That's what. There was no chance now of getting to her today.

He. Had. To. Wait.

Sin shook, his knuckles cracking in his tight fists. He had waited years. Then, since she arrived among the Sung, the most glorious of all sunrises, he had waited months. Had watched Anda leave, and Elu, and Adara. Day by day, he had become more crazed, had become a beast trapped in the cage of his own making, the bars made of his honour. Her choice. Her Song that would sing him in.

So the bars held him. Barely.

"One—more—night." The sound that pressed through Sin's clenched teeth was feral and violent. The people around him were raising eyebrows and edging away to create a buffer of space. Male gazes were sharpening on him in spite of the seductive, overwhelming distraction of the Queen's Dance. Sin's self-control was unravelling at terrifying speed, transforming into its own chaos-wrecking storm to rival the one visited upon them by the heavens.

This could not be happening. His muscles were spasming, his throat convulsing with a building roar.

No.

No, he was better than this. If he wanted to have any chance at all of meeting her, he had to be better than this. She had an established Court by now. He was new. No Sung male of her Heart Court would allow him to get anywhere close enough to her to even hear her voice if he lost it now. There would be no excuses. His time on Amea would be done. Over. Gone. And that was not an acceptable outcome.

Zajasang. Sin closed his eyes. *Zajasang.* He focused on the feel of his tongue wrapping around and caressing her name. It had become his meditative ritual when his bars were threatening to break. *Zajasang.* After she'd vanished more than half his lifetime ago, he knew who she was. *Zajasang.* Her name could finally become his prayer.

His breath was slower now. Good. Not only had he at last learned who she was, when her name was passed from Circle to Circle several months ago, the day after he'd felt her at sunrise, he'd also known where she was. And now they were in actual reach of one another.

She had Sung him in.

He had followed her call and came.

Though what had he imagined would happen—that he'd waltz right up, and be granted a formal introduction, and she would know him at first glance? That she'd know in her soul who he was like he'd known who she was to him? That she would just accept him without question? Disdain needled Sin's neck as he blinked his eyes open.

But Wicked Wild, not this! He hadn't imagined arriving to this. Hadn't fathomed being plunged into the fire of feeling her so intimately and sensually, and having to share it with the whole Court.

The murmurs of the Sung ebbed and flowed. Sin whipped his head around, taking in the outer open courtyard of the

Dark Palace and the archways leading off it, searching, assessing, unable to register the magnificence he had heard tales of since childhood. He needed to get out of the crowd, find a place to rein himself in for the next few hours. Jealously and doubt roiled in him in an unholy joining. He knew none of the tittering Sung surrounding him were experiencing quite as much as he was receiving from his Queen through their... connection. But what of her Bonded? She already had three. Anda from Ember. Yako from Crystal. Tavo from Vigil. Friends, theoretically. Rivals and enemies in his current reality. What if one of them was witnessing her Dance? Images flashed through his mind of a different kind of dance, an innocent dance of a young girl on a lonely beach, and how entranced he'd been even then.

Faster. He needed to get out, away, faster. His movements as he manoeuvred across the courtyard were becoming more fatally smooth and graceful still than was habitual to him. The snarling, possessive beast in him was thrashing, was close to ruling him. Baring his teeth at all the...eager, awakened, *hungry* —

No, that was *not* the way to introduce himself as a new male to Court. Sin ducked through the archway and blindly hurried down the colonnaded walkway, his gait an elegant stalk even at speed. Every step was a prowl, was his body's way of saying *mine, mine, mine* in rhythm with his heavy heartbeat.

He should have come months ago, taken the risk and use his one chance to petition for Court acceptance without being Sung in. Songs, give it another week and his cage would have lain in slivers, and he would have done exactly that. There had been no way he was staying away from her any longer, keeping them from knowing each other. Had she not Sung him in, he would have come here and fought for her, shown her what he could offer her that she might not have known she wanted.

Sensation flushed through him again, *her sensation*, in blazing licks along his bones. Wicked Wild, he had to find some nook this instant.

So he could ride out these waves.

Privately.

Sin swung left, half right, and swept up some spiralling stairs seemingly suspended on air. Similar to how he was feeling. He had known, in theory, that there was no experience that compared to witnessing the Queen Dance. No way to feel as alive, to feel life itself. This was the gift of females: How sensitive they were, how close to life they stood, how much they sensed and felt. How they rode the waves of life, exuberantly howling at the crests and glorying just as much in the valleys. The males of his world thirsted for that drink of life, that immediate closeness and vivid experience of it, hungered for that soft vulnerable strength that outmatched their own physical prowess and soothed their heart unlike anything else.

Not theory anymore.

At last on his own, no other males in sight that his wild animal wanted to shred so as to eliminate competitors, Sin surrendered to the surges of bliss coated in spine chilling frissons. His body rocked, and he moaned loudly. Yes, their females had the power to channel the essence of life. But Zajasang? She didn't sense the world around her, she *was* the sense and she *was* the world. She was the elixir of femininity itself, the deep serenity and wicked wildness, she was the howling rage and storming passion, the burning beauty, soaring freedom, and vulnerable sensitivity.

She is the Sacred Song.

And never more so than when she Danced. And she was Dancing now.

Wicked Wild, if this is what he felt when he wasn't even witnessing her Dance—Sin couldn't divine what it would be to have that privilege. He'd give his heart and his body and his soul to have that privilege. If only she'd give him a chance.

First, he had to meet her. And for that, he had to make it through the night.

Songs help him.

* * *

"Don't you look the picture of relaxation, brother."

Sin glared at Anda. The energy and tension that had gotten worked up in him last night hadn't fully abated by the time the sun had risen, and now his nerves were stretched taut again for a whole other reason. His friend's cocky grin as he looked him over did not help his constitution. "I need to see her."

Anda's eyes flashed at him, his muscles flexing. "When she's ready." The sharp glint of Anda's Dedication, the plain gold band worn by a Bonded, felt like a stab in Sin's heart.

A growl rose in him. "I can't wait for a formal introduction." Sin's thoughts were starting to spin, his breath burned, and the only clarity he had was that he needed to find her. This was her true home, her Dark Palace, and he could scent and taste her everywhere. She was in the air, in the light, in the vibration and hum and caress of the Song penetrating him with perplexing potency. It was torturous teasing. He didn't have the strength to take it any longer.

Anda softened his voice. "She's gone to take her breathing space, brother."

So she wasn't here. Sin pivoted. He'd find her.

"Sin," Anda said in a warning tone. But he didn't stop him. Whatever Anda saw in Sin's eyes, in the coiled power pacing before him, it convinced Anda to yield. To clear the way of access to his Queen. But he did call after him. "You're making the wrong choice."

113

Sin snorted. No. Going to find his Queen could never be the wrong choice.

For a half hour, he picked his way through the jungle. He didn't know where he was going, but he let his sense of urgency, his sense of *her* guide him. The lush beauty surrounding him, the vibrant life of flowers and birds and teeming jungle, was lost on him. The only animal that pulled him from his frenzy for a ferocious moment of honed awareness was a large white-and-ash tiger with aquamarine eyes.

Cool calculation met his gaze, beast to beast.

Impatiently, Sin stilled. He was so close to her now.

Heavy tension strained between him and the tiger. One moment, two.

Sin moved.

The predator let him pass.

And followed.

He was going to be watched. Irritation, mixed with grudging respect and understanding, churned in Sin. His jaw clenched. He pushed aside leaves as big as his torso and clambered over the mossy trunk of a fallen tree. He wove his way through a tangle of hanging vines.

Then every thought eddied from his brain.

There she is.

Relief and contentment flooded him like golden sunlight rising on a new world. His heart stumbled a beat and he actually had to brace himself on the nearby bamboo stalks for a minute.

The girl by the water.

She was sitting at the edge of a natural pool, one foot dangling, the other knee drawn up. Her body curled in on itself as she hugged her leg and rested her cheek on her knee. Her thin gown left the whole of her back exposed. The sun shimmered and sparkled along her skin, tracing the curve of her spine. Her long hair was pulled together in a thick, loose braid, rebellious wisps escaping it here and there, and adorned with a piece of jewellery made of gold, turquoise, and pearl. She looked blurry at the edges, as if the chasm that separated who she was and what the world around her was had been half-crossed.

She seemed utterly peaceful. Resting in her solitude.

Sin heard his own heartbeat throbbing in his ears. Realisation washed over his brain like ice cold water.

This was wrong—the wrong choice, like Anda had warned. He was intruding. He should leave, right now, and hope to the Song she hadn't noticed him there, so he could try this again the right way.

One heartbeat banged out. Three. Five. Sin hadn't moved a muscle, couldn't even take his eyes off her. *She is real. She is here!* He'd finally found her, his lost Queen, was finally seeing her, close enough to walk up and touch.

Some critters bustled in the foliage above him, tipping a large leaf and sending a small deluge of collected rain down over his forehead and nose. Mother Nature delivering a chastising flick, snapping Sin out of it. He tossed his head.

Songs, she is Dark Queen! She'd clearly come to seek out peace and quiet. There was a reason her time alone was guarded, protected, and defended in blood if necessary. With the amount she felt and experienced and had to process every moment of every day, the solace of solitude in nature was life-sustaining for her. His brother—her actual Bonded—had been right. He'd lost every good sense. He should have listened to him, should have been patient, should have waited until she was ready and he was invited to a formal introduction. What would another few hours have been after half his lifetime? He was messing this courtship up before it had started.

Sin hardly dared draw a breath, paralysed in indecision. What now?

He had to walk away. Sin swallowed. The idea caused him physical torment, a tugging in his gut.

The Sung revere. We cherish and offer our devotion. Most of all, *we honour choice,* he reminded himself while chomping his tongue.

When he tasted blood, he sighed inwardly. For now, she had chosen space. He had no idea if she knew who he was. If she felt what he felt. It didn't matter. He'd have to wait to find out until she was ready. Painfully slowly, pulling on every single piece of hard-earned control he possessed, Sin backed up. He prayed to the Wicked Wild that his trespassing had gone unnoticed by her, that her seclusion hadn't been disturbed by his presence. He placed his feet with the utmost care, step by silent step.

There was no point deluding himself—he wasn't going to return to the Dark Palace. But he'd take a page out of the playbook of that other wild animal prowling nearby. He could stay close without encroaching on the space she'd claimed for herself. So he purposefully moved far enough to no longer have her in his sight, and faced the opposite direction for good measure, sinking down against smooth bark onto damp soil.

An hour ticked by in agonising sluggishness. The image of her bare back was branded in Sin's mind. Every muscle in his body was tense, only his fingers ever-moving as they ripped a fern into smaller and smaller pieces. His tongue was chewed raw. He reached for a new fern, the previous one ravaged, breaking the stem—

Their connection stirred. Sin froze. Even his heart stopped beating.

She was on the move. She was coming toward him.

This is it.

He shot up.

He wasn't prepared.

He'd been prepared for years.

Sin stood tall, his shoulders back, his arms relaxed.

Now.

Zajasang ducked through the fragrant blooms of an angel's trumpet and lifted her head. Pollen dust and water mist sparkled in the sun like tiny diamonds in her hair.

Their eyes met. The world stilled and the Song soared in his cells. One endless, breathless moment.

Then her lips quivered and she broke into a run.

Past him.

Away from him.

Sin whirled around, distantly recognising the awful, bitterly mocking familiarity of the movement in his body. Zajasang flew up the jutting cliff that stretched out like a runway to heaven. Her tread was light and surefooted, her movement graceful, at one with the nature around her. Her now loose hair billowed behind her, matched by the spidersilk of her flowing, barely-there dress, and she was the picture of unbounded freedom.

Sin was trapped in place from shock. *She ran from me. Again.*

But she was getting close to the edge now, where there was nowhere for her to go, and she wasn't slowing down. Sin jerked himself from his daze. She was going too fast, she wasn't going to be able to stop herself, she was going to—cold sweat broke on his forehead at the realisation and Sin bounded into a sprint. His mind whirred as fast as his feet pounded the ground. It was pointless, she was too far ahead, he was never going to catch up to her in time. And why? Why did she run? For one foolish, brilliant blink in time he had thought she was running into his arms. He wanted to drive his head through the rock below for that arrogance.

Sin's heart cramped. Why was she always running from him? Then. Now. He hadn't even said a word to her, hadn't even had the chance to finally say her name.

Three steps away. She was going so incredibly fast. Why was she—? Songs, she needed to slow down! He couldn't lose her, not like this. Not now.

Not ever.

Two steps. Desperately, Sin drew air into his lungs to holler her down, everything else be damned.

One step—

She leapt, as if the next step into thin air had been just another along solid ground, as if she could continue running into the sky. Her arms spread in soft grace, her legs long, her hair and skirts flowing free, her whole being opened and offered wholly to the world beyond her.

For an eternal heartbeat, Zajasang hung suspended.

She was devastatingly beautiful in her wild freedom, in the power of her surrender of herself to the air, the winds, the gaping abyss beneath her.

She shattered his heart.

And then she fell and disappeared from his view, taking all breath in his lungs and feeling in his body with her.

* * *

My heart is galloping. I'm buzzing like a swarm of fireflies is erratically lighting me up. Too restless to sit down as I wait for him to find a way down the cliff and follow me to the beach, I'm tempted to swim and swim out into the ocean. *What, you expect him to follow you out there, too?*

Classic Zaja—up and flee. Always running. So I focus on standing still as I look out over the sparkling blue.

From the moment this man—this *male*—arrived yesterday, I felt his base melody twining with the Song of the island—my

Song. It was different to any other male who'd come to join the Dark Court these past five months. But the Sacred Song was sweet and showed me grace. The storm came, giving me an outlet for my whipped up emotions, and an excuse.

Or maybe it was wicked. A giggle slips out of me, and I slap my hand over my mouth. That was quite the Dance last night. Quite unlike any other. *I wonder why...* I swear Zuzu laughed at me when I got up and started snapping at him this morning. I felt—skittish. There was some amusement from my Constellation, too—along with concern. My disquiet honed their temper, and their need to protect took centre stage.

I shake out my hands. Protect... Years of memories flash through me, of stolen snatches of the colour of eyes, the sound of a voice, the feel of a touch, a scent. Years of *him*. I'm certain of it. I don't know this male—but I know it's him. And I feel that whilst I might not know him, he knows me intimately.

My breath stalls. He made it down the cliff.

He's real. He's here.

I sense his approach. Slow. Cautious. As if each step closer is as vivid and vital for him as it is for me.

That scent that has never failed to soften me reaches me, and the calming cocoon of his shielding strength envelops me. The calls of the birds and seals have fallen silent, the whales have paused in their singing, even the palms don't seem to dare rustle. All of Amea seems to be holding its breath.

So I draw a big one, and I turn around.

His Song is a flower petal velvet caress of my soul. It is a raging ocean maelstrom of yearning and devotion, devastation and elation. It is darkly pulsing sensual power that drags soft lips from my shoulder to the soft skin beneath my ear, that is the feather-teasing brush of a thumb on the bottom curve of my breast, that is warm breath and small licking flames high on my inner thigh. It is pure calm crystal. His Song invades and touches every cell of mine, slinks around every one in a seductive dance, and withdraws.

Our eyes hold.

My Song sings back.

"I've been waiting for you," I say to him. This hour. This morning. This night. This lifetime.

Delight, desolation, desire. They bleed into one in his eyes like wet watercolour, like the sunset on the ocean, like the swirling swathes in the Dark Song. He takes another step, reaching for me, then seems to think better of it, and sinks to his knees instead, his eyes never leaving mine. Knees that are scuffed bloody as if he just recently crashed on them. Green eyes I've seen for years.

"Queen Zajasang." His voice is quiet but steady, ringing with the sort of assured, confident power that doesn't need to shout to assert itself.

"Zaja," I whisper.

He looks up at me as if he wants to bare his soul, and hand me both the keys and a sword to do with what I will. *What do I do?* What does one do with devotion like that, with power and responsibility that weighs as much as a heart and a soul?

For years I have longed for his touch, have known nothing I longed for more fiercely. Now I'm scared to receive it. I'm terrified to accept the oceanic force of his emotions, thoughts, intentions, that are so intense even without touch connecting us. So I keep one step between us, one foot of air that changes nothing and everything, and hang on to his gaze as the sensations of his Song sweep over me.

Drown me.

Fill me and slake me.

And still, the world is quiet around us but for the Song.

Thank you for finding me, I want to say. *Thank you for being the solace in my dance on the edge of sanity.*

I want to ask, *Who are you? What is happening?*
Where have you been, I want to beg.

"Will you join the Heart?" I settle on, my voice bleeding with everything I don't know how to say.

A shudder travels through him. "It would be—," he swallows, then continues, raspier, "my pleasure and privilege."

And suddenly I remember. Suddenly I'm on a different beach, in a different part of the world, in a different time. A page flipped—but into my own body, my own life. Before my parents had called for me, agitated, angry, and bundled us away in a hurry, I had met a boy, and I felt he might have been a friend. He had been my—

"Sin," I breathe in wonder.

12

Sin felt like the young fool he had been when he first met her, a Bondling with nary a clear sense in his head. What should he do with his hands? His breathing was loud. Should he make conversation? About what? He knew everything about her, and nothing. So he remained quiet and left her to her thoughts as they walked, though he couldn't help himself and glanced at her face every third step. Hoping to glean a hint of insight, he told himself, though that was only part of the truth. He had some sense of what she was feeling through the connection, and he didn't need to look at her for that.

But he wanted to. He wanted to look at her for hours, drink her in, learn her every feature, her every expression.

Zajasang kept looking ahead, or up, or out into the jungle. Only once did she glance over at him, and when she found he was already there, ready to catch her gaze and keep it captive, her focus skittered away again as if she'd been burned.

Sin wanted to groan. *This will take some time.*

They wove their way along narrow paths. Where he couldn't walk beside her, half a step to her left, he followed behind her. When they travelled along the same foot-wide cliff path he had taken to find her on the hidden beach, with rock face to their left and a steep drop to their right, he walked close enough to have his nose buried in her hair. He had no idea how she had made it in one piece and one swoop from the top of that cliff down to the secluded cove below, but he wasn't going to take any chances.

Close to an hour later they finally reached the Dark Palace, and Sin felt so antsy he thought he may have to run back there and jump off that cliff himself. Smiles bloomed on every face they passed, and the warm air echoed with the reverent greetings directed at Zajasang. Sin drew his shoulders back and held his spine straight. He watched as she responded with slight inclines of her head and a timid, gentle curving of her lips.

While also drifting closer to him.

Pride and purpose trickled down his neck. His hand was itching to meet the small of her back in a steadying touch, but he held himself back. Not yet. Soon.

They stepped into an expansive inner courtyard. It flowed out before them in nooks and curves, with tree canopies offering shelter in some areas, and woven roofs in others. Gauzy swaths undulated in the breeze, creating a soft separation and private places here and there. Where bright flowers were abundant, prisms also danced and glinted, where the night blooms reigned, candles were scattered. There were wide open spaces, allowing room for plenty of movement, and others, where various shaped settees or hammocks invited rest.

Casually interspersed throughout it all, somewhat clustered toward the entrance through which they came, were the Queens and males of Zajasang's Heart Court. The Heart, amongst all Heart Courts. Though if Sin knew anything of Hearts, it was that casual as they may seem, the positions they had taken up were quite intentional. *Good.* He was a new male at Court, and in the sole company of one of their Queens. He would have been concerned had they shown any less attentiveness than this.

Sin met Anda's steely gaze as he prowled toward them. When Anda, in an action without active thought, an action that spoke of naturalness and familiarity, lifted Zajasang's wrist to his face and ran a soothing thumb over those delicate veins, Sin bit down on his tongue with the sour feeling shooting through him. He took a quick step back from her. *She doesn't need to feel this.*

Then his breath caught when she twisted around, and at last allowed their eyes to connect again. In a clear and soft voice he was certain was heard by everyone present, and in which he thought he detected the slightest tremor, she said, "Welcome to the Heart."

And she disappeared behind one of the billowing pieces of fabric.

"Wicked Wild. Sin Zielliatu." A strong hand clasped his shoulder. "Congratulations, brother."

Sin dragged his eyes from the swaying gauze. Amusement and warmth had replaced Anda's earlier steel. "Thank you."

Many of the assembled males Sin recognised, thanks to all that travelling between the Circles he had done. He shared a nod with Elu. He greeted Jave and Jalen. He sized up Tavo and Yako, his eyes snagging on their Dedications, and felt them do the same to him.

"Fancy seeing you here." That teasing drawl belonged to Mrak. She was ambling towards him with Adara and another Queen on either arm, all three of them wearing big grins.

Sin grinned back. "Ladies." He lifted his fingers to his crown, spiralled them down to his heart and extended his arm palm up towards them with a slight bow. As he righted himself, he noticed Adara was wearing two moonstones around her neck. He looked over at Elu in surprise. Another male had joined him, standing arm to arm with Elu, Dedication on his finger, eyes on Adara. Not just watchful, but blazing with the same sensual intimacy that simmered in Elu's. That was an interesting new development.

"That's Dashuri. Adara-Bound." Adara winked at him. "From Crystal." She gestured across Mrak. "And Queen Tama originally of Vigil."

"Sin, from Storm," he introduced himself. Tama's eyes lit up at that. Unholy amounts of mischief were brewing in them. Sin inwardly groaned at this wall of wilful witch before him, with their linked arms and bright smiles. Those three should not be allowed together.

"Run into Zuzu yet?" Tama chirped at him, her expression just a little too innocent.

"Zuzu?"

Yako nodded at the majestic white tiger padding into the courtyard at that moment.

"Oh. Ooh." Sin's voice rose about as high as his brows on that one syllable. "We've...met."

Yako hid his mouth behind some fingers. "Zurea. But following Zaja's example, the Ladies have taken to calling him..."

"Zuzu." Songs, if the Coven were calling a predatory prince like this prime example of teeth and muscle *that*, he had a good idea of the tempests that truly raged underneath those sweetly swaying gossamer gowns. Sin shared a look of understanding with his brothers. He'd need all the skill and strength he possessed to contribute as a male amidst the female power running through this Court. There was no doubt these females would keep him on his toes.

The one female his eyes kept searching out where she was hidden behind gauze most of all. If any part of him had deluded himself that if he only found her, things would finally be uncomplicated and easy, he found himself thoroughly liberated of that notion. Whether it was the tiger before him, or the Queens grinning at him, or, most likely, that exquisite ethereal laugh floating from behind the fluttering fabric and making his heart stutter—a sudden certainty dropped deep into his gut that the years bygone had nothing on the years coming.

Sin swallowed hard against the strangled noise erupting from his throat.

Without ever once trying, this confounding, vexing, enchanting, glorious Queen of his was going to test everything he was.

* * *

Deep into the night, Sin woke up with a start. He felt clammy, his heart was drumming. He cast his eyes about to determine the threat. There was nothing. Then his sleep addled brain understood it wasn't his terror he was feeling, it was hers. *Zajasang.*

He leapt out of bed and sped through the Dark Palace. New Court or not—since those cobwebs had been blown away, he could find her unerringly no matter where he was. When he reached her suite, he drew up just short of barrelling through her door. Sin hadn't been in her personal space before. He hadn't envisioned the first time would be him barging in uninvited.

In those seconds he wasted hesitating, her Bonded arrived. Sin felt a grim satisfaction that he'd been here first. Their quarters were sure to be considerably closer than his.

For now. They might meet and marry a female in the Court one day who wasn't a Queen. Or a male, if that was their preference. He couldn't accept, couldn't contemplate a world where any one of them would have reason to move into the suite adjacent to Zajasang's. Where their Bond with her would be cherished in a way that was much more than friendly, and distinctly not brotherly.

"Why are you here?" Yako's growl was flat out hostile.

"I—" Sin realised all three of them were a blink away from pouncing on him. Wicked Wild. They thought he would have done something to make her feel like this? Rage rose in him, swift and brutal, having him bare his teeth. Yet he promptly turned his back on them, causing every hair on his body to stand up.

He ignored it. His priority lay behind that door.

"Zajasang?" he called out, knocking twice, then pressing his hand flat against the intricately carved wood. Another time he might have appreciated that his hand landed perfectly lined up with that of the female Dancing in abandon amidst the spirals and mystery frothing around her, almost as if he was about to pull her close in his embrace and join her in her passion. As it was, he was absorbed in the female behind the door, rather than the one on it.

And the frantic panic he'd been sensing from her had been doused by cold shock. Sin swallowed. "Zajasang," he called again, softer this time.

The lovingly carved fingers his own were gripping into gave way as the door opened. Wrapped in a thin, nearly sheer floor-length gown, her hair huge and wild, she looked up at him with wide eyes, swimming pools of swirling galaxies. Sin's breath hitched. He tipped into them, shivered from the intensity of the Song's caress that rolled over him in her presence, the power of the hum he could hear.

"Zaja," she whispered. She'd said that before, corrected him in the same way at the beach.

His eyes did a sweep over her person. She seemed alright. Physically, at least. She wasn't in any danger. She was safe. The steel band around Sin's chest loosened a little.

"Zaja." The melodic sound flowed from his lips as a sensual kiss dragging over her skin. Songs, he had to rein it in. But her shoulders dropped a smidgen. Triumph flared, until his sense returned. "Darling, what happened?" Yeah...that had been a purr.

He was bowled to the side as Tavo elbowed his way past him. Sin had forgotten those three were behind him. They made sure his ribs would remember. He only now noticed Zurea pressing into her leg, too. *Sacred Song and Wicked Wild.* Sin observed through narrowed eyes as Zajasang's Bonded surrounded her. Only Tavo reached out to lay a gentle hand to her neck, and only after closing his eyes and taking a deep breath. They were careful not to overwhelm her, not to force any touch on her that would heighten the tornado of sensations she was already struggling to contain. Tavo was likely concentrating to ensure only comfort and caring concern emanated from his hand where it rested against her skin.

Sin wished desperately it was him doing so instead.

"Talk to us, Zaja," Anda urged her.

Sin watched them, watched her, but he stayed on the threshold. The gold of the males' Dedications glinted in the moonlight as they moved, but no moonstones were resting on Zajasang's chest in this moment. Sin fingered the one hidden deep in the pocket of his loose linen pants.

Zajasang's eyes flicked over to him, then she focused back on Anda. "I'm fine. Thank you."

You're not fine. Sin opened his mouth, ready to prod, then closed it again. Not his place. Not yet. It gritted like sand between his teeth.

It was going to be joy enough to be questioned by her Constellation on how he wound up by her door, when supposedly only a Bond afforded a male the glimpse of insight into his Queen's emotional state that had brought the other three running. It was time for him to shut up, step back, and allow them to act on what was their privilege. But that didn't keep Sin from raising his brow and fixing her with a piercing glare when her eyes flitted over to him once again. At least she was as aware of him here on her threshold as he was of her, a few feet away from him and still miles too far.

Her lips pursed briefly, then she blew out a breath and looked to the ground. "It was just a dream." Her hand buried in Zurea's fur. "There was a harsh note in the Song. A rip." Zajasang lifted her eyes to return his glare, daring him to challenge her further. But, Songs, did she look haunted and vulnerable.

Sin's jaw clenched and he gripped the curved doorframe so hard his joints hurt.

Not. His. Place.

But he could try what he'd been trying for years. He could attempt to push something back at her. So he thought of the awe and bliss he felt all those months ago when the sun rose over the ancient plains outside Ember, and for one thoughtless, ecstatic moment, he had felt her in every aspect of his being. Had felt not her pain, but her glorying joy. It wasn't hard to dredge the power of the emotion back up again—the memory had been his daily companion since it happened, as much his prayer as her name.

He concentrated on it, and he pushed.

Her eyes widened, her mouth fell slack.

His heart thumped. She felt it. *She felt it!* Sin grinned at her, grinned so wide it was near indecent.

"A rip?"

Zaja snapped her mouth shut and her eyes to Tavo. "It was just a dream. Never mind. Sorry to wake you. Let's all just...go back to sleep."

Sin chuckled. No way that was going to happen. Not for her, and not for him—not if he knew her at all.

* * *

"Exciting night."

With his hands stuffed in his pockets, Sin came to a stop and turned to Vala. Zajasang had gone to take her solitary space, which he wasn't fool enough to intrude upon this time. So here he was, trying to not have his thoughts circle around her with every breath, and take a simple walk with a good friend. "I didn't realise Dark Court had a gossip mill."

Vala threw her head back and laughed. "Darling, a Coven lives here. But no." She shook her head and smirked at him. "My rooms are in the same wing. I felt you lot rushing past and tempers riding high."

"That's..." Sin sighed, though he couldn't help the quirk in his lips in response to her cheeky expression. "That's accurate, I suppose."

"So how did that conversation with her Constellation go?" Oh yes, that was the Vala he knew. He gave her a full smirk back. He had been glad to see her amongst the Queens in the courtyard yesterday, excited to reconnect with her, now both belonging to the Heart. She may have understood him better these last years than most—when she still belonged to Old, and he didn't really belong anywhere.

He'd also noticed that it had been her who had gone after Zajasang when she ducked behind that damned piece of a gauzy barrier.

Never before had he felt envious of a Queen. It was an odd experience.

"Hm. They won't be surprised when I offer her a moonstone."

"I don't think anyone will be, Sin." Amusement danced in her eyes. "I think the *mystery of Sin* was finally solved for the Sung the day Vigil confirmed a Dark Queen had come."

Sin snorted. "And thank the Songs for that."

For a minute, they strolled in companionable silence. The island stretched before them, lush and green, the waves rippling blue and singing their lullaby beyond. It made him wonder if Zajasang was sitting by the foot of the waterfall again, her dangling foot rippling the water where it had calmed by the edges of the—

Sin barked a short laugh. Who was he kidding? It was impossible for him to spend a minute of his life and not have it be about her in some way. There simply was no him devoid of her.

Vala cocked her head and slanted her eyes up to him. "When will you?"

He exhaled. "Today, if I didn't worry she'd be overwhelmed and pull back." He shrugged his shoulders. "I've only just arrived. She doesn't even know me."

Vala's sage eyes turned on him. "Doesn't she?"

Doesn't she? She'd felt what he pushed to her last night. Those years when she was lost and alone in the Loud—maybe she'd felt it then, too. He prayed she had. But it was pitiful, so very little he'd been able to do for her, far too little and far too late in their time apart.

When Sin kept silent—lest all his wretched fears and fervent hopes tumbled out—Vala asked, "You have a stone for her?"

"Yes." His fingers tightened around the smooth surface he had been caressing in his pocket. Hidden away as it was, his mind could nonetheless picture it perfectly: The marbled blue-turquoise depths, the white feathering like the softest, fluffiest clouds streaking the sky, the strong lines, the nested layers, the changing play of translucent shimmering and opaque mystique. The beauty of the ocean and the heavens, the maelstroms of tempests, and still waters of serenity. Everything that had lived in a girl's eyes on a beach long ago.

It seemed Vala had expected his response. Of course—she was Vala. She nodded. "Trust your instincts, Sin." Then she tacked on, "Maybe make friends with Zuzu in the meantime."

A brief laugh escaped him. Well, it probably was good advice. "Thank you, Vala."

"You're welcome." She flapped her hand, but her smile was true. He knew she meant it.

"Lady Vala, how are you?" She looked well, but there was a murky vastness in her gaze that had sat there for a while. Sin recognised it—had seen it before, more intensely, in Zajasang's. "Would you like me to stand guard for you?" Conspiring with Vala was the most obvious thing he could provide for her.

"Mmhmm. A tempting offer." Vala touched her fingers to his forearm. "I do believe you have other priorities, though."

He did. "I can make time."

"I know." She picked up a delicate flower that had sailed to the ground and twirled it under her nose. "But how much more fun would it be to celebrate Bond Song next Bright Moon?"

She meant that, too. Well, he supposed he should be heartened by her belief in him. *Celebrate the Bond Song on the next Bright Moon.* Songs. Sin wasn't sure whether he felt hot or cold, whether he should laugh or cry.

"Bond and Song, brother," he muttered to himself. *And may the Song be sweet and show him grace.*

* * *

"Lady Zaja!"

The Song was kind, indeed! It seemed Zajasang had returned from her morning jaunt moments before them. Come to think of it, maybe the random timing of when he had gotten peculiarly anxious to turn back, with no apparent reason for the urgency, hadn't been so random after all.

Sin made an apologetic face as he looked at Vala. Zajasang was gliding through the colonnade some distance ahead of them—by herself—and he could neither pass up the opportunity to spend time with her, nor let her walk about unprotected.

He realised that second thought was overzealous. She was in her own Dark Palace, and that tiger likely wasn't far off, either. He'd have to be careful not to turn into a smothering jellyfish. The ladies in any Circle had never been shy about making their feelings about that sort of *highly annoying* behaviour known. Even so...

The image of Zajasang's bare back as she sat by the clear pool during her escape to solitude the day before ghosted through Sin's brain—again. He gave himself a vigorous mental shake. *Focus.*

Vala sent him an indulgent smile and made a shooing motion at him. He could have kissed her.

"Zaja!"

Zajasang stopped and turned around. She watched him warily as he hastened toward her. "Sin," she said, and smoothed an errand strand of hair away from her face.

"May I walk with you?"

She blinked at him for a moment, then bit her lip and looked beyond him to Vala. Sin guessed Zajasang was now the recipient of her own shooing motion, and the corner of his lip twitched. His eyes never left her face, fascinated with every emotion and expression passing over it like he had been as a young boy. Unlike then, he now also admired the play of colour and depth in her eyes, the hue of her lips, the lines of her face, the luminosity of her skin. He clamped his hands together behind his back. And, Songs, the power of the Dark Song's caress whenever he was near her...

"Yes?" Her answer came out as a question more than a statement. Her voice was a little breathy, and he was sure he'd seen a slight shiver tremble through her. But she resolutely turned and strode on, requiring him to chase after her for two steps.

Sin gave it another two steps, before daring the first move in his overture. "How did you meet Zurea?"

He'd wanted to ask her about last night. He'd wanted to talk about the fact that'd he felt her...and she'd felt him. He wanted to beg her forgiveness for all the years that had separated them. But he got the impression she'd already been questioned about last night by her Bonded, and the whole topic felt rather heavy for such a sunny morning. And for hardly knowing each other— sort of. He wanted her to be able to be at ease around him, not look at him in that wild shy way she had been looking at him so far.

The surprised pleasure taking over her features told him he'd been right. The unexpected giggle bubbling out of her made him want to do a million more right things.

"I," she darted a glance up at him and looked away again, "woke up with him."

"You—what?" He hadn't been prepared for that. Then again, how does one meet a tiger?

"Yeah, my first night on Amea, I woke up with him snuggled around me."

Wicked Wild, he wished he had that tiger's courage. She didn't seem to hold a grudge against Zurea for that bit of boldness, but somehow, Sin doubted it would go over the same way for him. Females tended to have different rules for allowing males into their beds when they were human rather than animal.

"Are you happy amongst the Sung?" Argh. Sin groaned quietly as soon as the words were out. So much for light and easy. He half wanted to take it back—but he also desperately needed to know.

"Yes." An immediate answer—too immediate. Sin kept silent, kept watching her face, watch her chew her lip as she chewed with whatever she was feeling. Her eyes snuck up to his once more, and got caught. She let out a big breath. "Yes, I want to be," she said softly. "The Sung are..." A flutter of her hands. "Beautiful. Truly beautiful."

She swallowed back whatever else she'd wanted to say. Tried to pull away from him, from the truth.

Oh no, he wasn't having that. Sin dipped his head to catch her eyes again. "But?" he said as gently as he could.

They'd ambled to a halt. Held captive in his gaze, she stared back at him, revealing in her gaze what she didn't have the words to say. The worlds he saw in those eyes were so vast. The Sung could have been dancing circles around them and he wouldn't have noticed as she stared and stared at him. What was she feeling? Sin reached for their connection to understand it, something he'd never been able to do this purposefully before. It had never been this clear and tangible. He found an icy sea of uncertainty so cold it made him freeze even with the sun hot in the sky.

It was awful, and Sin hated what it meant.

"You are not alone anymore, Zaja." He needed her to know that. "Whatever you're scared of... I'm here with you."

He was so focused on his conviction of what he was saying, and her hearing it, that he stopped thinking. He reached out, watched his hand move closer to her, closer still—and then the tips of his fingers whispered over the side of her neck, his thumb grazing her jaw.

Her eyes widened and her breath hitched.

The hum of the Song was a roar.

He could feel her pulse thrumming as hard as his own.

"This is the truth of who you are." His voice had dropped a note into huskiness. "Forget about everything else."

Zajasang swallowed. Her tongue wet her lips. The icy sea shifted. "In the Loud—that's what you call it, right?"

He nodded. It was the Sung's term for the world outside the Circles.

"Well... It was loud." The sea welled in her eyes. Her voice nearly disappeared. "So loud."

"I know."

"I was—I thought—"

Sin dropped his hand. He had no right to touch her. He had caused this. He felt like dropping to his knees and howling. "Zajasang. I'm so, so sorry. So deeply sorry."

Her brows bunched. "What for?"

"Leaving you alone." Regret was a harsh and bitter abyss gaping wide inside him. "Zaja, I wish..." Sin shook his head. He could wish all he want, it didn't change what he'd done. Failed to do. His chest rose, fell, even as he wouldn't allow himself the luxury of dropping his eyes and evading her agonised gaze.

That pain... If she never forgave him, he'd understand.

For a long, unbearable minute, there was only silence. Was this it? Was it going to be over before it ever really began? His world began to crush and crumble.

"But you didn't, did you?" The smallest of smiles rose on her lips. "You never left me alone."

Sin's world halted.

A tear welled over and kissed its way down her cheek. She denied it with a rough swipe. Looked away into memory. And murmured between barely moving lips, so quietly he didn't think he had been supposed to hear, "Sometimes, that made it even harder."

And Sin's world tilted again into smoke and flames.

13

You're not alone anymore, Zaja.

Sin's words from the other day echo in my head while I ignore my guilty conscience over keeping Tama waiting, and eek out another quarter hour in my oasis of solitude by the waterfall.

He's right. Even now, here, where I come precisely to be alone... I let my muscles mellow, soften the tight holds I keep on myself, and relish the sensation of flowing apart just a little, of seeping into the earth and water and rock and trees...

Alone becomes all one. A soft sigh sings over my lips.

Deep down, I'm content, I realise. *And what a strange sensation that is.*

I've relaxed so much I flop over, land on my side, and roll into the water. Snorting with my own private hilarity, I flap about and pull myself back onto the bank. If you'd told me in my old life that I'd ever slump over myself from being too loose, it would have been ludicrous. My body used to be a constant ball of tension. It's a small wonder I never hardened into a gargoyle.

Now, though? My voice hums out the same pleasant hum I feel inside me. Yes, I'm content, and in fact, I have been for a while. Since...since briefly before Sin arrived. Stopped ghosting around in my head and turned up in the flesh. *Huh.* It's like—like I crossed my own inner ocean, and then he stood on the other shore.

Shaking my head to dislodge the philosophising, I reel my energy in with a sensation of solidifying back into my self. It really is time to get going. Tama is waiting so we can Dance together.

My jaw clacks. I cast one more longing look over the peacefully swaying rainbow lights reflected by the rushing water, then turn to head back to the Dark Palace. Itchy energy thrums through me. "Knock it off, Zaja," I mutter to myself and get moving. The heavy sourness of reproach coats my throat.

Lately, I've been feeling...hesitant whenever heading into the deeper layers of the Song. Like I'm meant to do today in my work with Tama. There's a harsh note that scrapes through me sometimes, leaving bloody ribbons in its wake. The Dark Song is far from gentle as it is, but something about that note... I recoil from the memory of it with a shudder. And the other Queens haven't said anything—which is half my problem. I don't know what it is, and apparently it's more to do with me than the Song. I'm scared to acknowledge what that might mean.

Just like that, I feel cold.

There are so many kinds of alone, Sin.

When I register the jungle around me, I realise my feet have carried me not to the Palace, but to the beach. The murmuring of the ocean washes through me, wave for wave a pouring of peace and me the chalice. A humpback breaches his hello out over the blue. The chalice flows over, flooding a smile onto my face. The whale and I have swum together before, a few times—and it's time we do it again.

Many kinds of Dance, too, Tama. Forgive me, Sister.

* * *

Returning to the beach some hours later, thoroughly emptied of thought and satisfied, the seals call to me, and I flop down amongst them. We roll and we rest. Nothing but sandy sunny salty happiness.

Then they begin to chatter. The two I'm sandwiched between join in. Voluminously. Right over my head. I clap a hand to my ear and rub at it. Sounds like quiet cuddle time is over. Groaning, I lift myself onto my elbow—and lock eyes with Sin.

"Hi," I creak.

"Hi back." He shifts more of his weight onto his arms, leaning back on the big rock he is lounging on.

I lift my hand and waffle it around. "How long...?"

His lips press together and the corners of his mouth quiver, but he doesn't say anything. He doesn't have to. His emotions are doing plenty talking for him. Though the jittery, sweetly tangy feeling...

"Your connection to animals never ceases to amaze me, my Queen," he interrupts my musings over the out-of-place sensation. Amusement and honest wonder war in his eyes and the tilt of his lips.

"You say that like—"

"Like it's happening all the time? Like it's utterly mind-baffling and magical? Like it's beautiful?" He graces me with his gorgeous smile, all traces of teasing gone. "Because it is, Zaja. All of those things."

Well. Is that what I'd meant? I unconsciously shake one of my cuddle buddies' front flippers, then stop when I notice I'm fiddling. "Did Tama send you? I'm sorry, I know—"

"Tama didn't send me." He slides off the rock, his unerring, focused attention on me as intense as ever.

"Oh." I eye the hand he extends down to me. "Good."

"Walk with me?" He pulls me up, our joint hands nearly coming to rest on his chest. For a moment his other arm snakes around the small of my back, holding me close to him. When he lets go and puts a foot of air between us, his exhale is too controlled to be natural.

Nervousness! I suddenly recognise and place the emotion billowing off of him. Nerves, that's what I'm tasting, and not just my own. My eyebrows rise in curiosity. I've not known Sin to be nervous since—no, I don't think it's ever been a predominant enough emotion on him to overpower all others.

We meander along the beach until I get the impression that there is no specific destination. I bite my lip, and saunter along, and listen to his Song, and try not to combust. Eventually, Sin turns to me, blocking the sun from piercing my eyes. Bending to the side to look between him and where we came from, I swallow a giggle. He just wanted me away from the mouthy seals hogging my attention!

I've not yet fully straightened up, my grin huge and toothy, when the words burst out of Sin like it's beyond his power to hold them in another second. "I know you hardly know me, Zaja. That all of this is a lot. You've probably not thought about me since that day on the beach half a lifetime ago, and you had no reason to. But I've thought about you every day. Every single one, Zajasang."

Oh. Oh! He wraps his tongue around the sound of my name like a caress. Songs. He wanted my undivided attention? I've grown stock still. He's got it.

"Because in those few minutes I got with you, I felt things I never had before. It doesn't matter how young I was—I was born Sung. I knew you were my Queen. And all I've wanted to do ever since is to cherish you, and shield you...and revere you. To devote myself to you. All I've wanted to do is to offer you everything that I am. To contribute to your Dance."

His declarations spill out of him without pause or hesitation, his sincere, heated eyes never straying from mine. My body begins trembling.

"You, your Dance... It's already been my life since that day, Zaja." Sin reaches into his pocket. "It would be my greatest honour if you gave me the gift of allowing that to continue."

Absolute silence falls when he finishes. It roars in my ears as he closes my fingers around the stone he withdrew from where he had it hidden on his person. He holds on for one long, weighted moment with his hand enveloping mine enveloping the stone—and he leaves.

My eyes roam up to the bright blue sky.

Even now at the height of day I can sense the searing fire of the endless canopy of stars, can hear their Song carried from another time.

They will shine in splendour tonight. It's Dark Moon.

Which means I have two weeks to decide whether I wish to return the stone humming urgently in my still closed, immobile, extended hand...or accept Sin's offer.

Tingles and shivers spread and spread up through my arm and into my heart and down to my womb, reaching my feet and spearing my crown. I burn where I stand.

It's infinitely more than a stone he placed into the palm of my hand, for me to hold and do with what I will.

I can barely hold myself.

Sin.

Sin.

* * *

Sin's hand reflexively reached into his pocket for comfort, feeling for a stone that was no longer there.

Because he'd offered it to Zajasang.

Within mere days of entering her life.

Songs. His stomach turned. If his reckless eagerness and need for her was his downfall—if she chose not to accept his Bond... He had to steady himself to breathe through the churning nausea that thought brought on.

"You alright there, brother?" The careful balance of gleeful hilarity and honest concern in Yako's voice was an impressive feat.

So was leashing the flash of jealousy and aggressiveness that rose up in Sin. That primal predator and protector slinking beneath the surface was as on edge as he was. "How about a round with the sticks?" Sparring would allow him to vent some of his wound up, territorial insecurity, while forcing him to pay attention—and make a valiant attempt to stop obsessing over Zaja and her choice.

"Uh-huh." Yako's brows were riding high, but he strode off with Sin to find some sticks. Good. The first clash couldn't come soon enough. "So, you chose today, huh?"

Sin stopped in his tracks. *Wicked Wild, it's a Dark Moon!* He groaned. Foolish. Foolish, foolish. All because of his impatience.

With the flow of her moontime his Queen dropped even more deeply into Song than she usually stood, amplifying Sin's pull to her further. For her, it meant an intense, inward, deeply spiritual and attuned time...during which a male's presence and attention wasn't necessarily welcome. For him, it meant extra charged protective and possessive instincts, and a whole lot of crazed gnawing at the bars of his self-imposed cage. Honour.

Reverence. Respect her choice. For a male to actually be invited to stay, or, Songs, lie with a female during her moontime—rare, and a significant honour. Sin could only hope he should be so lucky one day.

Judging from Yako's tense movements, Sin wasn't the only one struggling. Their sticks flew with the force of their frustration. "Probably did her a favour," Yako panted. "Coven's meeting. Gives her an excuse to scurry from you."

Sin grunted. Yako was right—there was no chance he'd get to spend any time with her tonight. Dark Moon night itself belonged to the Sisters, to their circles of visions and power and who knew what feminine mysteries.

"Just Coven?" Whether Heart or not, the females of a Court gathered to celebrate in their own sacred way. Sometimes they came together in one big circle, sometimes they gathered together in smaller ones. There seemed to be a feminine, harmonious rhyme and reason to it. The males didn't presume to understand it. Sin knew they cherished it for the opportunity to intimately connect with one another, when their daily life may often keep them separate in Court and Heart out of simple practical necessity. But if it was just the Queens tonight, just a darling circle of witches... Dark Court's Coven was small. Maybe—

"Don't go having any ideas, brother." Yako rubbed a spot on his upper arm, looking uncharacteristically put out. "Don't want to mess with this lot when they're riled. How's a little lady like that got that kind of strength..."

The sun cycle days were when the males came together to share in brotherhood, learn from and lean on one another. The females didn't disturb the males' gathering—and they *expected their gathering to be equally honoured and respected, male instincts or not, thank you very much.* Though a male could sometimes get away with a little fussing by providing some unobtrusive assistance in making sure their space was prepared and their comfort seen to. Oh, he would be sent away in no unclear terms sooner rather than later, but just that brief time around the witches could be the balm his wild animal needed to calm the ferocious instincts riding him. Enough to enable him to give the females the space they demanded for themselves for the night. The females were gracious enough to accommodate male instincts that much, despite their piqued protestations to the contrary.

Sin banged out a hoppy little rhythm with his stick, abruptly a whole lot more cheerful. How much threat could a handful of moody moony Queens really pose? Maybe he could go and help with building the fire later...

* * *

The six Sisters allowed him all of two minutes before they started shooing him away with the fearsome force of frowny females. He'd managed to see to the fire while covertly watching Zaja take a sip of the herbal brew he'd brought for her. She'd thanked him, but given no other indication in any way of what she might be thinking or feeling.

Sin poked and stabbed at the smouldering logs. He wanted to pry into that open channel between them—it felt muted, refusing to blare out what he wanted to know of its own accord —but that wasn't fair. He couldn't satisfy his own desire by invading her privacy beyond what she freely shared and revealed—not as long as he wasn't truly and officially her Bonded.

Giving up all pretence, Sin turned to study Zajasang openly. He was about to be booted in unmistakable fashion anyway. There. A slight scrunch and pinch of concentration in her features. She looked like she was battling through pain, and trying to do so quietly. He abandoned the fire, stalking back over to her. And was asked—again—to leave.

Well, they could put up with him for another twenty seconds. "Zaja." Sin brushed his thumb over her cheek. She was so unbearably beautiful to him, and yet that scarcely played a role in what he felt for her. It was her, her being, that was an irresistible lure, that was everything to him. He never wanted to be apart from her again.

"Sin."

Yes, that was pain in her eyes. Guarded pain. Sin hated it.

For a few breaths, he simply stood there with her, his thumb softly sweeping back and forth, doing his best to hold her with his presence, his eyes. It was nowhere near enough, but he was wary of pushing any further touch onto her. She was sensitive to touch at the best of times, and during her moontime... Still, his muscles strained to wrap around her. For years, he'd felt her agony, the many facets and faces of her pain. For years, all he could do was try to send comfort through the quasi bond.

Now he stood before her. Soon, if the Song showed him grace, he'd be her Bonded.

"Please... Use me." Could she hear the quiet way his heart was turning itself inside out in his urging? Choose me. Accept what I so desperately want to give. Let me be shelter in the Dark Song for you. Let me share the burden of the pain and do what I can to save you from it. Whether mythical or mundane.

Her beautiful eyes were wide. Mesmerising. Suspending him in a moment of infinity. But all she murmured with a graceful incline of her head was, "Bond and Song, Sin." Not a yes, not a no. Only the Song's most basic greeting, which gave him nothing.

Other than that he'd clearly reached the very limits of his welcome. At the risk of really riling the Coven, Sin stayed put for one last drawn out moment of breathing her in, before finally pulling himself away from Zajasang and leaving the Sisters to their Dark Moon rituals.

He almost laughed when he came across Zurea not far into the foliage. *Being a tiger has its advantages.* Like sharing beds. Or allowing a male to stray where he shouldn't...and stay close to his female. Not close enough for human ears to make out words in the hum and ebb of the Lady's voices, but close enough to have a finger on the pulse of the gathering. Close enough to keep watch over a certain Queen.

He locked eyes with the feline, molten emerald to crystal aquamarine. To a passing observer they might appear like different species, but anyone who could see beyond the apparent would see they were one and the same.

Two protective males. Two agitated beasts. Two Sung unconditionally devoted to their Queen, Bonded or not.

Throwing sense to the wolves—well, to his own inner wild animal—Sin pivoted, dropped into a crouch, and stayed. Stayed as the Sister's came to sit in a circle around their fire. Stayed as they talked, and laughed, and cried. Stayed as they reached their arms out and placed their hands on each other's shoulders, forming one continuous circle. Stayed as, as one, they rocked their connected bodies in spirals and wove a particular kind of feminine magic no male had likely been privy to before.

Stayed and witnessed when he knew he shouldn't.

Stayed and only left when he was satisfied that whatever pain Zajasang had borne, she had found a way to ride.

Hopefully, she would never know he'd been here.

Hopefully, when it shone Bright, she'd welcome him under the moon to stay with her. Through every pain and every joy and everywhen and beyond.

Sacred Song...please gift me this Bond.

Hopefully.

* * *

"You've done this before, Zaja," I tell my reflection.

The turmoil in my blood for once my very own, I smooth my trembling hands down the spidersilk fabric of my elegant, whisperlight dress. Gown, rather. The Sung—they know how to do clothes. Twisting side to side, I study myself in the ornate and gilded, free-standing mirror. My favourite part of the ensemble is the cape that hugs my shoulders, traces my clavicles until it connects, yet cowls low in the back. Almost as if wings were left their breathing room.

This feels different, the girl in the mirror seems to retort. *Deeper. More.*

My eyes land on the moonstone clasped in my fingers. It's breathtaking. I haven't stopped admiring it since I first opened my hand to see what it would reveal when Sin left me on the beach two weeks ago. This morning came, and I haven't stopped being enamoured by the stone... Haven't given it back. Which is what brought me to tonight. Getting ready for Bright Moon night.

Bond Song night.

No one held me to tradition last time, since Yako, Anda, and Tavo offered their stones to me so shortly before a ritual night, and conveniently failed to explain the significance of not returning the stone by the morning of a Bright Moon. This time though...

"You look like...like Dark Song."

"Thank you, Vala." Both our smiles are a little watery.

"You don't have to add it to your necklace." Tonight, I've chosen to leave my décolleté bare. At other times, it is graced with the necklace that holds three stones so far—Tavo's, Yako's, and Anda's. "You are Dark Queen. It wouldn't be preposterous for you to wear it in a diadem."

I'm relieved to see the wink that accompanies that statement. "Good to know." If absurd. "But no. I'll wear it over my heart."

"Good choice, Sister," Vala whispers.

"You think so?"

"He Sings to you, doesn't he?"

Maybe we're not talking about how I will set the stone anymore. I swallow and hum. "More than anyone ever has."

Vala watches me carefully. "As terrifying as it is delightful?"

Oh, she sees so much. Why isn't she Dark Queen? Shoving it all to the side, I straighten my shoulders. With the storm raging through me, I'm surprised no male has barrelled down my door yet.

The moon is calling, lilting her seductive, comforting Song. It's time.

"What's one more Bond, right?"

* * *

Sacred Song and Wicked Wild.

My mouth is dry, my hands clench, and I rock between my heels and toes. Every single member of the Court is here, every single inhabitant of Amea. Including the animals. I could swear I even feel the presence of the Sisters from the other Covens in the Song. The crowd's hungry curiosity and eager excitement is a wave trying to drown me, to batter me down and shatter me apart.

A burst of hilarity fizzes through me when I realise that maybe the whole to-do isn't about me this time. Maybe it's the fact that the legendary Sin has finally chosen to Bond to a Queen that's drawn everyone.

Oh Songs. I suck a breath through my teeth.

My Bonded press closer to me at feeling my distress, and then find themselves torn between wanting to stay close to shield me, and wanting to hang back to respect my choice in entering the ritual and accepting the new Bond.

With Sin.

I make the decision for them when I step out of their protection, beyond the inner circle formed by the Heart, and towards the centre of the clearing. I focus on the power vibrating in the rich earth beneath my bare feet. I focus on the night-bloom-scented breeze sighing through the leaves. I focus on the hum of the vast darkness, and the glint of the moonlight on the prisms. I focus on the beat of my own heart, to remind me I'm whole, and I'm here, and this body is mine.

And then every sensation, every foreign emotion clamouring for attention is completely conquered and swept away by the intensity of Sin's joy. His bliss roams through me like the sun stretching out, like warm sap, like flowing, glissading light.

The last time I stood here, I was joined by three males, my attention divided between them, my mind distracted by the multitude of impressions calling to me within the circle and beyond it. Now, I don't even notice Adara stepping forward to Honour this ceremony.

There is only Sin.

His Song, his eyes, his scent, and the spiced sweetness of his euphoric devotion. A sense of rightness pervades me, and I feel it echoed in Sin's emotions. The whole island might have hushed or it might have howled, I wouldn't know either way.

"My life in your Dance." His resonant, velvet voice is sure as he speaks the first of the sacred words, words with which he freely offers up all that he is. They twine and wrap around my soul, causing me to shiver with their sensuosity and sincerity.

In the short, silent moment during which his gift hangs suspended in the charged air between us, laced with his yearning, a hand stretched out in hopes of being met, every instant of our connection flips through me. Memories of all the times that I felt his comforting strength, smelled his familiar scent, before I ever knew it was him. Years that he has already revered me as his Queen in the way of the Sung, since meeting me once, by the ocean, so very briefly, oh so long ago.

It feels like a soft sigh to at last answer his call. "I receive your Bond."

The dazzling smile on his face is the most handsome thing I've ever seen. Hot pleasure tingles through me as Sin bends tradition, steps into me, and trails his fingertips down my cheek and throat, before sliding them around my neck.

The final words of the Bond Song are intoned together. We speak them almost privately, though no less intently. "For the pleasure of Song."

I reach to braid the energy cord, to Weave the spell and complete the ritual—and gasp. Tears spill over when I find the crystalline confirmation of what I have suspected for weeks now, and still don't understand. The thread extended by his will is not new and unbraided. There is no need for a Bond to be woven between us, because one already exists. One that feels strangely wild and ancient, its root buried in my core. One that reverberates and hums and lifts in glorious harmonies as it wakes from being dormant.

Like a string being tuned, a vow reaffirmed, my Weaving work is one of shaking off dust, not creating anew.

Sin's eyes roll back and close on a slight groan. "Zajasang..." His voice is rough, reverent. "I can *feel* you. It's like...like gray gauze has been ripped away, and finally there you are, in vibrant colour and stunning sharpness." He tips his forehead to mine, his free arm wrapping tight around my waist. "Songs, I feel you..."

Adara clears her throat next to us. "Congratulations, Sin Zaja-Bound."

"At long last," Elu mutters not so quietly. More than one amused chuckle, and even some teasing whoops, travel through the circles surrounding us.

In grand, dramatic fashion, Sin lowers himself to one knee. Filled with radiant pride, it's as if he's shed a weight he carried, a doubt that dimmed him. He is brilliant.

And a Heart male through and through, the sumptuous eroticism and sultry carnality oozing off of him. *Uh-oh.*

His cute, satisfied smirk and the cocky gleam in his eyes speak of long-hatched, well-formed plans. "Zajasang Maaya Zatinsa... My Queen."

Dangerous plans—and potent promises.

14

I lurch into consciousness like being flung against the bedrock that forms my ceiling. My eyes flick open to the empty dark of my suite.

In my old life, this used to feel like sandpaper rubbing me raw while being stuck in a car press. Not accompanied by any specific vision, it's just the feelings of a million souls in a million places bearing down on me. All at once. The pain of the world...announcing itself for an uninvited visit to tea.

Now, with that mental veil removed and nothing held back, I gasp with how much more potent still the experience is. My bones want to groan under the weight and my heart impale itself on my ribs. It is awful—but it's also no longer stagnant and lifeless. *I am* no longer stagnant and lifeless. I am no longer a powerless victim at the hands of universal whim. So instead of gritting my teeth, locking my muscles in place and bearing it, I grit my teeth, swing my legs out of bed and begin to walk.

This feeling, this pain, it is alive, it is born of life. And life demands life.

My feet step faster and faster. The halls and courtyards of the Palace blur past me. I'm aware of nothing but the tearing ache, asking to be felt, asking to be expressed, asking to be honoured as all life must be honoured. My flayed-open senses guide me through the black night, the light of the moon not penetrating the thick of the jungle. I don't know where I'm running to, I don't know what it is that I'm chasing, but I know it's not here yet. This is not right, yet.

On, and the jungle is behind me, the rich earth and mud below me replaced by sand. Finally, the ocean laps around my toes, crawls up my ankles, hugs my shins, caresses my thighs, welcomes my thinly clad hips. Like a lover's arms, the water wraps around my waist—and at last my frenzied race stops.

For one moment, two, I stand in the ocean, still and silent.

Then I tip my head back to the glittering infinity of stars above me, open my mouth, my throat, and I howl. From the emptiness in my heart...from the truth of my root...from the night dark whispers of a thousand-thousand souls, I howl the pain, and the longing, and the belonging.

The wolves raise the song with me, and together we sing the pain, for pain must be felt. For in the Song, there is the moan, the howl, the laughter, the tender whisper, the joyful shriek, the wrenching cry. The sacred and the wicked wild.

For the Song is life.

And only the whole makes the circle.

Tears stain my cheeks while the ocean holds me. Minute upon minute, the wolves and I dance with the pain. We become the chilling beauty of our mournful song, held in reverence by the silent night. All of the jungle has hushed, all the birds and monkeys fallen quiet to listen. Only the whales, far out in the watery depths, join their harmony with ours.

We sing sorrow.

Then—warmth in my back. A soft press of lips to my neck. A strong arm settling like a band from hipbone to hipbone. Another snaking around me; until a warm and steady, sure hand comes to rest between my breasts, with a new gold band worn proudly on its fingers.

A wordless vow that my heart will be held, no matter how many pieces it shatters into.

Sin tips back his head and joins in our song. Together, we howl the pain, the longing, the belonging.

We sing for the honour of Song.

When the stars have journeyed a handsbreadth across the sky, the crushing weight ebbs from my bones. With a last nod and courteous bow, the pain releases me from our dance and moves on.

I draw a breath to fill the hollows inside me. Slowly, the world around me filters back into me. I latch onto the feeling of the clean, healing moonlight soaking my skin like dew, heralding the birth of a newly born dawn after death in the darkest night.

With the moonlight sinking into me, I sink into Sin, strong and steady behind me, his hand held tight to my chest.

You're not alone anymore, Zaja.

Other than one soft sigh, no sound or movement passes between us until the sun rises out of the ocean.

No. Here, now, in this, I don't think I am.

* * *

"Four moonstones?"

Well, that's one way to introduce yourself. Maybe she's so shocked she's forgotten she just arrived at a new Court? I glance around to assure myself I haven't missed a slip into a vision. Nope, still perched on the same settee in one of the courtyards of Dark Palace looking as it did two minutes ago, my

Constellation clustered around me, and about to head out for a Dance. I'm pretty sure this is real and happening right now. A voluptuous Queen I've never met before with an apparently equally voluminous personality is...asking about my Bonded. "Uh-huh."

The horror in her eyes is almost comical. "What's that like?"

"It's only been a week and a bit since the fourth joined my Constellation, so... I'm still finding out." Close enough to the truth. Regardless, I haven't even spoken with Vala about the strange familiarity and prior existence of Sin and I's Bond. I'm not about to try and explain it to—

"Lady Zaja, meet Lady Feny of Storm." Thank you, Sin.

"Those your males?"

"Uh-huh." Her fantastic irreverence seems to have reduced me to syllabic utterances. I think I like her.

"Songs. Intense." Her head nods up and down sagely. "Respect, girl. I don't know how you're still standing. I'd be flip-flopping between being a puddle on the floor thanks to all that hot yumminess," she fans her hand toward my Constellation, who suddenly all seem to feel very satisfied, "and being an enraged banshee thanks to all that...male...bossiness."

Sadly, the satisfaction doesn't wane.

"What are you off to? Dance? Plants? Pleasure?"

She really is something else. Sin's Song swirls low and deep, Yako not far behind him. I don't need to be able to feel them to know they're thinking about that last one. The Sung's practices in pleasure are a harnessing of sacred power, enjoyed on one's own—or shared, energy to energy, through body to body. Once, it was well-known and practiced in many cultures besides the Sung, throughout the Loud. Once, long ago, before it was forcibly forgotten, and the Loud became loud, while people's voices became quiet. I hug myself.

Feny is cackling, a picture of joviality, her brows waggling. That's right. She is shameless in letting her voice be heard.

Among the Sung, everything we do is a manner of dancing and singing, in energy and pleasure and sound. The Dance itself. Plants—when we tend to nature, and grow and gather and grind and concoct. And pleasure. My arms slip from my waist to my womb. The Sisters have been teaching and initiating me in the mysteries of the Goddess since I arrived among them, of owning what always has been, is, and always will be mine. Like all else, it's breath, and energy, and movement, and touch—yet another form of the Dance, another way to Weave.

As beautiful as everything the Sung do.

Sin slides his hand over mine, interlinking our fingers. His Dedication is a cool, soft vibration against my skin.

"Dance. Some deep work in Dark Song." Untangling myself from Sin, I get up. Surreptitiously stretch and rub my neck, and try to massage away the clog at the base of my throat.

"Need assistance?"

"No." I offer Feny a smile. "Thank you."

With a shrug of her shoulders, she flounces off. "May we meet in the Dark Song, Sister," she tosses over her shoulder as she goes.

"Feny." My lips stay curled in bemusement as I stare after her. *Welcome to Dark Court.* It doesn't seem like Lady Feny requires any encouragement to make herself at home. I watch her run into Tama, exuberance dimmed none.

With a sigh, I turn to my Bonded. "I may need all of you. If that's alright." There is a lot of pain in the world today, straining on the energies. An escalation in a senseless war. Many injured. Many grieving. Many filled with fear and hate. Many children left alone and abandoned. Pain.

"Alright?" Yako bounds up and hooks his arm around my neck, wailing into my hair. "Thought you'd never ask, Zaja-Queen-of-mine!"

I pat his dangling hand. I appreciate the attempt to get the sun to peek through the clouds of my mood. Of course, they all picked up on it. *Who was I even kidding?*

And so we Dance.

I dive into the Song, pulling my Bonded with me. For one brief moment, I allow myself to drink in the easy grace, allow us to linger in the pleasure and comfort of the shared experience of the Song. Then I turn toward the depths. The burning darkness calling to me. Here, too, there is grace...but it is not always easy. Here the tidal waves of life and death, of emotion and sensation, slam into and crash over me. Volley me to ecstatic heights and swallow me in endless agony. Here, the Song jubilates and rages, howls as much in glory as in sorrow.

This Song is Dark. A black that is alive and a gold that glows. A *place you belong*, it sings. It taunts and tempts me to become it —easier to become it—but I need to keep myself in order to do the work I've come to do. Keep myself and weather the torment. That is the price I need to pay.

Strand by strand, thread by thread, I pluck and probe and weave. I feel what is Sung and honour it. People tend to try and ignore their pain, or they're overwhelmed by it—but life demands to be honoured. So I feel it for them. I share their burden. I weave webs of healing and comfort.

When my strength gives out and exhaustion threatens, I draw on my Bonded. I recede from the depths a little, find them like a lighthouse in the night, an anchor at the end of the chain showing me the way back, and seek shelter for a while. But there is more pain, tugging me in where my Bonded tug at me to come out. So I slip into the sea of wailing agony again, deeper down the spiral.

Eventually, I am too tired to weave. All I can give now is my willingness to carry the burden. Float while clinging to the raft that is my sense of self, and ride it out. Hold on until balance is restored. Then come back another day and weave more love and understanding into the Song, for a different world.

Just hold on and hold out...

My thoughts wander, thin and wispy, when I feel intangible arms wrap around me. That scent... The pain doesn't lessen, the sadness doesn't turn less cutting. But I'm no longer just clinging to myself. Somehow, even though he can't follow me here, Sin has managed to send himself—or if not wholly himself, then the comfort of his presence—along our Bond. Somehow, he found a way to be here with me, ride it out with me, so we can cling to one another. So he can help me stay on the raft.

My Sin, saving me from temptation.

At last, I abandon the raft. Not to give myself up to the black and gold sea, but to spiral up, dragging myself out fist by fist, reeled in by my Bonds. When I return from the Song, my legs are folding under me. Tavo snatches me up before I can hit the ground, and I hazily notice Anda prop a supporting shoulder under Sin.

"Too much, Zaja. Too far," Yako snarls in my face.

"Needed...to be...done," I mumble.

"No. Not at the expense of yourself." Anda's voice is gravel.

Tavo gives me a shake in his arms before burying his face in my neck. "I don't care how much better off the world is now. I care about you."

"Let me have her." Sin.

More growling. "You can barely stand."

"Let me have her. I need to..."

He may be drained and exhausted, but Sin's arms are adamantine bands as they enclose me. The slight tickle against my temple caused by his humming of a soothing, tender melody as they hustle me to comfort is the last thing I'm aware of before I slip into a blank sleep.

Until the blankness fills in like ink blotting paper. In the realm of what has been and what will come, in the realm where the soul wanders when the tether to the body is loosened in sleep, I'm running along my favourite cliff, running towards the edge, towards the leap into the feeling of freedom. But I stop just before going over. The world changes around me—another cliff, another ocean below. I take a calm, determined step. Release and euphoria lap over me, far greater than the familiar leap.

The raft is gone.

* * *

Sin startled awake. His heart was racing at an agonising gallop. He should be getting used to these nighttime panics, should be versed in handling them, but this—

It wasn't real. *Oh, please, Sacred Song and Wicked Wild, let it not be real.*

He fumbled for the Bond while grappling with the sheets to scramble out of bed. *She's still there.* He could feel her, her sense of...confused exhilaration? Sin overshot and crashed into smooth obsidian. Well, that was much better than the terror he was going through. He pushed off and skidded onwards, summoning the strength of a panther to his shocked limbs, but managing no more than the gangly grace of a newborn giraffe.

Most importantly, it meant it hadn't been real. Songs, he'd just watched her fly along that runway into heaven again, jump off again. He'd watched her do it a few times now, often enough to try and focus on the joy she clearly found in it over the near heart attack it gave him. He didn't even want to consider how many times she may be taking that leap that he didn't know about.

This time though, she didn't fall. No, it was worse. This time she...disappeared. Dissolved. Disintegrated. Was there suspended in the air, and then...gone. Colour bleeding apart. The brightest of lights returning home to the darkness.

Beyond his reach.

Lost to me. Sin clamped down on the wretched sound somewhere between a sob and a cry of rage that clawed its way up his throat with the memory. It felt so real. He'd lost her.

But he hadn't. She was alive and well and *here*, on the other side of the artfully carved portal he pulled up short in front of. What was he going to do, barge in there because he'd had a nightmare? She may officially be his Queen now, but she wasn't *his* in a way where he could lay a claim on her private time, her night hours. *Yet.*

As long as she was evidently fine, the rules and subtle dynamics of the Court Dance gave him no good reason to disturb her. Sin leaned his forehead against the hefty wood of her door and released a heavy exhale. She was fine. She was here. If he strained, he could even hear the quiet sounds of her moving about in her suite. Zurea, that lucky cat, was likely in there, so she certainly was protected.

Flipping over, he slid his back along the door until he was sitting on the floor. This would do for the remainder of the night, no matter how strenuous the day had been, how harrowing that Bonded Dance this afternoon. He preferred the reassurance of her proximity, the promise of her closeness that the visceral hum of the Song sung to him, to the comfort his bed could provide a hundredfold.

Only once the birds announced the dawn did Sin return to his own quarters. He took the fastest shower in the history of mankind, went to the kitchens to scrounge up some fresh juice, rich cacao brew, sweet fruit, and still-warm bread, and headed back to knock on Zajasang's suite.

"Lady?"

Sin decided to interpret the responding tug on the Bond as an invitation and opened the door. The breakfast dishes narrowly escaped meeting their fate on the ground when he saw her. Even mussed by sleep, the fire in her shone brilliantly. And there, over her heart, lay his stone.

"You brought me breakfast?" Oh, he was going to do that every day if it put that adorable, delighted expression on her face.

He set down his oblations on the low table in her sitting area. "Did you sleep well?" *Did you get more rest than I did? Are you recovered after that Dance yesterday? Is it like that for you all the time?*

"Mmh-hmm." She tinkered with the breakfast, completely unbothered.

Well, that made one of them. "Zajasang... I felt what you felt yesterday." Sin paused, gauging her reaction. It seemed her breakfast became spectacularly engrossing. A minute passed in silence. "What—what did you do before me?"

"Bore it."

"On your own?"

The stark look Sin got in response was answer enough.

Wicked Wild! He wanted to punch the walls. "Promise me you won't." Maybe shake her, too. "You won't Dance this Dark without me to support you. Ever."

Her haunted eyes, so alive, so beautiful, darted to the side. Escaping him like she hoped to escape his demand. She drew in a soft breath, as if to move on to some other topic.

No. "My Queen." That got her attention. Zaja's inhale stalled and her mystic, sepulchral eyes returned to his. "Let me contribute to you. Let me fulfil my vow."

A faint frown worried her brow. "Sin—"

"My life in your Dance. Those are not just words from an old ritual. Those words are my truth, my desire, my purpose." Surely, she could feel the sincerity and determination in him. Sin cupped her cheek. He needed her to truly hear what he was saying. "My life in your Dance. Whatever I can give you, Zaja, I want to give you. You're my Queen." *You're also my everything.*

For an endless moment, she merely looked back at him. Searching. Likely seeing more than he could fathom. Then, slowly, she nodded. "When I intend to go that Dark... I will call on you."

Sin ground his teeth. Not a full promise, but he would accept it. For now. He gave her a terse nod. The silence lingered.

"Thank you for breakfast." Her voice was low. Sad, almost.

Sin's shoulders dropped. Songs. He hadn't meant to get this serious with her this morning. Where was his charm, his playfulness? But she'd rattled him, and the urge to protect her, take care of her... He blew out his breath, gave his limbs a light shake. Then he stole a berry from her bowl and conjured up his best wicked smile. "Any exciting plans for the day, sweetheart?"

It had seemed like an innocuous enough question to him. Just a way to break the tension, shift the mood. Although as soon as the words were out of his mouth, he fervently hoped her most exciting prospect for the day was petting Zurea.

"Ooooh." The corner of her lip quirked up. His darling Song witch had picked up on his surging agitation. "I was thinking how it's been a while since I've—"

Please don't say leapt off a cliff. Or anything to do with a cliff, period. That, today, would be... He was strong, but he had his moments of doubt if he was strong enough to survive the tempest that was Zajasang.

"—jumped—"

Songs, no.

"—into the pool by the waterfall."

The memory of her trilling laughter accompanied Sin throughout the day, bright and vibrant. In contrast, the rest of it was a blur. All day, he dreaded the looming nightfall, and his focus was shot because of it. When evening came, at last and far too soon, and the Coven's chattering ebbed to a temporary end, he escorted his Queen to her suite. It was neither a particularly far, nor difficult or dangerous distance—from where they had gathered, one of the Coven's favourite courtyards to while time away together, to her rooms, the heart of the palace —yet Sin still enjoyed offering the small act of attentiveness. Zaja remained quiet the whole way, but a soft smile graced her face when she turned to him.

"Goodnight."

Sin lingered. He normally considered himself rather suave. When it came to Zajasang... He might as well be on his knees in front of her whenever he was near her. Sin had enough confidence and self-possession now not to dance on his feet, but his heart pattered like it was preparing to flee from his chest.

At least he had no doubt where its destination would be.

"Zaja." Deep breath. "May I stay with you?" He didn't need the Bond to parse out the elated surprise she felt, or the touch of anxiety. He'd studied her face, her body, enough to be able to read her even without the extra help. Most of the time, at least. "Just to hold you?"

She had accepted his closeness in moments of crisis, where there was no time to think or question. This was different. This was asking her to allow him to get close just because.

Her hand fluttered to her chest, alighted to caress her moonstones. His Bond stone, in fact. The sight sent a thrill through him. His fingers sought out his gold band in response.

A shy smile crept onto her face, like a fawn's graceful, cautious steps into a meadow. "You may."

Songs, yes! Sin hadn't realised he'd been holding his breath, holding on tight to his hopes, until it rushed out of him. Yes. He was invited to share her bed, to hold her through the night. A shiver ran down his back while his heart soared as he followed her into her rooms.

Before she could change her mind, Sin placed a soft kiss on her forehead, then pointedly turned to stand by one of the large, open wind-eyes to look out over the night. The waves murmured far below. The air was peaceful. She could take as much time and privacy as she needed to get ready for bed. He would wait forever for her.

But he didn't have to wait long. A soft tug on the Bond spurred his heart into a gallop once more. Zaja was tense when he slipped underneath the spider-woven wisp of a sheet behind her, stiff when he gently wrapped his arms around her and pulled her close.

Breathe, Sin commanded himself. *Give her a minute.*

He had a good idea of what her past had looked like, knew what touch meant for her. Reminded himself how little time she had in a day to feel like her body and her sensations were her own, and her own only. Even if his touch brought comfort, even if it was filled only with good things and his presence was a shielding cocoon for her—it remained an invasion of her space, feelings beyond her own that she had to process.

Sin resisted the urge to run his fingers along her skin. He stayed as still—and relaxed—as he could, doing his best to ensure his embrace evoked in her nothing but calmness, peace, and solace. Bit by bit, breath after breath, she softened. Gave herself to his hold, until sleep washed over her and took her out to a sea of dreams.

His own need for sleep long forgotten, Sin was consumed with the wonder of her, at ease and trusting in his arms. Enthralled with her exposed shoulder inches from his mouth, silken and fragrant. Roses blooming in darkness and stars burning below the ocean. Her scent was filled with worlds he'd only ever know through her.

It was as much of a mouthwatering lure as yielding to it would be a gamble. He'd been dreaming of this, needing this, for years. Aching for it since being accepted into her Heart Court. To kiss and caress her, in such an intimate way. To breathe her in and in and in.

Finally living it was sure to incite a riot within him that would risk ripping her from her slumber.

Still Sin succumbed to her spell.

* * *

My heart is a drum marching into war.

Space, I need space. My thoughts spin into a carousel. *Need room.* My skin is hot. *Breathe—need—can't*—arms wrapped around me, a body pressed to mine. It's too much. *Too close.* I need space, need air, Songs, *I need*—

I've kicked myself out of bed and across the room by the time my rational mind chimes in. Why am I freaking out over this? It makes no sense. And yet, I'm gasping and gulping like a mermaid in the desert, flapping my tail—no, that's the wall I'm banging against. Frustration melees with overwhelm, cooking into one unholy soup, and boiling over into tears running down my cheeks. *It makes no sense!*

If there's anyone I've ever felt safe with in the core of my being—it's Sin. If there's anyone I've ever wished to share this intimacy with—it's Sin. I want this. *Songs, I want this!* Why can't I revel in it, relish it—like any sane person would?

"Forgive me, Zajasang." Oh Songs, his voice. It sounds so broken, it might as well be a splinter in my heart. And stupidly, I can only cry harder. "Zaja..." His horror is shuddering acid in my veins. His hesitation freezes my bones.

He thinks he caused this.

"No," I gasp out.

Sin misunderstands.

From the vat of acid I go, wholly dumped into an arctic lake. My struggle to breathe in-between my intense, unwelcome sobs makes it impossible for me to string together a coherent sentence and explain. The only thing I can think to do is hold out my hand.

It won't help to have him touch me now. It'll amplify what I'm already feeling from him to beyond agonising levels. But it's the only thing I can do to keep him here.

To pull the splinter from his heart, and then maybe mine will follow suit.

Carefully, ever so tenderly, Sin weaves his fingers through mine. It's an awkward position we end up in—me hunched and curled over myself, crying, only my hand extended. Sin hovering close by, cradling my hand instead of cradling me.

But somehow, miraculously, he understands.

Patiently, silently, he stays with me.

Until the first full breath fills my lungs. Until the tears stop flowing. Until I can feel his hand wrapped around mine, and the sunshine-warm pleasure it brings.

My eyes rest on our intertwined fingers. It seems like a safe place to look while I muster up the courage to face him. *Woven together.* "What's woven...is strong," I whisper.

"It is." His voice is low, a little rough. But the unmistakable velvet prevails. The lovely sound is a treasured cloak wrapping around my heart. The night a cocoon wrapped around our bodies. My chest expands.

I make myself look at him. "Sin. I'm sorry."

His emerald eyes enchain mine as he pulls our joined hands up to his lips. "Don't ever be sorry for being yourself, Zajasang." Pressed into my fingers with his kiss, so softly it might have been a thought dropped into Song instead, he murmurs, "I want all parts of you."

My heart accelerates again for a whole different reason. Dawn hasn't come. Maybe the night isn't ruined. "Will you hold me?" He already holds my heart and my soul. Has held me for years. I can learn how to allow him to hold my body, too.

Silently, we settle back into the pillows. Just before sleep embraces me once more, Sin mumbles into my hair. "My Queen. My Everything."

Everything. No limits, no constraints, no trying to suppress parts of me. Accepting all of it. Could that be possible? For him. For me?

Among the Sung... Maybe anything is possible. Faint hope paints a smile on my heart as slumber scatters me apart.

15

MY FINGERS COLOURED BLUE, I pop a berry between my teeth and enjoy the satisfying burst of skin into a rush of sweetly tart juice. "Alright, Sisters, let's—get ba—"

My words trail off, all responsible plans and intentions lost to fascination.

Tama is gasping with her lips stained, eyes teary, and holding her tummy. "Nooo, no more!"

She doesn't mean me.

Hooting, Feny reaches up to wipe a drop of juice from the corner of Tama's mouth.

They have been dancing around one another—with their words, their glances, even small touches—since Feny arrived from Storm. I'd learnt early on that Tama's Bond with Sehe was not, and never going to be, a romantic one—they'd grown up together in Vigil and been best friends since childhood. Their Songs had called to one another's as Queen and Heart male, and they had honoured the call and formed the Bond.

But Tama and Feny... In each other's presence, those two balls of golden frizz and sunshine have become supernovas, and I'm enthralled by the romantic comedy they're playing out in front of me. Transfixed by the ease between them. Their ease in expressing their attraction and interest in one another.

I wish I could be that easy with people.

"Ladies."

My heart shoots off. *I wish I could be that easy...with him.*

Sin performs the customary greeting, then beams at me and steps in close. Zuzu scrutinises him from where he's lounging by my feet. Those two share a relationship that would be highly entertaining if I wasn't so dumbfounded by it. It's like they can't decide whether they are blood rivals or brothers in arms.

Leaning in until his cheek is a breath from mine, his lips close enough to my ear I can feel their warmth, Sin whispers, "My Queen," before ducking his head to briefly, covertly, draw in my scent by my neck.

He takes care to never actually touch me when he does things like this, and with him, I've recently discovered that is somehow...worse. He gets electrifyingly close, sets me ablaze—but doesn't offer the water to vanquish the flames.

Seven weeks since he arrived at Dark Court. Seven weeks for me to learn that nothing makes time feel as solid and real and slow and immovable for me as spending it burning.

I'm still hung up on the feeling of his husky voice brushing over me, still trying to keep my knees locked in the face of the sensual inferno he seems to unleash every time he's near me lately, when he's long since drawn back and is now patiently, with great satisfaction and amusement, watching me collect myself.

Zuzu huffs by my feet, equally pleased.

Males. And weren't they in rival mode just a second ago? How has that already flipped again?

Without ever looking at anyone but me, Sin says, "I'm sorry, ladies, but I'm whisking her away."

"You are?"

"I am."

He presents his arm for me, never once doubting that I'll come. And Song's mercy if my hand doesn't reach out for him before I think to ask, "Whereto?"

All I get in reply is a smile. An unfairly breathtaking, brain-scrambling one.

But I can't go. My hand stops a smidge shy of settling into the offered crook of his elbow. We may have been lounging about for the moment and having fun, but we'd been intending to get back to work in a minute or two. Just as soon as we could all get over our captivation with the berries. "Sin, there's more Weaving—"

"You need a break."

"I've just—"

Sin cuts me off with a soft finger to my lips. My heart stutters. Sizzling lava and soothing cascades, fire and relief in one. A barely there touch that I feel in every part of me.

I don't know, for once, if the sensations are mine or his.

"As your Bonded, it is my privilege to protect you. No arguing with your Bonded."

I struggle to make out the words through the roaring rushing inside me, struggle to get my own out through the haze. "I don't think that's how that works."

My lips moving against his index draw his eyes to my mouth. As if dragging it through honey, he lifts the pad of his finger and traces the tender skin, teasing the sweetness to its breaking point. Finally, his eyes lift back to me.

Scorching.

"Please?"

* * *

I take in the sight before me, glorious enough to outweigh the other constant distraction of the last hour—momentarily, at least. "Firefall."

I loved this place the one other time I've been here. Absolutely devoured its serenity, and magic, and beauty. It's just as stunning now as it was then. "Mesmerising," I sigh. The fall floods through me, taking with it all tension and leaving only clarity and spaciousness and power behind. "Thank you for bringing me here."

"You're welcome, Zaja."

For a while, we do nothing but admire Firefall, feel its fresh kiss on our skin, and taste the coming dusk in the air. Nothing to do but be, and enjoy, and soak in the peace. Until Sin places his hand on the small of my back.

His thumb draws small, firm circles that take off and fizz in my belly like spinning buzz bee fireworks. My breath catches in my throat, and I glance up to him.

His gaze is already waiting.

With a light press of his fingertips, he turns me towards him. Swallows. Draws in a breath as if to say something, and doesn't. Drops his eyes to my mouth.

Then he tilts forwards.

Excruciatingly slowly, he leans closer—and closer—and closer...and stills. He hovers right there, close enough that just one breath deeper than our shallow ones would bring us together. Hovering maddeningly.

Waiting.

Asking for permission.

A moment in which the world could tip over, be birthed anew or break apart.

He waits for me to choose.

The heartbeat of the Earth itself pounds once, twice. Three times.

I take a deep breath full of Sin.

As if freed by my choice, the moment our lips touch, there's nothing shy, or hesitant, or controlled left in him. Only untameable, indelible passion remains. His kiss is a dam released, a soul deep yearning answered.

His kiss is the purest worship.

The world spins out around me.

When, with one last nib, our lips part, the rest of us remains wholly entwined: Bodies colliding, arms embracing, Songs tangling. We touch our foreheads together, and breathe. There's nothing but drinking in each other's presence.

A soft golden feeling unfurls inside me. My heart blooms and billows open. So...vast.

"I've never felt so peaceful." And I haven't. The peace from before—the peace he so rudely...ravishingly...ravenously... interrupted—was a world removed from this.

Sin hums a deep, contented sound. He places a kiss on my brow and tucks me into his chest. "I know."

He kisses my crown, and tingles shiver all the way down into the rich earth beneath me. We stand bathed in the golden-orange glow and molten mist of Firefall, and hold each other.

"This is everything." I don't know where the words come from. Where the certainty, the sense of recognition, of remembrance of this feeling comes from. Of finding something long lost. "This is eternity." The words make me smile.

Sin's arms tighten around me before his hand cradles my cheek and tilts my face up to him. For a long while, he just looks at me—into me. Looks at me with eyes brimming with emotion.

Emerald eyes that have looked at me for aeons.

When he kisses me again, it is soft, and soul-achingly tender, and full of an infinity of searing vows. "My Queen. My glorious Dark Queen." His feelings say the rest.

I wish I could stay in this feeling, caught in his eyes, forever. It's so familiar.

And it's fraught.

16

Dark Court

"I've decided to ask Jaymin for the privilege of becoming her husband."

Tavo's declaration was calm and filled with quiet joy, true to his nature.

Sin clapped him on the shoulder and squeezed. "Congratulations, brother. Strong heart and Song's caress."

They were seated next to one another on a long, sturdy log during this month's sun lodge—his fourth at Dark Court. Where the females had their Dark Moon circles, the males came together each month when the sun moved into a new sign. It was their time to pass wisdom between elders and youngsters, to find support and guidance from each other, to celebrate and relax in brotherhood. The strongest among them rotated out to miss a lodge every few months so they could stay behind and ensure the safety of the females of the Court. A measure taken for their own comfort and peace of mind, rather than that of the females, who graciously accepted their *overprotectiveness*...and muttered about jellyfish.

"I hope to take her out for the devotion ritual this coming week," Tavo said, while passing Sin a fermented brew.

He took a sip and swallowed while eyeing the gold band on Tavo's finger. If all went well for him, it would soon be joined by another—this one proudly bearing a stone reflecting the colour of Jaymin's eyes. She was a good choice for him, a wonderfully kind and loving female who helped care for the young ones on Amea. She had been part of the early wave of Sung called to Dark Court, same as Tavo, and helped establish the Circle. Sin could see her and Tavo creating a bliss-filled life and family together.

"Have you spoken with Zajasang?"

Tavo nodded, a serene smile spreading on his face. "She agreed to Honour the Wedding Song for us."

"What a Queen you have." Sin gave him a friendly punch to the upper arm.

"The very best."

Their shared grin was full of satisfaction.

"What are you two so pleased about?" Anda's voice arrowed target-sure across the circle, despite its softness and gravitas.

"Our glorious Queen, dear brother. What else?"

"Good. I want to talk about Queen Zaja."

Any sense of playfulness bandied about the lodge vanished. Even the rest of the males, engaged in their own discussions, fell silent to listen. "Is something wrong?"

Anda's expression was thoughtful. Concerned.

"Anda?" Yako prodded.

"I believe your Bond with her is strongest, and the closest, Sin. What did you feel from her the day she asked us all for our first Bonded Dance as a complete Constellation?"

"Hesitation. Wariness." Sin's muscles clenched at the most salient aspect of the memory. "And pain."

"More pain than what you've experienced a Queen take on before?"

"Yes." Yako and Tavo nodded in agreement. "But not more than I've felt from her all her life."

Somber silence sat heavy in their circle. Sin hadn't openly spoken before about the unofficial bond he'd shared with Zajasang for so long—but he thought his Bond Brothers, at least, might have had their suspicions. If anyone was surprised at his statement, the implication of it weighed far more significantly right now than its revelation.

Anda rubbed a hand down his face. "It may be that it comes with her nature. It fits with what else is passed down about Dark Queens."

Dark Queens were rare. Sometimes generations lived and died before one arrived—or she, rather, *for there was only ever one,* as the stories said. During those times, when she didn't walk among them, only those stories kept their knowledge of the Dark Queen alive. Like the one originating from the time of Daina that was distractingly, worryingly dancing in Sin's mind as he stared into the flames of the lodge's fire.

Of the moon, Dark Queen wears four stones.
Three surround, with the fourth, love abounds.
The three close the frame.
The Dark Destined knows her pain.
He stands with her in the centre.
He follows her deep.
Even the Destined can't hold her
When she takes the Dark leap.

Sin had been dreaming of being Zajasang's Bonded since meeting her half a lifetime ago on the beach. He began dreaming of being her lover not long after. He just hadn't known he was dreaming of becoming Dark Destined. He certainly hadn't known how petrifying that last line was until she'd returned to them.

"Wicked Wild! I don't like it." Yako's expletive snapped Sin back to the here and now.

"Neither do I. We may still have to accept it," Tavo said.

"Her hesitation to Dance, though... I worry about it." Anda sought Sin's gaze again. "Then wasn't the only time I felt it."

Sin sighed, roughing his hands over his head. "Yes, she's been hiding something. I've...approached the topic. But she's guarded about it."

Yako started pacing. "She doesn't trust us?"

"She's still learning to, I think," Anda said. "Herself as part of the Sung, as well."

Sin tried to think from her perspective, tried to comprehend her—an impossible feat—from what he knew of her. "She was raised to the Loud. She's had only herself to rely on all her life. And the world she lives in, the depth of Song she constantly stands in—none of us can understand." He blew out a breath. "Even have an inkling, I think. Every sliver she allows me, every bit she lets me in..." Sin grunted and shook his head.

Silence sang between them.

"She is Dark Queen, brothers." An acknowledgment of a truth that caused him both awe and terror, the more he came to glimpse what it meant. His Zajasang was Dark Queen, in all her glory and horror.

"Have any of the Coven said anything? Or behaved... differently?"

Negatives all around.

"So we wait."

"And watch."

"Do our best to help her fully trust us, open to us, and lean on us."

"Contribute, protect, revere. Trust in her." Sin nodded, then sighed again. Gave himself a hard nudge to add, "And honour her choice."

Until she chose to tell them what was going on, they couldn't make her.

All he could do was love her.

Love her, hold her, and fear the Dark leap.

* * *

"Will you let me wash your hair for you?"

I startle at the question. My moontime has sapped my energy and carried me into visions and dreams. I'd been lost in listening into the Song, its wisdom and knowings and mysteries, and forgotten Sin was even here. Keeping me company in the sitting room of my suite, the sweet and salty breeze flowing between the wind-eye and the open courtyard, twining around the columns, lifting and caressing the petals of the flowers, the wings of all that hums and sings...

Stay here, Zaja. Sin is here.

Yes, Sin is here. And a scarily capable master at balancing the tightrope of my moony moods at that, often managing to stay close and around without making me feel hemmed in or rustling my feathers.

He asked you a question.

Right. I guess I had been absently twirling and messing with my hair, and it does need a wash, and I am too exhausted to move... But even so, I don't know what to make of this proposal. Through these past several months of moon cycles, I've come to expect the various small ways he finds to fuss over me—*Cherish you, Zaja. It's my privilege as your Bonded. No arguing with your Bonded*—so Sin says—so there are the herbal brews, the food trays, the fetching of things and books and knickknacks. A gentle touch when he is sure it will be welcome.

This is new.

"I'd like to," Sin says.

My brows rise high. "You would?"

Golden calm and tingling. Sincerity and anticipation. He would.

"Yeah."

"Is that a Sung thing?"

His lips quirk up. "No." Then thoughtfulness enters his expression. "I mean, I don't know. Maybe. It's—"

"Intimate."

He draws in a breath. Holds it. His green eyes are embers. "Yeah." More tingling.

Songs. I chew my lip as I watch him watch me. Wash my hair? Not even my mother... *Will I—will I be in the bath?*

"Just say no, Zaja." There's no disappointment, no misgivings whatsoever in his voice.

Though the fleeting, momentary somber taste of bitterness can't escape me. Of dashed hope. Still, his eyes are nothing but kind, and open, and patient. So... "Caring."

"Hm?"

I try to imagine it. I think I might like it. I think it might feel intimate, and caring, and—

"Loving. It's loving."

And I'm thinking that the minuscule smile that now plays around his lips might be very dangerous for my heart.

For the next twenty minutes, the lapping of water sings me a gentle lullaby, weaving me into a cocoon spun of warmth and comfort.

"Sin?"

His voice is a touch husky when he replies. "Zaja?"

"It's actually amazing."

"Good." He clears his throat, tapering off as he says, "That's really good."

I'm pretty certain my hair is clean by now, but his fingers don't stop. He continues to massage my head, somehow managing to not once pull my hair beyond what is deliciously shiver-inducing. The whole experience is as new to me as it is heavenly.

Too soon, his hands still. "You're all done."

Sin is the perfect gentleman as I wrap myself in my long and flowing, gauzy muslin robe. I know, because I watch him every second as I rise from the water and dress, dripping wet as I am.

"Thank you. I liked that."

His eyes dip down to the clinging fabric only once. Then he ruffles his hand through his own hair, and the crooked grin that comes over his face should be forbidden. "So... does that mean you want me to brush it for you, too?"

"Hmmm... Full service, huh?"

Sin winks at me and holds out his hand. I trail behind him as he leads me from the bath, only our fingertips hooked around one another's. When I'm seated, he bends around me from behind for a languid kiss. From there, his lips trail kisses to my ear. "Whatever is your pleasure, my Queen."

And he oils my hair, and brushes it, and when that is done, he begins braiding it. Intricately.

His fingers on me are a bliss I've never known, while the peaceful, quiet contentment of shared closeness that is expanding between us feels like an old, familiar, but long-forgotten coat. One you slip into after finding it again, and it feels like home.

"How do you know how to do this?"

"Hm?" Sin rouses from the trance he worked himself into with the complicated, stunning art piece of looping and interwoven braids that I can feel he is conjuring into my hair. They snake and curl, form webs and roses. "Oh. I practiced on mares."

I sit up and twist around. "Really?"

His lips twitch, and I could swear the tips of his ears tinge red. "And stallions. Really."

My mouth opens, then closes. The bashfulness that has slipped over him makes this revelation even more fascinating. "Why?"

"Because you had this incredible, beautiful mane even then." He tugs gently. "I began dreaming of—of this. Of being able to do this for you. So, I wanted to make sure I'd be good at it."

I shake my head in baffled disbelief, my smile spreading wide.

He tugs again, an answering grin gracing his sensual lips. "Turn around. Let me do what I'm good at, my Queen."

The simmering fire in his eyes sweeps through my lower belly in a sultry swirl. My tongue flicks out, laving my lip before my teeth restrain it.

Any trace of bashfulness disappears, the confident, prowling Heart male returning in full force. "Not that." Sin's velvet voice is dripping honey over tree bark. "That, later."

"You sure?" We could untangle all those braids again right now, in delicious slowness or frenzy...

He snarls at me, his tug a little less gentle this time. "I'm sure, Lady."

Oh, but does his Song say differently.

* * *

Sin jolted into alertness.

Zaja was snuggled against his front, warm, alive, her unique siren song of a scent teasing more than just his nose—but she was tense. His hackles went up, his arm around her tightening, as he assessed the space of her suite. Sin watched, and listened, and sensed.

Nothing.

She was safe.

Which meant it was either something in the Song—or it was him. The thought turned his stomach. He loosened his arm a fraction.

"What is it?" Sin held his breath.

Zaja flopped onto her back. Her eyes were still closed. She grumbled.

"Zaja?"

She turned towards him and smashed her face into his chest.

Sin felt his heart start beating again. *It's not me.*

He kissed her ear. He'd protect her from anything—even if what she needed protection from was him, and it meant having to remove himself from her equation. He'd do it even if it'd shred him, if it was what she asked for. He hoped to the Sacred Song she never would. "Sweetheart?"

"Ugh. Nothing."

Clearly, it was something, or she wouldn't be so tense. Sin trailed his fingers over her hair, the flower petal soft skin of her cheek, then he gently tilted her head back, and kissed her brow, then her nose. He felt into the Bond while he did it...and his brow lifted a smidgeon. There was annoyance, and a hint of embarrassment.

He waited.

With a grand dramatic huff, she flopped onto her back again. "I'm too lazy to move." She blinked her beautiful eyes at him, her long hair wild over the pillow and a slight pinch to her mouth. "And I need to go to the bathroom."

Sin broke out laughing.

She glared at him.

Oh but, "Songs," he gasped, his mirth fuelled further by relief and that look that had taken over her face, "you are adorable."

He was bellowing now.

Thus, predictably, she cracked, too. Chuckles spilt through her soft lips, followed by radiant, flowing laughter. "No," she whined, holding her stomach. "That's not helping!"

"Darling, do you want me to carry you?"

She swatted at him. Moaned. Rolled and puffed and escaped him.

No, no—his arm stretched after her, grasping only air. He missed the feel of her already. Sin groaned and turned over into the pillow—and smiled. He'd just remembered what day it was.

Sacred Song was coming up.

* * *

Vala and I place the last petals. The morning sun, filtered by the leaves of the ancient jungle trees towering above us like sentinels, teases our backs. We share a smile, send some gratitude into the soil beneath our hands, and stand up.

From the higher vantage point, we can see the whole of the spiral coiling and unravelling before us. White lilies and blood roses. Rose quartz where they swirl together. Black and gold obsidians to hold the frame and tethers. The elegant, graceful beauty of it speaks to me, singing a calming Song I try to cling to.

"The white river and the red river," Vala says with a serene, mysterious tilt of her lips.

I cock my head, thinking back on things I read in a library a life away. "The heart and the womb?" Bending down again, I reach to adjust one of the blooms just so.

Vala nods sagely. "The virgin and the whore."

My arm halts, trembling the tiniest bit. My eyes grow a bit rounder.

Another spiral not far from ours bleeds from ice blue to pink, to purple to orange. A fire of nature. All across the

Court, spirals and mandalas have been laid with flowers, seeds, stones. On the beaches, they're made from shells and driftwood and algae. They are like the moondalas that grace the Court for the Bright Moon celebrations, only that now they have blossomed into exuberant, overflowing life.

We are ready for Sacred Song.

Supposedly. I finish nudging the lily into place, bob up, and shake out my hands.

"Excited?" Vala asks.

"Yeah." There's no way not to get caught up in the charged anticipation that's flushing cheeks, making eyes glow, and making the males that bit sharper still.

She looks me over and narrows her eyes. "You'll be fine, Zaja. It'll be instinct."

I give her a wobbly smile.

"What part are you worried about?"

All of it? The massive responsibility and expectation placed on my shoulders to lead this thing? And...cryptic announcements like *the virgin and the whore?* "I've heard some things among the fluttering whispers."

"About?"

"About the Dance during Sacred Song." I warily eye her. Then I bite out, "Its *positions.*"

Vala breaks out into trilling, resonant laughter that I'm sure is heard on the other side of the Court. "Sacred Song," she gasps. "Ah, Sister, you—" She tries to calm down, to talk, but no luck.

I'm beginning to flush with embarrassed resentment when Vala grabs onto my forearm as she bends under the force of her hilarity, and I feel the pure spun sugar delight of it bubbling along my veins. My shoulders relax. I give her another moment.

"Yes?" I say sweetly.

"Zaja, all of us females among the Sung, we are all virgins." She nods meaningfully down at the fragrant blooms.

I snort. "Yeah, right—" Her face is serious. Still amused, but serious about this. "No, you're not. I mean, I know you're not. I mean, I don't actually know about you. But Adara, Mrak..."

Vala's grin is huge, her next nod so pointed it's comical. "We are also all whores."

"Vala," I whine, pathetically tugging on her sleeve.

"Alright, Sister." All the spunk and spark hidden within her quiet waters is on full display, whipped up to the surface by the torrents of thrill and expectation snaking over Amea. With both her hands on my shoulders, she unceremoniously pushes me back to the ground, into a cross-legged seat opposite her.

"The virgin—in its original meaning—is our freedom, our wholeness unto ourselves. The whore—hor—is our truth and power. It used to mean womb—the sacred dark place of life and creation."

This does ring a bell from my reading. "Temple priestesses." Temple...whores. Women who retained their ownership over both their sex and their lives, were revered, respected—and powerfully alive both sexually and spiritually. "Wild and holy. Passionate and pure."

Vala sparkles at me. "Two rivers spiralling as one."

The heart and the womb... Blossoming in unity as love that is as sensual and erotic as it is compassionate and innocent. "Alright—that's beautiful—but—"

"We're getting there," Vala waves me off. "The obsidian?"

My mouth hangs open. Really?

"The obsidian." I swallow my sigh, hold back my glare, and let my gaze wander over the stones swirling with and framing the red and white rivers again. "The tempest, the power of the abyss. Dark Song."

"Where you will lead us in the Dance."

Right. So everyone keeps saying. And no one will explain what I'm actually leading people in, or to, or through. All they keep hinting at is what the Dance looks like outside the Song. Neither is reassuring. Both are steadily, infuriatingly exacerbating my nerves about Sacred Song.

"I may lead myself off a cliff and this island before then," I mutter.

"Tsk." Those waving fingers again. "You've witnessed and spoken the words of the Bond Song. Do you know the Wedding Song?"

Memories of a vision rise in my mind. A male before me, such love within me, such power and charge in the air around me. He looks deep into my eyes as he holds my hands. With conviction, his voice strong and steady, offering his heart and soul before me, he says, *My sanctity in your choice.* I feel the weight of those words, and reply, *I choose you as mine.* Together, we seal the bond so woven. *For the pleasure of Song.*

Heat tingles over my skin and I clear my throat. "Choice," I tell Vala.

"Always. Our Bonds do not tie us. We are free females, defined only in our own being, independent of anyone else. We are our own sovereign and our own most important lover. We belong to ourselves." She studies me, gauging if I understand.

"Virgins," I whisper.

"Yes. We may choose to share ourselves, but that does not mean giving any part of ourselves away. The Wedding Song, our most sacred Bond, is still based in the eternal honouring of our choice." Her smile turns crooked. "Now of course, our males won't lie down and let you walk all over them, giving in to whatever. They'll fight for what they want." Her brow raises, and my own lips twist in amusement thinking of Yako...or Sin. Neither have any qualms about being bossy. "But at the end of the day, the males trust in the female's choice. Honouring her choice trumps all else."

"Why?" My voice breaks on the single syllable.

"We are nature, we are Earth..." She skims her fingertips over the vibrantly coloured ground, covered in leaves and rocks and flowers. "We are life and blood and vision and creation. We are sacred."

Vala scoops up soil and petals, slowly opens her palms as if revealing a treasure, and lets it all trickle through her fingers.

"Think about the Song. We, the feminine, open into ecstasy and surrender, and the masculine is called to honour, protect, revere, and contribute. We can take us both, feminine and masculine, into the abyss and bring us back. We can go places... find pleasure...the masculine can't access by itself."

Another searching look, so I nod my understanding. In this I know she's right. Without a Bond to a female, males, at best, hear the hum of the Dark Song. Only the hum, when there are symphonies.

She continues. "Sometimes, the masculine can help take us deeper than we can go by ourselves, thanks to their power, strength, and direction, or because they can push us into opening beyond our own resistance. It's what we love and worship them for." She thinks for a moment. "But it is only thanks to us that there is even a place to go. It's like—like they may steer the ship, but we're both the compass they navigate by and the ocean they're sailing on."

I blow out a big breath.

Clearly channeling a meerkat today, Vala revs back up into scary levels of animation. "That truth holds whether in the Dance or in the bedroom, Sister. Contributing to us—offering themselves in service to the pleasure of the female... It is the desire and the way of fulfilment of the male." She chuckles. "Oh, the satisfaction in making us sing..."

I flop onto my back, bringing my hands up to cover my face. But Vala isn't finished, chortling away.

"Among the Sung, sex is revered, Zaja. It is an honouring of life, a form of the Dance. Our female sensuality is an expression of our wholeness and divinity. Human divinity. We own it."

She leans over me, pries my hands apart, and drills her eyes into mine. She wants me to get this, to understand something here.

"The whore?"

"Two sides of the coin. Virgin and whore—both are our sovereignty, power, and ownership over our own body and pleasure. Different flavours, same thing. *Our choice.*"

I'm sure my eyes are swimming with spirals like those all around us. "So," I clear my throat, "Sacred Song. No assumptions?"

Vala tugs me up. She pulls on me to get us moseying back toward Dark Palace, swinging our hands as we walk like we are little girls. "No. While many choose to celebrate that way..." A shrug. "Others don't."

"And if there are several Bonded..."

Vala snorts. "I'm sure they'll be ecstatic if you invite all of them to participate in the ritual with you."

"You mean platonically. Like any other time we come together as a full Constellation for a Bonded Dance."

"Well, Tavo, yes. The rest of the lot..." She wiggles her shoulders side to side in a sinuous little dance. "I'm sure they'll eagerly accept the invitation if it's non-platonic, too."

I thump her with my elbow. Hard.

"Alright!" She laughs. "I'm stopping. I know yours won't be. And Sin would freak out. Now, Adara on the other hand..."

Images flash through my mind. Intriguing images. Vala and I look at each other. Look away. And burst out cackling.

It's a while before we manage to settle.

"However it goes down—none of them will allow themselves to hold any resentment either way. Your choice, Zaja. They'll respect whatever it may be." The closer we draw to the heart of Dark Palace, the more Vala regains of her usual poise. "Also, the night is long. There's time for more than one Dance."

"Hrm." It's an odd, choked sound that makes it up my throat.

We pass through one of the inner courtyards, climb up a few levels, and eventually turn into the hallway that leads to my rooms.

"You know," she says with careful nonchalance, "your bed remains yours. Even when Sin becomes your husband as well as Dark Destined, it will always be his honour to be invited to share it. No assumptions."

My next sound is positively strangled. Complete with the comic book popping eyes, scarecrow freeze, and a hue that flashes between dead and overheating. I *had* been about to thank her.

"Sovereignty, Sister," Vala sings gaily. She throws an arm over my shoulders, flushed with her mischief. "Last word of advice? Since he won't ever violate your boundaries or choice...it's up to you to let him know that you want it."

Oh Songs, swallow me now.

17

"Queen Zaja." Sin pushes off from where he was leaning against one of the columns of my sitting room, smirks at me, and sketches a bow. "May I escort you to your first Sacred Song?"

Warmth flutters inside me even as my lips tilt up and I shake my head at his antics. I'm not sure I feel any readier now than I did this morning. Then again, whatever this is going to be, it'll have to beat the annual routine with my parents on this night of the year.

Right? I take another deep, trembling breath.

Zuzu presses himself against my leg. There's the steady weight of comfort and support flowing from him, but also dry tanginess.

"Zuzu thinks I'm being ridiculous."

Sin still has his hand extended to me, watching me with affection shining in the green of his eyes. His lips twitch at that observation, but he makes no further comment. Wise male.

With a huff, I steel my spine and place my hand in his. Everyone else is long gone. It's time. "Escort away."

We wind our way through the Dark Palace. It's so quiet and empty, I'm reminded of the first time I walked these halls and breezeways, explored the courtyards and balconies. Before I learned I was Dark Queen. Before I'd met Zuzu. Before I realised Sin was real and out there somewhere. Before the Sung had welcomed me, embraced me, become...friends and family.

Well ahead of reaching the celebration grounds, I feel the merry twirling energies and hear the sounds of mirth. Laughter is punctured by gleeful shrieks. Music sways between fast and wild, then thrumming and sensual. Fire flickers under the clear deep night, singing to the glittering stars above, and the air is scented with cinnamon and spice.

There is not a single Sung on the island who isn't part of the celebrations.

As we draw close enough to begin making out shapes and colours through the jungle, Sin nods to one of the chalices. "Fires, as a symbol of the heart around which all life revolves, and also the ebb and flow, glow and darkness, clarity and mystery in the Dark Song. We celebrate this night as a time of the veil thinning between all beings and spirits, seen and unseen...between all dimensions." He looks at me with a queer expression I can't read. "Sacred Song is a celebration of life in all its glory."

We stop on the edge of the tumult. I clutch Sin's hand.

This is different to the times the Sung assembled for Bond Song rituals. Those were occasions of serene unity. This? This is wild and roiling, teeming with life and emotions. I spent a life avoiding crowds like this one. Crowds mean pain. Exhaustion. Madness.

My muscles tense up, bracing. My impulse is to turn tail, and only my locked down frame keeps me rooted.

Never releasing me, Sin steps into my line of sight. He lifts his free hand to cup my cheek, his thumb stroking back and forth. Silently coaxing me to focus on him.

Green eyes. His scent. Rose and violet velvet in his caress. Moored might.

My breath evens out. My panic recedes. I realise I only feel him. I'm shielded and sheltered in the cocoon of his strength. No stray energies pinging through me or pounding at me. There's just him and me.

Just him and me. My thoughts clear.

These are the Sung.

I'm not the same Zaja I used to be.

This is not that. This can be like—like Dancing in the Dark Song. Rather than trying to stand against the wave... I can let it flow through me and sweep me up with it. For a little while, at least.

"Don't let me get lost," I whisper.

Another swipe of his thumb, then a soft pass across my lips. "Never."

Sin bends and places a gentle kiss on my forehead before stepping back to my side. Freeing my line of sight.

I take in what wholly escaped me when I slipped into old anxieties.

A vast majority of the Sung is...dancing. Slung around one another tightly, they are moving in concert, their hips churning, chests gyrating, backs arching, hair flying. All of a sudden my throat feels thick and my skin hot. Their dancing is the most beautiful, connected, and sensual I have ever witnessed. Subtle movements of hips, legs, chests, and hands of one partner seem to guide the other. Both are fully sunk into the communication of their bodies, listening with their whole beings, asking and answering. Many of those surrendered into following their partner's lead have their eyes closed.

This dance is a moving embrace. It is a worshipping of each other, of their bodies, their ability to feel one another, their willingness to open to full connection. A worshipping of the beauty of life itself.

They take my breath away.

"Sin..."

"Let me show you."

He pulls me into the throng, wraps his arms around me and brings my body snug to his. For a moment, we merely stand and feel into one another. Then he begins to move, and I stop thinking, and I follow where he takes me.

I become a whirlwind of limbs, a maelstrom of sensations, but always, always, I'm spooled back in to safety in the frame of his arms. He may be teaching me how the Sung dance, but he may as well have taught me how to fly. Moving like this, with him—it is like being lost to the best parts of the Song, without any of the fear or the pain.

Hours later, my bones feel wobbly, my smile is hurting my cheeks, and I reckon my eyes are as bright as those I see around me. "I'm a sweaty mess," I gasp out.

"That's the best kind of mess," Sin says, waggling his brows at me. He kisses my temple. "You're beautiful, my Queen." His voice is so low and husky I barely make it out.

Damn if contentment doesn't hum through me.

"Found her!" Mrak suddenly shrills into my ear.

She's grabbed my hand and spun me around before I know what's happening.

"Well done, Mrak," Sin mutters behind me.

I clap my fingers over my lips to hold in my giggle.

Mrak deftly manoeuvres us through writhing bodies. "Night's calling, Sister," she chirps.

I glimpse the rest of the Coven flocking on the edge of the celebration grounds, the Heart males hovering around them.

The latter's faces spell eager anticipation, though some appear torn with dry sympathy when looking over my shoulder to the male trailing after me.

None of that in Yako's eyes though—only impatience there. A simmering fire in Anda's gaze, and open joy at my approaching form in Tavo. They close around me when I reach them, each of them bending or reaching for one of their favourite spots—temple, wrist, or curve of my neck—to scent me.

Just as I'm opening my mouth to tell them to back off, a hand sneaks in and snags me out from under them.

"You'll get her later, gentlemen."

Their expressions are rather wonderful, I have to admit.

With the revelry continuing on behind us, we cluck back to the Dark Palace, picking our way through the subtle pathways of the jungle, laughter and chatter flying through the air the whole way. One of the monkeys decides to ride along on my head like that first day in Vigil, causing a loud chuckle from Tavo, which is met with curious glances.

I want to float along on the levity of it all. Only now that I'm no longer spinning and whirling out of my mind...my nerves are coming back.

Vala quietly takes my hand. Of course. What did I do to deserve her?

Based on everything I've heard—everything I've been fretting over—I expect the group to break apart once we reach the Dark Palace. Instead, the clucking continues, the Queens ambivalent to having crossed into Palace grounds. Caught in the middle of them as I am, I let myself be bundled along. When we arrive where the Coven's been heading, I wonder how I could have forgotten.

The Witch Harp.

Evidently never shy about anything in her life, Adara strides forward first, confidently beginning to strum the glinting strings while swaying past them.

I'm entranced. Usually, her strong sultry presence has an edginess to it—but seeing her playing the Witch Harp... Her lines and edges seem to soften, leaving nothing but splendid beauty behind. The clear notes of the instrument merge into the symphony of the Song, each a sprite twirling along my spine and a burst of pollen dust teasing my nose.

The lilting melody tilts. Adara's song builds, and the energy in the room shifts like a drop of nectar released from petals that could no longer keep it contained. Spice mixes in with the flowery scent. The warm silky smoothness like that of a snake's languid, scaly body twines up my legs. Heat flows through my blood.

The sensations draw my eyes up to Elu and Dashuri. Their focus on Adara is intent. My regard strays back to her swaying form. Where before I saw only dance, I now see sensuality in the way her fingers graze or pluck a string, her neck arches into the flight of a melody.

Beyond playing the Witch Harp, it's almost like... *She is making love.*

When we stepped onto the balcony, I thought I might play tonight. Vala and I have spent hours here together. Talking. Laughing. In silence. She instructing me in the art of playing the Witch Harp. It has become one of my favourite retreats in the Dark Palace.

I feel very doubtful about the idea now.

Clearly having no such qualms, Tama takes three sure steps forward, idly caressing one of the Harp's crowns as she goes, and seamlessly joins in with Adara's song.

The tiny hairs on my neck lift with the feeling of roses blooming in each of my cells as the melody splits and opens, layering into two where before there was one. A new membranous page in the folds of the worlds, in the book of the dimensions sleeping snugged one alongside the next.

A rise and a fall, a dip and a swirl later, Vala slips in among her Sisters with the grace of a ballerina's glissade. One by one, the Queens join, to bring their notes to the harmony. With each layer it becomes richer, fuller. With each Queen entering the song, the energy thickens and its power rises. It is mesmerising, and it calls to me.

But that is not what causes me to join.

When I finally take those steps to the strings, to complete the circle of the Coven slinking along them, it is because I feel drawn to belong. Belong in this moment of time. Belong with my Sisters. To no longer stand aside but be a note in the music. To be more than a receptacle holding on while life rushes through.

To not be the Witch's Harp...but the Witch.

I pluck the first string that answers the melody's yearning. My Sisters smoothen their movements. Each steals a moment out of time in the endless silence existing between each note—if only you know to listen for it—to meet my eyes. Warmth from Vala. Joy from Tama. A spark of fire in Adara's eyes. A glint in Mrak's. Wicked pride from Feny.

Our senses stretched wide and connected with each other we undulate in delight, we quicken to crescendo, we rise and fall. We are a Coven joined in sound and vibration, dance and glance.

So this is what it truly is to play the Witch's Harp.

No way Vala could have ever explained this to me. Maybe the Sung weren't purposefully oblique in revealing their world to me whenever I tried to pry information on one thing or another out of them. Maybe they just preferred not to use words where there weren't any.

The longer we play, the more I can sense what is coming. Whereas the earlier dancing out in the celebration grounds was its own magic of unbridled wild joy, grounded and earthy... This magic wrought from the Witch Harp's strings, woven by our playing, tastes of the otherworldly. Evoked by each gliding step and each vibrating thread, it is like we are dancing into the folds between the worlds, preparing for the full step through.

More keenly than ever before I understand. *This is our gift, our burden, our privilege.* As Queens, as Sisters of the Song...as Witches.

The velvet weight of certainty unfurls in my womb. The time for the ritual has come. I feel for a space between the notes to take a deep breath, and reach for a low vibration to slow us down. "Sisters, shall we Dance?"

One by one, like helicoptering maple seeds, my Sisters spin out of their frenzy, releasing themselves from the Witch Harp's trance. Bursts of tart anticipation in my mouth are tempered with the sleek gravity of their sincerity, and a soft cloak woven of ribbons of recognition of the sanctity of this adventure settles about my shoulders.

Mrak is the first to reply, serious and solemn. "May we meet you in the Dark Song, Dark Queen."

Watching her walk to the archway opening to the hall, my belly jitters and my throat is clogged. I hardly register the flush of Jalen's cheeks as he follows after her.

At the last second before she flounces around the corner, Mrak turns back to me and offers a wink.

Oxygen floods through me once more, and I sag a sliver in relief.

One after the other, the Queen's repeat the vow and disperse, Bonded in tow. In less than a minute only my Constellation remains. Every single one of them looking at me expectantly.

My eyes flit about the shadowed space, my fingers knotting in the light layers of my skirts. "Umm... So..." I catch a hint of amusement in Tavo's gaze and silently plead with him to come to my rescue.

He remains as mum as the lot of them. Of course.

My breath seems really loud in the silence.

The silence turns heavy and crushing.

Wicked Wild. Where did all that surety go that had so brazenly taken up residency in my womb?

None of them offer anything, still simply looking at me. The one time I could really use their bossy opinions and jellyfish habits...

Right. Alright. I shake the thought—all thoughts, preferably—out of my brain. *This is my show to run.*

Trying to block out how my awkwardness is volleying between us, feeding on itself, my growing discomfort escalating into my Constellation's unease, I cast my eyes around the dusk-darkened balcony again. The world feels far away with only stars glimmering above us and some of the Palace's candles lit below. Echoes of the Harp's magic still swing in the air. Maybe we can just stay and do this right here?

I open my mouth to tell them as much—

The sensation of a knife scraping against my skin breaks through my wilful ignorance. *Huh.* We are well tucked away in the middle of the Court—I wouldn't have thought they'd have an issue with me Dancing here. *I guess everything is a little more... intense...tonight.* The males' need to protect is riding them hard.

"How about we go to my sitting room?"

Their immediate response—cool sighs slinking through my veins—affects me as much as it does them. Still, the males cluster around me as we traverse the vacant halls, colonnades, and breezeways. Sin directly to my left, Anda in the lead, Tavo and Yako bringing up the rear. Zuzu pads along on my right.

The jellyfish back in full force. I find I can't hold it against them.

When the door to my sitting room snicks closed behind us my Bonded relax another smidgen. With the room's open, wallless layout letting in the subtly scented breeze from the private courtyard it doesn't feel stifling or enclosed in any way—yet it is protected and safe.

And utterly silent, only my heart hammering away in my ears. *Songs, not a word or peep even out of Yako!*

The realisation brings me up short. I mentally roll back the last hour—nope, none of the Court males have said a word since we entered the balcony where the Witch Harp reigns. They've offered their reverent presence and focused attention… but only that and nothing beyond. Almost as if they're afraid to disturb the half-finished spell we've woven—the Witches have woven.

Fine. No further direction from them forthcoming…that's fine.

I know that in essence the Sacred Song is a Bonded Dance.

Only that the Dancing can be a bit different to most days.

If I wanted that. Which I don't.

Focus, Zaja.

Reining in my wayward thoughts before they can lead me further astray and my blood burn any hotter in my chest, I suck in a deep breath and give my patiently watching and waiting Bonded a resolute nod.

Anda steps forward, his lovely dark eyes churning with emotion. Respect and honouring shimmer over me like pixie kisses, drawing a shiver out of me. He leans in to scent my neck. For a split second I worry that I read this situation wrong, that they read it wrong, and don't know I'm not ready for anything more than the Bonded Dance the way we know it. Then Anda pulls back, and in a gesture oddly reminiscent of my old life, of a world before the Sung, places a soft kiss on the back of my hand.

Yako comes up to replace him, clasping my hips and resting his nose by my temple. I feel him sink into the sensation of holding me. Breathing me. We stay like that for long moments, long enough for me to lift my hands to rest on his back. They've mentioned to me often how my presence surreally enhances their awareness of the Song for them. I imagine that's what Yako is taking in most of all.

An overwhelming restlessness and suppressed frustration steals over me. *Sin.*

Apparently, this is not a good night for Sin to watch Yako... being Yako. I give him a gentle push. My lips twitch at his muted grumble. He holds on for one heartbeat longer, and another—this *is* Yako, after all—before stepping away.

Tavo never takes his eyes from mine as he moves in for his turn. Warmth and joy sparkle in them as he lifts my wrist. Sunshine floods me, and I think of that first sun-and-salt rich moment we shared when he sailed me to Amea. *Almost a year ago.* I cup his cheek, awash with gratitude for his steady and gentle friendship.

Tavo retreats and links with Anda and Yako to form a three-pointed frame around me—leaving Sin with me in the centre.

My heart skips into a new rhythm that would make springbok envious. *In and out, Zaja.* Sin places a kiss on my forehead so sweet it nearly swells my pronking heart to sundering.

The emotions in his gaze are overwhelming. I lower my eyelids before I become completely distracted and forget what we are here to do. My senses follow his hands as they slide down my sides until his forearms settle against the small of my back, holding me close. He touches his brow to mine, and I'm enveloped in the divine scent of him, laden with all that shone in his eyes. The spiced sweetness of his devotion. The bright bouquet of his disbelieving awe. The warm cinnamon of his gratitude.

In and out. I breathe through the tears welling up in a great surge, threatening to drown all reason and intent in sensation-drenched senselessness.

Then I take a mental pivot into the Song.

This Dance is mine to lead.

The howling glory of love and loss, joy and pain, defeat and triumph, of the colours and melodies of life itself becomes all there is. Only the smallest part of me remains in the Dark Palace, feeling Sin's touch and the others' nearness. With the males tethered to me, I ride the swells and falls of the Song, lead us through the rainbow kaleidoscope, and deeper towards the beginnings of the gilded black depths where the Song turns Dark.

I slip into the dimension of the Song that is beyond space and beyond time, the fold between worlds, and meet my Sisters. From the Heart and every Heart, from Dark Court and every Court, from all around Earth, we come together to link up in a circle. Our males position themselves behind us, a larger, looser circle surrounding our own, there to witness, honour, and add their strength to holding the space.

Oh!

Serenity floods me. I recognise this moment from one of my visions—one that visited me in the Loud. I identify this feeling as a familiar one, and find I *know* that I've done this many times, done this for aeons. Finally—

I am ready for Sacred Song.

My Sisters by my side, my Bonded behind me, I begin to gather the threads. I Weave the grand tapestry of energy that will scoop every single Sung like a billowing sail. The Weave that will safely lead them into the shallows of the Song, so they may bathe at depths just one wave deeper than what they can access any other night of the year.

Fleetingly, I wonder if it couldn't be woven to scoop the Loud, too.

Then the Weave is complete, and we give ourselves over to the celebration of Sacred Song. For the rest of the night, we don't Dance for a further purpose. No specific work is wrought in these hours. We simply embrace one another and dance in our Dance, glorying and jubilating together in the Song as we did separately in the Courts.

For life must be honoured. So we meet in Sacred Song.

18

"How did you like your first Sacred Song, sweetheart?"

Sin's voice laps over me in a warm ripple. I'm not sure how much time has passed. My heart is still pounding, my skin tingling, my smile rooted deep within. Moments—minutes?—ago I returned from the Song, bringing the males out with me. We all held onto one another to keep each other steady as we grounded back into this realm. Before I'd reoriented myself and puzzled apart what was me and what was other, Tavo, Yako, and Anda had slipped out of my suite.

"Mm-hmm. Web...strong..." is all I manage. My brain hasn't reassembled yet.

Sin's rumbling chuckle trails me as I totter through my bed chamber, past the yawning starlit night beyond the balustrade—*the beauty of a true, pure night! For how long has the Loud forgotten the night?*—and into the hidden private courtyard I've come to think of as the real heart of the Dark Palace. The night blooming flowers, lush vines, and serene presence of the heaven-reaching tree greet me.

I'm sliding down a deep sigh when a stretching coolness tugs me around. Sin is hesitating on the courtyard's threshold.

"I loved it," I finally answer him. I get lost again in his beautiful green eyes until I remember that he isn't stepping closer. "Come."

My belly flutters low when Sin prowls towards me, all elegance and power. This is the first time anyone but Zuzu—who is conspicuously absent—has been in this courtyard with me. My skin pebbles with vivid awareness of the solitude the cloak of night is casting over us.

"You were—" Sin stops, swallows. Starts again. "Experiencing that..." His thumb caresses the delicate bone under my eye. "My Queen," he breathes so softly I might have imagined it.

For ever and ever, we drown in each other's gaze.

"I didn't tell you all of it earlier. When I explained about Sacred Song. It's our highest celebration of the year not just because we honour life—"

"What about death?"

"Part of life. Another side of it, part of the circle." Sin smirks and nips my lips.

"Good," I mumble. "Sorry. Continue."

But he doesn't. He spins out the moment—his fingers ghosting over my clavicle, while his other hand moves up on my spine. His focus wraps around me like perfectly black, thick water, his verdant eyes luminous and deep.

Sin's voice becomes rough, reverent velvet. "Sacred Song is the night of celebrating Dark Queen, who is life itself, who is from beyond that veil. Who hears our yearning, and comes to us on this night." A small, boyish smile graces his face, and I swear I feel him tremble against me. "Happy birthday, Zajasang."

I don't know why his words shudder through me like they do. Why I suddenly feel like I want to weep.

Also, I never told him that. Any of them.

"Anything else Sacred Song is about?" I half croak, half whisper.

Sin grunts, then nuzzles his face in the crook of my neck, inhaling deeply. "Mh-hmm." He places small kisses all the way up to below my ear.

"Are you going to tell me?" The words come out breathy.

Kisses along the other side of the column of my throat. "We celebrate..." The lick of his tongue is warm, and as weighty as his meaning when he utters his next word. "Union."

I moan a question mark.

"The dance of give and receive..."

His mouth dances over me, travelling lower, giving so much.

"The melding of the earthly and the divine..."

Yes, heaven surely is found in this.

"Every act of pleasure becomes a celebration of a force larger than us flowing and expressing through us..."

"Songs," I gasp, when his teeth tenderly clamp and graze through layers of gauzy fabric.

Sin chuckles darkly, hungrily. "Yes, a way of worship of the Song. Of the life force that is all and sings in everything."

When his mouth travels lower still, leaving a wet, hot trail on my dress until he finds a place even wetter and hotter, I think we're beyond words.

But Sin croons in a cadence that speaks of words well-loved and long-shared, "In her Dark symphony she surges forth enraptured. In her Dark cascade, life is restored. In her true Bond and Song, reverence redounds." And with just one, long, open-mouthed kiss, teasing with the promise of so much more, he rises back up.

I stare at him. Slap the tops of my fingers over my mouth. And a nervous, overstimulated, hysterical giggle breaks free. "What?"

Sin's brows shoot up while his inflection dives down. "What?"

I croak a nonsensical sound. Resort to my apparently limited vocabulary, and repeat myself while fluttering my hand, briefly covering my eyes, then uncovering them. "Sorry. Continue." My teeth worry my lower lip. "Please?"

His warm, bemused eyes meet mine, steadily returning to sultry, then infernal, as they slip down my face. He doesn't use his thumb to tug my lip free this time.

"This," he says, and kisses me—at last melding his mouth to mine and breathing my soul—kisses me with the most wicked and wild worship, kisses me more ardently than he ever has before, "is our most sacred prayer on Sacred Song."

Then he releases me and steps back, leaving me reeling in more ways than one.

By this *he did not mean his kiss.*

Maybe this thing I feel is a wild herd thundering on the plains of Ember. Maybe those are roses blooming open in Storm. Maybe that is a golden eagle soaring in the sky, high above a beach.

Or maybe it's all my heart.

Sin watches me, attentive, patient. No words, now. But a question spoken nonetheless.

And I decide that I want this. I want my pleasure to be my prayer. I want to honour life with this dance I've never fully shared with anyone before. I want to know reverence that redounds.

I want him.

"Yes."

Sin is frozen fire, like my dancer in the library that shattered me into a new world. Then he shatters, too, ready to dance me into a new world once more. He rushes to me. His hands cradle my face, urgent, tender. "Yes?"

"Yes." A memory surfaces with the golden eagle of my heart. "Be my Sin today."

The request seems to ravage him, and his groan ravages me. His lips return to capture mine as he has captured my soul. Reverent. Demanding.

Firm yet gentle hands smooth from my neck over my shoulders, taking my dress with them. The touch so warm, filled with so much intent, I feel it to the tips of my hair. His desire is...oh...is a deep sea he has kept tightly contained behind a dam while it whipped itself into a tempest.

But no sea, no tempest, will forever be contained.

Every last vestige of restraint obliterated by my consent—my plea—Sin claims me with unfettered abandon and delicious, ravishing male arrogance. Minutes later, hours later, bliss is all I know. Every sensation is doubled by everything that flows into me from Sin with his every kiss and every caress. I am suffused with the warm golden haze of his worship, taking up residence within me like the thick and tranquil fog that leads to other worlds.

With each quivering of my awakened flesh, I feel a mirror sensation, an echo. Maybe a memory. Each spark of pleasure lights up a layer of realisation in my mind, coaxes me into letting go of my hold on the here and now. Calls to me to give myself over to the all.

Enrapture...

Cascade...

You are the ocean, it says to me, *you are the wind.* Pulling, teasing. *Not the drop.*

Not the drop...

Like a sigh joining the wind, I let go and become all sensations.

In the Song the witches dance, and in the Courts they writhe wildly, freely riding their Bonded, limitless and sovereign in their femaleness. I become their primal pleasure as I am mine, giving myself over completely to it. With each circle of our hips, surrendered in power to beauty, we fulfil our ancient role. We are the Liliths to the Eves, the Eves to the Adams. We are the seductive garden itself.

Joy surges, and love, and we flood these avalanches through that web we hold around the globe in wave after wave, and that is our delightful, delicious, holy work tonight. That is our sacred prayer.

We are Queens, Witches, Sisters, Goddesses... All the same thing, isn't it? Tama's voice echoes through my mind. Only now, almost a year later, do I truly understand.

The sliver of personal memory orients me back into one body. One body wrapped around another. Seated lap in lap. Those are my hips drawing spirals, those are Sin's hot hands roving my spine even as our chests slide against one another.

This is our sacred prayer, our sacred union.

The ecstasy of this joining feels slow and undulating and near never ending. Sin is strong underneath me, holding me safe in his intense presence. My head thrown back and heart splayed open I unleash myself, unshackle myself, and claim my very own freedom and power as I dance this ancient dance. Nothing of my sensuality stifled. Nothing of my desire diminished. This body is mine, and its pleasure is mine. This pleasure is for me, and I live it entirely.

But not alone. Not on my own. This glory is shared.

My gaze finds Sin's—as so often, already there, waiting for me, always on me, only on me. Brimming and blazing. His love for me wraps around me in tendrils and strong bands, an ethereal embrace mimicking his physical one, invading and claiming me with his being as much as with his body. My love for him streams in a powerful rush from my heart into his.

The cycle is complete. We are tethered in gaze, in body, in soul.

For once, I have no fear of losing myself. I feel so very present with him in this moment, so very, wholly within myself and here with him, even as parts of myself are claimed by the vastness of the never space. So I Dance in the embrace of Sin's love.

Here, I am the virgin and the whore.

Our pleasure is shared and amplified through the Bond. Our mingling moans' song of bliss is the crowning melody to the Song's symphony.

I become divinity alive...the bridge between heaven and earth.

"Sin..." My voice flows from me like wind stirring around crystal, careful not to disturb the magic of the infinitely beautiful thing between us. "...this is everything."

"You, Zajasang. You are everything."

My vision swims...and where there were his green irises, I see gold looking back at me in devotion, then blue, brown, hazel, grey, crystal, many of them, one after another playing over those eyes I have looked into for years. In each colour, each pair of eyes, I see Sin. Always him. Looking at me. Loving me.

So I'm not afraid.

I am anchored in every sensation singing between us, revelling in my rapture. Carried away on it. It feels natural, in the never space, to Dance deeper and deeper into the incandescent darkness.

Fearlessly, Sin follows me into the Dark as I take him into the tempests and torrents and thrills of the Song. Trusts me beyond the edge of reason or control, without doubt or question. Sure of his strength. Willing to go wherever I lead.

I marvel when I understand the truth of his vow, the significance of the words he spoke to me at our Bond Song.

Where I go he follows, mine avowedly and completely, offering all that he is.

His life in my Dance. His life in my life.

Softened, opened, surrendered to the sumptuous Dark symphony, I follow where the Song calls me and go. Cascading down and down into the Dark. Deeper than I ever have gone before. So far into the heart of Dark Song, I spiral through frozen ancient rage, I become the night and the starlight, and I discover the place where deep silence sings as loudly as the Dark Song itself.

Here, the cacophony and the glory are one.

Here, I find a circle of Sisters.

Some old and some young, they welcome me home as one of their own. There is nothing about me to hide here, nothing to change about the truth of who I am, nothing to tweak in even the smallest way. A full laying down of the weapons, lowering of the shields.

Together, we sit in companionship. We lean on one another, and soften into each other's embrace. We laugh and we rage. We weep and we howl. We talk and sit silent.

We are many and we are one.

We are forever and never.

Seconds pass that house minutes that contain aeons.

I stretch and release into the circle and the Weave...like opening the fist with which I've held on so tightly. Loosening the corset strings I've lashed around myself, trying so hard to hold myself together in sanity and a sense of self.

At last, with a great, sweet exhale, I lay my body down on the rocks and let myself slip underneath the waves. Moving further and further from *I* into...

Zajasang?

The flicker of a voice halts my blissful undoing.

Distant, but familiar. Welcome, always welcome that voice.

In the *We* it makes us wistful.

Yes, the *We*... It pulls on my threads again, shimmering me apart a little more, unravelling me further into nothing but presence, life, Song. Into becoming the circle more than I am me.

This is like honey melting into every cell. This is good.

I want to stay here, just a little while longer...what is time?... just forever.

Sweetheart.

Something about that flicker that makes it push through the richly vibrating silence like a trill... A taste of copper.

Disquiet. Worry.

Come back to me, darling.

Velvet soft bands wrapping around me with a shrill hum.

Come back.

Urgency.

Zaja.

The voice is a trembling shiver dripping tears and hissing fire, kissing and caressing bones and skin into awareness.

Everything. You are Everything.

And the voice carries the knowing of a name, and the remembrance of a male.

I remember.

Like an exploding star reversing and sucking back in on itself, I remember myself.

Like the crystal cold water of a mountain spring, I remember my Sin.

My love and longing for him tie the knots on the strings that cinched me, back into one distinct whole.

Him. All I want is him. I want to go back to him. Back home into his arms, his strength, his love.

He is a bright gold in the inky darkness, up, up, high above. He becomes my homing beacon as I arrow up through the Song.

Then, like slipping back into a breath I had left behind, hanging suspended and forgotten in another dimension, I feel gentle, determined hands again.

Finally, I see emerald eyes again, and notice the moisture pooling there. Sense the shock, the fear, the despairing love in the lips pressing to my forehead now.

Hear Sin when he whispers, "Zajasang," his voice as tight as his arms, rocking us, kissing me over and over, and whispering, "Zajasang. Zaja. Songs, Zaja..."

* * *

He'd been losing her. He'd only just genuinely gotten her—her trust, her love, her surrender to what lives between them—and in the space of a breath, he'd lost her.

"My Queen. My Love." Sin couldn't stop rocking her, rocking himself with her in his arms, couldn't stop scenting her, grasping her tighter, whispering to her over and over again. To make sure she was here. To keep her with him.

She had literally begun to dissolve in his arms.

His life. His everything.

But I can't, can I? He scoffed, because it was better than howling.

Sin suddenly gained a whole new appreciation for that blasted old verse he had recited to her, seasoned with a heavy dose of healthy fear. He was beginning to learn it spoke of a lot more than sex. No, he'd never be able to hold onto her. She was like water running through his fingers. She'd never be his to hold onto, to grasp or contain.

A sound that was equal parts groan, dark laugh, and sob escaped him. *You can't grasp onto life.*

All he could do was Dance with her. Step off the cliff with her. *And*—Sin forced himself to finish the thought. *And be strong enough...to love her enough...* If she chose to return to the ocean one day, like the river rushing home... If she chose to truly take the Dark Leap... *that I'll let her go.*

But not tonight.

With his teeth still gritted and his jaw still clenched, he lay back on the ground that hummed with power—power that he and Zaja had generated together. Gently, he guided Zaja down with him to rest on his chest. Where else would she be? She was his heart.

No, more than that. It was her heart that lived in his chest—a most precious and otherworldly golden bloom that he cherished with everything that was in him and would give his very life to protect. When she breathed, he breathed with her. When she laughed, he felt the glow of her heart. When she cried, he felt the breaking. *In her unfathomable aliveness, I feel alive.*

She. Was. Everything.

"Stay with me, Zajasang."

His Queen lifted her head and kissed him, so sweet and delicious. Her touch so delirious to his senses.

Kissed him, but didn't say anything.

Maybe it was a promise she knew she couldn't make.

Sin tightened his arms around her, feeling the weight of her, listening to her breathing, drinking in her glorious scent. She was here now. He would cherish every single moment he would have with her, every second of her that he was gifted.

Zaja had gone back to dazing on his chest, her beautiful body so trustingly draped over him. Slowly, he caressed her silky back in smooth, soothing strokes, grounding her here to him and pouring all of his love and devotion into her. His acceptance of her exactly as she was, of exactly what she could give. He needed her to know that it was more than enough, more than he ever dreamed…

Even while he wanted more, everything, and forever.

Sin had fought for her his entire life. He wouldn't stop now. He would do everything he could to help her live with who she was and the tidal waves of sensations clawing at her, ripping her away from herself. Everything he could to make her stay here with him as long as possible.

Sin's thoughts mirrored the idle circles of his fingers on her skin, entirely lost in her. His Dedication glinted in the silver light, and he dreamed of the ring he was determined to place next to it. He wanted to fully bind himself to her in every way he could, to fully be hers and know that she chose him, too. In the mysterious, teasing play of the low light, he could almost see his Devotion sitting on his finger next to his Dedication, the gold bands identical, the stone of the Devotion reflecting the mesmerising colour of her eyes. He'd have the honour of calling himself not just Sin Zaja-Bound, but Zaja-Chosen-Bound.

A thought occurred to him, splitting his face in a giddy grin. A Devotion may still be a fanciful dream of his desired future, but…

"Sweetheart?"

Her answering grumble was adorable.

"Zaja." He lightly shook her shoulder.

Zajasang lifted her head and propped it on her fist, raising one lazy eyebrow at him. Knowing his smirk was nothing short of roguish, Sin was gratified to see the desire winning out over the suspicion in her warring eyes.

"You're Dark Queen," he stated. Until now, that fact had simultaneously filled him with awe—the good and bad kind—and been irrelevant to him. But if it gave him an opportunity to officially claim a part of her beyond the claim others had on her, claim a special position and privilege in her life...

She raised her other brow.

"Has anyone explained to you what the empty suite across the courtyard is about?" He was definitely pushing her. Likely overstepping, according to the subtle complexities of the Court Dance. He found he didn't care one bit.

"Oh." Her slight blush when she understood the implication of his hinting was so enchanting, Sin wanted to ravish her all over again.

He waited while she chewed her lip, wondering if she could feel his heart hammering away under her hand.

"Do you...want to move in there?"

Sin cupped her face in his hands and drew her up until she was hovering above him, his lips a breath from hers. "Zajasang," he whispered, "may I have the honour of being your Dark Destined?"

Songs, he hoped she'd say yes. He wanted this, wanted this so much.

One breath.

Another.

Wicked Wild.

Another.

Why wasn't she saying anything?

Panic bloomed in him, hot and acidic. Had he pushed too far? Was she not ready for this? Or willing? Had he—

"Yes."

Yes.

For one second, his bones turned wobbly and the wild beast in him rolled around on his back with his tongue lolling.

I am her Dark Destined. One more way that Zaja had accepted him as hers.

The next second, a wildfire of energy swept through him, demanding to either consume her or offer itself in service to her.

Zajasang was life...and her willingness to let him care for her, love her, was the source of his life. As long as she accepted him and trusted him with her happiness, he'd never grow tired, would never run out of strength to offer her. His life in her Dance, indeed.

Sin closed his lips over hers, and spent the rest of the night making sure that in between her helpless mewls and sated moans, there was no damn doubt or hesitation left in her mind over having him as her Destined, her consort—the only one who she would share in this kind of intimacy with from now on.

Oh, he was going to make use of this privilege to the fullest, this night and each one following, and every day, too.

He just didn't know how many they'd have.

19

Standing under the rush of the water the following morning, his dusky bronze skin gleaming in the sunlight and the water running rivulets down his sculpted body, Sin is...well, sinful. His linen clad hips disappear beneath the surface, though not before teasing with the image of wet fabric clinging tight to masculine lines and powerful, lithe muscles so good at feline prowling.

I let myself be captivated by the sight of him. *My Bonded. My...Dark Destined.*

He tips his head back, then shakes out his lush hair. Green eyes open and grow luminous when they meet mine on the edge of the natural pool. His steady, simmering love licks at me like a bath of flower petals.

I breathe in, and the warm scent of sun-dappled moss in a forest clearing blooms in my chest. Invitation.

His focused attention on me never wavers, the calm intensity of it never lessens.

Inch by inch, I lift my hand and begin sliding the fabric of my gown over the curve of my shoulder. Sparks burst into flames in his eyes and low in my back. Trailing featherlight caressing fingers across my décolleté, I push down the other side.

Dark berry coated in cacao slicks down my throat in tandem with Sin's chest broadening, the air between us as charged and crackling as the Bond. A whisper cool kiss along my body, and sheer silk pools at my feet.

A muscle tics in Sin's jaw.

I glide into the water, momentarily distracted and shivering with the bliss of feeling it roll over my skin and through my bones. But over it swathes the Song of Sin's demanding yearning for me, and my eyes lock back onto him.

Languidly, I move towards him. The Bond is a honeyed elastic between us, each inch of closeness we gain a tangible sensation, thickening more and more.

Finally, the waterfall cocoons us both.

I stop—a sliver of air between our bodies, our mouths—and we breathe each other in. In and out, him and me, nothing else in the world. Standing there facing each other, sharing presence, souls tangling in our gaze, each cell attuned to the other—it is gold.

Gold flowing within me, out of me, through me, from me, to me.

Everything. My lips trace the word without any sound.

We drop our foreheads together with the bliss of our connectedness brimming over.

Ah, touch. The marvel of it!

As our faces nuzzle and slide along one another's, Sin smoothes his hands up the backs of my thighs, my curves, up to the small of my back, pulling me close.

I come to rest buried in the crook of his neck and sheltered in the safety of his chest, his arms holding me flush to him in a strong embrace.

Waves and waves undulate and radiate through me while we stand unmoving with all the time of eternity, doing nothing but holding one another.

Serene ecstasy. Shared space. Togetherness.

Who could ever disturb this peace? Who would ever dare to?

Sin lifts his head, his eyes focused beyond my shoulder. A deep, long growl rolls out of him, his teeth bared.

And I start to laugh.

Of course, Zuzu would.

* * *

Zuzu and I race, each step becoming longer as we fly along, the ground propelling us, the air buoying us, the sun energising us. Then only his roar and my laughter sail through space side by side, when I go over the cliff, and Zuzu digs in his claws to keep solid ground under his paws.

This leap I only ever take on my own.

Down in the secret cove, the sand is warm between my toes, the water cool and soothing. Where they meet on the edge of the cove, black rock rises high, polished smooth by nature and shining in the sun. The thick tropical forest begins here, too, the rock a part of both worlds.

Maybe that's why I like it so much.

I clamber up top, to the area overgrown by moss, and mottled with spots of shade from the lush leaves and juicy, fragrant flowers hanging heavy above. I've spent some nights here, and many hours of day.

The dark hum of Amea...it vibrates through the rock, wrapping me in a comforting embrace. The Song is strong and pure. With my gown shrugged off, I meet it in equal purity and bareness. The wind picks up and twines around me in a greeting caress, lifting my hair and tickling my sensitive skin, while the sun's warmth sinks into me in loving worship, and the ocean rolls in in a tall wave, strong enough to jump up and kiss me when it meets the rock.

A smile tugs on my lips, and I send a hello back before reclining onto the plushy green. The stone carries my body, and the hum of the Song carries my soul. With a grand, grateful sigh, I let myself float on its melodies, let my mind drift. The life around me sinks into me, and I release myself into the web of nature's energy.

When I'm alone like this, I become all one. My consciousness travels, skips and hops from stone to leaf, from branch to breeze.

Deep at the bottom of the ocean I stay awhile. Cocooned in the strength of the ground beneath me and the water above me, I feel held. Safe and soothed in the darkness, quiet and peaceful. Sometimes, shafts of light dance down.

Gilded darkness.

Sanctuary.

The ocean—she is a Sister patiently loving and full of fierce relentless strength. There in the depths it is quiet—but for the Song...and, often, the haunting, graceful song of the big-winged whales. Sometimes, the males sing while hanging vertically suspended in the water, singing energy into the grid to stabilise it as their females Weave it, just like we do with our Dance in the Dark Song.

Slow and resonant, it ripples and ripples through the darkness. The whales' song is full of beauty and grief, love and longing. A perfect harmony to the Song, sung to the heartbeat of the universe. A *divine duet.*

The whales—they remember...they hold the memories and knowing. They swim in cosmic consciousness, in the star-sparkling black of the sea of space. They swim between the worlds, between the folds and layers and dimensions. They live in this world as much as the dream, awake and sleeping at once.

For hours, I listen to the whales sing, listen to their bonds that stand strong across space and time. My tears are drops of the ocean, joy and pain, flowing together as one. More than any of my Sisters high up on Earth... The whales are like me.

When I flow back into a body, it isn't mine left behind on the rock. The air smells just as sea-drenched, but different, and the hum of the ground is not the vibration of Amea.

Neither am I alone.

The gown on this body is even more accentuating and revealing than what I've become accustomed to among the Sung. Soft layers of fabric fall in elegant layers, ruched together in places by delicate, shining chains of gold, gemstones, and pearls—all to caress and reverently display bare breasts. Yet there is no sense of shyness or self-consciousness as I look upon the male I'm kneeling with, only utter confidence—and grief. Such grief.

His supple golden skin glistens in the sun. The cloth covering his hips and thighs is rather minimal. This world, these people, this encounter is foreign to me—but the soul shining in this male's eyes feels familiar. Maybe it is their expression I recognise. Love beyond reason or hope. Devotion.

Only this devotion is slashed by pain so stark it strangles, an ache that fractures. Tears freely run down his cheeks. This strong, proud male is fully rendered in his love-fuelled torment. "My Dark Queen," he whispers in a language I don't know and yet this body understands, his hands cupping my face.

His touch is the spark that catches on the pyre and lights the infernal blaze. The force of his emotion wrenches my bones out of their sockets. I'm suspended motionless in the shared agony between us.

Until, just as harshly and suddenly, I'm wrested back into the here and now.

My body, my time, my reality.

I'm gasping, shaking, my arms outstretched, grappling for someone long past my grasp—but there is only Amea singing to me, only the Song all around me and in me.

And a note that doesn't belong, a harshness that scrapes against me shrill enough to make me shudder in my womb, clap my hands over my ears, and bow forwards and back. Like another inescapable pyre.

What was that? What is that?

I try to tell myself that it's an echo of that old anguish, a cry from long hence. The Song doesn't know time—it makes sense. It's a good explanation for a wrong, tainted sort of discord in the harmonies of the Song that houses all. An illogical situation—the Song *is* all, how could there be anything that doesn't fit?—with a logical, reasonable answer.

"It could be true," I mutter, prodding the mossy growth beneath me in a jerky staccato as if it would become true if I only stabbed it in hard enough.

You know it's not. Because the vision may have been unfamiliar. That particular pain may have been remembrance newly unearthed in such clarity. But the wrong note in the Song—I recognise. Because I have been shying away from it in the Dance for weeks.

My skin feels too tight. I shake my head wildly and growl, flashing and gnashing my teeth in a way that could rival Zuzu.

The only answers I'll find dwell in the Dark. Where, as last night most viscerally showed me, I'll also find...and may lose... so much more. In the most sacred of unions, when I'd found the holiest of homes, such blissful belonging with Sin, so long longed for—the Dark still snared me.

Sin's fevered words come back to me. *In her Dark symphony she surges forth enraptured.* Enraptured, indeed. Captured, in plain language.

Each time I dive down, with every Dance into the Dark, the terrifying temptation to stay in the wild depths becomes just a sliver stronger. Lose myself to the madness. Strip myself of sanity, of sense, and surrender to sensation.

"No," I whisper, for no one to hear but the wind. My cramping fingers dig into the moss, convincing my body to hold on as much as my mind. I've fought my whole life to stand strong against the onslaught, to not let myself be obliterated between one vision and the next. I've finally found something worth the fight, someone worth keeping my shards and pieces glued together for.

With the Sung, day to day, it has become easier—and in the Song, it has become harder.

"No," I repeat, more fiercely.

The deep Dark of the Song may call and cajole...but that doesn't mean I have to listen.

20

"Home", Tama sighs, snapping me out of my brooding.

I make myself focus on the world around me. The sky is a black womb enveloping us, reminding me of the depths of the Song. We are on our way to gathering in our first Dark Moon circle following Sacred Song. Which comes with its own precariously piled cornucopia of memories.

Soft notes of vanilla, orange, and cinnamon, spiced with some bark and expectant deep cherry, flow through the circle from Sister to Sister. Tama's pronouncement sings true for all of them.

Home.

I thought I'd found it amongst the Sung. And yes, part of me shares in the lifting lilting melody the Song is bending into with this strong coherent emotion the Coven is experiencing. Why can't it be all of me?

Mrak tosses an elbow into my ribs. "You joining us, our highness?"

She gets a stuck out tongue in return. The laughter rising up around us and hop-skipping up my thighs manages to at last shake my gloomy thoughts loose.

"You don't want to miss out on this one." Vala is practically glowing.

I raise my brows at her in question. We've arrived, so I suppose I'll find out soon.

"Aaah, yes. 'Tis a good one, even I have to admit," Adara says.

"Yes, yes," Mrak throws back, "we know you're all soft goo behind that intimidatingly sensual warrior Queen."

My brows don't have any further to go at this point.

While Mrak and Adara rib each other some more with big silly grins on their faces, Tama waves it all away with an impatient hand. "Let's get started, shall we?"

Feny beams at her. "Yes, let's."

Usually, this is a time for storytelling. For sharing joy and pain, laughter and tears. For passing on wisdom, and speaking of mysteries closely guarded. For weaving spiralling magic out of the darkness of the womb and the moon. Our blood flows into the Earth, where all red rivers connect and flow into one. Our hearts connect to the moon, and as below, so above, in that web, we are connected, too.

Apparently, today will be different.

Vala places a hand on the ground. "Mother, this is your daughter Vala."

"Mother, this is your daughter Tama."

"Mother, this is your daughter Feny."

One by one, we go around and greet the Mother who carries us. This is familiar—this is how we open the circle, the circle in which we offer our moon blood back to the earth, and are nourished in our connection of the Dark red tide.

My turn. I place my hands on the ground, feeling the vibrant hum. "Mother, this is your daughter Zaja." Warm pulsing, like a resonant drum beat, returns my greeting.

When the circle is open, a soft energetic weave cocooning us in the Sung's version of the age old custom of the red tent, I look around in expectation. What now?

Mrak and Adara lead into a hauntingly lovely melody. It's all hums and aahs, rising and falling, opening into crescendos before softening into vibration again, a simple phrase repeating in an infinite loop. Feny and Vala quickly fall in.

I know better how to sing with my energy than with my voice, but it doesn't matter here. After a few loops, I join in, too.

When all of us are singing together, Tama moves into the middle of the circle.

We are witches. We Dance to Weave the energy. Tonight, it is our hands that do the dancing and weaving, and it is a spell of deep love, compassion, acceptance, and welcome that we cast. We thread love back and forth from our hearts' to Tama's in an endless loop that mirrors our song, until at last she sits in the centre of an unbreakable web born of feminine power. Pinks, golds, and greens are glowing all around us, and Tama's cherry-tart joy saturates the air. The Song rolls through and under us in big and gentle swells.

We all smile at each other with tear-bright eyes, before Vala moves into the middle and we begin again.

Until each receives her turn.

When the last note fades and the Song settles, tonight's circle is closed. For a while, I hang suspended in the beauty of the rich love that permeates the space. Faintly I register Tama chattering away to Feny, and Mrak's trilling laugh. But gradually, like tar slicking down my scalp, my nagging worrisome thoughts return. I let myself fall onto my back, staring up into the darkness.

It doesn't take long for Vala to lay down next to me, only the two of us remaining.

"What is it?"

For many minutes, I stay quiet. Vala waits next to me as they tick by, content to lie in the darkness with me. Presence and openness without demand. Veritably, she is the best friend I ever could have asked for.

So here goes nothing. I release a big exhale.

"I saw...a private moment. Between a couple." The emotion of it surges back up in full force, and I coil my arms around me. "Private, and painful. I was in her body, experiencing it through her, and the male she was with, her Bonded..." I blink the wetness from my lashes as my voice grows hoarse. "She was a Dark Queen, too. I suppose he was her Sin."

Vala and I turn our heads to look at one another as I continue.

"What they shared, it felt special." My shoulder lifts in a light shrug, even as my lips pull into a gentle smile that is mirrored in Vala's eyes. "Her Sin was—he—" I swallow. The longing, the love, the loss, the yearning, they're stealing my breath again and burning my throat as if it was all happening right now. "He really, truly loved her. Loved her beyond—beyond reason and sanity and understanding."

"Well," Vala carefully clasps her hand over mine where it grips onto my waist, "the Sin of then. The soul remains the same. She was you."

She pauses, her words hanging between us.

"And I think I just realised that the same applies to him. The one you love. Love in every way—the Dark Destined." Her eyes take on a distant look. "I wonder if it was known."

"I—" What is she saying? I shake my head. "Explain, please."

"The knowledge passed down among the Sung is that there is only one Dark Queen. *One who is many.*"

The refraction of firelight by one of the prisms that grace every nook and corner of Amea catches my eye. During the day, they paint the whole court in rainbows. My head cocks as understanding dawns. "Vala? How long have prisms been hung in Dark Court?"

Prisms. They reveal the facets, the different colours, within the whole. The rainbow within the white. Just like all humans are different expressions of the one Song. Just like the one whole soul of each human travels the journey of life and death wearing many different faces.

Vala looks around with me, then turns back with an owlish mien. "A long time."

On Sacred Song night, I saw all those eyes when I gazed into Sin's, all those different shapes and colours, wearing the one, same expression. They were the eyes of Dark Destineds past, maybe Dark Destineds to come, and all of them, all of it was him. Other bodies, other names, other times, yet always him, looking at me, loving me.

And maybe, those Sisters I met in the heart of the spiral...

"She was me." One Song, fractured into different Dark Queens, different lifetimes.

The visions—not the ones of life beating through me from the far reaches of places and times, of moments of pain or magnificence, terror or sheer delight—but all the visions that felt so personal, that, looking back on them, I eventually understood were visions of moments taking place among the Sung—

Memories. Memories of lives long gone...lives yet to come?

"He was him." Vala smiles at me, her eyes shining bright, full of excitement as the true meaning of the lore she grew up with settles into her. "It was both of you in another time, another... incarnation."

One who is many. The notes of the one Song.

I blow out a breath between pursed lips. Wicked Wild. "You think it might have been helpful if I'd actually remember?"

For just a moment, Vala cracks a grin. Then she sobers. "Maybe other times, you did. There's—" She inhales sharply, sympathy and sorrow swirling from her, "there's never been a Dark Queen who wasn't born and raised among the Sung."

Huh. Another mystery. Another question to add to my many. "So why now?"

We look at each other as if we might find the answer in one another's gaze. Why now, indeed?

"The Song will tell."

* * *

"Destined's privilege!"

The triumphant shout blasts my ears a split second ahead of the arm snagging me around the waist and hauling me back against a strong chest. A hot mouth meets my neck before I've even been able to draw breath again.

I *had* been trundling down one of Dark Palace's outer colonnades. Peacefully and quietly. Now I look up to see a boyish and satisfied grin that melts me a bit, against all better judgement. Sin has wasted no time in making the most of his new official status.

"You're making that up."

"You wound me, my Queen." Sin pretends to have been speared through the heart. "I do believe you granted me that honour?"

"Yes!" I throw my hands up. "But I swear it can't mean all these convenient fussing privileges!" Like dropping in half naked last night to check if my feet were cozy, or if I needed any help keeping them warm. The whole night.

"I disagree." Sin's eyes sparkle. "Why else would the suite be right there next to yours, in prime fussing proximity?"

An eye roll is the only deserving response I can come up with.

"Where are you headed?"

"The beach."

"With whom?"

"No one."

Sin's gaze traces my face. He likes to play, and his instinct is to protect, but he would never abuse the Court Dance to cage me or force anything on me—be that touch or company—when I have a need for space or alone time.

"Will you accept your Dark Destined's escort?" He accompanies the question with more featherlight kisses and nibbles along my neck. The sheer sensuality emanating from him is so dizzying my answer comes out breathy.

"Alright."

Sin swipes his tongue over a particularly sensitive spot and grazes the skin with his teeth. The responding sensations I feel in deeply intimate places leave no doubt that the intent behind his touch is definitely erotic in nature.

"And not off the cliff."

My hazy thoughts take a minute to parse his literal rather than metaphorical meaning. But that gives me an idea—after all, two can play this game.

"Fine... Off a different sort of cliff once we're down at the beach then."

Sin's dark chuckle does justice to his name. "See? That's what I said. Destined's privilege."

I daresay he hastens me down the path to the beach.

Amused, I take a little longer than strictly necessary to choose a suitable patch of sand. Before he can get ahead of himself, I tell Sin with an imperious air, "I'm still here to work, you know."

Biting his lip over a grin, Sin inclines his head. "As my Queen commands."

He watches me with searing eyes as I make a show of getting myself settled—and may have undone a button and bow or two for reasons of debatable logical value.

"Comfortable?"

"Quite."

"Where would you have me?"

I stretch my hand out to him, which he kisses, then takes. I lead him to sit down behind me, supporting me in a slight decline as I open my legs to the ocean.

"There better be no-one coming within a mile of us for the next hour," Sin grumbles into my shoulder.

I laugh out loud, causing him to add a growl to the grumble.

"Focus."

"Already am." Lips meeting said shoulder. "Always am." Meeting my ear. "On you. Only you..."

So for the next hour, Sin offers *assistance* as I pull the vast ocean's energy in through my sex and send it up through my body, changing and transmuting it to match my intent for love, harmony, and healing, before sending it out into the Weave through my crown.

Until at last I do charge off a cliff.

And indeed, we are undisturbed—until we're not.

* * *

"Oh, you didn't!"

I freeze up where I had been leisurely basking in the afterglow, puddled into Sin's embracing strength.

"Yes, you did," Sin chuckles into my ear. "But she doesn't mean you, sweetheart."

Songs. No, of course she doesn't. These are the Sung, after all. I snicker along with him. Still, the arrival of the rest of Heart on the beach just a ways down from where Sin and I created our little piece of paradise is rather suspiciously serendipitous timing. For my own sanity I have long since decided not to question these things further... *Best I don't now either.*

Tama and Feny keep shrieking as the group rambles over. Sin helps me fix my dress and generally sort myself out—which includes one last brazen kiss that robs me of any composure I managed to collect—until they reach us and we join up.

It's a beautiful, gentle sort of day, the colours soft and vibrant. The Coven is feeling light-hearted as we wander and play on the beach, so the males ambling behind are content and relaxed, too.

I know for a fact that Sin is...since he invoked his 'Destined's privilege' to make entirely sure that I was. I shake my head with a grin. Satisfied and unspooled, I let my gaze fly free along the turquoise waves, let my senses stretch and uncoil with it. The laughter and tumbling voices fade into the background, and I wonder...

"Sisters!"

There must have been something in my voice that makes all of them stop and look around. There must be something in my face that makes them all pause and cock their heads, like a mesmerised murmuration of starlings.

"Ooh." Mrak gasps, her hands meeting in delight. "A bit of mischief?"

I bite my lip, swaying my head from side to side, and look back out over the ocean. "A bit of magic." If this works. If this can be done.

When we cluster together, whispers floating on the draft from hands waving in excited motions, I feel male awareness perking up and taking note. I feel it sharpen rapidly when we wade into the waves, wispy dresses and all. Of one mind in this as in many things, my Sisters and I happily ignore it, a privilege afforded to us by our abiding trust in their love and devotion.

Once we stand waist deep, we enter the Song and sink deeper. We sink into the wave, become the wave, and meet again in the Song, in a place beyond space and time.

Expectantly, my Sisters circle around me, faces glowing with delight and glee. Begin, they nod to me.

And so I open the Dance and this particular Weave, letting desire and instinct guide me in creating in the void what hadn't been before. My Court Sisters pick up the threads and join the pattern, and the call flows out, out through strands, out into the grand Weave, out into the Song, until it reaches our Song Sisters in the ocean.

Far out in the waves and deep below, they listen and respond.

Near each one of them, a male escort gracefully moves his large body into position, suspended motionless in perfect vertical alignment, a column of utter strength and stability right above a crossing of threads. They send out their melodic vibrations to flow into the crossing and on through the threads, cocooning and sheathing them in protective power, while their witch sends her beingness along them, on and on, far beyond her own body. As the water flows around her physical form, so she flows the essence of herself into the Weave, mending it with patient love and ancient memory, with the knowing of stars and other worlds.

Carefully, the Coven and I braid the living strands and the precious beingness they hold, united in the purpose of Weaving this wreath.

When it is done, we return to ourselves, swaying in the waves, sweat dotting our brows, hair flying wild and snarled. We turn to see, inevitably, a wall of males lining the beach—having closed in to watch over and protect, their attention ensnaring and holding us the way their bodies yearn to.

Unless they deemed it absolutely necessary, they did not dare interrupt a feminine ritual they hadn't been invited to. Though where they might normally have been filled with an adoring sort of exasperation, in velvet cinnamons and furry caresses tasting of berries, they are now caught up in nothing but crystalline awe.

The sand, the air, all of it is thick and resonating with song. A song carried from the deep and rarely heard, now flooding the whole of the island, every inch of the Court. *We remember,* it says. *We honour.*

Whale song of the big-winged ones.

As one, my Sisters and I raise our hands to our crowns, spiral them down to our hearts, and send them out, palms up, towards the males facing us.

21

THE WARM NIGHT AIR IS holding a charge that chills me. Side by side, Yako and I are leaning on the balustrade of one of Dark Palace's balconies.

He just valiantly launched into yet another Sung-favourite tale about Sin's more infamous—meaning incongruous, infuriating, intriguing, or plain idiotic—adventures. "Ah!" Yako interrupts himself, clapping his hands and pointing at my face. "That's a cruelly cute crooked smile I spy—"

Concentrated fire flash floods my veins. My eyes flick up to meet the crackling fissure cleaving the night a split second later.

Then I'm falling, falling backwards off a cliff, falling into endlessness. The feeling is faintly familiar—during the height of pleasure, I have chosen to let go into this fall. In those sacred moments of bliss, it is a graceful arching lift backwards, a surrender into ecstatic dissolution in the Song. But this—this is cold. This never-ending fall brings a fear that frosts my spine. This is a yawning abyss of emptiness, the opposite of the richness of the Song. This is not the stillness of death, which is part of Song and as beautiful as life. This is not the void which itself is fertile as the womb.

This is not sacred.

This is an abject absence that withers me in horror.

A scream works its way up my throat, struggling to pierce the terrifying absence, to throw upwards a hook that may break this fall. But before any sound conquers the oppressive vacuousness, I'm ripped away again—

Now a wildly wailing young child, caught in a sea of fire overtaking the land all around me, choking me in smoke and searing my tender skin—

Now a cub of the most magnificent white coat, but oh, oh I am so tired as my little legs paddle, have paddled so long, far too long, and then only icy water rushes down my throat as I sink into the darkness—

Now the great big mountain is thundering down on me, crashing me—

Now the big eyes of my kin swimming in front of me as betrayal spears me, and I bleed out and out, and with the blood the hate flows out, and I can see below the surface in those eyes the arrant anguish, and an understanding blooms deep within, a forgiveness, though before the seed can crack open and blossom, my end has come—

Now a gargantuan wave takes hold of my frail body and smashes me against rock—

Now the fire again, ravaging my fur and delving deeper, setting in, no escape—

Now back in the endless cold fall—

At last in my body.

The lightning that is brightening the night has just finished stretching out its forked legs to their full, is just beginning to fade into darkness, the fire in my veins receding with it. The full storm won't visit us tonight—no, this is merely a portent of tomorrow.

Not even a second has passed.

So much has passed. So many lives.

"...Dance."

Yako looks at me, startled. "Come again?"

"Need to Dance. Now. Full Constellation."

His brows bunch, his mirth dimming into seriousness. He dips his head regally. "Lady. Wait here while—"

"No need." Sin. Of course, he felt it. Of course, he is here. "Find Anda and Tavo. We'll meet you."

In minutes, I am diving deep into the gilded Darkness, this abyss that is roaring with its fullness even where there is emptiness, four sacred flames far above me to offer strength and shelter.

If there is wisdom to be found, I will find it here. *The Song will tell.*

For hours, I locate torn thread after torn thread, strained and tangled knots, strands that burn like live wire dipped in acid, and I Weave and soothe and mend and heal. Bit by bit, I grow more exhausted, and more relieved. There is much pain, there are many wounds, but all is familiar. All is as we've come to expect in the Song. Within all of it is that flaying, rending beauty; the vivid glory of life. All of it is part of the harmony, and inspiring of reverence. All of it is the truth of the Dark Song: glorious and terrible. It is the Wicked Wild.

All is as it should be.

There is barely a drop of strength left in me, and the urging to return from those flames above becomes intense to the point of discomfort. *Come back to us*, they say.

I send a pulse along the strands, a silent beat of the drum amidst the cosmic cacophony. *I'm coming. All is well.*

And I slip and fall, flailing into a tear in the Weave.

A tear that caterwauls the very note I've been trying to forget and hoped never to feel again. A note so harsh and discordant it bleeds my ears and scrapes open my skin. A note so agonising and shocking, my deepest survival instinct has me recoil and violently snap back along my Bonds, and I have neither strength nor desire to fight against it.

Anda's snarl greets me. "Was that necessary, Lady?"

"We get Bonded's Privilege." Tavo growls—growls!—next to him.

Vibrant, irreverent Yako looks so forlorn it makes my heart turn over, and Sin's lips are pressed in a thin line.

So I don't protest as they lay me down in soft pillows and blankets, as they massage my limbs. I stay silent as Sin smoothes a hand under my neck and a hand under my sacrum, every movement cautious and tender, and the others place crystal and flowers on the energy centres of my body. It is such a beautiful custom, as all of the Sung's customs are. It is a beloved aspect of being a Bonded for the males; being able to care for their Queen after she offers her unique gift of the Dance, being able to support her body and hold her.

It ought to feel nothing but beautiful and loving, and I ought to be nothing but fulfilled.

But for once in my life, all I feel is numb, and underneath the numbness something terrible is building.

Nothing is as it should be.

A silent tear slips down my cheek.

* * *

Late into the morning, obscuring the midday sun, the storm comes.

I unfetter myself, loosen my chains of politeness into the Queen's Dance, and let the clawing, feral rage unfurl that has been simmering and roiling in my gut and my blood. With each whip of wind and hair, each drop of rain and sweat, each swing of hip and thunder, I let the rage slip out of me, seep through my pores, screech into the sand.

I become the Earth, and I bleed her wrath. I surrender to the Song, and I rage.

Funny, how by fully giving myself over to the all, I can at last feel and face my own emotion. Balanced on a sword's edge only, oh yes, every moment just as likely to tip me into losing myself as knowing myself.

I cackle and yowl.

This is life. The life in which I am invincible, in which I am all. Who can destroy that? My darkness will always be deeper. And the life in which I hover like the butterfly in the wild kiss of the hurricane. Will it destroy me this second, or the next? For destroy me it will.

And yet, what choice do I have but to feel it all, live it all, rise again and again, the phoenix from ash? What choice would I ever want to make, but this wrenching, heart-aching glory?

Caught in the maddening liberation between pleasure and torment, delight honed by fury, I rail against the world and myself. I rail against everyone I have to feel. *Too much, always too much.* I rail against the carelessness of the Loud, the daily disasters needing me to flay myself open over and over in the harshness of the most wicked melodies of the Song. I rail against this wrongness I feel—only I feel—and the consummate loneliness that brings.

That was meant to be over. *I was meant to belong now.*

And when it comes, I lash out against the seductive call from a Circle sitting in sisterhood in the deep, deep depths.

You belong here, they sing.

I kick my leg high, leap in a twirl, twist and stomp. I raise up on my toes, stretching higher, arms extended above, becoming the bow pulled taut. The pressure snaps, I break at the waist, and the arrow flies. *How can I belong when there will be no me left?*

On and on it goes, a battle in my mind, against my mind. There is no way to win when your foe flows as lifeblood in your veins.

Then there is fire.

Four flames of different flavours. Four beacons of strength beckoning. Teasing, tempting, with their empassioned storm-eye calm. So innocent in their potency and direction, their essence of clarity and claiming, protecting and prowling. Their essence of death and nothing, where I am life and everything. I am power in chaos and spiral, and they are might in focus and service.

So gloriously beautiful and beloved.

So easy to seek shelter with.

So unwelcome.

With each step closer to me, I feel their desire and excitement rolling over me, sliding under my skin, taking up space that for a few sacred minutes had been washed clear. Had been my own, filled only with the everything, and the everything had been me.

Now there is me and them again, always so much them. Even when the them is loved.

"Mine," I snarl at my Bonded, turn my back and dive back into the Dance.

But they are there. Flames in the endlessness.

I flash my teeth—why, why have they come.

I whine—why, why must they brush the frissons of my frenzy.

I shiver and they groan.

Sin growls—and I moan.

A bolt of primal violence singes through the plain.

Three flames recede. One closes in to burn me up.

I writhe in the caress of his heat, thrash the ember sands into clouds of dust that do nothing to douse the blaze. "Why," I snarl at him, and still he doesn't retreat.

Ever closer, he stalks circles around me. "Mine," he purrs.

Lightning hits the ground near enough I could have stretched out my fingers and called it into my palm.

"No." Thunder explodes around us, inside my every molecule.

His heat coils around me, stroking my neck, my calves, my thighs. "Mine."

Enough.

My eyes snap open and my lips draw back, poised to gnash and fight—but he's right there. Storm-drenched and immovable, animalistic eyes lighting into mine, so close he is all I see. Before the sound can tumble free, my snarl is swallowed by Sin's kiss.

Wild and forceful, his hands gripping my slipping, soaked, heated, dusted skin, he gives and demands everything, and then more. He will not let me go. He will not give up. He will not stop fighting, even when he has to fight me to fight for me.

He will remind me to transform my pyre even when I forget.

I burn hotter and hotter. I burn with him, and I burn with rage. The temper and temptation mix, mingling into a glory I hadn't known. Higher and higher, the flames of either whip each other into a conflagration in the cauldron of my being.

Finally, with a strangled death cry, I am the phoenix leaping to heaven, propelled by frustration. My lips wrenched from Sin's and my head thrown back, mouth ajar, my searing shout dissolves, gradually slipping off into a tangled moan.

My knees give.

Rain washes the ashes of my cheeks and the blood of my soul. The freshness of the storm-cleansed land expands in my cells. Gently rising laughter dances up only to be absorbed by

Sin's soothing kisses. Life bubbles up in me anew, and still Sin holds me, still he loves all of me.

Still he stokes my flames and welcomes the fire of the witch.

For a while, I know bliss again.

Nearly perfect peace. Hampered only by dread of the day when the fire will immolate him, and still he won't let go.

* * *

"What's wrong?" Sin gripped the back of the settee in Zajasang's suite, his short nails digging into the wood and fabric. He appraised his Queen where she stood gazing out the wind-eye. Her shoulders curved inwards, her lower spine was stiff, everything about her tense. A tree robbed of its sap. Had she heard him? Noticed he was here at all? "Zaja?"

Sin lifted his clawed fingers one by one before he caused any damage.

This had been going on for too long. He was still shaken from that horrifying minute where he thought he was losing her on Sacred Song. Short weeks later, that self-sacrificing Dance deep in the night from which she had returned so cold and frozen. So shut in. He thought her explosive, raging, formidably hot Queen's Dance during the storm that smote down on Amea the day after may have made things right again, may have helped her process what she seemed to be choking on.

Apparently not so.

He sidled around the room until he could at least see her profile.

Zajasang opened her mouth. Closed it. "I don't know."

Wicked Wild, he loved this female with all that was in him—and sometimes he wanted to take her by the shoulders and rattle her into trusting him. "Talk to me." He pushed it out through clenched teeth. "Please, sweetheart. What's wrong?"

She turned her head to look at him. Her tongue flicked out to wet her lip under his intense scrutiny. Maybe he could kiss her into forgetting her fears and opening up to him. It seemed to work just fine in the storm.

Zaja cleared her throat. "I need to talk to my Sisters."

Well. That wasn't quite talking to *him*, not quite how he'd hoped this would go, but then again, she was a Queen. There was—literally—a whole world of things she would be able to ask another Queen about in a way different to anything he could provide. Sin sighed.

At least she'd told him what she needed. Giving her what she needed was one thing he could do. Excelled at, even, and *lived* to do.

"The Coven?"

"The whole Coven. My Sisters in the other Circles."

Pale murkiness trickled down the Bond to him. Her eyes were so wide, her whole posture so unsure it reminded him of that damn feather teetering on the edge again. Easily blown away by the slightest puff. Sin couldn't stop himself from going to her and drawing her into his arms, making sure she was safely enveloped in his embrace. He rubbed his hands down past her elbows and to her wrists, treasuring every inch as he went.

He didn't like it, not with the way she'd martyred her body recently and expended herself, but if it was going to help her move past this... "Alright, let's Dance."

Zajasang emphatically shook her head. "No, I need to feel—" She stopped herself.

Oh. The problem wasn't that she didn't trust him. Satisfaction flared before coals dropped into his gut. *She doesn't trust herself.* She didn't know that her sensitivity was the realest form of magic he'd ever witnessed, and that it gave her instincts he would trust his life to.

Alright, he could solve this for her. Something made her feel the need to check in with the other witches of the Sung, and for some reason, she didn't want to do it in the Song. "A tour of the Circles, then."

"Yes." A soft sound of relief, accompanied by a strong nod, as if to convince herself.

Sometimes Sin wished he could be in her head as well as her heart.

Smoothing his thumb over her jawbone and lifting her face to his, he said, "We'll leave in three days."

Her beautiful, troubled eyes flitted away from his while she nodded, more slowly this time. She sucked that lip between her teeth and began mistreating it.

Sin took her face into his hands fully, waiting until she met his relentless gaze again. He lowered his mouth to hers, softly nibbling on the lip she released on a quiet gasp, then soothing his tongue over it. "Tomorrow." He pulled back to watch Zajasang's reaction. "We'll leave tomorrow."

Those eyes. They were his life and his death. A glorious, delicious death. The expression in them right now...

Her voice was quiet, but surer. "Thank you."

Sin kissed her, deeply, unhurriedly, until she finally relaxed in his arms and the Bond no longer sang of tension and strain. "My life in your Dance." He allowed himself to bask in the simple bliss of holding her and feeling her soft form surrender into him. Feeling her emotions calm and her heart settle.

He wondered if she realised how much each of these small, forgettable moments meant to him. He was *here* now. He could give her his strength, and feel the difference it made. Love her, cherish her, devote himself to her. It wasn't just the Dance, the big moments, that filled him with the warming fire of purpose and made him proud to be her Bonded. It was this, the moments she wouldn't think twice about, the moments no-one else would know of or see.

The every moment kind of moments. Those were his everything with her.

Once Sin had taken care of his Queen, he went out to take care of business. He would provide for her whatever she needed, give her whatever was in his power. After all, she gave him the world.

He had tried to give her any solace he could, and prayed it was enough. He hoped the Coven would be able to give her the solution he couldn't. And prayed that would be enough, too.

* * *

Usually, the ocean brings me calm, so that is what I came in search of after Sin left me. This dusk, the water couldn't douse the acidic boiling in my belly.

Now I'm crouched in the sand, hair snarled after tumbling through the unforgiving waves, again and again draping itself over my face. Relentless. Obscuring my vision. But also sheltering me, caressing me, mollifying me.

Toying with me, tossing me like the waves, back and forth between grumble and growl.

I like feeling like a wild thing, uncivilised and untamed. More part of nature than humankind. It requires less effort.

Frozen into immobility until my feet have sunken enough to topple me off balance and I need to readjust, my gaze is fixed. It helps me distance myself, illusion myself into some kind of numbness. It's not real, of course—I feel so much, too much, everything. But when I freeze like that, I almost freeze it with me. Nearly succeed in screening it all out.

The acidic boiling is muted to a simmer.

At last, the sand carried out from under me once more, I'm a statue moving again, the stillness shattering. I rise and turn, decided on leaving. This beach, for tonight. Amea, tomorrow, after thirteen months. Months filled with more aliveness—even in the despair—than all the years before.

After a few steps, I turn back. I touch my fingers to my forehead, then sweep them down and out in a spiral offering, Queen to Queen. There is contentment, at least, in the familiar ritual. The waves continue to roll in as my gaze lingers for a moment longer.

In the foaming whites and upset blues, I hear her whisper. *I'm here.* She flows back even as she returns. *I'm always here.* Always ready and waiting, an embrace overflowing with love and compassion, tenderness and belonging.

The grey hollowness cracks. The ocean seeps through the ruptures, and the tide rising in my eyes tastes sweet. It tastes of returning to life.

Maybe I ought to be more positive. We'll tour the Circles. We'll figure this out. We'll return. Amea will be waiting. The ocean will welcome us home. All will be well.

"I know," I answer her. I shudder through a breath that crackles my heart into warmth. *I know.*

She will be here. Even if I no longer am.

Even if I don't return.

22

Old Court

"Welcome home, Vala," I say quietly.

Another journey, another arrival. I'm reminded of setting my soles onto the lands of Vigil for the first time. This heading into the unknown and to unknown shores feels as significant as it did then. Though I almost envy that Zaja. She had nothing to lose and carried only hope. I have everything to lose and carry only foreboding.

Yet you were her dream, Zaja.

Expelling a harsh breath through my nose, I focus back on my new surroundings. The playful melody emanating from the regal birdflower on our left. The heat of the sun sinking deep into my pores, the warmth smooth like a snake's scales. The beautiful, large spider who climbs on my foot and settles on its arch. Grounding me. *Thank you, Sister.* Through it all, the rich hum of the Earth rolls through me. Its harmonies feel vibrant, readily available right beneath the surface, and yet layered to infinity...old. The Court is aptly named.

And of course, most pronounced, the assembly before me glowing at me like a swarm of fireflies. Bright eyes and white teeth shine from vast stretches of bare skin—what else did I expect in a Sung Circle, though? The style of dress is distinct and markedly different to Vigil and Dark, the fabrics of the loose skirts less sheer and bolder in colour. And yet the comfortable sensuality of the clothes and their wearers, the freedom, the generous adornment of feathers and pearls and delicate chains, are decidedly Sung. Not to mention the telling gemstones on necklaces and rings.

"Nah." Vala's hand finds mine and squeezes. When I look over at her, her eyes are closed. "I love this land, but home... That's inside."

Is it? Amea feels like home to me. Zuzu. Sin.

One of Old's Coven steps forward. Well advanced in years, Janaina is slight and sprightly, a twig with bark so rough there's beauty to be read in ever ripple. She smiles at me and places her hand on my chest. "Queen Zaja. It is good to meet you again."

Not that we have technically met—physically—but the lines of reality have become a lot more blurred since I found myself part of the Sung. I have Danced with these Sisters in the Song, in places beyond space and time, and it felt no less real and immediate than her weathered brown skin under my fingers when I complete the circle. Doesn't make things any more straightforward for someone who is reality-challenged to begin with.

I bite back the grunt directed at myself and return Janaina's greeting. "Thank you, Sister. It is."

But suddenly all I want is to get on with things. My Constellation's been hovering protectively around me the whole journey, shielding me in their steady cocoons. Thanks to them I arrived worn, not delirious. And I suppose I'm no longer that same girl who arrived on Vigil, for good and for bad. So I may not be a barely knit together bundle of bones and wildly firing nerves, yet a restlessness is niggling at me. There's an echo in the Song—even now, even here—that's making me itchy.

I address the Coven gathered before me. "I know we only just arrived, and there's much to see and talk about, but would you join me in a Dance? I would like to go deep."

I glance behind me at my Bonded apologetically. Anda looks calm as ever, while Yako draws up straighter and Tavo gives me a minuscule nod, his eyes tired but warm. I look to Sin last. The concern in his eyes is stark and rubs against me like heavy fur, a slight crease forming between his brows.

"Zajasang," he murmurs, lifting my wrist to stroke his thumb over it and kiss it tenderly. Warm shivers tingle up my arm.

"Sin."

We don't need to actually have the discussion that's playing out between us to follow it to its conclusion. I sense his strength and dedication to service beneath the superficial exhaustion—which is why I made this request of them in the first place, and why I know his concern isn't rooted in doubts about himself or his brothers. He senses my urgency and disquiet—which is why he'll give me what I need. But not without negotiating.

"You'll eat and sleep after. And rest until tomorrow night. No further Dancing."

When my eyes try to veer from his in exasperation, he cups my chin with his strong, agile, oh-so-gentle, oh-so-demanding fingers.

"Fine."

"And you won't deny us Bonded's Privilege."

"*Fine.*"

He leans in to brush a kiss over my mouth, then, his lips still caressing mine, says, "My life in your Dance, darling", before kissing me once more and letting me go.

I huff. Male.

Thus, in short order, we bustle into the favourite Dancing courtyard of Old Court's Coven and enter the Song. I dive in, torn between trepidation and the familiar, undeniable sense of relief and rightness that slips over me. For weeks, it's been the same thing. The embrace of the Song's magic beckoning to me, even as it wars with the wrongness calling to me from the depth.

One by one, as I spiral Darker and Darker, spinning out the thread keeping me anchored to my Bonded, my Sisters drop away and stay behind as they reach the limits of their Dance.

My edges bleed apart, and it becomes harder to hold onto who I am. But I know where I'm headed, know where to look, know to approach carefully. I find the tear. The wrong note is unmistakable. As clear and awful as it was on Amea. As out of place and painfully scraping as before.

And yet, none of my Sisters shudder the way I do.

Even if they did, none are close enough to reach these fraying threads and assist with the Weave. Still, they should hear it, feel it. All threads are connected, Dark and Light, deep and shallow. The Song travels through all of them. They should feel drawn to take up the far threads, to Weave where the echo reaches.

So why don't they? The question that has been haunting my every moment since Sacred Song. *Why don't they sense what I do—at all?* Not on Amea, and not in Old Court either.

I'm beginning to think that it isn't the Song.

It's me.

My own shattered mind, my scattered self, come apart in the Dark. The tear the first taste of how I'll end in tatters. Or simply the place where it can no longer be denied how ripped my mind has been for years. No Dark Queen's grown up in the Loud before. Maybe that's left me unprepared somehow, unable to withstand the Wicked Wild, or just too worn down. Sandpaper that has lost its traction. Maybe it isn't the Song that's shrieking, but my disintegrating sanity, protesting as it's sliding right off.

Then so be it.

Or maybe something is seriously, seriously wrong with the Song.

Then I will Weave until my soul bleeds.

And maybe there's no difference between the two.

I grit my teeth and Dance in the indignant fury, the endless pain, the weeping sadness of the jagged-edged sound.

I Weave and Weave until I finally retreat and collide and collapse into the shelter of Sin's beacon. It's more him than me towing us through the tether to Anda, to Yako and Tavo, up, up, until the world crashes back into me, and my body folds under me to a now familiar chorus of my Bonded's curses.

I'm just glad I'm here to hear them.

* * *

Sin watched Zajasang as she stood immobile, her arms slung around herself.

Not good. At all. Stillness was for her what pacing was for most.

She was positioned off-centre in one of Old's courtyards. It was on the edge of the court, deserted, and open to a shrub-dotted, red sanded plain. Only his Queen wasn't taking in the view. She was facing a seemingly random direction, looking at nothing he could determine. Just—stalled. A ball that had been rolled until it came to rest in any odd spot, getting lost in the dust. Wouldn't move until someone came, found it, picked it up. Cherished it again.

He'd found her. He'd pick her up.

Sin walked towards her as though he were wading through water. She hadn't attempted to argue with him today, hadn't tried to convince any of her Constellation of another Dance. But she'd also uttered a grand total of seven words since the morning.

Her emotions were doing the talking she refused to do herself. Bewilderment. Worry. Frustration. Each growing and growing. Whatever she'd wanted to circle the Courts for... She hadn't gotten it at Old. She'd been near catatonic in her exhaustion after the Dance yesterday, accepting a bare minimum of food they'd coaxed into her, receiving Bonded's Privilege, and settling into sleep wordlessly. In the middle of the night she'd woken up, sobs wracking her frame. Sin had pressed himself against her, wrapping himself around her, doing his best to cocoon her in his love and the strength of his body as she cried.

The memory burned through his chest. She had grabbed his hands and moved them to hold her heart and her womb. As if she would come apart without him holding her together.

He would hold her forever if she let him.

Sin sighed, his brows drawn. Since dawn...this. Choking, scalding blankness. Screaming silence.

On the plain, the blood-red sun was seeping into the sand, nearly bled out, about to give way to the encroaching darkness. In its dying flare, Zajasang looked forlorn. A little otherworldly. And always, to him, heart-achingly beautiful.

"We can leave in the morning." He winced—his tone was harsh. He hadn't meant to bark at her. The combination of the building maelstrom of misery inside her and her continued silence over it was fraying his temper. They needed to talk about this. Had been needing to talk about this for a while.

Sin opened his mouth again, then paused as his eyes caressed her form. Lingered on the brittleness with which she was holding herself.

He exhaled forcefully. Now was not the time.

Crossing the remaining distance between them, he aligned his body with hers until he could shelter the bones of her hips in his hands, and her delicate back in the expanse of his chest. There was something about her tonight—something that made him feel wary. Made him feel that, if he didn't touch her, to ground her to this reality with him, he might lose her. Truly lose her.

Zaja didn't react to his touch, didn't soften into him.

He rested his lips on her neck and waited.

The cool night air spiralled around them, a sensuous snake coiling in the dark.

Still, Zajasang didn't move.

With each joint beat of their hearts, Sin sank deeper into her. Every thought, every sense honed in, until the world was nothing but her warmth, her fragrant skin, her silken hair, her breath, and the river flowing to him of the ocean of perpetual explosion of emotions and sensory experience rising and falling within her.

At last, Zaja breathed in sharply. "I should—"

Sin's jaw clenched. That was the problem. She was controlling and taming herself, instead of listening to that unique, uncanny insight only one who felt everything could have. Some part of her was still warring against herself...was still refusing to trust herself.

"What do you need, Zajasang?" Sin interrupted her. *Let me care for you*, was what was underneath the words, was the unceasing expression of his heart flowing back to her no matter what came the opposite direction. *Let me love you.*

For a moment, even the clamour inside her stilled.

Then she leaned back into him.

Finally. A rumble worked its way out of Sin, the vibration traveling into her where his lips rested on her skin. He slowly rubbed his thumbs into her lower back.

"I need to make sure."

A soft mewl escaped her when his thumbs found a particularly sensitive spot, but she shook her head and tried to swallow it. His rumbling turned into a soft growl, but she ignored that, too.

"I don't think there's much time. I think—" The misery flowing out of her then froze his thumbs in their ministrations. "I think I've waited too long."

Kissing her ear, Sin tightened his hold. "So to Ember?"

Zaja sighed. "Vala..."

"Hasn't been at home here in a while." He bit the shell, skilfully blew a warm breath aimed to elicit a shiver. The more his Queen came to life in his efforts, the more the prowling wildness in him calmed. "Besides...there's a certain beach at a certain court further along on our agenda that I'm eager to re-introduce you to..."

And he gave her a generous preview of just what he had in mind.

* * *

"Sin."

Sin turned from the little packing there was to do to see Zaja critically staring at nothing—again. Her brow was bunched and her teeth were worrying her lip. She hadn't done much sleeping during the night. He was ready to get them going, to have her focus ahead, to Ember and beyond.

"Come see this."

He made his way over, the woven mat covering the ground smooth under his feet. He placed his hands on her waist when he reached her and a soft kiss on her neck. Then he looked. And saw—nothing.

"What am I looking at, sweetheart?"

She stretched out one pointing finger, an ever so slight tremor upsetting the grace that so effortlessly filled all of her gestures. "I've been noticing it everywhere...even back on Amea. But I didn't—I didn't understand. Didn't listen well enough."

The wave of frustration and fear that hit Sin through the Bond coiled his muscles and had him work to hold back a growl. He slid his arms fully around her to pull her against him.

"Sweetheart, it's a web." Wasn't it? What could she see that had her this jumbled up?

She shook her head and made a sound in her throat that tore at his heart—a tortured little sound full of despair.

So not just a web. He studied her, studied the web, and her again. He'd never tire of studying her. "What do you see?"

Zaja twisted her head, doubt written starkly in her eyes. But she pointed again, and her quiet voice was sure when she spoke. "She wove a hole into it, a hole that doesn't belong." Pleading now filled her gaze, though for what he didn't know.

Songs, he'd give everything to know what it was she needed from him, and to have the ability to give it to her.

"They're all weaving holes that don't belong. Every single spider web I've seen."

Licking her lower lip so she'd stop mistreating it, Sin said, "Alright. A hole that doesn't belong."

She crumpled. "You don't see it."

What did that matter? There were whole worlds she could see that he didn't. He didn't need to be able to see it to trust her call on it. Sin lifted her chin until her eyes met his, so she'd know she had his fullest attention. "What do you think it means?"

One long second, another, she stared back.

Drew in breath as if to speak—and stopped.

Eyes closing once, slowly.

Then a tear slipped free, and she whispered, "That it's me."

EMBER COURT

"Adara. The land... How does it feel to you?"

"Familiar." She squints at me shrewdly, and smokey grapefruit spreads across my tongue. "How does it feel to you?"

So she's not even noticing anything off. My teeth grind. She is a strong Queen, she has two Bonded, we are on her land. If the tear really was a wound in the Song, *surely*, at least Adara would—

"Sister?"

"Warm. Pulsing." My lips stretch in the imitation of a smile. Feverish, is what I don't say. Because apparently that's not the land.

Adara keeps me trapped in her aware gaze, but then I feel— and she must see—smooth, quiet strength approaching us in my back.

"Lady," Anda saves me, "would you like to go out for a tour?"

I spin around. Omulara is beaming at us from behind his shoulder, an eager grin lighting up her face. Meeting her last night upon our arrival felt like stepping into a bath of starlight.

Remembering it loosens the cords of my neck enough for me to nod. "Please."

Anything to discover and learn more. Or to distract me.

We get our little group together, then head out on foot. Anda, of course, showing me his homeland. Yako insisted on coming with—to see if 'the majesty of the land can hold up against that of Crystal'. Leave it to Yako to find enthusiasm for competition in anything. So he roped Dashuri into joining alongside Adara, for a qualified second opinion, while Elu is spending some time with his younger sister. Omulara and her Bonded Quaden complete the party.

We have not long passed the intangible boundaries of Ember Court, Yako and Omulara quipping back and forth, before the power and grace of a herd of wild horses flows through my flesh. Their hooves whip up dust against the burning horizon soon after. When they reach us, there is much snorting and pawing until I become the centre of a star of equine bodies, tails swishing sparkles on the outside while heads butt and soft lips nibble me in the heart of the constellation. I dutifully caress noses and stroke jaws and necks —yet the pawing persists.

"Alright, alright! Let's fly together."

Renewed jostling meets my words. Amusement wriggles in the Bond, and I look out over the horses bumping each other.

Anda is shaking his head and snickering. Of course, a small bird of the most magnificent iridescent plumage chooses this moment to alight on my head, claws securely burrowed into my hair. Which becomes a marionette's strings as each pull of the talons only serves to widen Anda's grin.

"Sister, are we all good to ride?" I ask Omulara.

"Don't think we're given much choice in the matter!" Though it doesn't look as if she minds. "You know how to ride, Yako?" she asks sweetly.

"Lady," he says, and performs an elaborate bow. Then he jumps up on a magnificent ice grey stallion in an admittedly very impressive acrobatic manoeuvre, and winks at me when he catches my eye.

My mount is more supported by the suave finesse of the stallion who wins the herd's jostling contest than my own skill, but either way we all end up on horseback, and no sooner are we all mounted than my stallion takes off in loping gallop.

Flying, indeed.

The sensation is its own kind of miracle. Our heartbeats become one, and our hooves touch down in rhythm with the Mother's heartbeat. Hot power flows along the fibres of my muscles, a heat so different in texture to that of the unbridled sun. The pure aliveness of the herd mingles with the delight of my fellow riders. A bouquet of joy flowers in me, a sublime combination of flavours like the sweetest dessert. All around me, personal melodies are soaring in a mirror of our flight across these plains humming with ancient, primal power.

Beside me, Anda is a hot sun unto himself, radiating with steady strength and contented love. He stretches his hand out toward me. Like the wingtips of two eagles brushing mid-flight, our fingers graze for one second, two. Anda's eyes widen. His smile grows even bigger, and he shakes his head a little. His wonder becomes a third dark sun in my solar plexus.

The wind teases my hair and draws tears from eyes, but those sensations are eclipsed by the uncanny feeling of galloping along the Song itself.

I give myself over to the exhilaration, thirstily drinking down this divine gift.

Until the awareness that we are flying towards a great accumulation of life pierces through. Life, and wisdom, and emotion.

Pained emotion.

I was too distracted, too elated, clinging to these harmonies of freedom and joy—but now the rumbling red of worry becomes unmissable.

Ears waving, trunks swinging... Deep in these lands, far away from any people, hundreds upon hundreds of elephants have gathered, huddling, as if holding congress.

No—not as if.

There is much activity flowing through these Sisters and brothers, much passed on from one to the next. Though most of all, they are connected in the tangy, metallic notes of fear and distress, threaded through with the sweet grace that is the comfort of togetherness.

I slide off my stallion as if in trance, carefully winding my way through these beautiful beings. My hands trail along their large dusty bodies. Trunks curl around me and gift me with kisses as I pass. The feverish impression I've had since arriving in Ember is clear and pronounced, a cleanly bleeding knife's edge. The Song rises in a lamenting wail, gaining in power the deeper I progress into their midst.

I round another great body, and one more. Nausea rushes up my throat. And then I see what I've been feeling.

In the centre of their congregation, the matriarchs have gone to their knees.

Trunks entwined, these strong Queens at last have buckled.

Two unfurl their trunks and wrap them around my waist, weaving me into their circle.

Not just a wound deep in my mind.

I buckle, too.

23

"Dark Destined, brother?" Fern stepped back from their brotherly embrace, clapping a hand on Sin's shoulder. "So that's what you were holding out for all those years?"

Sin took in the familiar face full of mischief and more rugged handsomeness than was good for its owner. He took in the whites and blues and greens, the rusts and beiges around him, vibrant in the sun. Tasted the salt on his tongue, and listened to the rolling and rocky sounds of bits of chatter sailing on the strong breeze, sounds that mirrored the craggy hillsides and cliff faces. Storm Court. Coming here, returning here—it always felt the same, and always a little different to arriving in any of the other Courts.

"No. I was holding out for Zajasang." A difference. An important one, to him.

"Who happens to be Dark Queen."

Sin's hackles raised—and his lips retracted to bare his teeth.

Wicked Wild, this is Fern! Returning to his home Court may always have felt the same—but clearly Sin now felt different.

He rubbed a palm down his cheek and focused on the playful glint in his best friend's eyes. "Yeah." For a moment, he stared into space. Returned his gaze to Fern with a slow shake of his head and slight raise of his brows. "Yeah, she is." An incredulous laugh broke free.

Zajasang had turned out to be even more spectacular than he'd imagined.

The Song had deemed him worthy of her.

And she'd accepted him.

Fern threw an arm around his shoulders, his lips pressed together. "Strong heart and Song's caress."

"Oh, you have no idea, brother." Sin ran his hand through the hair at his nape. He'd never known just how accurate, how vital that well-wish was, until Zajasang came back into his life. "You have no idea."

Whatever Fern saw in his expression... It was enough to have him wheezing and gurgling.

Finished with his guffawing, Fern unbent himself and danced from foot to foot. "Do I get to meet her, then?" Usually, he was akin to a tree stump that had planted himself.

Sin fought to hide his smirk. "Where's Ivy?"

Instantly, Fern's eyes mellowed and crinkled at the corners. It told Sin all he needed to know.

"She's resting after our Dance earlier."

"I'm happy for you, brother."

"Yeah, I'm happy, too. Took us long enough to sort ourselves out—though not anywhere near as long as it took you!" His grin was broad. "Now quit stalling and keeping the Dark Queen to yourself. Help a brother out and introduce me."

Oh, Sin would make an introduction with the Dark Queen. But Zajasang? The girl before the title, behind it, for whom the title may be part of who she was, and still was besides the point? *She is all mine.*

They sauntered across the Court's central gathering space to where Zajasang was talking with Seren, her back to them. Not that it made a difference for Zaja—she was so acutely aware of the world around her, she might as well have a dragonfly's eyes.

"Lady." Sin slipped a hand around her waist and dipped his head to scent her, before placing a gentle kiss in the same spot, where her neck curved into her shoulder. He revelled in feeling her lean into him a little, softening and opening a little. That she trusted him, allowed and welcomed his touch and responded to him in this way... It never failed to amaze and delight him. How could he not want to give her everything?

"May I introduce Fern Ivy-Bound of Storm Court." He cleared his throat. "Fern, meet the Dark Queen."

Zajasang glanced up at him with a slight lift to her eyebrow. He gently squeezed his hand on her waist in return. When she didn't leave it at that, questioning his peculiar introduction still, he grazed her neck with his teeth and held her in a tender bite for good measure. He didn't care that a considerable number of Storm's Sung were watching. In fact, he'd prefer if they all see clearly that she was his—and he was very particular, possessive, and protective of his claim.

His Queen cleared her throat to signal the end of that— though not before he felt a flash of desire from her. That, more than anything else, appeased Sin enough to play polite again. He loosened his teeth, laved the marks, and moved his head back.

That was the only part of him that moved back.

Wicked Wild. He hadn't been this bad in the other Courts.

With mirth dancing in his features, Fern touched his hand to his brow and performed the customary spiralling bow. "Queen Zajasang."

"Bond and Song, Fern Ivy-Bound of Storm Court. You know Sin well?"

"Oh yes. We grew up together."

"You did!" Glee spread across Zaja's face. "I'd love to hear any stories you have to tell."

Sin suppressed a groan. Of course she would. And Fern would stretch it out as long as he could and hog her for hours—if just to rile him up. Well. *He* had privileges Fern didn't have. Sin appreciated seeing her gayety—it had been far too rare in recent weeks—but he was well-equipped to—

"If there's time." And as quickly as it had come, the levity fled Zaja's frame. The girl stepped aside and the Dark Queen took over. "Please excuse me, gentlemen. There are questions I..."

She trailed off. Her focus had already moved beyond them. The lines of her body as she turned from them spoke for her. There were answers she needed to find.

Sin stared after Zajasang as the other Queens closed rank around her and took her Songs knew where, for conversations he both hoped and feared to learn the contents of.

"As full of secrets as the Song, huh?"

Sin grimaced. His chest was burning again. He'd have gone after her had it not been for Fern's strong grip on his shoulder. Being back here, where he had first met her and lost her, where he had longed, and longed, and longed for her... Every breath demanded he verify that she was here and his.

His oldest friend studied him.

Sin searched for the right words, and inflated with each he found. "She's embraced by the Dark. Songs, she's the Queen of it. So incandescent. Illuminating the world for us, radiant with her life. When she's fully open to me, and shining like the moon in the night—" Sin grunted. His arms fell. "But the moon disappears. Withdraws. Hides. So elusive and mysterious..."

He huffed. "I lose her all over, no idea how to reach her. The Dark swallows her up."

Fern just listened, giving him the space to face what he needed to.

Sin scuffed the ground, like the boy he'd been so long ago.

He'd gotten his dream. Earned his place by her side.

But it wasn't enough.

"Fern. She's Dark Queen." He roughed up his hair, the movement choppy and violent. "How do I hold onto her?"

* * *

The longer the day dragged on, the more useless Sin became.

He ruined his mother's brew when he dumped the chopped vegetables in the wrong pot. (*Not those roots!*) Then he accidentally whacked a youngster hard enough to leave a weal when the males came together to spar. (*Well, if that brew wasn't ruined...*)

The sensual heat that always simmered in him scorched out his mind. His urgency to get his Queen to himself continued to build and build. Every part of him, rational or primal, wanted the kind of reassurance of his claim on her that only came from the throes of shared passion, the soothing darkness of her touch.

But he hadn't got to see her since they had arrived this morning. The Queens had things to discuss. She was busy. Everyone wanted a piece of her whenever she emerged. How was he supposed to have expected being back in his home Court to be so vexing?

Even being near his Bond brothers grated on him, so Sin tried to lose himself with the horses. Maybe ride hard, or at least sink his mind into the familiar complexity of achieving a good braid.

They all shied away from him, refusing to let him come near.

Wicked Wild, he had to get himself under control. But the fact that she was upset… It only added fuel to the fire. He never much liked being apart from her—he couldn't bear it now.

Sin kicked a wood bucket, sending it good and skidding. That interlude over the webs back in Old kept replaying in his mind. In Ember she had flipped into frenzy. Zajasang had been frozen in, then the ice cracked, and she hadn't stopped clinking since. All those brilliant, crystalline, jagged pieces jangling and rattling, like the most splendid chandelier in disastrous free fall. Her body talked to Sin even when she didn't.

Had she even noticed how she had been shaking continuously? Likely not. Which also vexed him.

He needed to take care of her. Banish the thoughts that were torturing her. Relax her body. Soothe her heart. Fix her like this wonky lean-to in the horses' pasture, securing the loose parts back into their right place, help her be whole again.

The sun was bruising the sky a dusky purple when Sin broke the plank he had been working on. He bellowed at the heavens and threw down his tools. Then he steamrolled through the Court he knew better than any other, finagled Zajasang away with as much politeness as he could muster—not a lot—and stole her to privacy.

To soft blankets under his favourite laurel tree.

For the next three hours, he seduced her with all he had in him. Which was what it took. Every ounce of his single-minded focus, skill, and perseverance. First to quell the inflamed blistering inside her, then call forth a new, differently throbbing heat.

But with each moment that belonged only to them, each shared moment that he was free to devote himself to her again, his frantic heart calmed and his pace slowed. *Thank you,* his nose traced into her cheek. *I need you,* his tongue licked around her spine. *You don't know how much*, his mouth growled high into her inner thigh. Touch by touch, the urgency receded until it was gone completely, and time or the world ceased to exist.

Sin enveloped her in the ocean of his love, catching all the tinkling pieces, stroking and smoothing every single one until they exquisitely chimed together in the waves. Until he could feel her love overflowing and spilling freely from her heart into his, a stream so clear and pristine it must have come from an enchanted other world.

They were slow now, slower than they'd ever been. A joining so unhurried, so present and transcendent, it went beyond passion, beyond sex. It took Sin's breath away, and he robbed Zajasang of hers. Her heart started beating to a new rhythm, and that was the pulse that sang in his chest.

"Mine." Sin's voice was guttural, commandeered by the wild animal in him. He held her captive with his gaze, demanding her complete opening to him, her fullest surrender to his loving.

Her face awash and glowing in pleasure, she arched her breasts up into him. Even half lost in her delirious ecstasy, he saw the hint of lightning flash through her eyes, the fierce storm raging deep in the abyss.

"Mine," Zajasang snarled through a gasping moan, refuting him, holding on to her claim to herself, defending her sovereignty.

Like every time before.

And then Sin watched in complete, knee-bending awe as her love welled up, softening her in a breathtaking flush, and she sighed, "and yours."

How would he ever let her go now? Even if that was the way to do right by her? She was the temple at which he worshipped. She was the Goddess bestowing her grace upon him. He never loved her more desperately.

For endless minutes stretching into more hours, dusk turning into night, there was nothing but her, him here with her, the two of them moving together in utter splayed open love. Deeper and deeper into bliss and Song Zajasang rose, and somehow he was the one who'd been granted the glorious gift of rising with her.

So Sin followed Zaja wherever she went, into a battle where he lost and won at the same time, for they soared, and then they shattered again. But they shattered together, and found all their shards gathered safely in the beauty and power of their embrace.

And through their flight and their fall, Zaja never hid from him. She remained all his, the fathomless star-filled depth in her eyes matching the pristine firmament high above them. There were only truth and reverence shining at him when she breathed out, "...and then there's this."

A memory arose on the edges of Sin's mind. The first night on Amea. The conviction that there was no experience that compared to witnessing the Queen's Dance. How wrong he'd been.

"And then there's this." He breathed it back into her, soul to soul, reverence redounding.

Dancing *with* his Queen—any of her Dances—that's what he was her Destined for. As long as she'd let him do that, they'd be able to figure everything else out.

24

ZAJASANG'S BODY WAS TENSE IN Sin's arms, enough to have woken him from the cavernous realms of contented sleep.

No. Not yet.

She had been so soft and unspooled. Had remained languid, serenely humming and nuzzling into his shoulder, when at who knows what hour he'd carried and nestled her into the plushness of this bed in the suite she'd been offered. He'd wished the night would last forever, and there would be no need to return to the light of day. No separation. No shards. Just bliss bundled into his chest.

So they'd slept in peace. Until now.

Sin glanced outside through the wind-eye. Dawn was a long way off. He mustn't have been asleep long. He wasn't likely to fall asleep again, with Zaja this uneasy in her slumber. Maybe he ought to wake her? No. She needed all the rest she could get. Her sleep was taut, but she wasn't tossing. He'd just settle in to watch over her.

Time stretched in the darkness like the late afternoon sun. Sin lay awake, caressing her and pressing soft kisses in her hair. It made no difference. His wish for forever turned into a plea for time to speed up and release her. His only gratification was that her body sought out his for comfort, pressing as close as she could, Zajasang's stiff fingers gripping into his hard muscles.

Then she screamed.

A hoarse, night-shattering, bone-cracking wail that sounded as if her heart was being wrenched from her chest, and it wrenched his soul right along with it. Her body propelled upright with the force of the sound, then contorted back onto itself as her scream transformed into an unrelenting keen.

"Zaja!" Expelled from his frozen shock of abject terror, Sin frantically ran his hands over her body. Was she in pain? Of course she was in pain, but was it hers? Was there something wrong with her body, or was she riding out something originating beyond her?

Sin grasped her arms and tried to straighten her out of her spine-breaking contortion. "Zajasang, sweetheart, please."

Her eyes were wide, her pupils blown, the sheen of her tears reflective in the scant starlight—but she was unseeing.

"Songs, no, please, please." Sin gathered her into his arms as best he could.

The wooden door flung open, banging hard against the stone wall, as Tavo, Anda, and Yako barrelled through it. They piled around him, muttering to her just like he was.

"What happened?" Yako barked.

It barely pierced the sphere that had descended on Sin, pressing in on him faster and faster where he was hanging on to Zaja, trying to keep her from being crushed, keep her with him, keep her *safe*. "Zaja, darling." He cradled her cheek, tried to find her in her eyes. Wherever she was, she was beyond their reach. "Zajasang, my Queen. Come back to me."

Sin clutched her tighter, but awkwardly, half afraid to touch her at all. She was so rigid in her convulsion. Rigid things can't bend in a storm—they can only break.

"Sin!"

"I don't know," he gritted out.

"What started it?"

"I don't know!"

Her keening was unending, as if life itself was straining from her while she was locked in herself. Each moment of it shredded him further.

Sin gently rocked her tortured body. It was all he could do. All of her he could reach. The Bond was obliterated with white hot agony. A tidal wave so intense there was no room to push anything back at all.

He rocked, and vowed he would hunt down whatever was drawing those awful sounds out of her. He would tear it apart until it was left in the same bloody pieces as his heart.

Sin rocked and Zaja keened.

When was it going to stop? He needed it to stop.

"Sin." There was an edge in Anda's tremulous voice.

It wasn't enough to pull Sin's attention away from his Queen. Nothing could do that. He was as locked in as she was.

Where was the dawn? Had the sun forgotten to rise? Maybe there was no more sun. Maybe it was suffering as gruesome a death here in Storm, molten in this crucible, as it had had a glorious birth in Ember.

"Sin." The vicelike grip on his shoulder clawed his focus and carried it up. Anda's eyes were fixed to the doorway which still gaped ajar.

Sin followed his gaze.

A huddle of crying witches and frenzied males holding them crowded just beyond the threshold. Mrak clinging to Jalen. Adara looking more fragile than he'd ever seen her. Ivy propped up by Fern. Tama and Feny clutching each other, Sehe and Syed holding on to both. Vala—enveloped in the arms of Moyo, one of Storm's as yet unbonded Heart males. They must have just met today. The whole of the Dark Coven, and many of Storm's witches, too. All of them as distraught as Zajasang, dissolved in a tormented threnody—but at least they were clinging to their Bonded or beloveds.

At least they still seemed to be *here*.

"Come in," Sin rasped, and turned his gaze back to Zaja's empty one, brushing his thumb over the delicate bones below her eyes to catch her tears.

Heart Court filed in and filled up the floor, settees, and wind-eye seats around them. A harmony of horror haunted the room, a dirge of grief and wrath sung in a dozen wailing voices, the gentle hushing, muttering, and husky pleading the bass line. Outside, the wolves had risen in a howl, and no other creature in the night seemed to dare make a sound.

Many long minutes later, each lasting as long as a lifetime, the symphony of sorrow never letting up, some of the witches began to calm. Between crying jags, their song stuttered to hiccupping moans and hoarse humming.

Zajasang remained unchanged, cold and immolated in his arms.

Sin held tight to his fraying patience, ripped back the impotent rage laying waste inside him. None of it would help Zaja. None of it she should have to feel, if she could feel him at all.

"Lady, what's wrong?" The urgent, insistent whisper came somewhere behind him on his left. It could have been any one of the Heart males, desperate for answers from their Queen.

Another soft sob, and muffled sniffle.

Then, at long last, one of their witches found her voice.

"They're dead."

* * *

The thready pronouncement echoed through the sickened silence that followed it.

They're dead.

Sin had never stopped monitoring Zajasang's catatonic state, had not wrested his eyes from her but the once. And yet, the declaration jarred him into a renewed flurry of movement. Feeling for her pulse, at her neck and her wrist and her heart. Checking her breathing. Running his hands along her limbs. Pulling the blanket tight around both of them as if that would keep her safe. Staring into her wide open eyes—and seeing only an abyss, and nothing looking back.

"Who?"

Sin didn't know who of his brothers had mustered the courage to rasp out the question. All of the females had quieted. The hush—only sporadic whimpers humming along below its weight—was more ominous than the harrowing grieving song had been.

In another corner of the room, a mewl shaped itself into a shadow of syllables. "Hundreds upon hundreds."

"Witches?" Anda pressed.

"Yes."

One broken word that broke their world.

Cataclysmic pandemonium rose and froze in the same heartbeat. Every male present rared to rage out into the world and find whoever was at fault—and instead pulled their female closer, behind them, into any defensible position they could. Their every instinct ridden by the need to keep their own witches safe and never let them go.

Anda, Yako, and Tavo had turned outward, too, facing off the danger they couldn't see.

Sin's eyes remained stuck to Zaja's face. He didn't think the danger was out there.

What about death? she'd asked him. *Part of life,* he'd said. Death hurt but belonged.

Not this death.

Somehow, without understanding anything, Sin understood that this death was wrong. And his Queen, his Dark Queen who was as good as life itself, was—

No. Not like this, Zaja.

Terse sounds ebbed and flowed around him, males coaxing and Queens choking out whatever revelations they could.

"Ocean Sisters..."

"...all at once."

"A rip in the web..."

Bile burned Sin's throat. The big-winged whales, gone. How could that have happened? Why?

"Without the Weavers of the Deep..."

"A wound in the Weave."

A wound in the Weave. All those times Zajasang had overexerted herself deep in the Song, had returned barely conscious, collapsing in their arms when she emerged. Now she had become the open, bleeding wound. How many deaths had she just died? How much could one person bear to feel at once before being eclipsed by it? He had held her before, deep in the Dark, when the Wicked Wild threatened to devour her.

He couldn't hold her now.

Songs, no. It couldn't be. Mustn't. Please, please don't let this be the Dark leap.

"...probably the only reason the tethers were still holding together, in the Dark, and the strain became too hard." Mrak's voice, garbled and distant as if she was shouting underwater. "The threads snapped, and they went with it."

Is that what happened? Had Zajasang gone with them?

"Without them... We can't hold the web. It's too much for us to balance."

"It's going to keep unravelling."

Like him. Sin pressed his forehead to Zaja's. The first time they'd touched in this way had been at their Bond Song. He'd felt invincible. But he was nothing without her.

He had to know. "What are you saying?"

He didn't know whom he was asking, which of the witches. Any of them, all of them. He finally looked around, and they were slowly blinking back at him. Forlorn and faded, like those flowers that had tumbled out of one his mother's books once.

At last, Vala responded, every word sodden with sorrow. "This world has no idea how much it needs its oceans. Doesn't see, doesn't care. The world—the Loud—is going to fall. We're not strong enough."

It was all looping in Sin's mind. He couldn't quite parse it apart. Nothing was connecting.

Tavo shifted. Carefully teased his hand through Zaja's hair again. Cleared his throat. "Were there no signs? Nothing in the Song?"

Everyone's head was swivelling, eyes large. *Owls*, Sin thought. *Don't owls know the way in the dark?*

But they weren't giving anything away, telling him nothing.

No, that wasn't right.

Tavo has asked about the Song. Warning signs.

"There were."

The croak snapped Sin's mind back into clarity like a narwhale's tusk breaking the icy water's surface. It had come from the Queen in his arms.

Her eyes were locked on him, and she was *in* them.

"Zajasang." Black spots appeared in his vision. "Oh, Sacred Song, thank you." He kissed her, kissed her nose, her cheeks, didn't care one bit that his Bond brothers were doing the same to her hands and knees and wherever they could reach. "Sweetheart, Zaja, darling..."

Now she sobbed and shuddered, a delayed echo of her Sisters, and clung to him. "So sorry," she moaned, "I'm so sorry," banging her head against his shoulder. Cried out, and smashed her wet nose into the crook of his neck.

Sin had never been so glad for her crying.

She was here with him. She was back. She was alive.

He hadn't lost her.

25

MORNING SUNLIGHT FLOODS THROUGH THE wind-eye, merry and bright. As if the world is the same as yesterday, and an infinite number of sunny tomorrows will follow.

Maybe for a different world. Not this one.

Because of me.

It's just as well my mind hasn't emerged from the night. Inside, I'm still mangled by the Wicked Wild. And any pieces that are left unscathed I maul myself.

The tomorrows are limited. The world is *not* the same. The witches below the waves...

Because I failed them.

Refused to listen, do more, do anything. Didn't go where the Song needed me to go. Failed to do the one thing the Sung were relying on me for...had embraced me for as their Dark Queen.

"I need to go."

Sin is shushing me, mumbling non-sensical sweet nothings to try and calm me. But the same desperate words keep tumbling around in my brain, sometimes tumbling out of my mouth.

When did the Court leave? I don't remember. I just know that like a pendulum swing, I went from one extreme to the other. Total stasis and freeze, into phrenetic, pulse-racing panic that has me in a chokehold and won't let go.

Songs, I actually thought I belonged. That there'd been a point to this horrid madness of my life, that all this wretched feeling was good for something. Welcome and needed and I could *do* something.

But I couldn't. Or didn't. I don't know. I fought to be me, to stay—but that wasn't enough. So what was I fighting for?

"I need to go." I struggle against Sin's arms, needing to pace, move, flee.

I can't. We've traded positions. Sin has completely locked up —around me.

"Where?"

"Away," I hiss. It's my only alternative to wailing and sobbing right now. "Away from the Sung." I didn't do you any good. I don't belong.

"What? No." The faintest part of my mind manages a vague, bitter sort of amusement when Sin grabs up the blanket I'd struggled out of to wrap me up in again, moves us both into the wall, and spreads his body over mine. As if I was worthy of that sort of uncompromising devotion. "Zajasang."

Sin. I batter against my cocoon. *Oh, Sin.* I have no chance against him. My hands don't even make it out of the blanket, but I can't stop. *I wish you could have stayed my only sin.*

"What are you saying? You want to leave the Sung?"

My ineffectual slugs stutter. Sacred Song, I don't. My fractured soul erodes with the mere thought. But how could I stay? They trusted me to care for the Song in the way only the

Dark Queen can. And my only legacy is damage too terrible for even the Sung to balance.

"You want to leave me?"

Pain sears into the very ends of my hair. His? Mine? I taste blood—real blood, not through my sense of the Song. My eyes fly shut to hide the damning evidence of my welling tears.

"You are my Queen," Sin growls, rattling me, somehow still managing to be careful in his touch. Never once has his formidable strength been turned against me. Whenever the fangs of the hunter living inside him have been bared at me, then only to protect me from a threat lurking in my back.

A rising, high-pitched wail presses through my throat. Sometimes it's not another's blows that break you, but their love.

"You are Dark Queen. You belong with us."

I snap my eyes back open—a whip against my own flesh when they meet his tormented ones—and snarl back at him. "The ocean witches are dead!" Finally, one hand is free, and I pound it against Sin's chest. "You got it wrong! I'm wrong!"

No matter how different their Court Dance may look, the winged whales are Sung. They are the holder of the memory, the guardians of the beyond. They are the Sung of the ocean. They were my Sisters in the Song. They were my Sisters...

I collapse against Sin, heaving and struggling for breath and drowning in my sobs and wondering why I haven't. Why are they gone and I'm not?

"No! Nothing about you is wrong, Zajasang." Sin captures my hand, gathers me tight to his heart. "Nothing about us—"

"I grew up in the Loud. No Dark Queen ever has. I didn't belong there, and maybe I should have fit with the Sung, but I still didn't, did I?" I swallow and gurgle through my snot, getting louder and messier as I go. "So either you got the wrong girl and I never was Dark Queen, or maybe—" Shards of shattered obsidian lined with gold flash in my mind. "Maybe the Loud broke me!"

"Zaja, listen to me." Sin clutches my face between his hands, long fingers smoothing along my jaw and cradling my ears. "You, Zajasang Maaya Zatinsa, are everything you were meant to be. You have always belonged with us, and you have always belonged with me. My life in your Dance, Zaja. Always. You've got this, and I've got you. I'll always have you. You are not alone. And you were born for this."

He's breathing hard. His insistent eyes bore into me, willing me to believe him, to agree with him.

But there's nothing I know to say.

"When is your birthday?" I stare at Sin blankly. He jiggles my head. "When is your birthday, Zaja?"

"May 1."

"Who named you?"

What—how does he know about that? I keep my lips pressed shut in a tight line. Sin's prodding, demanding scowl doesn't let up. "A great-grandaunt who was dead long before I was born," I eventually mumble. I don't even know any more than that. Why didn't I ask my mother what she knew when she made that throwaway comment?

"How did you feel when you first came to Amea?"

"That's not—"

"How long have you been able to hear the full Song?"

Always. It's not like listening with your ears, not truly. It's more like opening the doors of your soul and your heart, and you...hear it. For me, those doors have always been open. They were veiled, but I've always felt the wind blowing through. Always heard it. Hearing through my heart was as natural as hearing through my ears, whether I wanted it to be or not. I swallow and glare at Sin. His green irises reflect my large, defiant eyes back at me.

"Does Adara go as Dark as you? Mrak? Any of your strongest Sisters?"

I stay mute but for a minute shake of my head. I understand what he's doing, what he's wanting me to acknowledge, but—

"Spell it out, Zaja."

"No, they don't, alright? You know that they don't."

"Have you noticed animals and nature flock to any other Queens as much as they do to you?" Sin's thumbs begin stroking across my cheekbones as his voice gentles. "You are always giving access, sweetheart. You don't need physical connection for it. Everyone is gifted with the Song just by being around you. Songs, in ritual, you take us where no other Bonded gets to go. Do you want me to continue?"

"No," I whisper.

He does anyway, only now he's growling and pressing closer. "You're catnip to any Sung male. That dark, wild aliveness seeps out of you, emanates from you more strongly than any other Queen we've ever met, and we—"

He cuts himself off. His jaw works and the fire rages in his eyes. His face is so close I can taste him on the air.

"I've felt you for years. I know you. I know how deeply, overwhelmingly, you feel life. And I'm sure there are still worlds to you that I know nothing about, but I. Know. You." An actual, real animal growl rumbles in his chest. "I don't have the wrong female, Zajasang. Nor the wrong Queen. I've had the right girl since I met her on a beach, lost her, and spent every moment of my existence fighting to take my place by her side again."

What do I do with that? Tears spill hot tracks down my cheeks—again. Sin watches their path with a predator's focus before leaning in to kiss them away.

"Do you believe me now? Because, believe this, I will stay here and do this with you until you believe me."

He's got me up against the stone of the wall, his gaze holds mine, and I know we're reliving the same memory. The day after he took me to Firefall.

The day I was freaking out after our first kiss, when everything was too much, too new, and too close to everything I'd ever dreamed of. He felt me going haywire through the Bond, tracked me down, and refused to let me shut him out. Any resistance I put up, and barricade physical, mental, or emotional, he barrelled through. Until he had me trapped, and demanded I lay my heart bare to him. Spit out the words, however tremulous. Reveal my fears, however ridiculous.

So I did.

Is this real?

Sweetheart, he said, *I'm going to stay right here loving you until you believe this is real.*

That had been our second kiss, punctuated by Sin's unshakeable confidence. *This. Is. Real.*

Sin doesn't need to say the words this time for them to be reverberating through my being with his kiss.

This is real.

You are meant for this.

I will stay right here with you.

Finally I pull away, ready to drag myself to Storm's bathing spring. I feel frayed inside and out. I need time to process and think. Once again, Sin collected my shards. But it's up to me whether the pieces will glue back together.

With reluctance, Sin loosens his hold. As I move, his hand trails from my waist to my elbow, all the way down the length of my arm and hand and to the very tips of my fingers. Not keeping me if I choose to go—but making his desire abundantly clear.

When the wind at last conquers the space where touch existed a moment before, he clears his throat. "Will you stay? Promise me."

I don't know if what he reads in the Bond and my eyes is enough to reassure him. Judging by the pain in his, it's not.

But he lets me go.

* * *

The air hazy with steam, the spring is an otherworldly oasis of peace. Lichen-covered rock outcrops peak through the wafting mists when they part, rich with vibrant, heavy blooms draping over their cracks and crevices. It is the type of bathing place that goddesses of myth might have sought out. I feel so far removed from that it makes me want to laugh, but I don't have the energy left for even that.

Void of any grace, I lower myself into the soaking heat and close my eyes. My mind feels like a pestle has been taken to it in a mortar, before a cyclone came along to spin the dust into a tizzy. Like panicked sheep, my thoughts want to spring in all directions at once, and like an ostrich, they also want to burrow in sand and not emerge again. Or really, they'd love to just faint like a goat and fade to black forevermore.

One by one, I force myself to relax every cramped tight muscle. Then I make myself focus on every sensation radiating through me from my immediate vicinity. A melee of pure vibrations of nature. I make myself acknowledge them, really feel them. Eventually, the ocean fills my womb, the essence of wildflowers fills my sex, and soft sun-dappled coiling ferns cradle my heart. The steamy droplets pearling down my neck return the steel to my spine when the cool breeze teases them.

Breath by breath, I find a measure of comfort.

I sling my arms in a tight hug around myself, then I hone in on the contours of my skin and my own heartbeat. With enough clarity to think, I try to make sense of the senseless.

What do you know, Zaja?

And I make a list.

My swimming Sisters are gone. Our singing brothers will follow them into the beyond.

So the web will collapse.

The world is heading for disaster.

The wound in the Weave is too extensive for the Sung to darn.

I tried to reweave it, and failed.

I was the only one who tried.

That—it snags at me. The spiders wove the wound into their webs as the wind sung it to them. The elephants felt the feverish vibrations. I wasn't the only one aware. How could I have been the only one to try and reweave it? I chew and chew on it. I shouldn't have been. It doesn't make sense. I can't make sense, unless...However I twist it, only one answer remains, whispering to me from the depth.

Unless none, not even the whales, swim as deep.

I have to face the terrifying truth—it will remain the truth whether I shy away from it or embrace it. The difference, I realise, is whether it rules me, or I rule myself.

With a big inhale, I loosen my arms and look at my reflection in the undisturbed surface embracing me.

I am Queen. Witch. Weaver.

I am Dark Queen.

A dragonfly causes an undulation to travel through the water, animating my reflection until I see me nodding back at myself in the merest hint of a mysterious smile. Understanding ripples through me. I'm not Dark Queen because the Sung want me to be or tell me I am—that, alone, can never make me Dark Queen. I am Dark Queen because I own that I am.

Only then.

And also never because of what I do...or fail to do...but what. I. Am. It is in my truth, the core of my being.

I return to my list.

I am Dark Queen.

For the first time, the thought doesn't sit like a heavy stone in my belly, but like a night-blooming flower low in my womb.

I, Zajasang Maaya Zatinsa, am Dark Queen.

And I'm a child of the Loud.

The flower opens as epiphany hits. Songs. I tremble in the near-burning heat of the spring.

The Loud didn't break me. Those fires of hell wrought me, and hell locks from the inside. It's time I opened the gates.

* * *

"I'm going back to the Loud."

To all outward appearances, following my announcement, only the Song of silence sings. To the Sung, the silence is more or less filled with hum or melody, the portal opened to them through their own emotion or the touch of their Queen. To me, it is a clamorous woven web of every single feeling filling the courtyard.

"Lady." The pleading note soars above the symphony in heart-aching rawness.

Sin's single spoken word is the wave that topples the dam, and the others join in. Their refusals lap into one another, layering, all of them merging into one refrain. "Don't leave us, Zaja."

"I'm not *leaving you.* But I do need to go to the Loud."

Even if I dread the clogged, dirtied, aching cacophony that will overwhelm me there. My body is like a theatre. It's the place where all the drama of the emotions rising and falling in everyone around me plays out. Amongst the Sung, that drama is often intense and frequently distracting—but rarely is it truly painful. They live in harmony with nature, their intentions honest, their feelings clean and clear. Unlike the Loud...

"I'm the only Dark Queen from the Loud, right?" I continue. "There's a reason for it. There's a reason the Song didn't sing to my parents." It did sing to previous Dark Queens, and showed them what was to come. It sang to the great-grandaunt who left instructions for the girl born on May 1.

"The Loud needs to change if there's going to be any hope. They don't hear the Song, don't hear how nature is crying." My hand is gripping my throat. I do hear it. The continuous shrieking of a world tilting on its axis. I imagine the Titanic's metal must have sounded like this in its dying squalling.

"But I can be her voice. I grew up in their world and sat at their decision makers' banquets. I am Sung, and I am from the Loud." Deep breath. "I can be the bridge."

Too dizzy to remain on my feet, I droop onto the edge of the closest settee. Nausea is clogging my airways. *Back to the Loud. Seriously, Zaja?* Return to a life I ran from. No clear idea where I was running to then, and no clear idea of where the path takes me this time either. Desperate and half-delirious both times.

Yet the girl from then...is not the witch of now. She had no idea who she was. But finally, I do.

"Who will you speak with?"

Anyone? Everyone. Wicked Wild, I have no idea how to do this, only that I must. Who will listen? What can I say to make them listen? Bowed over, I bang my head against my knees. Allowing myself one shudder, two. Until my attention drops from my bleating brain...to my steady heart. A clear stream of confidence, trust, and certainty curls around it, buoying it. And I bop back up, like a flag planted, rising proudly in the wind.

My eyes find those of my Constellation. Tavo. Anda. Yako. Warmth and love shine at me. Kindness.

And Sin, always Sin, like a sigh of pleasure in my soul.

Gaze locked with him, my still grappling mind grinds to a halt on the memory of another set of kind eyes, of relief amongst grating pressure. Older, more watery. Sea blue. Perceptive, and understanding. A brief moment of contentment rolling through me with the tolling of a clock, signalling my escape from a stifling banquet.

My lips twitch with the realisation. We're at Storm Court, of all places.

"The ambassador of Greece."

26

THE LOUD

WICKED WILD, THE LOUD IS loud.

Machines roaring and humming and screeching. Overlapping sounds from people and devices all blaring in competition. Manufactured and dirty smells eclipsing natural and clean ones. Utter chaos of people and things moving in all directions, bumping and swerving. And below the surface, the deeper river. Raging suppressed and ignored feelings scrabbling to be heard, howling and scratching and kicking at me, from nearly every person going about their business.

In the middle of the road, we are a huddled pack splitting the stream of people, stuck in shock and blocking the flow. The irony.

With each heartbeat, I feel myself shuttering up, slat by slat unrolling. Protection. Survival. Shield and armour.

Hot breath tickles my ear before the growling velvet of Sin's voice tremors down my spine. "My life in your Dance."

Right.

A deep breath shudders through me, half halting the clanging condemnation of the slats falling into place. I'm surrounded by big, growly males. Bonded males. Males ready, eager, to take up weapons for me. If I lay mine down, they will take them up and stand strong and impenetrable around me. Leaving me...free.

Free to be me and do what only I can do.

"My Queen?" Anda probes.

If I surrender, I can be connected.

"Zajasang?"

My true shield is my trust.

Slowly, ever so slowly, I force my tense muscles to relax. I allow the rush, the rip-roaring tide, to flow through me. Instead of closing down, I stay open. But I let myself be anchored and carried by the calm strength of Anda, Yako, Tavo, and Sin. They are flames of warm golden light, each connected to me and one another, a web of glowing spider silk. And me in the middle, floating above the abyss, feeling but not falling, resting on the strength of the wondrous threads of the spider silk bonds.

My hands fall from my waist. I don't even need to nod my readiness—my Bonded read me as well and intimately as I read the world around me.

Time to do what we came for. Time to be both Queen Zaja and a Zatinsa.

* * *

"Zajasang Maaya Zatinsa requests an audience."

They are the only words I utter—not unkindly, yet confidently, and firmly. I had a whole childhood to observe and study posturing.

Before me stands a man like an autumn leaf: a little weak and brittle, but not without beauty and appeal. The secretary raises his eyebrows, preparing to question us—before swallowing whatever imperial remark sat on his tongue. His eyes glanced over all of us when we first entered, although now he holds my gaze. A leaf with some life and strength in it yet.

The silence stretches.

We must make quite the tableau. Our clothes match the location in degree of stylishness and elegance, though not reticence and conservatism. Our energy matches the locale's air of determined business—but it would be kind to describe my Bonded's expressions as anything less than menacing. I couldn't convince them just one of them would be protection enough—not on this first visit. It would have been fun if Zuzu had tagged along...

As it is, my Constellation encircles me, in lieu of the wall of steel I long to pull around me like a cloak. We swept down the carpeted corridors right to this understated door, past all the gaping mouths whose protests soundlessly floated out of them like bubbles out of a goldfish. Only for this secretary did we at last stop, heads held high still.

His phone begins to ring on his desk. He makes no move towards it. Simply waits for it to ring out. Watching us as we watch him.

Silence descends once more.

Then he turns, opens the door into the office on our left, barely a sliver to let him through, closes it—and we faintly make him out as he echoes my request word for word.

I have the silly urge to break into hysterical giggles.

The slight tickle of my Bonded's amusement resonates through me. I don't need to look at them to know the kind of looks they're exchanging.

"We haven't achieved anything yet," I say quietly. We need to actually be let in. We need to be listened to...and heard.

Anda's deep voice is soft but sure. "Who could deny you, my Queen?"

Let's hope not the Ambassador of Greece.

The door opens again. Wide. A portal to possibility. I return the secretary's nod, and we file past him.

"Miss Zatinsa." The Ambassador went to the trouble of standing and coming around his grand desk before we crossed over his threshold. His well-schooled face doesn't give away the intense curiosity cooking in him—but it is blatant in the slight burning on my skin.

"Ambassador."

His eyes are unchanged—sea blue, watery—in a slightly more portly body. They hold traces of bemusement, though they aren't empty of recognition. "It has been many years. Belated birthday wishes, I believe."

I incline my head. There's an eager puzzlement in this, too, lurking behind his words—but where would I even begin with answering that? It's not what I'm here for, and time is precious.

The silence sings.

"What brings me the unexpected honour of your presence?"

The warm rays of my Bonded's approval of his choice of words swirl over my shoulder blades. They kept themselves respectfully in the background, fanning out behind me while allowing me to step forward and command the ambassador's attention. There is no doubt in my mind where their laser sharp attention lies.

"I require your assistance. The world does, in fact."

Only now does it occur to me that I didn't even think of laying this plea at the feet of my parents—the most obvious people for me to have thought of reaching out to. Bridges in their own way, by virtue of their profession. Alas, they were not the ones whose eyes held kindness. They were not the ones who looked and were able to see. The thought holds sadness, but little bitterness. It is a puzzle piece that found the place where it fits. They did the best they were capable of, and played their part in the great symphony.

"As I'm sure you're aware by now, a large number of whales recently died simultaneously and seemingly without cause."

I do not try to hide the hoarseness of my voice, do not attempt to cloak my emotion. The banquets were a never-ending game of poker and deception, the dignitaries' daily interactions greased in oil, the diplomats mostly men.

But I'm neither a dignitary, nor a male. I'm a Queen.

"More death will come."

The ambassador remains unchanged before me, though the reverberations of this pronouncement return to me carrying the evidence of his distress, coloured in a cold metallic tang.

"First in the oceans, then on the land. Unstoppable, irrevocable death—if the people of this Earth don't change their ways, and fast."

Even now the screeching deep in the Song scratches at me. It's a wound that has been opened, any scab torn away. Now it leaks, and demands to be felt. A shiver crawls through me, and I feel my Bonded's concern spike in response.

For a long while, nothing but the ticking of the ostentatious clock fixed to the wood-panelled wall fills the room.

The ambassador's eyes rest on me, travel over my Constellation, then return to me. Only his finger ticks by his thigh, keeping rhythm with the clock. "You know this."

Slowly, gravely, I nod. "I know this."

The ambassador's gaze doesn't waver, his brows raised expectantly. Another ticking eternity later, he asks, "Is that all you're going to give me to go on?"

A sudden, unexpected firestorm climbs in me. My head cocks to the side, and I clench down before any other part of me moves. "A simultaneous mass exodus of the whales wasn't enough for you?" For indeed, the singers of the deep have followed their weavers. We are racing against his damned clock with every second he is ticking off.

The flames are crawling over my skin and through my bones. My rage stokes my Bonded's for whom it lives so closely under the skin—especially where it comes to me—and at the best of times.

This is not the best of times.

"I do not make the decrees." The ambassador's head tilts from side to side, like a billowing white flag, revealing the waver that his voice doesn't.

Still, my brows dance. "Yet you hold the puppet strings... And you sit at the banquets."

If I can't make *him* see, can't get him to understand, the one with the kind and perceptive soul—how will I possibly get through to anyone else in his circles? Maybe our Circles have been closed for too long. Maybe this conversation should have happened a long time ago.

Maybe that's the reason a Dark Queen from the Loud was needed.

At last, the Ambassador's chin lowers in concession and recognition. The sweet citrus of his curiosity brushes against me again. "The people of this Earth. You don't count yourself among them?"

"Oh yes." I snort internally. "Though to speak frankly, my people are more truly *of this Earth* than yours. We live by her Song."

It seems frankness is relative, if the ambassador's expression is anything to go by. "And the people?"

"Most are lost in the Loudness."

The ambassador's perusal of me remains steady. The corners of his eyes crinkle, a silken streak mingling into the sweet citrus. It is to his great credit, I think, and to my great fortune, that he has the capacity and wisdom to still be engaged in this admittedly unusual dialogue, and to take it seriously. Not many would.

"You were listening for her Song then?"

Ah, yes. If he ever gets Sung in, he will be welcome. His understanding does hold depth. Such stark contrast to those we were sharing the table with... I remember the various flavours of pain trampling through me, sharp, dull, pulsing, punching. A satellite dish reading every ricocheting emotional hit fired from beneath civilised, smarmy veneers. I remember the thunderstorm raging outside, and the cleansing, spacious relief it brought.

I remember the same eyes watching me then and now, missing very little.

"The Loudness didn't make it easy." I hesitate, then extend a few strands to him, a glimpse of the Song. He gives a start, his brows rising once more. My lips curve and voice gentles. "Strong heart and Song's caress, Ambassador."

The Ambassador swallows, slightly sinks onto his desk. Remains utterly dignified as he searches his composure. "Protect nature, then? That must be the priority?"

"Protect, honour, cherish. Revere. Earth—nature—and your women. For they are one and the same."

"I can see that."

Another trickle of amusement from my Bonded, wrapped in teasing affection. *Yes, yes, I am the storm.* Equally affectionate exasperation flows back to them.

"Ambassador, are you familiar with the prophecy that talks of humanity as a great eagle? One wing the feminine, one the masculine. We have lived through a time on Earth when one of those wings has been so weakened, oppressed, and beat back in fear, that the other has developed a kind of violent fury attempting to keep the bird aloft. Good intentions warped by much misunderstanding, horror, and pain. A forgetting that was intentionally introduced by the few and indelibly harmed the many. And so the great eagle only spirals towards its demise."

I pause there, waiting to see if the Ambassador will follow through to the prophecy's conclusion of his own insight.

"To soar, the eagle needs two equally strong wings—" he halts, his gaze wandering over my Bonded before returning to me. "And they must beat in harmony."

I smile at him now, genuine and wide, despite the constant underlying strain. "They must master the complex dance of honouring each other's unique gifts—contributing to one another. I hope to see you again, Ambassador."

When I head towards the door, my Constellation returns to their closed ranks around me, all of them subtly seeking touch. Taking and giving comfort, the Bond blurring the difference.

"Miss Zatinsa."

Yako's hand has just met the door handle when the Ambassador's voice rasps through the silence. I pause and turn back, blinking through the wall of male crowding me.

"Will it be enough?"

My stomach grows hot, the floor drops beneath me, and the whisper slips out unbidden. "No."

27

SIN SMOOTHLY MANOEUVRES TO ONCE more put himself between me and the traffic as we cross the street and near our destination. I fix my eyes to the hotel doors, commanding my body to make it that far and to the private room and bed waiting beyond.

This week has been one of constant travel in the Loud and of bulldozing our way into meetings with various political figures. There was no time for politeness and finesse. None of these encounters allowed for a conversation as conventionally opaque, yet clear with understanding, as that first with the Ambassador of Greece. We had to point to the signs, their cumulation, emphasise the significance... And still it was like shouting into a tempest, your words carried off before they're ever received.

Ten paces to the doors. Sin seethes next to me, growling like a very unhappy dog needing to get free of his leash. "I swear, Zaja, if you—"

My left knee folds on the next step before catching, making me wobble as if I was performing some goofy curtsy-gone-wrong.

"That's it." Ignoring my protests, Sin scoops me up and swoops us past the bellhops.

Unprecedented rainfall is continuing to visit regions that are normally almost entirely free of precipitation... The news anchor on the wall-mounted TV of the hotel lobby is largely screened out by the people rushing past, buried in their phones, or chattering away with one another. A few of them glance at us, and I wish I was holding up a poster board. With a big fat red arrow pointing at that damned TV at least. The Loud is glued to their devices at all other times—why aren't they paying attention when it matters?

All Sin is paying attention to is me. Carefully, he shifts me in his hold, adjusting his grip so my head rests more comfortably where it lolls against him. I know he is registering and cataloguing and comparing my discoloured hue and the tense lines of my features, the bruises blooming under my eyes and in the crook of my arms, the starkness of my collarbones and a million other things I'm blocking out like the Loud ignores that anchor.

Between every meeting, every leg of travel, in every free moment there is, I plunge into the Song to Weave. Since my Constellation literally can't stop me, they assist me. Hating it, but hating the alternative more. The Song is still awe-inspiring magic and beauty—what else could it be?— but being in any but the lightest layers of it is...a different experience now.

Even outside of it, there's a dull, constant echo of sandpaper scratching over my bones accompanied by tiny glass shards in my bloodstream. The proximity of my Bonded can shield me from much of the cacophonic pollution of the Loud surrounding us—but this particular misery isn't coming at me from the world around us.

No, it's coming from its marrow. It's in everything, changing everything. It's subtle and insidious, oh so easy to overlook or dismiss. Just like the heavy rains they're reporting on a là business as usual, without yet realising the significance of its pH balance being off. Just like the braced quiet in the forests, as mother tree after mother tree ashens. Just like the death fever spreading through the coral reefs, out of sight and out of mind. Just like the matriarchs coming together in Ember, the gaping wounds in the spiders' webs, the birds not completing their travel.

Strands unravelling, tangling, lashing...tearing. Fast.

And the Loud revels on, too loud to notice the unnatural quiet, too distracted to see, too disconnected to feel.

Yet I feel it all.

"Almost there, darling," Sin murmurs.

Almost where? There's only one place this can lead. A non-place. A cold, terrifying absence.

We reach the old-fashioned elevator and the youthful porter hurries to open the elaborate metal gates for us. It's gotten difficult to keep my eyes open, but I lift my head and make sure to find his gaze. "Thank you, Karl."

He steps in with us, cranks a lever, and sets the elevator moving. "My Lady." That, he seems to have picked up from my Constellation, and deemed it a suitable, if unfamiliar to him, address.

Of similar age to me, and clearly perceptive and intuitive, he's held other passengers back so we could ride alone, and is authentically courteous at all times. He also didn't bat an eyelid when a squirrel was clinging to my hair when we came to the elevator yesterday, which warmed me to him even more.

So like I did for the Ambassador, I extend a few rainbow strands of the uppermost level of the Song to him. "Bond and Song, Karl," I wish him, knowing that he will understand the undercurrent in those words, even if he doesn't know their true meaning.

I'm rewarded with a slackening of his features followed by a furious blush.

His reaction makes me smile, and for a second, I feel jubilant. Nothing but pure glory. Yes, that is the truth of the Song. That is the beauty it makes you feel.

If your mind is quiet enough to let it pass and your heart is open enough to receive it. My smile quavers and slips. The elation that so erratically erupted nosedives equally quickly, building up disastrous speed and force like a comet heading for impact. Those are not descriptions that apply to the people in power who we've been meeting.

"It's not enough, Sin." I look up at him, knowing I'm getting weepy but unable to stop it.

"They can't hear. I can't—" the tears are coming hot and fast now and I'm sniffly "—make them—" and Sin is making soothing noises and I blubber some more "—hear—" and Karl nearly succeeds in awkwardly patting my arm but "—Weaving—" Sin interrupts his hushing to bare his teeth at him and "—not enough—" the words spill like the blood under my skin. "What will be enough?"

* * *

I lie motionless in the dark, the cotton sheet cool below me.

Sleep has been erratic and elusive—pulling me under into total blackout for an hour here and there, then refusing to visit for days. When my body leaves me no other choice, allowing neither sleep nor further activity, I lie in Sin's arms, listen to his breathing, cocoon myself in his Song, and wait.

Once more, dawn arrives. The steel band around my ribs loosens a fraction. I manage to draw one breath that is a little fuller. And along with the light dawns the recognition that I'm back in the place where I began.

Metaphorically, and—literally. The estate is a cab ride away.

Suddenly I want to return to it. Need to assure myself that I'll feel different being there, that I'm not just back where I started. That I've changed, grown. I'm less of a spectre now. I'm solid. I have people who love me. I'm not alone. Not insane, either.

I know what's real.

I think.

And maybe completing the past will somehow open up a door into the future.

"What plan are you concocting, my Queen?" Still half asleep, Sin is rubbing a hand over his heart, as if to soothe the agitated determination he felt rise up in mine.

But I think I need to do this on my own. *Yes, I know I do.* I need to face my parents. Maybe...maybe they can even help me figure out a way. If they're even there.

"Uh-oh. I'm not going to like this, am I?"

Given that we're in one of the loudest centres of the Loud, calling me 'recovered' from yesterday would be generous, and I'm wanting to throw myself right into that forest of knives, without letting him shield me? *No, not at all.*

"Sweetheart." He wraps his arms around me, curls his whole body around me, as if to envelop me in his love.

I sink into more guilt, dredging the Bond down, down, down, like a rock in a thickly oily pond.

Sin sighs. "So you won't even let me accompany you on the way."

"I'm sorry," I whisper.

Sin grunts. Cinches his arms around me tighter. After several minutes, he grumbles back, "Don't be." But his arms stay locked for another few minutes, his face nuzzled into my hair, until he releases me with a groan.

Only because the rest of the Constellation comes knocking. They force some food into me before escorting me to a cab to at least safely see me off, however much they loathe it.

Soon—too soon—I'm churned up and chewed through from my unshielded trek through the Loud, and trembling with trepidation thanks to the gates before me that gleam in the morning sun. The estate. A place I frankly had no desire to see again when I ran from it.

The halls feel as cold as always, a stark contrast to the pulsing of warmth and life emanating from the grounds beyond. I'm tempted to beeline out there, find Dog and Cat and the deer and horses. Instead, my feet carry me to the library first.

It isn't unoccupied as I'd expected. I draw up short.

"Mother. Father."

My parents raise their heads from where they were poring over communications and newspapers, but don't get up.

"Zajasang! We—" Mother trails off. "What are you wearing?"

"Oh." I glance down at myself.

Father spares me from having to come up with an answer. "You didn't choose any of the programmes we spoke about."

We hadn't really spoken about it. It had been implied which programmes they were thinking of when they spoke of going abroad, and assumed that I would obediently choose one of them.

I just went abroad.

"We enquired after you after some time and were faced with some embarrassing conversations."

"I'm sorry."

"So?" Mother again, already seeming irritated with me after less than thirty seconds in my presence.

It's not the most exuberant or warm welcome from either of them.

Thankfully, I'm not the same daughter they saw last, over a year ago on my birthday. On Sacred Song, even if I didn't know that then. The night that was the pebble to the avalanche. The night that led me to open to the Song and follow it home. Because of that night, I can feel and hear the quiet baseline of my parents' concern, relief, and love thrumming beneath the sharper melee of feelings that find their outward expression.

"I found my people. I followed the Song, like you said. Thank you for that." I would have offered my gratitude for that incomparable gift either way. Knowing what I know now makes it that much easier. And despite the horror of the last week, a small smile hitches on my lips. "It gave me everything."

In ways they may never understand. But that's alright, because there are those who do. Which reminds me of something. "My great-grandaunt, what was her name?" Mother looks momentarily confused, and Father uncomfortable. "The one who left the instructions and named the girl born on May 1?"

"Oh. Daina."

Daina. *Thank you, Sister. You saved my life.*

"I see you have learned the art of secrecy. I trust you have at least been productive during this rogue mission of yours?"

My father's rough words fill me with amusement now, and I grin broadly at him. "Very." *Just not any way you can imagine.* Though that gives me an idea. "I've been travelling internationally the past couple of weeks. Been meeting with various of your colleagues." My smile slips. "I'd like to meet more." *Have to meet more. Meet, and make them understand.*

With that tiniest of morsels of insight into my life, Father's emotions flatten like the carpet in a study filled with pipe smoke. Content with the haze, my father is satisfied with this distant, distorted view of his daughter. His focus already returning to the documents in front of him, scanning a page, turning it over, and leafing through the stack below, he says, "There's a big international banquet coming up." He checks his calendar. "Three weeks. I'll see to it that your name is on the list."

Good—that's good. Lots of them in one place. It'll be awful. "Thank you. And Sinu Zielliatu, please."

"A colleague of yours?" Mother asks.

"Yes…" How can I explain to them who Sin is to me? "And more. He's important to me."

Father's head comes back up. He nods. "Bring him."

Would they understand if I tried explaining the Sung to them? Just how Sin and I are connected? We are partners in so many and signifiant ways; colleagues is as warped a description of our relationship as fledgling diplomat is of me. Then again, it's true enough that we are combining our strengths for a common goal. Maybe that shared language and understanding is enough.

"We have been working together, internationally, on the universal threat of the massively accelerated deterioration of the environment." This focus shouldn't surprise them—after all, it wasn't that long ago that I lived under this roof as a nature-loving half-savage who held biology and anthropology degrees. "I trust you're aware of the news around the gravely concerning recent environmental incidents and natural disasters. The news aren't even capturing half of it. This is serious and extremely urgent. Severe measures need to be implemented with immediate effect. We need all countries to come onboard, to work together for this."

The more I talk and try to get through to them, present the science alongside reports on the human impact, the more their eyes glaze over. The initial excitement and enthusiasm over their daughter actively sharing in their world vanes. This issue, what matters to me—it doesn't fit in with their beliefs and priorities. It doesn't touch or move them. To them, it is remote and easily swept aside.

So I try the only thing I can think of to make it less remote. To make it as real and alive and personal for them as it is for me. I extend strands of the Song to them—simple, pure, beautiful ones. And then I carefully extend a strand of the Dark Song. One that is heavy and dripping with the wrongness and harshness of the wound in the Weave.

"Do you feel that?" I whisper. "Can you hear that? That is what I'm talking about. That is what this is to me."

Their faces pale. Their eyes widen even as their lips press tight. Their Songs sing a minor key.

Then they blink, and I see them mentally pack me up in bubble wrap and put me on the hidden back corner of the shelf, where I'll catch dust and be forgotten. "You seemed to be doing much better, Zajasang."

I expect to see shards scattered all over the floor. Onyx, webbed with gold. Jagged.

Instead they hang suspended, caught in the warm golden light streaming through my Bond. There's nothing to cut my bare toes.

I start bleeding nonetheless.

* * *

"You're home." Sin felt his whole being relax when he could enclose Zajasang in his arms again. Three hours of her away from him—and unprotected—were three hours too many. He revelled in her warmth and softness against his hard torso, delighted in her unique, familiar scent. Burying his nose in her hair, then her neck, kissing her temple as he went, he murmured, "Right where you should be."

She made that little humming sound he so loved. In a voice like molten honey, Zaja said, "Right where I choose to be."

Sin's gut tightened and his chest swelled. If he wasn't the luckiest male in existence for it. He pulled back so he could look at her, marvel at her, kiss her.

And froze. "You're bleeding." His muscles tensed, the wild animal inside him prowling.

She hummed again—a noncommittal sort of sound this time that he liked a lot less. Her beautiful eyes gazing back at him were tired, strained—but there was a spark of her incandescent fire in them when she said, "Kiss it better."

Sin would never miss an opportunity to kiss her, so he gently closed his lips over the split in her lower one, taking care not to hurt her further. That didn't mean he was appeased. He had to watch her body suffer enough as it was. He didn't know whether to squeeze and shake her or wrap her up in the softest feather duvet he could find.

"So you get to go around hurting yourself, and you expect me to watch you do it and only swoop in afterwards to cauterise the wound?" Of course he always would, and gladly. In some ways it was what Bonded's Privilege was all about. It still didn't mean he had to like seeing her get hurt, and if he had anything at all to say about it, she wouldn't drive herself so far as to be hurt in the first place. Especially when she wasn't Dancing. Especially when it was damage to herself that was within her control. Sin drew himself up to launch into letting her know as much—

"Maybe."

"Pardon?" Wicked Wild, this female! "No, Zajasang, that's not good enough."

"No. Exactly. Not enough. Maybe that's what we need to do."

Sin deflated, his shoulders dropping, the incensed flare sputtering out with the rush of air escaping him. "Lady." He observed the faraway focus in her eyes. Her teeth worrying the already abused lip. Whatever page she'd jumped to, it wasn't back here with him and his concerns about her wellbeing. He sighed, and used his thumb to free and protect that lip he clearly cared so much more about than she did. "You've lost me."

Zajasang's gaze flitted and skipped some more, likely seeing things in the world in her unique way that he'd never be able to fathom. He waited patiently until she returned to him. He would always wait for her to return to him, no matter how long it took her.

"Cauterise the wound. Maybe that's something we can do, to buy ourselves more time." There was a slight hitch in her voice at the end of that sentence that made Sin uneasy, but she barrelled on. "We haven't been able to do the Weaving in the Song to fix it. It's so deep, so violent, we can't... I can't..."

The Coven Sisters couldn't reach it, and would be torn to shreds if somehow they ever did. And whilst his Queen could reach it—though Wicked Wild, he didn't want her to go there—and she could withstand it—at a personal cost he found unacceptable—even her incredible strength alone wasn't enough to match up against the tear in the Song, and the speed at which it grew.

"Talking to people here—it's not enough, and it's all too slow."

There she was. Her gaze had returned to his, and she was like a gem glinting at him from the far bottom of a clear lake. Still distant—but unmistakably present, and in reach.

"We'll continue doing that, continuing trying, but I think there's something else we can try as well. And I think we can start in Storm Court."

"So let's return to the Sung, sweetheart."

Zajasang nodded. "Let's go home."

As long as he was with her, he was already home. But Sin loved hearing her say it.

She had chosen to stay with them.

28

"Yes." I slow down and stop, kneading my toes into the warm, pliable earth the way Zuzu might do. "Here."

The air is humid and sweltering, thrumming with moisture and chirps and rasps. My senses are overflowing with the fullness of all that thrives here, the myriads of pulsing strands of life from an abundance of plants and insects and animals. The Loud is as full and overflowing, but there, the taint and jagged edges wreck me. This richness is pure—aside from the ichor emanating from the tear and coating everything.

"Here?" Sin smiles at me.

"Here." I return his smile. Simply being back in nature and away from the Loud has transformed us both. Has brought a levity humming between us that had been crushed for a while. There's a sense of hope to cling onto. My body is healthier. Things are wrong, but there also remains a sense of right.

"What do you need?"

I think on it for a moment. Come to a conclusion. Inhale and—

"Lady. Are you blushing?"

I wasn't. But the gleam in Sin's eyes and the curve in his smirk is rapidly making me.

"What do you...need...my Queen?"

Wicked Wild, he's enjoying this far too much. I pointedly turn away from him, though truthfully, it's a futile effort to hide from him how much I'm enjoying it, too.

"This is... Let's call it an anchor point."

Sin ghosts his fingers down my spine, leaving shivers in their wake, before massaging his thumb into a highly...sensitive...spot at the base. "Just like this."

"Yes." I breathe. "No! In the Weave...the foundational web that cocoons Earth."

"Mhmm." The skilled fingers of his hand splay across my back as his thumb continues its slow, persistent spiral, forming their own kind of rather magical web. "So the energy here is particularly...potent, would you say?"

A cackle splutters out of me. "Songs, Sin."

In the grin he flashes me I see a glimpse of the carefree, insolent boy I met on that beach so many years ago. He effectively swipes that image from my mind when his mouth sets to graze along the column of my neck.

"Major veins are converging here—"

"The blood runs hot and fast, as it were?"

"—so if I can pour myself—"

Sin clamps his teeth even as his tongue swipes hotly and his fingers dig in, and I break off on a gasp.

"What were you saying about pouring yourself?"

I growl at him, which only makes him chuckle. Wonderful.

I try again. "If I can Weave energy into the web here, strengthen the strands and flow in massive power at as many anchor points as we can make it to, it might—help."

Momentarily, Sin grows serious, holding me a little more tightly, and sweetly kissing where a minute ago he was lavishing.

"It might help," I repeat softly.

"So you need my power?"

"No, no it's not about magnitude, not massive power in the sense of brute force or undiluted quantities. What I mean is... the most powerful energy. The greatest power."

Sin kisses my neck again, thoughtful. Kisses my hair and my ear.

"My life in your Dance."

I wet my lips as I look out over the undulating sea of green and blue, land and water, spreading out before us. "Greater even than that."

"For the others, maybe." I feel Sin shaking his head behind me, a gentle growl in his chest resonating through me. "But for us... They are one and the same."

He speaks into my ear, making sure I hear him with perfect clarity. "You are my breath, you are my heart, you are my greatest Dance, Zajasang. My joy in your Dance. My pride in your Dance. My strength in your Dance." The swell and spill of his conviction is singing and searing through my cells. "My soul in your Dance, my Love. Your Dance—your life—you."

His truth.

I breathe a grand, gusty sigh, and blink the tears from my eyes. "Everything."

"Everything."

For a while, we stand entwined, Sin's sinewy arms holding me to his broad chest and his nose resting in my hair. Our love is a tangible, limitless force between us, glowing warm and golden as it flows through my veins, and I flow, flow, flow it out through my feet and my crown, into the web and out, out along the strands of the Weave.

It might help.

"Lady?"

"Hm?"

The beat of hesitation is enough to rouse me from my dreamy bliss and make me narrow my eyes in expectant wariness.

"That's not what made you blush."

"I didn't!"

"Darling, I happen to be an extraordinarily lucky and privileged kind of male who happens to have this precious Bond—"

Pesky thing, really.

"—which I highly covet, deeply cherish, and will rabidly defend, in case that wasn't clear—" at that I'm on the receiving end of an emphatic stare "—that allows me to feel your blush before it ever graces any part of your mesmerising, delicious skin."

Sin, once again, looks far too pleased with himself and the world.

I clear my throat, then adopt as nonchalant a tone as I can manage. "It simply occurred to me, for the briefest of moments, that the highest form of energy can express itself in various..."

"Flavours?"

I don't answer, merely returning my focus to the Weave.

"So...what do you need me to do?"

When I stay mute, he pokes my side and I squeak. Males.

"You were already doing a good job of it earlier," I mutter, and literally feel his chest puff up and expand behind me.

"Oh, I can do a better job." Sin's laugh is as dark and wicked as the deepest realms of the Song. His hand begins to wander. "A much better job."

"I have no doubt."

"I would hope so, sweetheart." A pause, as he gives his full, undivided attention to his wandering hands and mouth conjuring a different...flavour. As he ensures he has mine, too. "Who would have thought there could be so much fun had while saving the world?"

Songs. Sometimes the only thing you can do is to either laugh or cry, and often it is one and the same anyway. And isn't that the true beauty of life? So I stop thinking, and give myself over to feeling. Feeling all of it. Tear, tragedy, and thrilling exultation.

My last coherent thought isn't mine at all. It's Sin's promise —more devastatingly prescient than he knows. "My Queen, I will be on my knees for you, and you will pour."

* * *

"Do you need us for the anchor points?" Anda asked.

They were back in one of Storm's courtyards. Too soon, by Sin's account. He'd have happily stayed out there in the cathedral of sunshine and flowers and ocean vistas for several more hours, worshipping at the altar of his goddess and Queen.

"Yes."

Sin whipped his head around. *Yes?* A few menacing growls escaped his chest before he could snuff them out. After what he'd just partaken in with his Lady, he was reluctant to even share her presence with anyone. It was a Weaving, a kind of Dance, unlike any other. The closest comparison he could come up with was Sacred Song.

Zaja glanced over at him, her eyes full of mirth. It didn't matter that he'd cut off any protests he'd wanted to very loudly voice—to her they were equally loud whether given voice or not.

Fine. His Bond brothers were part of her Constellation. This was important. It all made sense. Still, he'd damn well make sure they wouldn't...assist...her the way he'd had.

At that thought, he found himself on the receiving end of another glance. With a quirked eyebrow.

Sin's jaw ground, and he forced himself to soften his coiled muscles.

...Unless that's what she desired.

Wicked Wild, does she? No. That was not the kind of relationship she had with his brothers. Yes, that was it. They were like brothers to her. Then again, there was Adara as a living example of a different way the Constellation relationships could look. Had he been so wrapped up in himself that he'd missed something? Something vital? Was this a factor in why she was so strained?

Songs, if—if that truly was a desire of hers, an experience that would bring her bliss, the Song knew he would give it to her. He'd ask that as her Dark Destined, he'd retain the privilege of taking the lead. He'd ask that it wouldn't mean quite the same. But he'd give it to her, and give his all to the experience.

Didn't change that he hoped desperately this wasn't what she was asking.

Mine. His beast was building up to a violent rage with where his panicked thoughts were taking him. He'd need to find a safe way to process through it. Away from Zaja, so it wouldn't hurt her. But being away from her wasn't tenable, either. *Mine.*

Sin's awareness snapped back to the present, noticing that Zajasang was still holding his gaze.

When he saw her eyes soften, felt the tender glow of her Bond, a deep breath rushed into his starving lungs. Oh thank the Song.

Wicked Wild.

That had been a trip. A wild one he never wanted to go down again. How in all the Songs had he even ended up on it? Possessiveness was in his nature, was part of who they were as Sung Heart males. It didn't always work in their favour—but this had been extreme.

Clearly Zajasang wasn't the only one bending under her burden.

Sin seethed and punched a wall. He wanted to be strong for her, not add to the weight. Losing his head wasn't going to do any good to anyone.

Tavo guffawed now, clapping him on the shoulder. Anda was shaking his head and grinning. And Yako...decided to rub it in by sweeping Zaja into his arms and giving her a big, exaggerated, wet kiss on the neck.

His Queen laughed and swatted him away, then reached for Sin's hand and kissed the tips of his fingers, then his knuckles. He didn't relinquish her hand when she dropped it.

"Whereto, my Queen?" Having already raced far beyond the moment, Yako was bouncing on his toes, endless boyish excitement and thirst for adventure thrumming through him like always.

"There are three anchor points I want to stop off at on the way, but then..." Zaja graced him with one of her brilliant, heart-stopping smiles. "Crystal."

29

CRYSTAL COURT

THEIR BREATH FROZE IN THE air, yet Sin didn't feel the cold as the clear night sung with crystalline notes and shivered over their skin. In the darkly luminous sky, colours shifted in rhythm, as glorious and spectacular as the vibrant Bond glowing between the five of them, forming its own little web of radial and tether lines... All of which converged with Zajasang. It was an orchestration of the whole Universe dancing with them, a dance expressed through every physical sense, the Song made sublimely tangible.

Zaja's laugh trilled through the night. The huskies responded to her...and so did Sin.

Despite his worst paranoid fears, Dancing at the anchor points with his Lady and his Bond brothers had turned out to be an experience of consummate beauty. Instead of concentrating on specific healing that was required, on fixing fissures and mending tears, instead of spooling away in the Song with only a thin thread leading back, their Queen stayed close.

315

Sin shuddered in delight. Sharing the Song was always intimate. But somehow, the way she connected and stayed with them in these Dances as the Song flooded through her... doubled it.

He stepped and circled. Leading and following were one. Their Queen moved with the melodies that lifted and guided her limbs, leading the Dance, and they moved in to guard and guide her body on the physical plane...leading that dance. She followed the Song and they followed her, and led her in turn.

Like the unique splendour of ice crystals, their dance was ever-evolving, flowing from one formation into the next. Now they were holding onto one another, spiralling around an axis, a star set to spin. Yako whooped, and Sin grinned. He had known Zajasang's Bonds with the rest of her Constellation were deep, and as valid as his own. But now he understood. Now he had tasted their flavour of love for her—and they had tasted his.

It had benefitted all of them.

Tavo dipped and caught Zaja as she surrendered into her body's deep sway, lifted her, and sent her arcing through the night to complete the impetus of her movement. Their very own meteor, rendering them breathless with her beauty in one eternal frozen moment of streaking through the dark. She was that magical, mythical fire that hurtled to them from distant realms, to be admired while she graced them with her presence, to pray upon before she was gone.

Seamlessly, Anda plucked her out of the air like a star from the heavens. No sooner had her toes gently touched the ground as that she twirled on. She was lost to the Song, trusting them entirely with her body. Had she even known she'd been flying through the air? There was no up nor down in the Song, no gravity and force of reason. Flying was her natural state.

Maybe the Song is where she truly belongs. More than with me.

But Sin had no time, no space or bandwidth for anguish. Rather then leading them into the Dark, Zajasang led them into diamantine love sparkling in facets he and his brothers didn't even know existed. The more familiar he was becoming with this indescribable experience of this wondrous kind of Dance that he was sure one could never grow used to, the more Sin began to tease out new notes in the energy. Beyond the specific flavour of the love flowing between her and each of her Bonded, he tasted the love flowing between her and the huskies...the Coven...the glaciers...the Song itself.

Life made love with her, and every new flavour Sin tasted infused and intensified the flavour of his own.

All of it, she channeled and wove and wove and wove into the web. It was a sustained, orgasmic experience of untouchable beauty.

It almost became easy to forget that there was a gaping wound in the Weave which scraped Zajasang raw every minute of every day, and his Queen was wasting away before his eyes.

That she would only waste away faster in the Loud.

And that they'd soon need to return to the Loud to attend the banquet and continue the fight on that other end of the bridge—before the bridge broke away completely.

* * *

Leaning into the icy wind rushing down the steep snowy incline and twining around us, I heave myself another step. Every inch of my skin is slathered in sweat and my thighs are trembling. Yet I'm determined to reach the plateau up ahead. Determined to share this Dance with Sin. Only Sin, and only there.

I don't even know why, exactly. *But I must.*

The sled and huskies are waiting below, the rest of the Constellation is back in the coziness of the Court. If Sin preferred to be there, too, instead of out here in the unforgiving white, he doesn't let on. Instead he's plastered so closely to my back it must be aggravating to take any step at all without getting tangled up in my legs.

"You know," I puff, "if you were in front of me—"

"No."

"But—"

"No. Can't trust you not to tumble down the mountain."

"You'd be a wind shield. And I could hold onto you."

Sin snakes his arm around me and holds out a crooked finger. "Hook into me then."

I do, using three fingers. He tugs. And slides out of my grasp without any resistance at all.

Scowling and huffing, I climb another step.

"Darling, we could just slide back down this mountain right now."

"No."

"It'd be fun."

"No."

"I could make being back at Court in front of a fire on furs really fun."

I growl and snap my teeth at him over my shoulder. Sin laughs, but breaks off and begins growling himself when the move causes me to lose my footing and slide backwards into him—all the five inches there are to go.

"Wicked Wild, Zajasang—"

"Trust me." *I must.*

We don't speak again until we reach the edge of the plateau and scale it. The view of sparkling plains of ice and snow extending before and below would take my breath if I had any left.

Sin keeps me well away from the drop, firmly holding onto me as if expecting me to hurl myself right off, or that the wind might swirl around, pick me up like a feather, and send me over any moment—never mind that he's seen me go over a sheer drop many times.

Who knows, maybe he's right. Everything's skewed. The wind didn't come to coax and lift me either in the last forty minutes, instead battering down on us mercilessly. The cold rage of a Song bleeding hot.

"I'm scared for you." Sin's fingers ghost over the bruises blooming under my skin.

I turn my head into the hand cradling my cheek and kiss his palm. "I know."

His eyes continue to trace my face, to track every sign of pain and exhaustion. "Is it helping? The anchor points?"

Is it worth it, is what Sin is asking. Is it worth pushing my body this way. "It's... keeping us in stasis." He stays quiet, allowing me to sort through my thoughts. As always, he just— stays. Offering me his presence, his strength. It's a gift I will never stop loving him for. "It was about buying time, right? I guess that's what it's doing. It's...staunching the blood flow. Without it, we'd have bled out by now. With it, it's not really fixing anything, not really saving us, but it's keeping us where we're at." My teeth are worrying my lip again, much to Sin's chagrin. "Alive, if barely. Keeping us in a space where we can still find a way to be saved."

All of Dark's Queens are spread out to anchor points across the globe and flowing love into the Weave the better part of the hours in a day. After that memorable first attempt in Storm, when I put the idea into practice with Sin and knew it could work, I'd called together the Coven. Mrak fell over with laughter after teasing some of the finer points of detail out of me about just how the experience had unfolded—all in the name of being sure to fully understand what I was asking them to do, of course. Then we all collapsed into a tragic heap of tears saying our goodbyes, and our promises to come together again in the Song. The males had been riled up and ruffled by the time we emerged from our feminine bubble of high emotion and fell into *their* arms, ready to set out in all directions of the compass to weave a web unlike any other.

"Alright, good." Sin's fingers sink under my hair and massage my scalp. I notice how carefully he is controlling his emotions, allowing nothing but soothing reassurance and trust to flow from his touch. "What else? There's more rumbling around in here."

Closing my eyes, I do my best to screen out everything but the smokey pine flavoured threads of thick honey seeping from his careful ministrations. Miraculously, it does help me put things in order.

"All Queens—from all Courts, the entire Coven—will need to join in now to help and keep it going. We all need to spread out to anchor points and flow the love in as continuously as we can. The traditional Weaving is becoming harder and harder to do for my Sisters as it is, with the Song becoming gnashing and snarling to the point of dangerous even above the Dark, so instead of trying to reach each broken thread and glue it, we need to just..." My hands gesticulate in an attempt to illustrate what I can see in the energy. "Pour glue over the whole thing and try to coat it in it."

"So that's good." I open my eyes to Sin nodding. "It's an intermediary solution of sorts, keeping things stable whilst we go into the Loud."

"Maybe." I blow out a breath, clinging to that certainty and assuredness in Sin's gaze. I can't fathom where he is taking it from. "For now, the Loud is raging on as always, piling on hurt after hurt."

A grunt, making it quite clear what he thinks about that.

"So what the Sung are doing, what we've been doing, the Queens pouring the glue—it may be enough to hold the scales even..."

Sin looks me in the eyes with fiery determination, as if he could make it so by sheer force of will alone.

"Or they may tip regardless."

He tucks me in against his chest and wraps an arm around my head, like he is hoping against hope to hide me from that terrifying possibility.

But I can't hide from it. "I'll gather all Sisters in Crystal and meet with the Queens in the Song tonight—and then we need to return to the Loud tomorrow." And worse, I'll have to split up the Constellation, send the rest of my Bonded off to different corners of the Loud to try and cover more ground simultaneously. But I don't tell him that now. It's enough for my stomach to turn over with dread at the prospect of that goodbye. *No way of knowing how final it'll be.*

"What?" Sin stiffens. "Zajasang, no. It's too early. The banquet's not for two weeks."

"Even so. The banquet is like an anchor point in the Loud— one place to impact that will spread out and reach many. But there are different Loud anchor points. Ways to speak to the people directly, not just those governing them. We need to find those. Find those who will hear us—more people like Karl—but who will also be heard by the greatest number of others." My voice grows hoarse, pleading. I think I'm pleading with myself most of all. "We need to do more. Everything we can."

"Lady." There is no question who Sin is pleading with. "Your body is breaking down even here. It'll be so much worse there."

All I can do is silently shake my head, helplessly raise my arms. Sin is right, of course.

Still. I have to go.

A muscle twitches in his clenched jaw. Then he cradles my head with his hands buried in my hair, shaking me as gently and ferociously as those two things can be done together. "I love you, and I love how much I love you, and I hate how much I love you, and how much it hurts to love you." An agonised sort of growl escapes him. "And I wouldn't ever give it up, and won't ever stop loving you."

Every word he lays at my feet punches through me in deep pink and fuchsia and blood red on its way there. Drawing in a tremulous breath, I reach up to caress his jaw where that muscle still tics, trace his lips, stroke his cheekbone...and catch the tear that slipped his leash.

"Sin. Do you have visions? Do you remember when we have loved each other before?"

He gives a wretched sort of half shake of his head. It's a no of the conscious mind completely contradicted by the utterly certain, rejoicing yes of his heart, his gut, his Bond.

I have his head in my own determined hold now, making sure his focus is fully with me, and he receives everything I have to give, no matter how blurred our gazes are from both our tears. "I even remember how we will love each other again."

A whimpered laugh. Sin melds his mouth to mine in a kiss of equal despair and awe. "What else would I do but love you no matter where we are in space and time? Everything, sweetheart. Everything."

More kissing, and more crying.

"But I don't want to think about loving you again. I want to love you now. Please let me love you." The unspoken words sing in the cajoling of his lips, the imploring of his tongue. Please don't leave. Stay.

Stay. Stay. Stay. It has been an internal chorus pulsing with my heartbeat for longer than he knows.

Still we hold onto each other's faces, gazes, souls. Unwilling to ever let go.

But we don't have ever.

I find the exact place where the strands of the web meet and the energy is the strongest, face out across the vastness, and securely plant my feet. Sin moulds his body to mine, unwavering strength at my back. When my arms rise and extend, his follow, two bodies moving as one. His fingers link with mine, keeping me present and anchored to him.

That is all the dance that is needed today, for this Dance of endless love.

So we stand together like a burning cross, a monument of the divine fire of sacred union amid the ice, riding the waves of love as if we're standing in the bow of a ship. The energy we channel is so rich, so powerful beyond compare that it rushes and roars through me into the web, wisps of it emanating outwards from us in heat that melts the snow and in light that gets reflected in the millions of crystals all around us.

High atop this snowy cliff, this one cliff I do not go over, we become our own Firefall.

For this moment, we have forever.

* * *

That night, I gather with the Sisters of Crystal.

Queen or not, the connections between females are vital and closely woven among the Sung. Queens may be the ones who work and meet in the Dark Song and can share the Song with others. But all females hear at least its hum when in the throes of strong emotion. We all have our own access. We are all female. We are nature. We are the Song and the heart of the Sung. All of us.

Outside, the males are guarding, watchful, their gazes turned outward. Protecting without intruding. Securing the boundaries of our space while honouring it.

Inside, safe in our majestic shelter of ice and wood and stone and fire, we talk and laugh and light candles. We tell stories and cry and sit still and listen. We shake and give expression to what needs to be heard. We prepare.

And then, together, we dance. We dance in joy, in celebration, for our own pleasure. We dance freely and wildly, fast or slow, following the call and flow of the earth, our blood, our bones. Elated, we meet each other's eyes, and settle into the sacredness of this gathering.

We remember ourselves the priestesses and holders of ancient embodied mysteries, remember those who have come before us to initiate us into these holy feminine secrets, and those coming after us to pass them on to. We know these practices to be ours, to enjoy for our own connection to divinity, and to share with those we are connected to in love and who honour us, so they may come to know their connection to divinity, too.

The air vibrates with the charge of holiness and remembrance and sacred recognition of truth. This magic, it is ours, uncoiling from the core of each of us, a snake rousing and rising. So we begin to dance with her sensuous glide along our curves, following her path with the tips of our fingers, enticing her with the press of our hands, feeding her into frissons of pleasure. We shed any layers standing between us and her, revealing ourselves to her fully, so we can fully receive her gifts. Sweat beads on our skin as our bodies begin to make their own music, weaving together into raw harmonies with the sounds of our Sisters, and with the Song thrumming in each of us. With each stroke of our hands on our body the energy rises, spiralling amongst us...the divine feminine force becoming tangible.

When we look around, we see the beauty of bodies writhing and enraptured, surrendered to the Goddess' gentle guidance, whispered to us in the language of erotic ecstasy. We witness our Sister lying on the ground, her heart wide open as her breasts arch to the moon she feels high above. We witness our Sister standing with her arms raised and her head thrown back as her knees shake from the force of the energy moving through her. We witness in love as it reaches her throat, and she sings the sounds of her pleasure, or laughs the joy of her delight in unleashed abandon. We are her and she is us and we are all Song.

This is the way of the witches. We dance the thunder of the storm without and within. We embrace the messiness and illuminate a path through uncertainty with our passion. We look the darkness in the eyes and see ourselves and we cackle. A space of witches is a space of the womb, that holy chalice of darkness where all beings are initiated into the glory of life. It is in the dark that all things are created.

So as our bodies become the harp we play, as we twirl naked and chase our pleasure and are wholly free however we choose to be, a wind whips up in this sacred space. A maelstrom comes to life.

Just like the spiral of the Song that infinitely opens up beneath us.

A peal of laughter glides over my skin—Mrak. A fierce bucking of freedom lifts my hips—Adara. Two vibrant dervishes intertwine and whirl around us—Tama and Feny come together in the Song. Vala sighs over us like a lowering veil of silk on skin. There is Janaina, and Aracely, Omulara, Ivy, Anthea, every Queen from every Court like the featherlight brush of a wing on the edge of our own experience, filling our hearts with joyous celebration for their existence.

Each of us our own note of sensation and pleasure added to the harmony.

Each of us a vibrating string on the Witch Harp of the Goddess.

This is the way of Sisters meeting in the Song.

This profound and pure love between Sisters, we pour into the web, too.

And in the space beyond space and between time, the Queens of the Dark Court pass on the dire knowledge and the urgent task, reverberate and sing it out, until it is humming in the Song, right below the surface, for every Sung to feel and every Queen to find.

For we do not know how much longer we'll be able to enter the Song, and when we'll be able to meet this way next.

Love, the message sings, *love as fiercely as you can, and share of that love beyond yourself.*

Like a golden healing lava or flood or ether, let it flow forth from you in your truth and essence and coat the web until it cloaks the world.

Go where many strands of the web meet, where the energy is the strongest. Share it there so it can flow out.

Give of your love.

I add the final whisper. An afterthought spun out of me in a flash of knowing. One last thing I need to pass on.

Watch the webs of our spider Sisters when the Song becomes too violent for you to enter.

30

The Loud

No matter the horror and pain, I get one moment of reprieve every day.

Always, I awake to the feeling of Sin's arms around me, his hands caressing my face and body, the touch flowing through me in velvets and pinks. His eyes on me are full of tenderness and fire, awe and gratitude. I bloom open under his emerald gaze, and the more I open, the more he looks directly into my soul. I watch him behold me and be overcome in love.

And in this very moment of each new day, every day is divine.

"Exquisite," he mumbles now, before pillaging my lips in a way that does honour to his name. From my lips he moves to my cheeks, my nose, my forehead, my eyelids. With maddening precision and patience, he rains gentle kisses on every inch of my body like rose petals settling on a tranquil pond in golden morning light. Each touch of his lips adds to the fizzling festivities in my blood.

"Sin," I breathe, when his warm hands slide underneath my back and arch me up for him to better reach.

"You're my violoncello," he says, smirking. I'm too melted in exultation to manage more than the imitation of a raised brow. "All gorgeous elegant lines and soft curves that I love to cradle... And the better I sway and play you..." He demonstrates his virtuosity. When he speaks again, his tone is reverent. "The more music I hear."

As if to prove him right, both the Song and my moans crescendo in symphony.

Sin has decided we ought to bask in bliss every moment we can.

Sin has decided blocking out the worries of reality as much as humanly possible, anytime we are not actively doing something to fight for the fate of the Earth, is the way to go.

Only a love and desire and determination as powerful as Sin's could keep it all from intruding and actually have made me forget for a few moments of paradise.

But a few moments is all I manage before I remember the hell that humans have been making of the heaven that is Earth. Deep sadness spreads through me, weighing down my limbs. I cling to the refuge Sin and I have sought in each other, try to hide us in it like a turtle in her shell.

It gets heavier and heavier alarmingly fast. I try to lift a hand —and find I can't. I try to speak, to call out to Sin, make any noise at all—and can't do that either.

That sadness isn't my distress over the overall situation resurfacing.

Only I obscured that truth even from myself by burrowing into that bony shelter—until I can no longer avoid it when my spine is nearly broken in half by a comet of pain blasting a crater into our canopy. It crashes down on me, its impact erupting out of my throat.

"Oh, no, no, no, no. No. Not happening."

But it is.

Sin grips my face between his hands, slams a hard kiss against my screaming mouth, and stares into my eyes as if to hold me there by sheer will alone.

I'm not sure he can. I'm going under.

"Not again. Stay with me, Zaja. Use me. Songs, stay with me."

His blown pupils are tracking back and forth between mine. It feels like he's trying to push the entirety of his essence through the Bond to me, like he's trying to wrap his being around mine.

Yet I sink.

Tears are swimming in his eyes, the sea drowning the forest. "Don't shut me out. Stay." Sin continues to mutter, continues to beg. "I'm sorry. I'm sorry. Please, Zajasang. I need you to stay."

He is breaking. He wasn't made to be broken.

So I try as hard as I can, try to cling to him and stay, while the pain steadily obliterates me.

Resisting it is harder. It would be easier to let go. To let myself be swept away in it. Like being caught in a vortex, fighting against it takes everything out of you. If you let it take you, you ride into the depths with it. You may come out—or it may take you too deep to come back from. Either way, resisting it is harder.

But that's what Sin is asking.

So for him, I try.

I try to cling to this cliff, even with my hands bloody and slipping, and the ferocious wind pulling me, and the hail pelting me. With the abyss of absence creeping up my legs.

Somewhere, my body is contorting, and shrieking sounds press between clamped teeth.

But I keep my gaze locked with Sin. Seeing him.

Sometimes, I slip.

Slip away, and down, and lose sight of him.

But then I fight until I see him again. Until I'm there again. I have to fight to give this to him.

Because I think we're too late for anything else.

It's not just the winged whales that are gone now. It's also most of the coral and fish.

* * *

I'm in a blessed haze of half-consciousness, distantly aware of my body wrapped up in Sin's. My thoughts trudge in delicate loops.

Bridge.

That's supposed to be me.

Banquet.

Where I'm supposed to go.

Together. With Sin.

Gone.

Too late.

A long silence comes after that.

Bridge.

I'm the one who can weave back and forth.

Sung. Loud. Sung. Loud.

Bridge.

Banquet.

Too late.

Sin.

Banquet.

No good now...

I slip off the loops into the memory of what it would have been like.

Too loud, too shrill. Surreal to be shut away in this detached delusional bubble of clinking glasses and shoulder claps in the middle of a collapsing world. Partying on while the Titanic sinks.

Sin there with me. We are here together, belonging together. Introduce ourselves together. Mother, meet Sin, my Bonded and Dark Destined. Father, meet Sin, who is everything.

Speak to people. Speak to everyone we can. Carried off to separate ends of the grand room, trying to make people hear and see and understand. *Too late, no good now...*

Too loud, too shrill. The to do and the fluttering, the boisterous forced laughter, the touches on arms and hands leaving smears. Balance so off, scales so tipped. Too much, can't breathe.

Too late, too loud.

Where—*there.* A glance across the gulf of noise. It's enough.

Outside, blindly stumbling, outside, *let me go, excuse me, please,* outside.

High terrace.

Breathe, I can breathe. Slow down. I unravel, I can think.

I am a person. *I am me.*

The air is fresh and light without toppling over into chill. Mountain on my tongue with each breath. The sky and the valley, vast and dark above and below, yawn open a cosmos in my chest. A thimble on the inhale. A universe on the next. The sparkling specks in the tapestry are glimmering tears in my heart.

Such beauty. So sad to say goodbye to.

I sense Sin's warmth behind me.

Greater beauty still. Impossible to say goodbye to.

One more mountain breath for courage. Then a pirouette.

We are lost in each other for eternity, a last time savoured like the first. He steps close and whispers a thumb over my cheek. One of those tears had become a diamond for him. His forehead to mine, shared breath, shared soul. Reverence for the energies between us. They are the softest, most velvety petals dancing in the wind. Weaving two harmonies into one symphony.

The agony of bliss, the tragedy of passion.

A kiss where a moment before we were connected, a kiss on my nose, a kiss on my eyelids—flying out of my skin with hunger for him—hunger that has built in the minutes since he followed me out here, that has built for lifetimes and aeons—that has built in the despair of a looming goodbye.

Whose trembling is whose when our lips taste one another?

Inside's humdrum has long since shifted to a murmuring.

Outside's silence remains complete, singing so richly for us.

Our Song.

Too late for the Song.

Too late...

Slowly, I'm rising through the haze.

The thick stupor is suffering punctures of the Loud seeping through with spear-sharp points. *No. No, no, no. Not ready for that yet.* Need this—this haze—

Need this space for something.

I stumble up like a muddled marionette.

"Zaja." Sin's voice is the string that jerks on my heart.

"Forgive me."

Was that his voice or mine?

The haze is thinning. Can't have it thin yet.

I reach the bathroom door and lock it between us.

* * *

The water of the shower pounds my skin like apocalyptic sleet.

I stand, numb, staring blankly ahead.

Waiting.

Then a shudder rises from my womb, crawls through my heart, and by the time it reaches my throat, it is a loud, awful, broken sound. It starts and it stops.

My hand juts to the wall, holding myself steady. For another second I stand, waiting, listening in the now edgy silence.

A tear trickles down my cheek.

Then I wail.

Keening, torn, terrible grief is a torrent that swallows me whole, and I wail. I clutch at my chest, my throat, my stomach, as if I could rip out the pain. When it is close to unbearable, I at last give in to it. Ride it. All the grief that lives inside me—for once, not the one the world shunts through me, but mine—I give myself over to it.

Finally, the grief I held in all those years growing up completely alone, the only person in my world, finally this grief, too, sings its song.

I grieve for the Zaja I was in the Loud, and for the Zaja I could have been among the Sung. For all of me, and all of the me who I have rejected and kept at bay.

I grieve for a past and future that could have been, and I grieve for the past and future that was.

For the present.

For the time that's run out.

For knowing deep down what I must do now, and what I will do. I grieve for the despair of it...and for the joy and relief of it. Oh, how it shudders through me.

But most of all, I grieve for Sin.

For loving him—and leaving him—and losing him.

I wail, and I grieve.

Until eventually, the grief has nothing left to sing, and I feel a hollow clean on the inside to match the flayed clean of the outside, and every shred of the haze is gone. And I know what must come next.

It was there all along, no matter how much I fought it.
Sin even was the one to tell me.
A shower, of all things, helped me accept it.
In her Dark cascade, life is restored.

31

Ｔʜᴇ Ｌᴏᴜᴅ

"Zᴀᴊᴀsᴀɴɢ?"

Sin's own voice rang like an echo in his ear. *Zajasang?*

It was what he'd said when she'd unlocked that bathroom door between them yesterday morning. When he'd felt as hollow as she'd felt. When he had broken while she had fallen apart. When he'd been scared to death that she'd wanted distance from him *because* of him.

It had taken only one look from her, one touch, to wipe all that away.

She had remained hushed, deep in thought, the rest of the day, but never far from him. Then she'd asked they travel here—a place they'd never been before and that didn't mean anything to him—and had stayed close again. Until an hour ago, when she requested space for herself. *To prepare.*

For what, Sin had no idea.

It was like she'd dipped under the surface and had held her breath since emerging from the bathroom. Everything halted. No frantic running around and contacting people. No self-

335

sacrificing Weaving. Not even the anchor point kind of Dance. Instead of desperately doing, Zajasang had spent the last two days... Being.

Sin had been glad for it—initially. He'd had enough days of watching her drive herself into the ground, no matter the noble, and very real, cause. The primal protectiveness of his nature wanted to get her into a soft bed and resting for weeks to make up for it all. But of course the whole thing was a conundrum—when she rested, the world unravelled, and the worse the Song got, the worse she got, but the more she tried to singlehandedly keep the world stitched together, the more that took its toll on her as well. And back around it went.

At least, since yesterday morning, there had been a hint of peace in the bouquet that was Zajasang, a tiny quiet bloom tucked in amidst all the sadness and pain. So he'd been glad for it. Until he'd caught her reflection in the mirror sheen of a window, when she'd thought herself unobserved. She'd held in silent sobs, and had furiously dashed away tears rolling down her cheeks before he might have discovered them.

With the subtle rumbling of an earthquake rolling through the seabed, changing the currents and building new waves, the serene reprieve of stillness had taken on the ominous sense of the silence before the storm.

And Sin had begun to worry, a more earnest wariness than the trepidation that had become baseline. He'd begun to fear the sort of Queen's Dance she'd dance with this storm that wasn't in the skies, and yet he felt looming.

My Queen... What are you up to? He'd waited through the hour.

Then she had brought him out to this natural half cave at the bottom of a desolate cliff—where else. He hadn't been able to help the half groan, half chuckle when they'd reached the bluff top, and her crooked smile had been adorable. Zaja had deigned to take the slow way down with him, until their feet had met coarse sand and their skin had been misted in the cold ocean spray. Hand in hand, she'd led him into the shelter of the massive rock, the rich darkness lit by dozens of candles, a woven blanket on the ground.

Where she had disappeared from him again. He would have panicked had he not felt her through the Bond in crisp vibrancy.

So he'd waited for her. *Have, my whole life. Will, always.*

He hadn't wanted to disturb anything, hadn't dared sit down. Sin had stood where she'd left him and waited.

And then there she was, coming towards him.

He drew himself up to his full height and broadened his shoulders as he watched her approach him. A simple, light gown flowed enticingly over her body, her moonstones rested on her chest, and she was carrying a small jar in her hand. Most of all, Sin was ensnared by the queer light of determination in her eyes. Which was why he called her name.

A question, an invocation, a prayer. The first time he'd learned it. The first time he'd kneeled before her. Every time until the last time.

"Zajasang?" It echoed through the cave like it had echoed through his mind.

His Lady kissed him sweetly—so sweetly the storm clouds cleared and the moon shone through, serene and bright.

Just for now, for this, he simply wanted to be here with her.

And she went about undressing him.

Oh. Sin's body tightened and loosened simultaneously. *Alright.* He could get onboard with this plan. But when he tried to return the gesture, when his fingers went searching for the places her gown knotted and clasped, she pushed his hands away. The side of his mouth quirked up. "My Queen?"

She kissed him again—just as sweetly innocent, and telling him in just as certain terms to shut up.

Well, his darling Queen clearly was up to something. With him. Right here in his arms and reach. Safe. And Sin lived in her Dance, so whatever she wanted to do, wherever she was going with this... He was more than happy to follow her lead.

He watched attentively as she set the jar to the side, guided him to a seat on the soft blanket, and kneeled before him. For a long time, his Lady looked deep into his eyes. The Song rose with every moment, standing his hair on end. Sin did his best to decipher its mysteries, its feminine language of emotion and aliveness. There was reverence and honour, dedication and devotion. That resolute determination. And love. The love filling the Bond was unmistakable.

It was a song of deep beauty.

Beauty—but not happiness. The storm remained waiting in the wings.

Sin's throat closed up and he swallowed against it, gulping air into a too tight chest.

Her eyes darkened. Rain began to gather in them, heralding whatever it was that was moving in on them. But before Sin could catch the tear welling over, Zaja bat at it and gently set her fingertips to his forehead. She began tracing every line of his features—slowly. With so much intent it became hard to concentrate on anything but her warm touch. The rain, the storm, it was all moved aside, to be remembered later. There was only her skin meeting his. Her fingers caressed the line of his brows...the more delicate skin of his eyelids and below his eyes...the line of his nose...the path of his cheek- and jawbones...traced the seam of his lips and then each one individually when they parted on his aroused intake of breath.

Like she's committing me to memory.

The fleeting thought was a sheep bleating across the dusty hillside before it was chased away by the blaze of the wildfire. Inexorably, the fire ravaged him, originating from the tips of those soft, magical fingers. She switched her attention between following where her fingers went, and returning to look deeply into his eyes.

Finding yourself the utter, full, and single focus of a being who constantly held in her experience the sensations of a whole world was more electrifying than being touched by lightning. Sin was panting, his body spasming with the energy shooting through it, before Zaja even touched his ears and ran her fingers through his hair and along his scalp.

Then she trailed her hands down his neck—and brought her mouth into play.

"Zaja," Sin groaned.

The Song was steady in its carrying melody. Her hands and lips kept up her ministrations. In sure strokes and caresses they glided along his shoulders. She moved around him and kissed her way across his back, came back to his front and ran hands and lips alike down his chest.

"Songs—sweetheart—"

All that he felt, all that there was, was pleasure and aliveness.

Around back again, kissing her way excruciatingly slowly down his spine...caressing down the sides of his ribcage... making him feel like he had actual wings when she explored the wide panes of his back.

Sin was trembling, his muscles in constant involuntary little twitches now, his skin dampening. He could taste her soul's essence on his tongue, so connected he felt to her, so bathed in her awareness.

Circling around once more, Zaja stopped her descent before she reached his abdomen and instead moved back up to his arms. Exquisitely torturous minutes later she reached his hands

—and he had never known this much pleasure elicited from the touch of hands.

Sin sucked air through his teeth and hissed it back out. "Wicked Wild." He was desperate to touch her, to hold on to her. When she moved to the sculpted lines of his core, his hands clamped on to her for dear life. When she moved lower, his moans became an accompaniment to the rousing Song.

On and on she continued, never wavering in her thundering focus, always returning those extraordinary eyes to look deep into him... Inevitably and irrevocably drowning him in the sea of stars that was her.

Sin had never been more honoured.

He gave himself over to the overwhelming bliss of feeling her feminine touch reach every part of his body, not forgetting a single inch. He was ecstatically exalted in her devoted attention, and gloriously conquered. Every single one of his cells deserted his control and chose to fall to its knees at her feet instead.

He was hers. Whatever she wanted to do with him, he was hers.

All he wanted was for it to last forever.

Zajasang—

Zajasang...

Zajasang.

When he knew only her, when he floated in a surreal state of utmost presence and blurry rapture, she deemed her worship of his body complete and moved to grab the jar. She dipped two fingers of her left hand inside, which came away covered in a rich, scented oil of liquid ore.

His Queen painted the oil onto him in sacred reverence. Sin felt himself a king blessed by the Goddess herself. And then, finally, *finally*, after her lips had gifted every part of him with their kiss but his starving mouth, Zajasang kissed him.

The Song is sweet and showed me grace indeed.

Sin gripped her neck and rolled her under him. He was overcome with the wild need to lavish and ravish her as she had ravished him. She opened her mouth to him, and through this sacred union of their kiss, breathing only of each other, Sin knew his very soul was wrapping itself around hers.

He would never, could never, let her go.

The resonant symphony of the Song unfolded in all its colours. It filled and pressed into the curves and reaches of the cave with a complex harmony that was both celestial celebration and driving dirge. Zajasang cried out, again and again, soaked equally in pleasure and tears.

It was a harmony that set the savage creature inside him on edge, pawing the earth and growling, even as it stole his every coherent thought. But Sin felt his Queen warm and alive in his arms, and he felt their hearts beating together as one... And all he could feel was the rightness.

* * *

It's a Dark Moon.

Having clambered back up the cliffside and followed its scraggly edge all the way to the point, I soak in the clear power of the black night, letting it seep through my skin. Like the lonely princess high up in the tower of her castle, there's no other human out here, at this rough and relentless end of the earth. Only infinite stretches of nature's untainted power and resplendence before and behind me in water and soil.

But no, that's not right. I'm not a princess—nor am I lonely. Since finding the Sung, I have... I have *become*. Wings unfurled. Crown accepted. Darkness owned. And beauty found. Gratitude and grief tear through me, waves as damning as those crashing far below. Oh, the beauty I've found.

My thoughts return to the moon, my regal Sister Queen. Even as she dies again and again, she remains immortal. Her darkest night is filled with the potential of new life blooming. She always comes back.

My chest expands with the thought. *I might come back.*

Even so, a cold tear tracks down my cheek. It feels like they haven't stopped flowing since the shower, though here the gale carries them into my tangled hair. How many years did I keep myself imprisoned, fighting against the truth of who I am? At last I've come to understand this gift I've been granted—not a curse that hobbles, not senseless pain, but the very magic of life itself.

At last, I want to live. *Songs, how I want to come back.*

And Wicked Wild, I'm willing to risk that I won't.

The two truths entwine around one another, twin serpents rising within me and helping me stand straighter. As the wind whips and howls, the cliff stretching out solid behind me, an abyss of ephemeral darkness before me, I slowly work through my emotions. Before dusk fell—was that only this afternoon?—I asked Sin for one hour. Aeons later, yet long before the arrival of dawn, I asked for three.

I know he will give me exactly those and stay far from me not one minute longer. My womb is still contracted from that exchange.

With each pulse deep within, each drop of blood flowing between my legs, moments snatched from time imagined rise up in visions along my spine. The many more moons and suns and Song nights we might have shared. The way his touch might have become engraved rivers of gold in me through the years, well-worn paths loved with such devotion that his touch became part of me. The things he might have murmured to me as gifts only ever given to me. The many more times we would have stopped time as our gazes connected, or the glory we would have revelled in, dancing in Song and in life.

Faster and faster the tears come, and I whimper. If I ever do come back, if that will be possible, puzzling the pieces back together into a shape of me... Will that emptiness gape open inside me once more, knowing I lost something vital, never knowing what it was? Knowing only that it existed once, I had it once, but with absolutely nothing of it left to grasp onto? Will I have lost us again, forgotten us, and still remember?

I feel brittle as I sling my arms around myself and taste the salt on my tongue. Only those serpents of fire and ice are keeping me upright as the wondering unravels me. Would it be kinder to forget altogether, no inkling even that something was lost? Or would it be worse to remember, and know exactly what was lost? Because Sin will. He will remember. In some ways, he always has. All those years he knew who I was to him and what lived between us, knew what he was meant to have but didn't.

And now I'm going to do it to him again.

My heart splinters open and the hoarse scream painfully clogging my throat at last thrusts free. I hope that even being the only one who remembers, it will give him some solace. I hope he will be able to hold onto the good amidst the pain. I hope he will forgive me.

Because I know he will care beyond hope, and never stop.

I know that even as it breaks him, he will respect my choice.

I know that I'm about to rip his soul in two, and still I have to do it. *In her Dark cascade, life is restored.* It's the only way to fix this. The only chance humanity's got. Oh Songs.

He is going to be my greatest sin.

Futilely, a part of me struggles and revolts. Refuses to accept that this is how it has to be, that this is my reality. Struggles against the truth of who I am as I have my whole life until I found the Sung.

Then even that part stills in amazement. Unfathomably, against all odds, a butterfly glints iridescently in the night. With her slender, membranous wings she doesn't try to fight against the wind that roars strong enough to nearly take the flesh off my bones. Instead, she embraces it...and the growling gusts become her dance. I open myself to the Dark Song. These wicked winds are as a caress to her, buoying and lifting her and letting her soar. The corners of my lips rise to meet her joyful, improbable ride.

And I understand. *In her true Bond and Song, reverence redounds.* I am Dark Queen. I, too, ride the winds. I Dance the Dark Dance. I can finally see that my strongest Bond is with the Song. Myself. So I can't be lost—even if I will forget that this was real, like I forgot that it was real before.

I'm returning home for the first time. True home.

I wish I could share it with Sin. "I'll find a way back." I whisper the vow into the wind, where it wraps around those fragile wings, ready to journey where life will take them. A way back to him. Not because I need him. No, need doesn't have the power to transcend space and time. *Because I choose him.*

First I need to take care of the wound deep inside me.

Time to save myself.

Time to be whole, even if it shatters me.

I feel the heat of Sin's love flare long before he reaches me and threads his arms around my waist. He kisses my shoulder, then looks out into the darkness with me as his strong body warms my back.

I revel in the feel of him, in his closeness, his scent. Like always, his steady devotion is my sure lighthouse in the storm. But oh, how glorious the storm. How precious this life blooming so recklessly here on Earth. The grief seeps through me again like a muddy lake dotted with lotus flowers. Slick and pervasive, yet the beauty lining it undeniable.

"I hate situations that involve you on clifftops," Sin grumbles. A surprised, rasping laugh snaps out of me. "My heart always hurls itself after you."

I choke on the air.

"Talk to me, my Queen."

But words have fled me. By choosing to let go of the deadlock I have on myself, by opening that cramping fist and letting go of clinging to *me* and instead becoming *all,* I also take myself away from him. Pluck myself out of his grasp, even if never his heart. *How can I do this?*

"I'm imagining all sorts of awful things right now." Sin rest his forehead against my neck, rubbing his nose along the column of my spine, where the serpents still twist. "Whenever I feel this kind of pain in you, and you don't tell me what's causing it, my brain takes off at a gallop."

He pauses, waits, but I can only silently shake my head.

A growl grumbles out of him as his teeth carefully set themselves against the curve of my neck. I suppose with his brain galloping away, there's no one left to keep the prowling, possessive, protective, primal wildness caged that lives beneath his skin. His teeth nip a little harder, impulsively followed by his soothing tongue. His lips send vibrations through the sensitive spot below my ear when he rumbles, "You're the only one who can hold the reins."

My body trembles in his embrace.

Sin's arms get tighter and tighter, his growling more and more insistent. "Please hold them."

I swallow, swallow again. Like miasmic ink blooming in water, I feel his fear spread through the Bond.

I have to do this.

"Sin."

The ink halts.

"It's the only way."

It spreads so fast, nothing but a stygian sea remains.

"If I become the Wicked Wild... If I Weave from there..." It must work. I'm sure that it will. The Song is beyond time. There will be a way to reverse this, fix this. Heal the Song, save the oceans, save the planet. Save Sin.

I remember the circle of Sisters I glimpsed deep, deep in the heart of the spiral on Sacred Song night. *The circle of me.* Answering that call... This is the way. I may lose myself in that depth, no longer know myself as I have. But I will own all of me. And that will be pure life force to pour into the strands of creation and shape the Song in its womb.

"No. Songs, no." Sin's grip becomes tight enough to be bruising. In a few moments, it won't matter. "Zaja." He scrambles trying to turn me around to face him, barely able to release me enough to move me. "Zajasang." His hands cradle my face, demanding I look at him. "Please. Don't leave me. I need you. *I can't follow you there.*"

I may be lost until both of us come back as different facets of the prism, and that facet will return to the circle, and so the cycle will continue. Yes. We lose each other now. Some other part of our soul will have the privilege of finding each other again. I know that much is certain.

"Darling." Sin touches his forehead to mine, hot despite the wind whistling around us. "I only just got you."

Yet what I want is to come back to Sin as me. This facet, this life. So I vow it to him as I vowed it to myself. "I'll find a way. I trust in our love, Sin. I trust in you."

I trust in you. Trust in me. Let me go. Never let me go.

We are a rattle the wind plays as we stand skin to skin, soul to soul, like so many times before. Like we had imagined so many times to come. Every sensation doubled. Such unbearable beauty living between us.

Even in this.

"Zaja, my Queen, my Love—" The squall steals Sin's ragged croak.

The pain piercing me shuts my eyelids, but I rip them open again to seek his vibrant, waterlogged green. Mirror waterfalls careen down the frozen plains of my cheeks. "I know."

Already, I feel the Wicked Wild tearing me apart, the Dark Song unfurling in the depth of my heart.

It is happening. I am doing this.

Sin crushes his lips against mine, for one heartbeat, two, five. "With all that I am, Zaja." His desperate eyes bore into mine. "Please, please choose differently."

Because the vow of his Bond is to trust, and to honour my choice above all. Even if it breaks him. The immensity of his love and devotion shines in those starkly glistening eyes, those eyes I love, those eyes I remembered before I remembered anything else.

When the sound of my cracking heart is his only answer, he kisses my forehead, pulls himself taller, and caresses my cheeks. "My life in your Dance," he swears into my lips. Briefly his iron will slips, that strength forged in love beyond comprehension, and his hands tighten reflexively. Grunting, he stills, before kissing me once more.

It feels like his whole self streams into me with that kiss, seeking and searching, until he finds what he was looking for. Dark velvet coats his voice when he continues. "My sanctity in your choice."

I collapse into him. Wedding Song. The most honouring, meaningful words a Sung male can speak.

I choose you as mine. Fiercely, the sacred response sings in my soul. It echoes down and down the Bond, a flaming feather until it settles on sand. *I choose you as mine.*

But those are not the words I can speak to him. Not until I make it back to him. So I breathe only the final phrase of the jubilant oath. "For the pleasure of Song."

I am Dark Queen. In this moment, I wish I wasn't. I wish I could accept his vow and choose him. And still, I live for the pleasure of Song.

This is my truth, and this is my choice.

And because Sin loves me, and he understands the truth of my being like no one else ever has, even as he repeats my name like a prayer and clutches me close with his eyes—

He loosens his arms and lives his Song. *My sanctity in your choice.* Even when everything in him begs for me to choose differently.

The sun births out of the ocean, a goddess rising.

We are caught in one endless glowing moment that could never last long enough, one infinite moment in which we are the world.

Then I step backwards.

Step off the cliff in a final leap, and become the wind and the wave and the rock and the butterfly. I become the dark and gilded sky folding around Sin in eternal embrace as he falls to his knees and roars.

I hold his gaze as if it could hold him together even as I am coming apart. Cascading into the Dark.

"With all that I am, Sin."

And I become the Dark Song.

EPILOGUE

FRAGMENTS. FRAGMENTS OF HER WERE everywhere.

On his way here, Sin heard her sigh in the wind twining around the branches of the trees. He heard Zajasang's laughter now in the clinking of the glasses all around him, up and down the long dining table laid in finery and heavy stark-white linens. Sin looked up from his food and found his Queen looking back at him in the Greek Ambassador's eyes. When Sin excused himself to take a moment of air on the grand balcony, he found himself surrounded by her scent, there in the open night air.

Sin stood like a fool, breathing deep and grinning widely.

Then his gut clenched and he had to fight against doubling over and losing his meal. They had been meant to attend this banquet together.

When the spell passed, he tipped his head back. The half moon hung high above him in the night, teasing and elusive, now there, now gone. Hidden one moment, basking him in her light the next. Just like these fleeting moments of her that overcame him no matter where he went or what he was doing, that simultaneously stopped his heart and called it back to life again. That soothed him and sliced him back open.

She was—always had been—had become—the very fabric of life itself. Zajasang had felt the whole world, and now the whole world felt her.

But he couldn't hold her and feel her soft warmth, couldn't admire her smile and listen to her voice, couldn't kiss her and make love with her. His hands stretched up above him as if that would allow him to reach her, then faltered and dropped to behind his head before he thumped them down on the balustrade with a grunt. Zaja had taught him that pain needed to be felt, life needed to be honoured, and remembrance was sacred.

She promised to come back. *And trusted in me to help her find the way.*

So Sin clung to his vivid memories of his Queen, was determined to never let her slip away. He could recall exactly what it felt like to hold her in his arms. Recalled it every day, in fact, as a matter of sanity and survival. She was as real to him in his dreams, memory, and imagination, as real in her absence as she had been in her presence. She was still the precious golden bloom in his chest, was still his life.

Pieces may be all he had of her now. But she was everything.

Sin turned around, leaning on the balcony's banister while surveying the civilised battlefield inside. He would soon need to join the melee again, where the fighting was all the more vicious for being cloaked in sharp smiles and cuttingly elegant words. He could see why Zaja had hated it. Didn't want to imagine what attending events like these had felt like for her.

At least he could take her place here. At least he could do that for her. Follow the path she had laid out. The Sung needed to open up and share of the Song, and the Loud needed to quiet down and listen. The sooner that happened... the sooner his Queen might be able to rise again from the depths.

Pausing, Sin tried to work through the din swilling out onto the elevated terrace to listen himself. There was the vibration of the Song, that caress gliding over his skin. He even thought he could fathom the hum. He huffed out a laugh. How his life had shifted to monochrome where it had been technicolor when she had been there. How ironic, when she was lost deep in the black and gold world of the heart of the Dark Song, whilst he was here in the rainbow world of this reality.

He cocked his head, an instinctive move to try and follow those hints of Song. With this new angle, a gleam caught his eye. There, in the corner above the doorframe, a spider's web had been missed when this place had been polished to welcome the elite mingling inside.

Sin prowled over to study it more closely. Found the gaping hole that didn't belong, that Zaja had taught him to recognise. But he also noticed how this weaver was dancing around the edges of this very hole—was slowly, slowly filling it in.

Closing the wound.

Tears rushed into Sin's eyes. *Thank you, Lady.* He gripped at the pressure in his chest. *Thank you.*

He wasn't sure if he meant the tiny Lady before him, or the beloved one who had been ripped from him. He wasn't sure it mattered, if they weren't one and the same.

But he knew what his Lady was telling him.

It was working.

Holding his breath, Sin focused inward. The Bond was stretched beyond what he'd thought possible, was more obscured than even in all those years before he'd found his lost Queen again the first time. Her end of the Bond felt frayed like a rope unravelling, torn apart into tender filaments. Any evanescent impression or feeling that travelled through to him was barely more than the ripple lapping against someone's skin, caused by another's movement on the other end of an ocean.

But there is an ocean.

Somewhere, Zajasang Maaya Zatinsa still existed. She was Dancing.

The Bond remained, and through it, he heard the glorious tones of the echo of the echo that was her Dark Song.

ACKNOWLEDGEMENTS

*For only the whole makes the circle…*and only the circle makes the whole! My deep gratitude and appreciation to the circle of wonderful souls who supported me in making this Song whole.

Mama, thank you for your steady presence on the other end of the phone, your constancy and patience, encouragement and love, as I race up and down my emotional rollercoasters. I love sharing a hysterical giggle fit with you. Krissi, thank you for surprising and gifting me with a reaction far beyond anything I expected to my first trembling steps towards sharing my word weaving with the world. It meant so much. And for diving deep into design dilemmas with me (until we emerged on the other side!). Papa, thank you for always being willing to help when I ask for it, and imparting a sense of adventure and a daring to dream and leap off cliffs.

My sisters of my soul and havens for my heart: Marieke, thank you for letting me feel beyond certain of being loved no matter what, offering your pocket to carry my doubts, and jubilating my joys. Miri, thank you for being there from the beginning, listening at length to my ramblings, cheering me on step for step, and fevering through the story, back copy brilliance, and tag line triumphs with me.

Sonali, thank you for getting excited with me and helping me trust that *everything will be awesome!* Chacko, thank you for blowing my socks off with your enthusiastic response and requests for 'framed copies of my paragraphs of poetry'.

To the early readers of my writing, thank you for sharing your time and your thoughts. To all the kindred souls and early readers of my writing in the VITAverse, thank you for being so vocal in your appreciation, and your melodies in the Song. You inspire me.

Thank you to Ruth and Howard for hosting me and taking such good care of me during the last two weeks of edits and the first steps from screen to real world book.

To the authors who were courageous and foolish enough to write the books that became the breath in my lungs, sheltered the spark in my soul, tore me apart and put me back together more true to who I've always been: You've left me crying, ecstatic, and laughing myself silly in the dark (and the Dark), and my gratitude is boundless.

To you, the reader: Thank you for dancing in the Song with me.

PLEASE LEAVE A REVIEW

Thank you for reading!

Happy to help with a three-minute favour with massive impact, so this story can reach more people?

Please leave a review on Goodreads, Amazon, and all your favourite bookish sites!

Thank you.

May you sing your soul's song and may your heart bloom in love,

Your Word Weaver,

Mera Akiana

JOIN MY NEWSLETTER

Be part of the magic, madness, and merriment of my writing & publishing journey and receive exclusive peeks between the pages...sporadically.

Sign up now at https://meraakiana.com.

AUTHOR BIOGRAPHY

© Emma-Jane Photography

Mera Akiana weaves words as a way of singing the song of her soul, and braiding bridges to remembrance and reverence for the glory of life. She might have been Florence + the Machine if she could *actually* sing.

She read Psychology & Philosophy at the University of Oxford, UK, after growing up in Germany acting on the professional stage, sailing in the youth elite, and training at ballet boarding school. Later she whirled about Hollywood and danced in the realms of somatic empowerment and sacred sexuality.

Her entire life she found solace, shelter, and her sanity in the stories of books. Today Mera Akiana writes transcendent fantasy romance full of epic emotion and deep devotion…and just maybe, her stories will sing your soul home, too.

Learn more at https://meraakiana.com and join her newsletter.